Holger entered the ~~...~~ ~~...~~ of
the lintel-capped st~~...~~ and was slammed by
a stench of corruption and decay like that of a
battlefield on a hot summer's afternoon. He
gagged and fell choking to the ground, retching
until his stomach ached and his throat burned.

The harbinger laughed at him. He could
feel the amusement reverberating in his head.

Behold the dragon slayer.

That was what he had come to be, but
curled in a tight fetal ball, he wasn't doing a
very good job.

*Behold the frail and unfit man, the flawed
vessel into which petty tyrants pour their hopes.*

He struggled to his hands and knees and
looked at the harbinger. The thing had grown.
It was more dragonlike now, having grown scaly
limbs and clawed feet. Fetid and twisted, it had
none of the majesty video makers put in their
dragons. Such a loathsome thing had no place
on the earth.

"To hell with you," he told it.

ALSO BY ROBERT N. CHARRETTE

A Prince Among Men

A King Beneath The Mountain

Published by
WARNER BOOKS

A KNIGHT AMONG KNAVES

ROBERT N. CHARRETTE

WARNER BOOKS

A Time Warner Company

For JG. It's a different trip but that doesn't make the companionship any less important.

WARNER BOOKS EDITION

Aspect is a registered trademark of Warner Books, Inc.

Cover design by Don Puckey
Cover illustration by Keith Birdsong

Warner Books, Inc
1271 Avenue of the Americas
New York, NY 10020

A Time Warner Company

Printed in the United States of America

First Printing: December, 1995

10 9 8 7 6 5 4 3 2 1

As our story opens . . .

With the awakening of heroes held for centuries in magical sleep and the release of the spells binding Caliburn, the alignment between our world and the otherworld has grown stronger. Where once the doorways were closed, they now stand open. Creatures both horrific and benign make the crossing with greater ease, and magic is loose in the world. Yet the otherworldly manifestations remain mysterious and, to most, unknown. Science still denies the magic, as do the governments and megacorporations that rule our world. But there are those who know the truth: the world has changed irrevocably.

The scramble for position in the new world is under way. Some seek to save our world from the revenant magic. Others strive to exploit the magic and make it their own. Still others seek to use the magic to accomplish a greater, more sinister change in the order of the universe.

The enigmatic elves of the otherworld have sought the reopening of the ways between the worlds. The secretive dwarves, long hidden in their underearth homes, have fought against the convergence of the realms. Humans are caught in the middle, often as unknowing pawns. Those who are aware of the conflict, depending on their beliefs and affiliations, make efforts to aid, to hinder, or to pursue their own agenda. Alliances form and dissolve. Yesterday's opponent becomes today's collaborator and trusted partners become dangerous adversaries. Nothing is as it seems.

Prolog

Charley Gordon's spine didn't appreciate the shock of the verrie's landing. The Omni Dynamics MRVWC-7 Mamba™ was no luxury air taxi, but then an air taxi wouldn't have been able to make a landing pad out of a Providence city street, as the Mamba had. Dank night air swirled into the cockpit as the canopy swung up.

Hagen hauled himself out of the pilot's seat and dropped to the ground, disdaining to use the climbing ports. He sank to a crouch as he landed, absorbing the impact with the practiced ease of a paratrooper. He scanned the surrounding streets and buildings before scowling up at Charley.

"Come on, Gordon. You're not going stone on me, are you?"

Going stone? Maybe. Why *shouldn't* he be scared? He'd seen what the guy they were chasing could do. Going after him with a flight of milspec aircraft had seemed almost reasonable, but what Hagen proposed doing now was considerably less so. But it had to be done, didn't it? *Something* had to be done. A monster like Quetzal couldn't be allowed to run loose.

The flight coveralls Charley wore were made of Wear-Iron™ ballistic cloth, pure milspec; Charley had recognized the smell when he'd put them on back at the Mitsutomo command center. Their oily odor now seemed to overwhelm the other scents rising from the Mamba and mixing with the dirty Providence air. "Comfortable protection," the manufacturer's slogan said. Charley felt neither comfortable nor protected.

"Gordon?"

Charley couldn't pretend that engine noise drowned out Hagen's question. The Mamba's engines were idling, no louder than a car's engine. Their companion ship hovering overhead was only a little louder; the sheathed turbos of Mamba gunships were remarkably stealthy.

It was time to get moving, like it or not.

"I heard you," Charley said, doffing his flight helmet. He immediately missed the amplification circuitry that had made the dark night no more an impediment than a hazy day. He tried not to think about the advantage he had just surrendered and hauled himself out of the cockpit. Disoriented by the decreased visibility, he had a little trouble climbing down. By the time Charley joined Hagen on the pavement, the little man had dug a pile of stuff out of the verrie's cargo compartment and was burrowing into the Mamba for more.

Milspec required survival equipment to be stored there. Hagen pulled an assault vest from the heap and handed it to Charley. It was heavier than the police tactical vests that Charley was used to, but the fabric cover looked similar. Charley strapped it on without a word. He took the helmet Hagen handed him as well. Relieved to see that it had amplification circuits, he switched them on at once. The toys in Hagen's pile were not standard military-issue survival gear, but they'd do more to ensure survival for the crew of this verrie than the usual stuff.

He looked at the man he was about to trust his life to. Hagen was short, barely up to Charley's shoulder, but built like a tank. Sturdy, no doubt—but reliable? Charley had no idea, and he couldn't help worrying. Hagen was corporate, and Charley hadn't met a corporate yet who could be trusted to do more than watch out for his own butt.

Yeah, Hagen was corporate all right, flashing his masters' logo all over everything he wore. His coveralls, vest, and helmet all bore the logo of Yamabennin Security Services, a member of the Mitsutomo Keiretsu. All the equipment that Charley was using belonged to Mitsutomo, too, but Charley's stuff was unmarked. Somebody not only had anticipated the possibility of something serious on the ground, but had gone out of his way to make sure that Charley would not be wearing anything that could tie him to Yamabennin.

It hadn't been Charley.

This whole thing had blown up so fast, and the pace seemed to be accelerating. He wondered again how smart he had been to get involved. Not very, he decided, as Hagen handed him an Adler Arms KAR-99 assault rifle.

The weapon was popular with security firms and common among European tech runners in the sprawl; Charley had taken familiarization training with it, but the cylinder mounted under the barrel like a bayonet was new to him. Wires ran from the base of the cylinder to the scope and to the shoulder stock. The setup looked a little like a laser targeter.

"High-actinic spot," Hagen said, snatching up the weapon's dangling data cable and snapping its terminal into a socket on the side of Charley's helmet.

Data appeared in the air before Charley's eyes. It startled him; it had been a while since he had used a helmet with a heads-up display. The glowing lines, bars, and numbers provided targeting crosshairs with range readout as well as data on the spotlight's power level and the ammo status on the weapon. As he expected, the crosshairs moved as he shifted the barrel of the weapon. Very smooth. Very sharp. More milspec equipment, much better than the department's SWAT helmets.

"Selector switch responds to verbal commands of 'single,' 'burst,' and 'light,'" Hagen told him. "Or you can use the manual switch on the stock. Usual position. The light is one position past the burst setting. The fire selection indicator will stay at burst."

"You think this is enough to take on that thing?" Charley asked.

"It's all we've got at the moment," Hagen answered, sounding unhappy. Charley understood; he wasn't happy either, but the job had to be done, and soon. Before Quetzal killed again.

This whole operation was on very shaky legal grounds, but it wasn't the first time Charley had stretched the rules to do what needed doing. Hoping it wouldn't also be the *last* time, he fished out his shield, flipped the wallet open, and tucked it into the vest's breast pocket. At the moment, it was the best he could do to show he was a cop.

They were using his authority as a detective in the New England Cooperative Police Department's Special Investigations Unit to justify the application of Mitsutomo's corporate muscle in order to expunge the abomination that was Quetzal. Things like Quetzal weren't supposed to exist, but they did. Everyone in Special Investigations knew that they did. Hagen and his people knew, too. But no one publically admitted knowing. Somehow it was easier to go on living in a world with such things when you didn't have to admit that they were real. You dealt with them when you had to, and only when you had to, and then you did whatever you could to get them out of your world.

That's how Charley had always thought about it—the stuff of childhood nightmares didn't belong in the real world. Certainly Charley didn't want things like Quetzal in *his* world, and in his five years with SIU he had always been willing and able to do something about it. Now though, he was walking toward a dark hole in the side of a mountain and he wasn't quite so confident. He kept thinking about the twisted iron that Quetzal had left behind him at the university gate. Anyone with the power to do that to iron would be able to do terrible things to flesh.

This was not the time to think about *that*! Charley started forward. They had to go in *there* and do what they had come to do.

There was an abandoned railroad tunnel running through the hill that made up the bulk of Providence's East Side. The maps on the Mamba's nav console had shown only two entrances, both of them supposedly sealed. Two others of their Mamba flight had gone to watch the far end; they reported it sealed but were holding station anyway. Their airborne partner hovered at this one, its spotlight trained on the wall only a dozen yards away. Centered in the beam was the dark jagged shadow that was the hole through which Quetzal had entered the tunnel.

By unspoken agreement Charley and Hagen stopped just outside the cone of the beam. Hagen shook his head. He seemed as hesitant as Charley now. The short man's visor was still up; his face was pallid. His mouth drew in, disappearing into the bush of his mustache and beard, and he muttered, "We shouldn't be going in there without more backup."

There was debris around the opening, ordinary trash of the sort Charley had seen in innumerable areas of the sprawl. Syringes and chip shells were as common as food and drink trash. All so ordinary. The sort of thing you saw wherever the homeless had forced their way past the power structure's barriers and laid a squatter's claim to a place.

There were at least two squatters in there right now. The fools had ignored Charley's warning and gone in. He hadn't been able to tell them what had gone into their hidey hole ahead of them—what could he have told them that they would have believed? Charley was the badge, the establishment, a tool of the system that had jettisoned their kind. Charley knew streeters well enough to know that they wouldn't listen to him. Even if they did, they might have preferred Quetzal over Charley. Charley was the devil they knew, Mr. Authority—while all they would know of Quetzal's evil would be what Charley told them. To them it would all just be more establishment propaganda.

But this time the cry of wolf was real. There really *was* a monster in the dark of the tunnel, and it was past time to do something about it.

The hole in the retaining wall was stark and ominous in the verrie's dazzling spotlight. Their quarry was somewhere inside, in the dark. Quetzal should be trapped, cornered like a rat. Cornered rats had a reputation for fighting back.

Hagen was right; they shouldn't be going in without backup. But could they wait? What mischief was their quarry up to in there? Might he have some way to escape the tunnel that they didn't know about? Going in wasn't bright, but given what they knew about the quarry, not going in might be considerably less bright.

There were other reasons to get this operation wrapped up. The Mamba had put on quite a show in the last few minutes. People had noticed—how could they not? If a bunch of verries had been buzzing the airspace over Charley's district, *he* would have been poking his nose into things, wanting to know what was going on. Lights were winking on in residences up on the hill. Calls were undoubtedly being made. The district's police would be here soon, looking for answers. The university cops, too. Mooks from probably half a dozen private forces, as well; there were significant corporate interests in the neighborhood. There would be matters of protocol and procedure.

And Quetzal would escape while they were answering questions. No justice there! He didn't like it, but there seemed only one thing to do.

"Let's go get the bastard," Charley said.

He rushed toward the crack in the wall, trying not to think how stupid he was being. From the sounds of the footfalls behind him, Hagen was being just as stupid. Could it be that Charley had fallen in with a corporate with a conscience and the guts to back it up?

Charley's shadow raced ahead of him, disappearing into the dark of the entrance. But instead of following it into the tunnel, he crossed in front of the entrance and flattened himself against the retaining wall. He covered the opening with the muzzle of his assault rifle. Nothing reached out of the darkness of the tunnel to grab him. No arcane light lanced out to spear him. Had he really expected it to?

Yeah, he had.

Hagen put himself against the wall on the opposite side of the narrow opening. The corporate's visor was down now. Charley couldn't see the man's eyes. Was he as scared as Charley?

Hagen was making no move to be the first one in. Keeping his hand on the trigger and his muzzle pointed into the dark, Charley signaled to Hagen that he would go first. Hagen nodded agreement and crouched in position to provide covering fire. The little guy wasn't a long-time reliable partner like Manny, but he seemed to be trained in this sort of thing. Well enough trained? Charley would probably learn too soon. He hoped he'd like the answer.

He went through, into the dark.

The helmet's circuitry made day of the tunnel's night. A hazy, dark day, but enough for him to see the shantytown of discarded boxes. A lot of streeters could be squatting here. God, Charley hoped not. He couldn't see anyone, but he didn't know if that was good or bad. He and Hagen began a sweep through the makeshift "homes." They found no one.

It turned out that the streeters hadn't set up their squats very deep into the tunnel, just ten yards or so, near enough to the opening that some light might filter in. The tunnel took a bend not far in, stretching away into deep darkness. There, at the fringes of the shanty sprawl, they found the first squatters.

When Charley saw the corpses, his first thought was that they were the two streeters he'd seen go into the tunnel. A second look told him that they weren't. One of those two had been a woman. Despite the condition of the corpses, Charley could see that these two were both men. The bodies looked rickety, hollow somehow, almost as though they had been sucked dry of the life that had once filled them. They looked like some of the pictures in Charley's Modus 112 file. Myocardial infarction was what the medical examiner would say, heart failure. Nothing more than that.

Like hell. This was the work of Quetzal. The monster had to be stopped.

The other two streeters—and maybe more people—were in here somewhere. He hoped Quetzal wouldn't be using them as hostages. It would make doing what had to be done harder, and he couldn't let Quetzal stop him by threats to innocents. Quetzal wasn't the type to let hostages go after he dealt with Charley and Hagen. Everyone would end up dead, unless Quetzal died first.

Charley didn't intend for that to happen. He liked being alive. Any streeters that got in the way of taking down Quetzal would have to take their chances.

They left the squatters' pitiful hovels behind and moved deeper into the tunnel. The light leaking in from the hovering Mamba's beam was cut off by the bend, its glow fading away as they advanced. The helmets' circuitry was good enough that they might have been walking through a dark night rather than utter darkness. Still, they had to spread out to keep both walls under observation. Using their underbarrel lights would have made the going easier, but it would have shouted their presence to anyone lurking in the darkness ahead. Besides, the lights were supposed to be a weapon against Quetzal, and there was no sense in warning him that they were carrying such weapons.

Without warning Hagen halted, scanning the space around him in apparent consternation. "Do you feel—"

Charley did. The earth beneath his feet was shaking. The air was suddenly colder. A rumble, deep and ominous, filled his ears and reached into his bones. The East Coast wasn't supposed to have earthquakes, but it seemed that the rock around them hadn't gotten the word. Dirt and grit pattered down from above. Were they about to be buried alive?

The entrance to the tunnel seemed very far away. Too far to reach, too far to run. Hagen was standing his ground. Charley did too.

The tremor stopped. And though the air was full of dust, they weren't buried.

Hagen switched on his light. The beam speared past Charley, illuminating an archway in the tunnel's wall. Gritty clouds billowed out from the choked opening, fogging down Hagen's beam. Charley added his. Rocks and debris continued to spill from the opening as the shifting stone ground itself into a stable mass. The sound and vibration died away, and Charley began to believe that the whole tunnel wasn't about to come down on his head.

Hagen leading the way, they moved toward the rockfall. Something dripped sluggishly among the rocks, forming a small pool. Charley put his light on it. The dark stuff shook and began to roil. "What's that?"

"Look's like blood," Hagen said.

Blood? The color was right. "But it's bubbling."

"Take the light off it," said Hagen, shifting his own away.

Charley did the same. Seen by the helmet's circuitry, the liquid lost its color. When the direct glare of their lights was no longer on the liquid, the bubbling ceased.

"Quetzal's blood," Hagen said.

The monster had shown an adverse reaction to light; that was why the actinic lamps were a weapon against it. This blood boiled in the glare of the light. Could it be true? Could the monster have been killed in the cave-in? There was a lot of blood. Had Quetzal done himself in, and saved Charley and Hagen the trouble? "Think it was in there?"

"Seems likely," Hagen said.

"You're not sure."

"Are you?"

"Nothing human could survive losing so much blood," Charley said, trying to convince himself.

"You know what we are dealing with here."

No, he didn't, but Charley did understand Hagen's point. Quetzal wasn't human. They couldn't be sure that the monster had been trapped and crushed in the cave-in. It seemed a reasonable conclusion, but they just couldn't be *sure*.

Hagen advanced to the face of the rockfall to examine it more closely. Charley didn't see what the man could learn; it would take a major excavation to unchoke whatever passage had led from that archway. No one would be finding Quetzal's body anytime soon. *If* it was even there to be found. Charley played his light over the loose debris around the edges of the rockfall, looking for anything that might offer a clue to what had happened.

He caught a glimpse of motion at the edge of his searching light—something long and sinuous that seemed to squirm. Thinking *snake,* he took a step back and put the beam directly on it, weapon ready. It wasn't a snake. It wasn't moving, either. In fact, it didn't seem to be quite there.

"Hagen?"

"Find something?"

"You tell me."

They found that they could see the thing best when the light wasn't fully on it. It appeared to be a sculpture of some sort, a serpentine shape faceted into segments. Charley had never seen anything quite like it.

"Quetzal's?"

"Likely." Hagen restrained Charley when he reached down to pick it up. "Not wise."

"This some kind of magic thing?"

"A powerful one, I think. Quetzal wouldn't have let it go. He must be dead."

Charley didn't see that the connection was inevitable. "What do we do with it?"

"I don't think that's going to be our problem. Look."

Charley looked back the way they had come, as Hagen was doing. There were half a dozen men with lights advancing toward them. In the backglow, Charley could see that they were wearing federal-issue field rigs. Charley and Hagen turned to face the newcomers. Light swept across them.

"Freeze!" an amplified voice ordered. "Put your weapons down!"

Very slowly and carefully, Charley and Hagen did as they were told.

A trio of suits came up behind the field agents. Two of them were cookie-cutter feds, but the third wore clothes too fancy to be government. That guy wore a corporate affiliation lapel pin, but Charley couldn't make out the logo. The fancy suit pushed his way past the field agents and went straight to the artifact, crouching down to examine it.

One of the fed suits stepped forward. "I'm Inspector Fletcher, and I want answers. We'll start with who you are."

"Charley Gordon, NEC Special Investigations Unit."

"Hagen, Yamabennin Security Services."

Charley was glad to see that Hagen understood that there was no messing with these kinds of guys.

The fancy suit looked up. "Gordon, eh?"

"You know him, Van Dieman?" Fletcher asked the man.

Van Dieman shrugged. "Heard the name before." He went back to examining the artifact. Fletcher didn't seem perturbed by the minimal response. He indicated Charley's shield and held out his hand. Charley handed the wallet over. The fed pointed his comp at the shield and flashed the code.

"Badge checks out," Fletcher said as he handed back Charley's shield.

No reason it shouldn't have.

"Your captain know about this operation?" Fletcher asked. "The aircraft outside belong to Yamabennin Security Services."

"This is an emergency pursuit situation," Hagen said. "To the shame of Yamabennin and all our corporate family, the detective discovered one of our clients in the commission of a crime. The detective called upon us to aid in the pursuit of our client, an armed and dangerous person. In compliance with statute 232 of our incorporation papers, Yamabennin is supplying supplementary personnel and equipment to Detective Gordon in performance of his duty. It is a community service."

Fletcher looked down his nose at Hagen, easy enough given the disparity in their heights. "You're pretty heavily armed for a public relations lawyer."

"Yamabennin prefers well-rounded employees, Inspector," Hagen said almost cheerfully.

"Yeah? Well, be a good employee and get your corporate butt back to your protected turf and out of here. I don't see any more need for 'supplementary personnel.' "

"Yamabennin is always pleased to cooperate with the authorities." Hagen gave Fletcher a corporate bow.

"I'm sure," Fletcher said, with exactly the same amount of sarcasm that Charley would have used if that line had been handed to him.

"You may as well go with him, Detective Gordon," Van Dieman said. "You're not needed here anymore either."

Charley looked to Fletcher. "This isn't a federal matter."

"Just remember to file your report," Fletcher said. "We'll be expecting to see a copy. We're in charge now."

Part 1

TIME FOR THINGS TO CHANGE

horizon panes showed the true color of the day: a sky. Still

CHAPTER
1

"Master Jack," piped the three voices, all off-key and out of sync.

Sleep-fuddled, John didn't realize at once that the voices were calling for him. John Reddy didn't use his real name much anymore. On the streets of old Providence he was known as Tall Jack, Lanky Jacky, Mucho Blanco Jacko, or just Jack. Street names for a street life. His mainline straightline life was behind him, his old home in Rezcom Cluster 3 a memory.

"Master Jack!"

Some called him that, too, but plain, unadorned Jack was what John preferred, although he had to admit that there was a certain attraction to the air of mystery that having a multitude of names gave him. Only Faye still called him John, but most of the people who could hear Faye were John's friends, so he didn't worry about it too much.

"Waken, Master Jack!"

Something snatched away his blanket, exposing him to the chill of the morning air. Hidden by the purloined mound of cloth, the thief scooted for the far side of the loft that John had claimed for his bedroom. The frenetic mound was the right size to be one of the bogies, and the voices were shrill enough to fit as well. They were being uncharacteristically bold, to disturb him.

Dirty windows grayed the light striking them. Only the broken panes showed the true color of the day's sky. Still morning? It seemed so. He hadn't been asleep long. If he were more awake, he'd be tired from his long nighttime prowl looking for Spillway Sue. There were no other blankets, but his leather jacket was within reach. He snagged it, dragging it over himself. The jacket was a poor substitute for the blanket, but he felt warmer. He had been exhausted when he'd hit the slump, totally whipped out, and had crashed hard. He wasn't ready to be up and about.

"Go away," he snarled at his tormentors, wishing that they'd picked someone else, like maybe Bear, to annoy. But he knew that they wouldn't bother Bear this way; Bear made no secret of his dislike for the Faery folk sharing John's slump, and the bogies stayed as far away from Bear as they could.

"But Master Jack—" "We can't." "*He's* here." The bogies wailed. "He will be upset." "After all—" "I'll tell him." "No, me!" "I said I'd tell—" "No you won't!"

"You two shush," said the deepest of the voices. That would be Kesh. "Master Jack, *he* has come to see you."

John didn't want to see any visitors. He just wanted to get more sleep. "Tell him I'm dead."

Which was true, according to the public records database. John Reddy was dead, killed in an accidental fire at the Woodman Armory Museum where he had worked as a guard. The datafiles were right that someone had been killed the night that John's life changed, but that was about all they had right about that night. The fire hadn't been set accidentally, and John wasn't the person who had died, although someone wanted the world to believe so, going so far as to alter the data records by substituting the dead man's physical description for John's in all public files. The substitution was a mystery John had yet to solve. But mysteries were for people who were awake.

"Master Jack, you must come!" Kesh pleaded. "*He* will not be pleased if you don't! Take it out on us, he will."

The bogies' continued importuning threatened to shatter John's fragile grip on sleep. If they would just shut up, he could go back to his dreams. He groped around the floor near his mattress until his hand encountered something small and throwable. He threw it, without aim or any concern. "*I'm* not pleased. Go away!"

That cowed them, but only for a moment. The shrill voices tumbled forth in chorus, chasing away John's last hope of returning to sleep. "Master Jack, you must rise." "The prince has come to speak with you. *He* sent us to get you." "*He* is waiting." "*He* doesn't like to wait." "Oh, no, *he* doesn't like to wait. The great ones never like to be kept waiting." "Have pity, Master Jack. The prince—"

John could only think of one prince who would simultaneously put such fear into the bogies and still wait upon their fumbling. Bennett. "Bennett is here?"

"Is it true?" asked a deep voice, Bear's voice.

John wanted to know himself. The bogies gave no vocal answer. Prying open an eye, he looked at them. All three had found niches that put them out of Bear's line of sight, but not John's. All three nodded vigorously. John looked to Bear. "So it seems."

"The elf is not to be trusted," Bear said with firm conviction.

Though Bear had regained his strength and self remarkably fast, he had been taciturn, keeping to himself since his rough time beneath the mountain. His disorientation from the dwarves' botched attempt to help him assimilate into the twenty-first century was gone, only the slightest trace of wasting he'd suffered while lying inactive in the dwarves' strange medical machines remained. Like a legendary hero— which was understandable since he happened to be one— Bear had recovered from his ordeal. Although relieved, John hadn't been surprised by Bear's resilience. As long as John had known Bear, the man had shown remarkable facility in recovering from wounds and fatigue. "A knack I picked up while I was sleeping in the otherworld," had been Bear's explanation. It was a knack that Bear described as "useful," as close as Bear ever came to saying he was grateful for anything that ever came out of Faery.

Bear harbored a lot of hate and distrust for Faery folk. What was it about Bennett's arrival that had brought Bear upstairs for the first time?

"Did you call Bennett here?" Bear asked suspiciously.

Did his tone imply distrust of John? Was this a sign that Bear's distrust of elves was extended to John? There were questions still unasked and unanswered between him and Bear. There had been little opportunity for a private talk since their reunion. For all that the old factory that was John's slump was huge, the building offered few private places these days, and the shadow that lay between John and Bear was one that John wanted to deal with privately. So far Bear had not so much as admitted that he knew John was an elf. So far it had been easier—for both of them—to pretend that things hadn't changed, that their relationship was still as it had been while they had both been members of the Downtown Dons, in the days before either of them had learned of John's true parentage. The few conversations they'd had revolved around current events in the world outside the slump, a world that Bear had yet to reenter.

"Have you seen him?" John asked, expecting that he already knew the answer. Bear and Bennett were a volatile combination. If they had already met, John would have been woken by the fireworks.

"No." Bear's answer was clipped. "Did you call it here?"

"I don't know why he's here," John answered honestly.

"Send the elf away. Tell it that there is no welcome for it here."

Bear was right: there was no welcome for Bennett here, but not just because he was an elf. Bear's hatred for Bennett touched on other, more personal issues. John had a few of his own. Though he didn't look it, John was an elf himself and allegedly Bennett's own son, though Bennett had shown him no fatherly care and concern, abandoning him to a life among the humans as a changeling. That accident of birth

had come between John and Bear, but now was not the time
to deal with their strained relationship.

Right now they had Bennett to deal with. It was tempting
to take Bear's attitude toward Bennett, but John found himself considering more than the emotional angles. The elf
prince was no casual visitor. What had brought him here?
Trouble, no doubt, but what kind of trouble? Could they afford to let irrational feelings keep them from finding out?
For the moment, at least, they had to put the problems of the
past behind them. John didn't know the history between Bear
and Bennett, but figured that his own reasons for hating the
elf had to be at least as strong. If John could look beyond
that, why couldn't Bear?

"Bennett's not your enemy anymore, Bear. You wouldn't
be here now if it wasn't for him. Without his help we never
would have escaped from the dwarves."

Bear scowled. "I didn't need to *escape.*"

Clearly Bear still believed that the dwarves were his
friends, as they apparently had been in his earlier life. John
had tried to explain to Bear that the dwarves were responsible for his deteriorated condition. If Bear still refused to understand, there wasn't anything new John could add to the
arguments. "You just don't want to accept that they duped
you. They are not our friends. They've got their own
agenda."

"I know that they have their own concerns. So do we all.
The dwarves are staunch allies. They are too much like the
rock in which they dwell; they will not have been changed
by the years, as you claim. Their memories are long, their
sense of honor keen. I have no doubt that there is deception
in this matter, but it is not theirs. They have always been
men's friends against the el—" Bear stopped short, displaying an uncharacteristic moment of discomfort. "Against
those like Bennett."

"If you *mean* elves, *say* elves."

Bear said nothing.

John had hoped that his remark would bring a denial from

Bear, an affirmation that Bear did not lump John in among the elves that Bear hated. But it didn't come. John had to have been crazy to think that Bear could find an exception in his hate, that Bear could think of John as he had before he'd learned of John's parentage. Bear was what he was: a self-important, bigoted fossil, an unenlightened product of his age. All that John had done for Bear didn't seem to be enough to prove to this man that John was not like Bennett.

"You didn't come up here because of Bennett," John said, almost making the statement an accusation.

"I came to return this."

Bear held out the combox that John had spent the first part of his long night scrounging, then getting cut into the slump's pirate tap. Just yesterday Bear had asked for the combox as a supplement to the net access John had already arranged for the slump, mostly for entertainment channels dumped to the monitor down on the main floor—the bogies were especially partial to the Nostalgia Comedy Channel™— but also to provide Bear with access to the news and documentary programming that fascinated him.

When John had returned from his prowling, he had logged on to check on the system's usage and seen that Bear had placed a call to Wilson, the dwarf who had kidnapped John and Spillway Sue while pretending that he was acting as Bear's agent. John hadn't realized that Bear knew how to contact the dwarf. Hell, he hadn't imagined that the dwarf might *have* a com code. Suddenly Bear's comments about the dwarves had a context.

"Are you going back to them?"

"I mislike staying here," Bear replied.

The slump was hardly a palace, but it was better than most of the places John had stayed since leaving Worcester. It was an island in the midst of the urban chaos of the sprawl, a refuge born of abandoned industrial decay, but a refuge nonetheless. And peaceful—if you discounted the disorder that occasionally erupted from the bogies and John's other "guests." A motley crew of Faery folk had followed him home from his last foray into the otherworld and moved into his slump as though it were the most natural thing in the world to do. And who was to say it wasn't? He didn't have many grounds to complain. Most of the Faery folk knew enough to leave you alone when you wanted to be left alone, which was more than John could say for the human neighbors he'd had over the years. Besides, since the folk had moved in, there had been no incursions from anybody else. Not even the Beasts, the biggest and most belligerent of the local gangs, had bothered them here.

"I thought I was your *comes*? Aren't I supposed to provide hospitality to you?"

Bear wouldn't meet John's eyes, but whether it was because of some discomfort or because the man was looking to a past long gone, John couldn't tell. Bear sighed. "The *comitatus* is a thing of the past. This is a new age. There are new ways."

"Meaning the old values aren't worth holding to?"

"I thought you knew better than that."

"Just what do you mean, then?"

Bear was quiet for a moment, but slowly he turned to John and met his stare. Bear's eyes were cold and distant, hard. Softly he said, "I can't stay here. You should come away from here as well. This place is . . . unwholesome."

John felt like he'd been kicked in the stomach. This slump was the closest to a home John had known since Worcester. He didn't like anyone disparaging it, not even Bear. "This place is mine. Are you saying *I'm* unwholesome?"

Bear didn't answer. He just looked away.

Damn him! Just being an elf didn't make John a bastard, even if he *was* an elf's bastard. Why couldn't Bear see that? "So we're quits?"

"Will you come away from this place?" Bear asked without looking at John.

John could be stubborn, too. "No."

Bear looked down at the combox, forgotten in his hand, then held it out to John once more. John spurned the box, folding his arms across his chest. Bear set the combox on the floor and turned away. At the door he stopped long enough to say, "You have my thanks for everything you've done."

Then he was gone.

If Bear couldn't accept John for who he was, John was better off without the man around. What business did Bear have expecting John to follow along and do whatever Bear asked of him? It's not like Bear was still the king. Any kind of a king. Hell, Bear wasn't even warlord of the Dons anymore. Here, John was in charge.

Maybe that was Bear's real problem.

Something tugged at John's pants leg. A bogie, Lep, the smallest of the three. Lep looked up plaintively and said, "Master Jack, the great one is waiting."

Ah, yes. Bennett. Another one who thought of John as some pawn in his game. Something would be motivating the elf to come here. Likely John wouldn't care for it, but he wanted to know what it was; or at least what Bennett would claim it was. The two would be different and, he was sure, almost equally interesting.

"Master Jack?" It was Metch, the third bogie. Offering John's jacket, Metch quavered. "*He* doesn't like to wait."

John took the jacket and slung it over his shoulder. Waiting would do Bennett nothing but good. John resolved to be polite and stay calm, figuring that courtesy and cool would give Bennett less to work with when he tried to manipulate John. Whistling Bard Taliesin's *The Elf at the Well*, John started down the stairs.

Bennett was on the main floor, in conversation with Gorshin. John wasn't surprised to see the two of them together. Bennett had brought Gorshin from the otherworld and left him behind. Bennett was good at leaving people behind.

Roosting somewhere in the main factory, Gorshin had become another of the uninvited residents that John called his guests. Dr. Spae said that Gorshin was a gargoyle. The bat-winged creature didn't look much like the gargoyles that adorned some of the oldest buildings in old Providence, but those were modern sculptural images and had little in common with classic medieval gargoyles. John had to admit that there was a resemblance between Gorshin and some of the more reptilian pieces that had once adorned Old World cathedrals, but none of those carvings had half Gorshin's air of menace. On the other hand, none of those carvings could move, either. Gorshin was not John's favorite among his guests.

But it was the real guest who drew John's attention. Bennett was wearing his walk-among-humans look, the human face that he wore subtly echoing his gaunt elven features. His clothes were stylish and rich, upper-rank corp—not the best look to wear in this part of the sprawl, but any sprawl scut who tried to muck with Bennett would get a rude, probably fatal, surprise. Despite his appearance, the elf was no rich mitch corporate suit ripe for plundering; he was an elven mage with the power to blast anyone who annoyed him. John had seen other magicians resist those powers, but a muscle-headed streeter wouldn't have a chance.

As John approached, Bennett said, "Gorshin tells me that you have been spending your time trying to track down your runaway woman. What was her name?"

Runaway wom— Sue hadn't run away. Not from him anyway. Well, maybe she had, but it was a misunderstanding that he'd straighten out as soon as he caught up to her. It was none of Bennett's business. And why was he interested anyway?

When John failed to answer, Gorshin supplied, "Spill-waaay Ssuuu."

Why did the gargoyle always have to sound hungry when he pronounced people's names?

"Hardly a name to conjure with," Bennett commented.

Bennett's scornful tone stung. Street names were street names, that's all. They weren't always dramatic. John himself was tagged with several he didn't much care for. What business was it of Bennett's? And what business did Gorshin have tattling on him? John's resolution to be polite evaporated like spit on a summer sidewalk. "What do you want, Bennett?"

Bennett smiled, unflustered by John's belligerence. "Circumstances are at last felicitous, Jack, and I have come to take you to the otherworld. It is time for you to step away from this sunlit world, and past time for you to claim your heritage."

Felicitous for whom? was John's first reaction, but the mention of John's heritage stirred up the confusion of feelings he'd been suffering since he first learned that he was an elf. His true world was the twilight land of the otherworld, but it was a world of which he knew little more than what he'd read in books and heard in songs and stories. How much of what he believed about it was true, how much false? He knew that legends had a basis in fact. Bear was proof of that—what greater legend was there than that of King Arthur? Bear, as Artos, was the basis of that legend, and he was as real as anyone John had ever met. The world had more to it than Horatio's philosophies. There was magic in the world, growing all the time. There was magic in John, too, and it was growing, though slowly. Dr. Spae's teaching helped, but she had as tenuous a grip as he did on the distinction between the reality of the magic-touched world and the fallacies of tradition. Bennett, born and raised a prince of Faery, knew. And now, it appeared, he was offering that knowledge to John.

What was in it for Bennett? There had to be something.

So Bennett was finally ready to take him to the otherworld. So what? Might Bennett finally be ready to be the father he ought to have been all along? So what to that, too. It was past time for fatherly concern. "I can get there on my own."

Nodding, Bennett said, "Yet you cannot partake of your patrimony on your own. An unguided ramble into our realm will not gain you that. I hold out to you what should have been yours all along."

"I don't want anything from you." Even as he said it, John

knew that it wasn't true. He wanted something from Bennett, all right. He wanted satisfaction for the years spent living a lie. He wanted compensation for the loss of his home and family, even if they hadn't really been his. But most of all, he wanted answers—honest answers—about his elven legacy. He knew so little, and most of that from other sources than Bennett. Hell, John couldn't even see his own true face, thanks to "protective" spells that Bennett had arranged.

"Jack, I know we have not had the best of relationships, but we have both been constrained by circumstances beyond our control. We have before us a chance to amend the mistakes that have separated us. This is a time not to look to the past, but to look to the future. Yours can be a brilliant future." Bennett waved a hand to take in their surroundings "You deserve much more than this."

John wanted to believe. But . . . "And you're going to provide it?"

"Indeed I will. After a fashion. I can set you in your place as a prince of Faery. The rest will depend on you, as it always has. But as to the opportunity and the starting place, I not only can but must provide it. It is not proper that I withhold that which is yours by right."

"You've done a pretty good job of withholding up till now."

Bennett sighed dramatically. "As I have told you before, that was not my choice."

"So you say."

"Though I find your questioning my word offensive, I can understand why you might doubt my veracity. The plain fact is that there is much of which you are ignorant, and you will remain ignorant so long as you remain content to dwell in the sunlit world. You cannot afford to remain ignorant."

"I've already learned all I care to from you." *Lots about deceit, for example.*

"Perhaps. But survival requires learning more than one cares to. Surely you wish to go on living."

"I'll survive."

"You have powerful enemies."

"Yeah? Like who?"

"This is not a time for names," Bennett responded.

More likely not a time to suit Bennett. *If* there really were any enemies. "Well, I'm not worried. I have powerful friends."

"Oh? Like who?" Bennett asked, echoing John's own disbelieving question. He shook his head regretfully and said, "I can see that you do not truly comprehend your situation."

"I *comprehend* that there is no reason why I should trust you."

"I am your father, Jack."

"So you say." But this time John couldn't put much conviction into his sarcastic response. He had come to believe that Bennett wasn't lying on that point, but he didn't like it. He really didn't like it at all.

"Do not judge me by human standards," Bennett warned.

"How *else* am I supposed to judge you?" John blurted. "I was raised by humans. I grew up in a human world. Humans are the only people *I* know. Theirs are the only standards I know. Those standards can't be so poor. After all, *humans* didn't abandon me when I was inconvenient."

"Neither did I," Bennett said earnestly. "The situation was more than just inconvenient."

"So you say."

"*That* is a tiresome response."

Hah! A hit! "Sorry if I bore you."

"Your remorse is unconvincing, but I will let it pass. Things move apace. It is imperative that you return to the otherworld with me."

Imperative? Were they getting to the real reason for Bennett's visit? John knew Bennett wouldn't have come simply for John's benefit. Time for Bennett to squirm some more. "No, I don't think so. I don't think I need to go anywhere."

Bennett's face darkened. "Do not be willful."

"Why not? Does it make me too much like my father?"

Eyes narrowing, Bennett said, "When you wanted my help to save your friends, you gave me your word that you would aid me, or have you forgotten?"

Why bring that up? "I haven't forgotten."

"If I must, I will call upon that promise to ensure that you accompany me. Will you come with me?"

Bennett had grown so earnest that John couldn't resist nicking him again. "Maybe you should just club me over the head and have Gorshin drag me back for you."

"I do not consider that an option. I ask again, will you come with me?"

"I don't want to," John said honestly.

"You will come with me to the otherworld. There is a matter in which I require your aid," said Bennett. The effort seemed to pain him.

Which was fine by John. Bennett's discomfort was just a tiny payback. Maybe there was room for a little more. "Why can't I help you here? This is the world in which you abandoned me, after all."

"I did not say that this world was uninvolved in this matter."

"Just for the record, I'd like to point out that you didn't say *anything* about 'this matter.' "

"Your oath put no constraints on the matter for which I required your aid. Are you finding this a convenient time to go back on your word? What sort of honor is Artos teaching you?"

Teaching? Bear was leaving. But like so much else, the affair was none of Bennett's business. "Leave Bear out of this."

"As will be. But now I ask a third time, will you come with me and aid me as you swore?"

John remembered the promise. He hadn't thought much of it at the time; his mind had been on other things. Despite Bennett's disparaging tone, Bear had taught John something about honor and about how a man kept his promises, no matter to whom he had given them. Would Bennett take his own promises as seriously as he was taking John's?

"Answer me," Bennett demanded.

"Is it that important?"

"You will regret it if you do not comply."

Appeals to self-interest, then demands on honor, now threats. Whatever was motivating Bennett had him spinning hard. John was intrigued. Bennett hadn't really told him anything about what was going on, but John found that he just *had* to know. "Will you answer my questions?"

"This is not a bargaining session."

"Will you at least have the disguise spell removed?"

Bennett dismissed the question with a wave of his hand. "A nothing. That is not a problem worth worry."

Maybe not to him, but John disliked living behind a false face. Was it really nothing to want to look in a mirror and see his true face? Bennett implied that the end of the disguise spell would be forthcoming if John went with him. If that was all John got out of Bennett, he'd be ahead of where he was now. So, if he went with Bennett to the otherworld, what would it really cost him? He knew how to make the transition himself; it was not as though he'd be trapped there. If he didn't like what Bennett had in mind, he could just leave.

"All right. I'll go with you."

Bennett nodded solemnly. "Gather what you wish to take."

"Hold on. There's something I'd like to do first."

"What?"

"It's personal."

Bennett shrugged, then he smiled. Now that he had John's agreement, his mood seemed more expansive. "Just don't take long."

CHAPTER

Holger heard voices. The voices were familiar, though not so intimate as Holger remembered them. He didn't hear such intimate voices so frequently now. He listened to these voices, taking in their rise and fall, stops and starts, all the tones and cadences, recognizing Gilmore the psych and Major Chartain. He concentrated on the sound, and the voices came to his ears more clearly. They were talking about the test. Chartain was expressing reservations about Holger's readiness.

Holger smiled to himself. Ready? He was more than ready. He'd been cooped up in rehab too long. He was tired of the white walls and the fussing labcoats, the constant buzzing of the air-conditioning and the goddamn controlled diet, the pointless physical therapy and the even more pointless psych evaluations, and the smells: the deadly clean, deceptive, antiseptic smells. Oh, he was ready. He wanted to see the sun again. He hadn't seen the sun since the accident.

The accident . . .

He didn't remember much about his accident. Traumatic stress reaction, the doctors said. There were bits of memory floating around in his head. He remembered lights and heat, pressure and pain. Voices. All a jumble. A needle? Too confused. They called it a training accident, but he wasn't always sure that they were telling him the truth. Sometimes the Department put a spin on things. Deceptive. It might not have been a training accident. The Department . . .

If only he could remember clearly. He remembered . . .

He remembered that he had been with Department M for a long time. This wasn't the first time that he had been injured. But the Department had always come through. Department M had always taken care of him, because he was one of their own; the Department always took care of their own. He felt good about that. He liked being a part of Department M. It was the best posting he'd had since he joined the Services.

He listened again to the voices on the other side of the door. Chartain was unsure. Gilmore clattered at a keyboard while he argued. The clattering stopped and Gilmore announced that the scenario was set. Chartain remained unsure about Holger's readiness. Well, Holger would show him. This test was his ticket out of hospital and back to active duty. He would show Chartain. Holger Kun was ready for duty again, and nothing, certainly not Major Chartain's doubts, was going to stop him from proving it.

The test he faced was a trial to ensure that he was ready for service again. It would start here, but would move outside to the real world—a real world he was anxious to see again. Being out in the real world added a complexity that just couldn't be duplicated inside a virtual theater. Besides, a virtual theater couldn't test a man's physical limits. Still, the Department's sponsors didn't sanction "live" testing, although Holger suspected that they knew of its existence and, for their own reasons, looked the other way. Live tests had been a part of the European Community Secret Service from the early, bad old days when there wasn't enough budget to train in controlled environments. It was tradition now, a rite of passage. Holger had been through it when he'd completed his basic training, and again after he'd taken the Department's special training course.

This test was just another hurdle for him. The scenario was simple. He was to retrieve some information from the facility's computer, simulating a data theft, and remove the data from the facility. Agents from Department M, and possibly other ECSS operatives, would be set on his trail. Some would be the hunters, others acting as obstacles, all trying to prevent him from delivering his package. Those agents were being tested, too, but not as stringently as Holger. According to the scenario, the hunters would have no special information about his destination, but Holger knew better than to expect that. There would be someone waiting for him at the delivery point. There would be at least one confrontation.

A thrill of anticipation ran through him. He was ready! So why wait? The real world was out there. He palmed open the door. Monitor screens on the workstations lining the room went blank as he entered. They would have been keyed to go to standby on the door's activation, as a security measure. He didn't mind. He had made a sufficient gain: by not announcing himself, he hadn't given his two testers a chance to get away from the console they were using, thus making it easier for him to select the correct one.

"Ah, good evening, Agent Kun."

Gilmore smiled the idiotic smile that made his bald head look like an overgrown infant's. His juglike ears bobbing above the collar of his white lab coat added to the caricatured scientist effect. Just from looking at Gilmore, one would never suspect that the man was near the top of his field—not with that idiot grin—but Holger knew better than to accept appearances.

Take Major Chartain's appearance, for example. Though Chartain wore the uniform of the French Légion Étrangère, complete with the European Coordinated Military Forces rank tabs on his collar and the ECMF wreathed eagle shoulder patch, the major was no soldier. Holger knew that Chartain had been military once, but not with the Légion. Now, like Holger, he was an agent of the Secret Services. Chartain's tight smile and economical nod were all the acknowledgment the major gave to Holger's arrival.

"You're a bit early," Gilmore said. "We weren't expecting you for a few more minutes."

"I didn't want to be late. Can we get started?"

"Nervous?" Gilmore asked.

Holger didn't bother to answer.

Gilmore's smile faded. "Yes, well, I don't see why we can't get started. The first part requires that you retrieve a preselected datafile. You remember the file's identity code?"

Pointless question. Holger never forgot the details of a briefing. "Westwind," he said.

"Good." Gilmore beamed again. "Shall we proceed?"

Holger shouldered his way past the testers to the console and stood, staring down at it, hands in the pockets of his greatcoat. This was not a simple workstation; there were two keyboards and a host of specialized input devices. He took his left hand out of his pocket and ran it across the keyboard and the other controls. So easy to tell which Gilmore had manipulated last. Too easy. Gilmore should have used a virtual control surface instead of allowing the trace heat of the psych's hands to identify his workstation. Holger dispensed with the tedious task of entering the protected file zones and simply keyed in a standard recall sequence, bringing the workstation back to life. Several subscreens appeared on the monitor. None carried the data he sought, but he hadn't expected that they would. He patched to the facility's server, called up the search program he'd prepared, and set it loose using Gilmore's access authority.

"Excellent," Gilmore commented. "I'll be collecting from Dagastino. He bet me that you wouldn't rely on thermal imaging to select the console."

Holger didn't care about Gilmore's bet. Anyone with the psych's credentials should know that heat was something you felt rather than saw. If Dagastino didn't know better than to bet against the psych, he was as stupid as Sp—

What was he thinking about? He had no time for idle speculation. He needed to concentrate on the job at hand. Yes. Do it and be done with it. Get free of the facility and back into the real world. That's what he needed to be thinking about.

"Data acquired," the console announced.

His program had done its job and collected the Westwind file, his ticket out. He dumped the file to chip and pocketed it.

"Good time on retrieval," Chartain said.

He didn't need to be told that.

Holger turned in place. As he did, he took his right hand from the pocket of his greatcoat. Gilmore and Chartain stared at the H&K Viper™ that he held in that hand. The weapon wasn't really a Viper, but it looked like one. Felt like one too, almost. The weight was the same but the balance was a little off. But to all appearances it was a standard-issue weapon. Were they wondering if he had replaced the test's surrogate with the real thing? Chartain's hand was sliding toward his hip and the holstered pistol there. The major would have seen that the safety on Holger's weapon was off.

"Entertaining doubts, Major?" Holger asked him.

Holger shot them both. A bullet in each neck. Chartain first. They looked surprised. They shouldn't be, especially Gilmore. They should have known that he would be playing to win this little game. Was he supposed to let them raise the alarm before he'd gotten out of the facility?

The anesthetic in the bullets was fast, but not fast enough. Holger had made the neck shot to minimize the delay in reaction to the drug. Chartain fought it. Holger had to step close and take Chartain's pistol away from him. Chartain didn't struggle long. Holger laid him on the floor beside Gilmore.

Once he'd instructed the door to seal after he left, and the workstations to simulate activity, Holger plucked Chartain's badge from his pocket and clipped it to the front of his own greatcoat. He took the major's hat from the rack by the door as well. The fit was satisfactory; he hadn't been sure that it would be. He was pleased. The security officers were considerably less vigilant about checking persons leaving the facility than they were about those coming in. Just as well for him—if anyone looked closely at the photo, he would not pass for Chartain. But no one would be looking closely at him. The hat, the military-cut greatcoat, and the mere presence of the badge would be enough to disguise him as long as no alert was on, and he had just arranged that the alert would be late.

The next step was to walk out of the Philips Sanitorium as if he had every right in the world to do so. And didn't he? The world outside was waiting.

CHAPTER
3

In weeks of looking, John hadn't found where Spillway Sue slumped. With no money to spread among the streeters, he'd gotten no talk from them. He was still new enough that the locals wouldn't open up to him out of kindness or in hopes of earning his goodwill. Yet, for some reason he didn't really understand, he felt that he needed to try again to find her before he left with Bennett.

He was sure Sue knew he was looking. *She* was well established on the street. Surely some of those John had asked were her friends or owed her favors, if not loyalty. They would have talked to her. So why hadn't she come out of hiding? She could have found him anytime; she knew where he slumped. Why hadn't *she* contacted *him*?

John didn't want to believe that Sue was hiding from him, but that seemed the inevitable conclusion. They had only begun to discover each other—he didn't want it to end without a word. He was afraid it already had.

He drifted through the neighborhood south of 195 near the river. Without knowing where Spillway Sue might be, all he could do was check places where she had been seen and hope that he would run across her. His path was nearly as aimless as the errant leaves that rattled and rasped along the pavement driven by the chill autumn wind. The leaves didn't know where they were going, any more than did John. John's thoughts were as tumbled as the leaves.

Sue—about whom he knew so little—had spent years on

the street, maybe her entire life, while he had been raised in safe, corporate turf. They had grown up in different worlds. What did they have in common? They had shared a harrowing time, confined by the dwarves who had taken Bear. Isolated from contact with anyone other than the dwarves, John and Sue had grown into a strange sort of closeness, two frightened kids as scared of what was happening around them as they were of their attraction to each other. Though he didn't understand the attraction, John couldn't deny it.

He also couldn't escape the feelings of guilt he felt whenever he stopped to think about it.

How could he be so attracted to Sue? What about Faye? John was living with Faye, if you could call sharing a slump with an incorporeal presence "living together." Faye was his confidante and friend, as she had been since he was a kid. But John wasn't a kid anymore, and only recently he had learned that Faye had never been one. She was one of the Faery folk, an ethereal being from the otherworld. Ever since he first saw her in the—was flesh the right word?—on his first trip to the otherworld, his feelings toward her had changed. She had become real in a way he had never anticipated. Since then, he'd been all too aware of the sexual attraction between them, an attraction simultaneously frustrated and enhanced by her intangibility.

In some ways, Faye was as much a mystery to him as Spillway Sue.

Faye hadn't understood why John didn't leave at once with Bennett, the guy who had once tried to kill her. She had been full of good reasons for John to go. In Faery, John could learn about his heritage. In Faery, John could be what he was born to be. In Faery, John would come into his own. But she had missed one of the best. In Faery, Faye would be tangible. Beautiful, loving Faye would be touchable.

But, in Faery, there would be no Sue.

Despite the marked differences between the two women, John found each of them strikingly attractive. Different, but desirable. Equally desirable? John wasn't sure. At best, in the right light, Sue was pretty, in an earthy sort of way; she was a real world woman, and she had been on the streets a long time. Faye was, without a doubt and by any standards, beautiful. Admittedly, John had only seen her by the fey and deceptive light of the otherworld, but he was sure her beauty was no glamour. Had the issue been looks alone, the choice would have been easy, but John's longing for Sue had a fierce heat that was missing from his slow burning desire for Faye. Lately he had been telling himself that he needed to see Sue again, that talking with her would settle his confusion.

He wondered if Faye knew how he had been spending his time away from the slump. *He* certainly hadn't told her. He still hadn't told Faye about what happened between him and Sue, that they had made love in the slump upon their return from captivity. Things had gotten dangerous shortly thereafter and there hadn't been time to talk. Later—well, later the time never seemed right. Faye had never mentioned the incident, and John had let it lie, lacking the courage to bring it up. Talking to Faye about the longings that he felt for Sue just seemed wrong.

And there was no one else to talk to about it. Even if he were still around, Bear wouldn't understand the problem. Talking to Dr. Spae was out of the question. Maybe if John's mother were still around. But no, even had he been able to find her, he would have found no solace there; no matter what she said Marianne Reddy still thought of John as her little boy, and little boys didn't have these kinds of problems. There was no one he could talk this out with but Sue. Only he hadn't been able to find her to talk to her.

Bennett had given him twenty-four hours to take care of his business. Even without Bennett's deadline, John had a sense that time was slipping away. The more he walked, the more he felt sure that unless he succeeded in finding Sue tonight, the opportunity to straighten things out between them would slip away. The seasons of the year were poised on the cusp of change, and the wind seemed to carry whispers that all would be different soon. Somehow he felt that the wind had the truth of it.

Most of the night was gone and John was tired. The wind started to pick up, so he took the first offer of shelter, the entryway of a building. He leaned against the wall, grateful to be free of most of the wind. He could hide from the wind, but he couldn't hide from his problems.

Why couldn't things be simple?

A leaf gusted into the alcove and fetched up against his boot, a fellow refugee from the rising tumult. Another leaf blew in and landed atop the first, clinging to it. A third tumbled in, fluttering over the first two and leaping the toe of John's boot to skitter about the alcove in an errant vortex. John shifted his foot. The first two leaves joined the third and all three were swept up and tossed back onto the street. John watched them flutter away, tumbling over and around each other. They whisked past a figure moving furtively along the street. A slight figure, wearing a familiar floppy hat. The figure wore layered clothing, pure bag-lady fashion, but the jumble of rags couldn't disguise the lithe, lively grace of the body beneath them. Spillway Sue.

He watched her approach, waiting for her to notice him. She seemed unaware of his presence in the shadowed entryway. She had almost passed by the time he realized that she wasn't going to acknowledge him. He stepped out.

And she spun to face him, pulling a pistol from somewhere within the tattered rags. She pointed the weapon at him. Streetlight reflections flashed from the three tiny chrome studs implanted on her cheek, highlighting the smooth curve of the bone and the delicate slope of her nose.

"Tall Jack," she said in a tone halfway between question and statement. Her eyes were narrowed, suspicious.

He couldn't tell if she was glad to see him. "Hello, Sue."

"Ya shouldn't oughta sneak up on me like that."

If a gun had become her answer to anyone approaching her, she was right. He kept his hands clear of his body. She sighed, and the gun disappeared back beneath the rags. He was glad of that. Guns were loud and ugly, not her style at all. "I've been looking for you."

"I know."

"Why have you been hiding from me?"

Instead of answering his question, she scanned the street around them. "Oughta not stand around in the open."

She led him back the way she'd come, back into the shadows from which she had emerged, the darkness was an alley mouth. They traversed several more alleys between the tightly packed buildings before she led him down a short flight of stairs to a door. Sue unlocked the door and opened it, gesturing him inside. He went in.

The interior was a rat's warren of trash, its only illumination a fading Bulbstrip™. She led him on a twisting path through the debris to another smaller room, less cluttered but no cleaner. Another Bulbstrip, somewhat healthier, lit the place. A mattress sprawled in one corner. In another, a perscomp, conspicuous by its newness, sat on a board supported by two sawhorses. A jury-rigged patch connected the box to the building's power line. Another cord, a communications line, snaked up and through a small hole in the construction plastic covering the window. There wasn't much else beyond a box holding a couple of apples, a three-pack of YoHo Choc Drink™, and a few Readi-2-eat™ meals.

"Is this where you've been staying?" he asked. The place wasn't really any worse than his own slump, but he didn't like the idea of Sue staying here. She deserved better.

"It's a place. Guess I'll hafta find another." She shrugged, fiddling with the keys of the perscomp and not looking at him. "Watcha want?"

He didn't want to lose her again. Impulsively he reached out and took her shoulders between his hands. Her muscles tensed under his touch. For a moment he feared that she would tear herself free from his grip, but she didn't. Slowly she turned to face him. She said nothing.

He was drowning in her eyes.

"I don't want you to run away from me," he told her when he found his voice.

Her answer was slow in coming. "It's not you."

"Then why?"

"It's—" She turned her face away. She seemed to be struggling for a way to express the problem. "It's that weird stuff. It's scary, Jack. That winged monster. The creepoid place ya slump. And that elf guy who says he's your father. I don't understand it, Jack. It's like a bad virtual, only it ain't a virtual. It's all too weird."

Sometimes John felt that way himself. Gently he turned her face back to his. "There's nothing to be afraid of."

"Ain't there? Ya telling me ya got it all under control?"

Her eyes were so deep, her warmth so near.

Under control? Hardly.

His lips sought hers. After a frozen second, she responded. Their hands groped through the barriers of clothes that separated them. His hand found her gun's hiding place. She didn't object when he put it aside; in fact, she helped. There were more important, more immediate needs. The mattress in her slump was dirty and it stank of mildew, but it was softer than the floor. He basked in her heat, bathed in her passion, and when it was over and they lay in each other's arms, he felt full, satisfied, sated. She curled warmly in his embrace, almost purring.

He would have been content to pass eternity that way, but she wasn't. From beneath the mattress she pulled a headset and put it on. Music, or something resembling it, leaked from the earpiece. John had thought that they might talk. He tapped the headset and raised a quizzical eyebrow.

"Crying Child™," she said, smiling, and slipped the headset onto John. "It's Willie Hunter's new album. I don't know if I like it yet. She's been experimenting a lot since she left Urban Wilderness™. Ya like?"

Experimental was a kind way of describing what John was hearing. The pounding, raucous beat trashed most of the lyrics, but at least it did have lyrics. Most popular sound only used words as another kind of noise, and John had never cared much for music that didn't have a story or theme. Words had always made the music's story clearer for him. He tried to find the story in the piece he was listening to. It took a few moments but he finally caught a bit of the tale behind the music, realizing with surprise that the song had something to do with the legend of Tam Lin. Willie Hunter's plaintive voice was complaining of the queen's "timely tithe to hell."

John was reminded of the passage of time.

"I have to go away for a while," he said.

The suspicion that had been in her eyes when they met on the street returned. To allay it, he said, "I'll come back."

"When?" Her voice was very soft, guarded.

"Soon."

The talk didn't go very well, but in the end, by the time he had to leave, she said that she understood.

"I keep my promises," he told her.

She smiled, and kissed him, and said, "See ya soon, then."

CHAPTER
4

Holger was driving south on the M27 heading for Southampton's old city center when the alarm went up. The agent he'd left active in the facility's computer had detected the signs, watched for and captured the alert, and narrowcast a copy to him. In reaction to Holger's neutralization of Gilmore and Chartain, the Department had chosen to break the rules of the test; the alert carried a directive from the big man to all involved agents: converge on the old city center. The free ride was over. Time to watch his back.

He checked the time. Not bad. He hadn't gotten as far as he'd hoped, but not bad.

He was a bit surprised by the directive. Vectoring the opposition in on him was contrary to the rules. Holger hadn't *broken* the rules of the game, just stretched them. Hardly a fair response to break them as a counter, but then it wasn't a fair world. In a fair world, it wouldn't be raining tonight.

At least the big man hadn't gone all the way and revealed Holger's destination point. Not yet, anyway. The game was still on. There was still a decent chance for Holger to come out ahead.

Someone passed him, horn blaring, and sluiced water across the windscreen. The wipers were momentarily rendered useless. When visibility returned to its previous miserable level, the taillights of the car that had passed him were already distant. That driver wasn't allowing himself much margin for error, given the road conditions. Whoever he was, he was in a big hurry. Someone heading to cut Holger off?

He wished he'd thought to have the computer agent primed to survey and relay the messages to his hunters. Even a simple counting function would have told him the number of operatives arrayed against him. Then again, maybe it was just as well he hadn't added any functions to the agent. More muscle would have made the thing more visible to the Department's safeguards. For all he knew, the agent had been detected and the message he'd just received was what the Department wanted him to receive. Operatives could be closing in on him right now. The hurried driver might be arranging a roadblock. Others might be—

Paranoia, he told himself. A useful survival trait, if not overdone. There was no good reason to think his agent compromised. He was ahead in the game. He was doing fine. He'd worked to eliminate problems and reduce the trouble he would have in the test, and he'd succeeded. Thinking otherwise was just paranoia.

Wasn't it?

Certainly. He'd built a proper fail-safe into the agent. If it had been discovered, its complex of programs would have dissolved and unleashed a code eater to devour the fragments. The only reasonable course was to assume that the agent hadn't been compromised.

He would have felt better if it hadn't been raining.

It had been raining the day of the accident. He didn't remember much about the accident, but he remembered *that*, even though remembering made his head ache. The doctors said that the memory loss and the headaches were to be expected. Typical traumatic stress reaction. They said that in time, when he was better able to deal with it, he might remember. For now, they said, don't worry about it. The doctors had done what they could; the Department took care of its own. Don't worry about the past, they said. Deal with the present. Concentrate on the present.

Good advice, given the road conditions.

He almost missed the exit onto the A33 because he wasn't concentrating. It wouldn't do to miss his meeting with the contact in Southampton. A headache had come out of nowhere to almost blind him. The doctors had said that might happen. It was mercifully brief; some kind of feedback problem, he guessed. A recurrence at the wrong time could be a real problem. He'd have to speak to the doctors about it. *After* the test was successfully completed.

His agent narrowcast him another alert being sent out on the monitoring system. His testers were putting out a general notice. Case D-23. Holger didn't recognize the code, but the prefix indicated a technical glitch. Not *his* problem if they were having trouble.

The rain let up just before he reached Southampton's old city gate, Bar Gate, but no bar to him. Almost there. Traffic was almost nonexistent as he headed down High Street, doing an impression of a cautious, poky, tired driver, to give himself a chance to assess the site. The streets were empty of people even though the rain had stopped. Given the hour and weather, the only civilians to be encountered would be those caught somewhere by the evening storm—or those who would have even less desire to encounter Holger than he had to meet up with them. That was good.

The Red Lion was ahead on the left. Light showed in the barely translucent old glass windows, advertising the pub remained open, but there was no one loitering in front, nor anyone in sight on the sidewalks. Holger could just stop the car, get out, and walk into the pub. The whole thing could be over in a matter of minutes.

He doubted it would be so easy.

Proof of his suspicion came when he spotted the lurker in an alley across the street. Any attempt at a simple, bold approach would be intercepted. Holger drove on past. He would come back on foot.

He ditched the car in the new carpark built out into Southampton Water next to Canute's Pavilion, a large structure enclosing a maze of restaurants, shops, and entertainment facilities that thrust out onto the Water. Though the rest of the old city seemed asleep there was still a crowd in the tourist attraction; the Pavilion blared sound and light into the night. Tourists, it seemed, didn't care about following the rhythms of the town. He left them to their pointless frolics and set his course away from the light and noise and toward the quiet city. He headed toward God's House Tower, intending to work his way through the back streets to the rear of the Red Lion. In the Middle Ages there would have been guards awaiting him at the God's House Tower gate; the town had crept out beyond the gate, and the gate itself was gone, and the tower had been made into a museum. A relic—as he would be if he failed the test.

The guns of the two men who stepped out of the shadow thrown by God's House Tower were not relics. They were Smith & Wesson Equalizers™, fourteen-round, semiautomatic, 12mm handguns. Powerful. Expensive. Reputed to be highly accurate, especially when fitted with the TRW Nightfighter™ targeting system, as these were. The muzzle of the weapon thrust into Holger's face was clean, showing very little wear. The weapons were new, their matte combat finish unscuffed except for small laser-cut channels where the manufacturer's serial number and the owner's registration number had been. That last datapoint told him that he was not dealing with run-of-the-mill street toughs.

Obstacles in the test? The weapons weren't standard issue, and the faces weren't familiar. He'd thought that he knew all the possible opposition. Whoever they were, they had caught him off guard. His own fault.

"Give us the chip," said the one with his weapon in Holger's face.

Holger could hand over the chip. Containing nothing more than bogus files, the chip wasn't worth anything. But that wasn't the point. The point was that he had been entrusted with it. The chip was not his to give up.

"Since you ask so politely, I don't see how I can refuse," he said mildly, in an attempt to put them at ease.

He slowly opened the left side of his greatcoat and lifted his right hand, as if to reach in and get out the chip. Instead, he struck out and snagged the talker's wrist. Holger pulled the man closer and drove his left fist into the talker's solar plexus. There was armor there. Not enough. The power of Holger's strike drove the air from the man's body.

His partner reacted, raising his pistol to fire. Holger shifted back and away from the man. The Equalizer's throaty cough sounded, a three-round burst. Holger felt two slugs hit the talker, his shield. One round ripped through the talker's sleeve and struck Holger in the ribs. Hard. It hurt!

Real bullets weren't part of the test specifications.

Red anger flashed in Holger's mind. He heaved the talker into the other man. The two of them went down. Holger was on the partner before he could recover, foot smashing into the man's chin as he struggled to rise. Holger felt and heard bone crack in the man's jaw. He went back down on the pavement, hard. More bone cracked as his skull connected with the concrete.

No movement. No breath. No pulse. Just the stink of feces, urine, and blood.

Dead.

So was the talker. One of his partner's bullets had found a chink in his armor.

Something was wrong.

Holger checked the bodies. He found no identification. Cards, yes, but only certified debit cards. Like the weapons they carried, nothing they wore had identifying marks. The communications gear they carried was not standard ECSS issue, and like the Equalizers, it was expensive stuff.

No ID. No standard-issue gear. Nothing obviously traceable. It all added up to corporate style, which raised other issues. Corporate special operatives might be unprincipled thugs, but they didn't go around jumping on random victims either.

Something was very wrong.

Holger crossed back to Canute's Pavilion, where he would be a more difficult target for any backup supporting the thugs. Once inside, he made his way through the meandering clumps of tourists and late-night revelers until he found a public perscomp bank. He selected the one with the best view of its surroundings, ran one of the thugs' cards through the reader, and punched up access. He added a security code that would identify him to the Department. The agent receiving the call asked for two more levels of confirmation before it transferred the call to a living being. Kun was surprised to see L'Hereaux, the big man's security expert, answer.

"About time," L'Hereaux said. A frown crossed his face. "Why are you using a public comp?"

"Read the ident on the card I used."

A moment's wait while L'Hereaux called up the data. "There is no ident."

Holger nodded. He'd expected that. "I borrowed the card from what I thought were two obstacles. They weren't part of the program, were they?"

"Where are you?"

"Use the backtrace if you really need to know. I won't be here long. Just tell me, were they on the program?"

"No one on the program has cards like that."

"Thought not."

"Wait," L'Hereaux said. "Don't disconnect."

Holger almost did anyway, but something in L'Hereaux's voice suggested more than a stratagem to keep him on the line while operatives were vectored toward him. That would certainly be happening, but there was more at work here. Holger was curious. He would listen.

"You didn't get a message, did you?"

Only from his agent. He'd locked out other codes to preclude tracing of the carrier signal.

"I see," L'Hereaux said. "There's a problem. We've discovered that someone made a substitution on the package you're carrying. It's something we'd rather not have out of our hands."

"You calling an abort on the test? You want me to come in?"

"No. Make your meet. We're compromised here. Your contact was to take you on to another step anyway. Meeting your contact is the best option you have at the moment."

"Calling off the dogs?"

"If they are attempting to use the test for their own ends, that would tip them to the fact that we know."

"Aren't you afraid that they're listening now?"

"I don't think that likely," L'Hereaux said, without offering any reason for his confidence.

Unlikely, eh, but not impossible.

"Be careful. If they managed the switch, they may have specialists working with them." L'Hereaux cut the connection.

Wonderful. If. May. L'Hereaux had no more information than Holger. And specialists—Holger's stomach soured at the possibility.

A "specialist" was what the Department called a magician—and not the stage kind, either, but the kind who did real magic. The Department's heads had long feared that someone else would acquire or train specialists to rival the Department's own. They had especially feared that one of the immoral megacorporations would be the ones to do so. The megacorps, with their global spread, were uncontrollable by any one nation, possibly even by a group of nations.

There had been nothing *special* about the two who had accosted Holger, but that didn't mean the affair wasn't tainted by such dangerous malignancy. Whether magic was involved or not, those two would have backup lurking about somewhere. There was no time to loaf.

Holger cut across Queen's Park and headed up High Street, thinking about the new factors in the equation. The new players were serious. Unfortunately, as far as tools went, he didn't have much to stop determined opposition who were playing for keeps. The Viper was loaded with tranqs, and a single load at that. He would have to rely on his personal abilities and skills, and though he knew how very lethal he could be without tools, the most effective applications required close physical proximity. Thugs were one thing, specialists something else. He had no desire to achieve close physical proximity to any specialists who might be working with this new opposition.

Magic, thank God, was rare. He wished it were rarer.

The possibility of specialists continued to bother him. Such people preferred to hide in the shadows; they didn't like anyone knowing of their unnatural abilities. Such a predilection could be turned to Holger's aid. If he could assure the presence of witnesses, the new opposition might hesitate to use anything *unusual* against him. If they tried anyway, he could try to make enough fuss to expose them. The emptiness of the streets no longer seemed fortunate. If he needed attention, he would have to draw. Gunfights made a lot of noise, attracted a lot of attention. But the Viper was rigged for quiet operation. He could fix that easily with a little time and attention, but he doubted that he had that time.

Besides, he had his own constraints. The Department wouldn't like him exposing magical things, even those arranged by enemies. Did that matter? Not just now. Holger's survival was somewhat more important to him than the Department's preferences. Alive, he could help them pick up the pieces, even help them focus any adverse publicity on the shadowy opposition. But only if he was alive.

At least his armor was real and reliable.

It stood him in good stead when he moved to take out the lurker watching the Red Lion from the alley across the street. Holger was easier on him than he had been on the thugs with the Equalizers. Fast and quiet. He looked down at the sprawled body, satisfied that the man was still breathing. This was Linkwater, an agent of the Department. Part of the test and not some unknown hostile agent. That comforted Holger, suggesting that the whole operation had not been compromised.

Time to finish the test.

He crossed the street and entered the Red Lion. He could hear someone in the back, in the kitchen, rattling dishes.

There were a few people in the front room. A couple at a table, huddled in a private world. A handful of working men at the bar. They ignored him. He recognized one despite his seedier-than-normal appearance: Pankhurst, another Departmental agent. Like the other patrons and the bartender, Pankhurst ignored Holger's entrance. That meant that Holger could expect trouble upstairs. The last part of the test would be there.

Warned, Holger started up the ancient, uneven stairs.

The floorboards above creaked under a heavy load, masking any sound that Holger made. Unwise of them not to be ready and waiting quietly. He could hear something being dragged across the floor. Holger's first glimpse of the upper story showed a pair of feet. They were quickly dragged out of his line of vision.

He freed the Viper and continued up.

A shadow fell over him as he made the landing. Something hard hit his arm, jarring him. Involuntarily, his hand opened. A hairy paw smacked against his fingers and the Viper went flying away.

Hairy paw?

Holger sprang ahead and to his left, away from his attacker at the head of the stairs. Holger caromed off the wall in his haste to get away. Not much space on the landing. He had lost his weapon. It would be hand-to-hand. He needed a chance to ready his defense. The old flooring moaned as he turned to face his opponent. Holger's eyes went wide as he saw what had attacked him.

The monster was a foot taller than Holger and stood hunched in the low-ceilinged room. It was massive, at least half again Holger's weight, and strange lumps distorted its outline. Dark, shadowed, piggy eyes glared from under shaggy brows; shaggier hair stuck out from beneath the red leather cap that it wore. A lopsided, snag-toothed grin distended its face.

Holger could hear himself panting.

A troll.

No tools.

Only himself.

"Come on, little man-thing," the troll said in a bass rumble. "Give me the chip and maybe I won't grind your bones."

There was a body on the floor behind the troll. The feet Holger had seen as he came up the stairs belonged to that body. No movement. No breath. No heartbeat. Dead. Evidence of how the troll would deal with Holger, probably whether he complied or not. Holger had to fight, even though the result was foredoomed.

Holger's breathing was shallow, rapid. His skin tingled. Everything he saw seemed sharp-edged, with digitally enhanced clarity. Someone—who? No time to think about that. *Look at what's in front of you!*—had once told him that you can't change anything you don't try to change. Heat crawled along his veins, exploding into flames. He launched himself at the troll.

Holger used all the combat arts he had been taught in basic training and every dirty trick he had learned since. He kicked and punched and clawed. The troll was pummeling him, but he put aside the pain. Pain wouldn't stop him. He couldn't let it stop him, not even slow him down. He fought harder. Smashing. Ripping. Tearing. He felt muscle and bone part under his assault. He felt his fingers go slippery with blood.

Then, without apparent transition, he was standing still, panting; this time from exhaustion rather than fear. He was looking down at the broken, bleeding body of the troll.

Somehow, he had beaten it.

The monster was defeated. By him. It had bled like a real animal, cried out in pain. It had been real. Too, too terribly real, but . . .

He had beaten it.

He felt . . . tired.

And worried.

This monster was evidence that another of the Department's fears had been realized. The troll was evidence that their shadowy opponent had done a deal with the otherworld and sent this minion here to intercept Holger. Who knew what other creatures might come to their call? There were things that physical force couldn't touch. Dangerous, deadly things. He knew.

Holger heard a door open behind him. He tensed, ready for a further assault, but it was only his contact Chalmers. The man looked as surprised as Holger had been to see the troll. Chalmers was fortunate that Holger had arrived when he did. Likely Chalmers would have been the troll's next victim.

At least the test was over.

Pankhurst came pounding up the stairs. Gaping, he stared at the troll Holger had vanquished. Kneeling by the body, he examined the wounds. "God, Kun, what did you do to him?"

"Took it out." It was a damned troll. What was he supposed to do? Kiss it?

"It?"

"The troll."

"Jesus." Pankhurst tugged at the skin on the troll's neck.

With a sucking, ripping sound the skin tore free. Pankhurst peeled the troll's face away. There was a man's face beneath it. Holger didn't recognize the face. No man's face belonged there.

"This is no bloody damn troll," Pankhurst screamed. "It's Leftenant Barkins from MI6. He's wearing a bloody costume, you maniac!"

Not a troll? But—

Holger looked to the body of the agent the troll had overcome. He saw what he should have seen in the first place. The body was not a body, but a dummy. No breath or heartbeat because it had never had any. And the troll—barely breathing, heart fluttering—the troll wasn't a troll at all.

"You do the same to Linkwater?" Pankhurst asked angrily.

"No." Holger blinked, confused. He shook his head. No. Not to a man. "No."

"Thank God for small favors." Pankhurst touched his head, behind the ear, where his implant would be. "Man down. Medical evac, stat. Make it bloody fast or just send a body bag."

Pankhurst stood, shaking his head. He was no more a doctor than Holger. There was nothing either of them could do for—was Barkins the name?

"Better check on Linkwater," Chalmers said to Pankhurst.

Pankhurst nodded and left. He left bloody footprints on the stairs.

Chalmers stepped up beside Holger. The man avoided looking down at the bloody mess that was Barkins. Yes, Barkins was the name. Leftenant Barkins, MI6. Not a troll at all.

"Looks like you've overcome your fear of the things from the other side," he said. "Do you still have the chip, Kun?"

Holger nodded.

Chalmers held out his hand. Holger placed the chip carrier in his palm. The last part of the test completed. Chalmers looked grim.

"I think Monsieur L'Hereaux will want some words with you."

CHAPTER
5

Ben Wiley was president of Datapik, the major information resource firm under the Metadynamics corporate umbrella. He wore the right suits, maintained the right home and the right friends, bribed the right politicians and media hacks, and never, ever left behind enough evidence to tie him to anything that might be deleterious to the company or to himself. Wiley lived up to his name, being sharp in his dealings and quick to take advantage of his opponents' failings. Young, ambitious Wiley was a rising star in the Metadynamics firmament, and a rival to Anton Van Dieman.

Van Dieman didn't care for rivals.

More than once Wiley had forced Van Dieman to restructure his plans. Had Wiley been more than mundanely oriented, he would have been a *dangerous* rival. But Wiley's time was passing, as was the mundanely oriented world. Van Dieman's stars were in the ascendancy.

The proof was there to be seen. Van Dieman had made himself a powerful man. His own Clemsen Bioresearch was no small part of the Metadynamics family. He had good connections in the megacorporation and in the government, but it was his other connections that had stood him in such good stead over the past year, and those connections would make his rise unstoppable. Opponents of Wiley's sort would soon be part of Van Dieman's past.

For the moment, however, Wiley still had the power to annoy. He separated Van Dieman from the herd as they left the last session of Metadynamics's quarterly coordination briefing.

"I hear you're losing the top brains in your research branch, Darney, Thompson, and Trahn, all at once. Quite a blow." Wiley made a mock sympathetic noise. "Hard to recover from, especially with a budget cut ahead. I'd say you're looking at some hard knocks in the market, my friend."

Where had Wiley gotten that information? "Those transfers have not yet been announced."

Wiley smiled a knowing and thoroughly smug smile. "Word gets around. Too bad—for you, I mean. I know how hard you worked to build up that staff. I hear the market's already reacting. I even hear that there's a rumor about you looking for greener pastures elsewhere." Wiley's tone suggested that he found such a concept very satisfying on a personal level.

"No need to worry," he told Wiley. "I will be staying within the family. I've accepted the executive vice presidency at NSC."

Network Securities Corporation's mission encompassed operations for most of Metadynamics's North American-based companies, including Datapik. Van Dieman's new position did not cover Datapik. Yet. That would change.

"I'm sure we'll be seeing more of each other," he told Wiley. Smiling at the man's stunned surprise, Van Dieman left him behind.

Upon return to his office, Van Dieman ordered both his secretary and his secretarial agent to shield him from any intrusions. He settled at his desk, noting the fine, expensive furnishings of his office, the symbols of his mundane power. Such power offered great rewards, but he wished to contemplate a different sort of power, one that offered greater rewards. He blanked the window for privacy and cut off the hologram projector nestled among the shelves of his office's inner wall. The false image of a rare Guthrie bronze faded away, allowing his prize to emerge from hiding. He smiled to look upon it again.

The object was a sculpture of unknown substance depicting a coiled, wormlike entity. The room's lighting was bright enough that the object appeared nearly transparent. He ordered the lights dimmed, smiling as solidity returned to the vermicular object. His eyes ran along the coils as he considered the fortune that had smiled on him.

It had been easy to convince Fletcher to place the object in his care, by telling the Federal Security Agency bureau chief that it needed to be studied. Who better to do so than himself, chief technical adviser to the FSA's top-secret Dark Glass program? No one among the agency's magicians could match Van Dieman's expertise, which was not surprising since half of them were charlatans. In its attempt to learn about and control the magic that was rising all around, the federal government had been less selective in recruiting for Dark Glass than it might have been, but even among the true magicians of Dark Glass, no one could offer a better chance of unraveling the object's secrets.

Of course, Van Dieman already understood some of those secrets; but his knowledge had come, not from study of the object, but from the cult of which he was a part. That cult, the Followers of the Glittering Path, understood what this object was for. They knew that it was what they had sought for more than a millennium: the Key. Not just any key, but *the* Key. The Key of the sacred texts, the Key to the Glittering Path. The key to power!

And who had a better claim to it than he? He had spent years learning the ancient ways and readying himself. When Quetzal, the Awaited One, he who had been called Quetzoucouatl, had come, Van Dieman had been ready to bask in his radiance. Van Dieman had exalted the Feathered Serpent and given him the honor due him. Quetzal had approved of Van Dieman's devotion and had seen his worth. Had not the Awaited One, from his own hand, given Van Dieman a taste of the glorious power that was the true follower's reward?

Quetzal had opened the way for him and set him on the path. When Van Dieman had received the sacrament from Quetzal's hand, his mind had been opened to thoughts beyond the ken of the sheep around him. Awakened, he saw more clearly now. He understood Quetzal's role as the Lord of Change. Van Dieman's life was changed by his contact with the Awaited One, as it was to be. Now he knew his role, understood his place in the opening of the Way. He was Quetzal's chosen successor. Had he not received the sacrament from Quetzal's own hand? Who else could say that?

All was moving as the stars decreed. All was becoming as it was meant to be.

Before his sharing with Quetzal, Van Dieman had struggled to maintain his position at the sixth degree. Now the power came easier. Already he had passed the test and achieved fifth degree—as high as Ryota Nakaguchi had ever achieved—and he was ready for fourth. Magical power meant political power among the Followers of the Glittering Path, and political power within the secret cabal meant secret but potent influence in the mundane world—influence that Van Dieman had used to engineer his own promotion within Metadynamics, as Nakaguchi had done for himself within the Mitsutomo megacorporation. Van Dieman intended not simply to equal Nakaguchi's successes, but to exceed them.

Quetzal's awakening had been Nakaguchi's greatest success, but ultimately his downfall. There was no denying that the Awaited One had not been exactly what the followers had been expecting. The teacher and guide of whom they had dreamed had turned out to be a tyrant, shaking the foundations of the followers' beliefs. Like Van Dieman, Nakaguchi had chafed under their new master. The overshadowing of Nakaguchi's power among the followers had prompted him to act, in an attempt to contain the threat posed by Quetzal. It was a logical and necessary rebellion, but one launched too soon. The Followers of the Glittering Path had spent centuries honing patience as one of their most valuable tools, something Nakaguchi had forgotten. The gleam of the path shining through the gray dawn of this new age of magic had blinded Nakaguchi with its promise of power, and he had acted hastily. He had paid for his impatience.

But the followers had paid a price as well. Quetzal was gone now, and with him the opportunity to learn from the Awaited One. But from each loss a good businessman finds a way to gain.

With Quetzal's passing the followers had also lost the brilliant mind behind the plans Quetzal had set in motion. Their councils remained divided about what to do next. But there were clues in their holy books, in what Quetzal had ordered done in his brief time among them, and in the key that Quetzal had uncovered. Especially in the key. Van Dicman's eyes caressed the twisted sculpture. There were secrets in the subtle, sinuous curves of the key, secrets that he was teasing out. Already he knew that the Awaited One and the Strong One of the texts were not the same person. The Strong One who would arise and lead the faithful had not yet come to his power.

But he would.

Van Dieman's time was coming. Already his team of specialists, monitoring Quetzal's magical resonators, had observed patterns in their functions. The secrets were unfolding. The resonators were enhancers, lenses to concentrate the effects of mundane processes. One exaggerated effect was already clear at the strongest focal point. There, at the bottom of the world, the rate of ozone depletion in the upper atmosphere was increasing. It was a sign. The spreading of industrial decay, what the prophet Luciferius had called the man-blight, was a major sign that the time of the Opening was soon to come. Soon harbingers would arrive, the heralds of the new age, and he, Anton Van Dieman, the Strong One, heir to the mantle of Quetzal, would be waiting to honor them and to receive their benisons and gifts of gratitude.

For Van Dieman, Nakaguchi's folly would become a blessing.

* * *

For Pamela Martinez, Nakaguchi's folly might become a blessing.

Or a curse.

The Quetzal incident had gained notice within the Keiretsu, especially when the fool Nakaguchi had managed to get himself killed by his resurrected monster. His actions had imperiled Pamela by exposing her secret Charybdis Project. No longer was she able to hide from her superiors her investigations into paranormal occurrences and the resurgence of magic. Nakaguchi would have a last use, however: she intended to lay all the improper secrecy at his door.

In his brief reign over the project, Nakaguchi had tumbled it into a shambles and perverted it from what Pamela had begun. She was still reassembling the pieces and trying to make sense of the chimera Nakaguchi had left her. Sheila Rearden, her best computer jockey, was still teasing her way into Nakaguchi's files, uncovering more and stranger data with every file she cracked. Already it was clear that Nakaguchi had made connections in occult circles that gave him access to information unknown to project researchers. Some of that information would be most useful in refocusing the project.

If she was allowed to continue.

There was still a chance. It had turned out that Nakaguchi had been acting on his own, without the knowledge or approval of Mitsutomo-sama. Pamela had used that fact to the fullest when her superiors had called for a full report on the Quetzal incident. She had been given an opportunity to distance herself from the disaster and she intended to take advantage of it.

The Mitsutomo board had assembled on the telenet to hear her report. Her strategy had been to cast Nakaguchi as a rogue and loose cannon responsible for the project's improprieties, while painting herself as the loyal company servant who sought to protect the Keiretsu's interests. She could not conceal that she had been instrumental in the direction of the

Charybdis Project, but Passerelli in Relations had helped her prepare her report, putting things in the best possible light, and Rearden had provided credible data trails involving directives from Nakaguchi in place of Pamela's own orders. She had made her presentation to the board, and now she could only hope that she had put the right spin on it.

Sitting and waiting in her office while the board considered her report made her feel as if she were waiting in a judgment dock; which, of course, she was, though her office was infinitely more comfortable. She still felt uneasy.

At last her wallscreen brightened as her node was relinked with the conference. A rank of subscreens showed a head-and-shoulders shot of each of the board members. Each and every one of them held his or her expression impassive and inscrutable.

"We must put the past behind us," said Kenji Kabashima.

Though Kabashima did the talking, his words were those of the elderly gentleman pictured on the screen to the left of Kabashima's: Hiroto Mitsutomo, the lord and master of Mitsutomo Corporation, the head of the greatest and most powerful of the world's megacorporations. The old man's participation in this vid conference was an honor.

Such honors had ended careers before now. She kept her expression correctly neutral.

"Your presentation on the Charybdis Project has been enlightening," Kabashima continued.

Not surprising, considering that the project had been Pamela's secret before it had become Nakaguchi's secret.

"Naturally, with such a complex subject, the ramifications will take some time to understand. For the moment, however, all the obvious questions appear to have been answered."

Not Pamela's. Was she still part of the Mitsutomo family?

Kabashima looked down, at a screen Pamela knew to be inset in the console in front of him. He would be receiving instructions there. The private screen allowed communication between master and mouthpiece without the embarrassing possibility of being overheard by other participants in the conference.

"At this time, Ms. Martinez," he began, "the board of Mitsutomo Corporation would like to express its gratitude for the efficient way in which you have attended to Mitsutomo's interests. The situation is, perhaps, not the best, but some matters are beyond any person's control. This is a fact of life that must be accepted. Your dedication to the interests of the corporation is commendable."

Pamela bowed her head in humble acceptance of the compliment. The bow gave her a chance to hide the grin of relief that threatened to overwhelm her face.

"Mitsutomo's interests are our interests," Duncan Middleton said. Duncan was Pamela's personal assistant, and he had her confidence. He also had a screen much like Kabashima's prompter with which she could guide him if necessary, but she wasn't planning to use it. She would have preferred speaking for herself, but there were protocols that one observed when dealing with Mitsutomo-sama. The old man was quite conservative in some respects.

"Much has been done in connection with this Charybdis Project, but the matters involved seem to breed questions. Clearly, there is a continuing need of answers," Kabashima said. "Data are power, as Gates-sama might say. Mitsutomo Corporation is always in search of useful data."

"The Charybdis Project, if continued, seems likely to provide much useful data," Duncan said.

"Indeed, that is the opinion of the board as well. Ms. Martinez is hereby appointed *kansayaku* for the Charybdis Project. The project will continue under the supervision of the Board, with all funding approved directly by Mitsutomo-sama's office."

Pamela couldn't have hoped for a better outcome.

Kabashima leaned toward the video pickup. "Nakaguchi-san misunderstood his role. Such a regrettable error is unlikely to occur again, *neh*?"

"Highly unlikely," Duncan replied.

In other words, Charybdis was Pamela's, but Pamela was Mitsutomo's. She understood that. It was an arrangement she could live with.

"This has been a most productive conference," Kabashima said.

"Most productive," Duncan agreed.

After the requisite courtesies closed the conference, Pamela opened the monitoring line where Sheila Rearden waited.

"Recall your recording and enhance the reflections in Kabashima's eyes. I doubt the old man is unsophisticated enough to have sent his orders in the clear, but I want to be sure. We can at least record the codes he uses."

"Roger-double-dodger, boss lady."

A most productive conference indeed.

CHAPTER
6

Putting down the coffee mug, Steve said, "Here you go, Gil. Radar says we've got a storm coming in."

"Thanks," Gil replied, taking possession of the steaming mug. It might be late spring down here, but spring in Antarctica was still too damn cold. She was supposed to be used to it by now. Well, at least the coffee was hot. Life-giving, healing warmth slid down her gullet as she swallowed. "A storm, you say?"

"Outer edge is coming across the Victoria Land now. Smart money says it'll be here in two hours, tops."

Steve might be military, but as a meteorologist he knew his stuff. Gil wasn't going to bet against him. "We've got two teams between Vickie and here. Should we call them in?"

"Put the word out. Sharon and her people will be able to make it back here no problem, but Jemal's team doesn't have a prayer. They'll have to batten down where they are. He should have listened to me when I told him he was going out too early. Call him first. They'll need all the time they have to get ready."

Why did Gil have to have commo duty just now? Dr. Jemal Dickinson was not someone she liked dealing with at the best of times. He wouldn't like losing time to the storm; he and his team had lost all of last season to storms. Alighieri, Dickinson's tel-op robot probe, was an expensive toy to have sitting around doing nothing when it was supposed to be exploring volcanic craters and the corp sponsors didn't like to see their toys sitting around doing nothing. Of course the scientists riding herd on Alighieri didn't like sitting around, either, but they didn't sign the paychecks so their yelps wouldn't matter much. Just like last year.

Gil pulled up the communications link to Dickinson's remote. Signal monitors flashed to life on the edges of her screen, showing the status of individual data streams piggybacking on the main transmission. The direct communications link was dark, and would stay that way until someone responded. Resignedly, Gil kept punching the call button. She watched the flashing digits and squiggly lines of the data monitors. Seeing that the video feed from the probe's cameras was running, she set up a subscreen to display the video transmission. The fuzzy false-color images from the probe's camera were more interesting than digital and graphical readouts. She punched the call button some more, and watched jumpy pictures of shadowy rocks until Dickinson answered. As she expected, he wasn't happy about being interrupted. And when she told him about the storm, he had some very colorful things to say, finishing with, "Alighieri's already running."

She knew that. "Can you call it back?"

"Don't be ridiculous. The sky is clear here."

If Steve was right, it wouldn't stay that way. "I thought I was being prudent by telling you."

He started to tell her what he really thought that she was being, but a call from off-camera interrupted him. "Dr. Dickinson! I think you ought to see this."

"What now?" Exasperation filled Dickinson's voice.

"There's something strange going on around Alighieri."

Without a word to her, Dickinson left the range of the video pickup. Gil felt a bit exasperated herself. She checked Alighieri's video screen. Dickinson's team member was right. It looked as if something was moving near the probe. The images didn't make any sense to Gil and before she could puzzle them out, the image darkened and faded to black. She checked the feed. Nothing.

Dr. Dickinson got back on the line. "McMurdo Station, are you getting video?"

"Negative. Other data feeds are okay. What happened?"

"We're not sure. Are you seeing any other changes?"

"There's a slight but steady drop in ambient temperature. Air pressure's down too."

"Yes, yes. We're getting that too. Anything else?"

"Care to give me a clue as to what I'm looking for? Probe telemetry is not my field."

"Stand by." He was gone again.

Dickinson was an *annoying* man. Stand by for what?

The data feeds from the Alighieri probe winked out.

Surely not *that*. She looked for the biomonitors on Alighieri's tel-op operator. That link was down too. Dickinson would be a very unhappy man if Alighieri had just fritzed out again.

Dickinson stormed into view of the video pickup. He raved at her. Gil tried to comply with his "requests" to find a clear bandwidth to reestablish data links, but everything seemed to be cluttered by the storm's interference.

"If it's this bad, you had better start battening down," she advised.

As he started to reply, a blistering indictment of her skill, the video began to flicker. She lost the video link entirely. Dickinson continued his insulting evaluation of her competence on audio alone. She tried to ignore him while she tried to reestablish the link. When the audio signal started to break up, she was almost relieved.

"The storm's going to cut commo," she tried to tell him, but he insisted, she thought, that the skies were still clear.

Well, from where she sat, the electromagnetic bands certainly weren't clear.

She bumped up the power, hoping to cut through the interference. She got through, sort of, but not to Dickinson. She found herself struggling to communicate with one of Dickinson's team. The woman was hysterical, practically babbling. It sounded to Gil like she was saying something about some kind of animal coming out of the crater. But that couldn't be right. The on-again, off-again link didn't help. Gil's requests for clarification only brought more garbled replies. Another boost to signal power didn't help. The interference was getting worse. Something came through that sounded like a scream. But it couldn't be a scream; it had to be some kind of electronic feedback. There was nothing but static after that.

Looking at the dead screen, listening to the static hiss, Gil didn't know what else to do.

The storm must have moved in faster than Steve had predicted, if it had already cut communications. She hoped the disturbance was west of the mountains between McMurdo and the research site, because if it was on top of Dickinson's team, there were six people in real danger of having their butts frozen off.

Could they send out a rescue verrie? Maybe Steve had an updated storm track that would tell her. Even if he didn't, he'd know what to do; he was a veteran of a dozen summers down here. She headed for the weather room and nearly ran into Steve in the corridor. His snow goggles were perched on his watch cap and he was pulling on his snow suit.

"Where are you going?"

"Going to go check the dish," he said. "That storm just dropped off the screen."

"What do you mean the storm's gone? It can't be. It just ate our commo link with Dr. Dickinson's team."

Steve shrugged. "It's gone. Vanished. Not there."

"You run diagnostics?"

"Sure. Everything's fine. Damnedest thing. Still got a track on the English verrie headed out to the seal station, but the storm's gone like it never was there."

"So there's something wrong with the dish." That had to be it. The storm was still out there fouling up communications.

"Must be." Twenty minutes later, he was back, chilled and puzzled. "Dish checks out okay. Still having trouble getting through to Jemal?"

She had been trying without success. "The airwaves are still fritzed. What's going on?"

"Damned if I know."

"Some kind of glitch in the radar?" It had to be. A storm couldn't rip up the electromagnetic bands like this one was doing and not show on radar.

"If there's a glitch, I can't find it. Wouldn't be the first time that happened, though." He shook his head ruefully. "If we've got a wild storm out there, you had better call Sharon and her people and tell them to get their butts back here. Better safe and all that." Gil agreed.

Three hours later, well after the storm should have arrived at McMurdo Station, the skies were still clear and the commo channels still fuzzed. Sharon's crew was back safe and sound, but Dr. Dickinson and his team remained incommunicado.

CHAPTER

7

"I don't understand why we're going to wherever the hell it is you're taking us. Why aren't we in the otherworld already?" John asked.

Bennett didn't take his eyes from the road, but he did remove one hand from the steering wheel and make an airy gesture. "One cannot just cross over anywhere."

Oh, yeah? "Dr. Spae says otherwise."

"Ah, yes, Dr. Spae. Quite the authority, isn't she?"

John didn't care for Bennett's sarcastic tone. "She knows a lot about magic."

"For a human."

"What's that supposed to mean?"

"She is quite talented. Again, for a human."

John was getting the drift. "But she's nothing much compared to an elf like you, hunh?"

Smiling, Bennett said, "No, she isn't. Not compared to an elf like either of us."

Despite the implied compliment, Bennett's put-down of Dr. Spae didn't sit well with John.

"He's right, John," Faye said.

John felt his face redden in embarrassment—he had almost forgotten that she was along. She was always very quiet around Bennett, and when an invisible person is quiet, there's not much to remind you of her presence. He felt even more embarrassed that she had broken her silence to chide him and side with Bennett. After all, wasn't Bennett the one

67

who treated her like some kind of lesser life form? Well, maybe Bennett *was* right, but John didn't have to like the way Bennett expressed himself.

Bennett seemed amused by John's embarrassment. "It seems I should not have argued against bringing the sprite along."

But he had, saying that Faye had no place in the life that was to be John's. Despite her apparent similarity of appearance, Faye was not an elf like Bennett and John, but a different sort of Faery being, a sprite. The news had dispelled his fears that he and Faye were closely related by blood. Which was great! Of course, he hadn't agreed to leave her behind; in the otherworld, they would be able to touch. Not that he let Bennett in on that reason for wanting her along. He'd just been stubborn, and Faye had backed his obstinance with her own, insisting that she accompany them to the otherworld—though later, privately, she had admitted that she thought Bennett was right about her having no place in John's new life. How could she doubt it?

"You know, Bennett, I'm not as good as you at abandoning people," John said.

"Really? What about your Spillway Sue?"

He *wasn't* abandoning her. He had told Sue that he would be back soon, and he would. As soon as he could. As soon as he got what was coming to him.

"Or Marianne Reddy? What have you done to further your senseless search for that woman?"

That woman had raised John, and he *hadn't* abandoned her. He'd been busy, working on acquiring the tools for his search. Having exhausted the obvious leads and his limited resources, he'd needed new ones, and when he got back from the otherworld, things would be different. He'd have access to the magic that was his by right of birth. He had plans for that magic, the first of which was tracking down his missing mother.

He really *wasn't* abandoning anyone. He was just taking

an opportunity to prepare himself, to get access to useful tools he had been denied.

"Jack, you must not concern yourself with such ephemera. You are an elf. Their kind can have only passing meaning for you. You will see. With time, you will come to understand."

Don't concern yourself? John was very concerned, but it was clear that Bennett was the one who didn't understand real feelings about people. Still, the elf had planted a seed of doubt. Was John fooling himself? Did being an elf make him *that* different? What would he see? How would passing time change his understanding? There was a hell of a lot about being an elf that he didn't know.

They covered a lot of ground while John fretted. Bennett took them off the state highway onto an even more rural road, and out the car's headlights. He drove on, unconcerned, apparently satisfied to rely on his elven ability to see in the dark. Had John not been able to see as well himself, he would have been terrified by the speed at which they were traveling. As it was, he decided to watch the landscape rather than the road.

The neighborhood started to look vaguely familiar, which puzzled John until Bennett turned down a long, wooded drive and he saw the house that they were approaching. It was the safehouse where the ECSS agent Kun had taken John after he and Bear had rescued John from the clutches of Mitsutomo. The place was dark, apparently deserted.

"What are we doing here?" he asked. "This doesn't involve Mitsutomo or spy stuff, does it?"

"You're unnecessarily concerned. Mitsutomo no longer has an interest in you, and the owners will never know that we've been here."

"The place has alarms." John had seen the systems and been impressed by their thoroughness.

"We won't be going inside."

John noted where Bennett was piloting the car. Unnecessarily concerned, hunh? "You won't have to go inside to set off the alarms if you drive much closer in this direction."

Bennett stopped the car and gave John an inscrutable look. "How do you know that?"

"While you were having your conferences last time, I wasn't included. I didn't have a lot to do, so I looked around the place. I got a look at the security system before Agent Kun chased me away from it." At the time, knowing as much as possible about the place had seemed like a useful survival move.

"And you understood the system?"

"Well enough."

Bennett seemed satisfied with John's answer. He shut the car down and turned to John. "You asked why we have come here. Consider. Have not your studies with Dr. Spae taught you that the symbolic content of some actions is as important, if not more so, than the actual actions? It was here that you made your first return to the otherworld. It is fitting that your return to your proper place begin here as well."

"So you've got some kind of magical thing cooking."

"Not all symbolic actions are directly related to things magical." Bennett cut off John's questions by getting out of the car. "Come. It is past time that we were on our way."

John opened his door and got out. "You ever going to tell me what this is all about?"

"I've already told you, Jack. This is about your heritage."

It *had* to be more than just ensuring John's heritage. Bennett wasn't that generous, and he had played hardball to get John to go along. "What do you get out of it?"

"An heir."

John stood, hand still on the car door. Was Bennett serious? What did it mean?

"All will come clear in time, but not here," Bennett said, walking toward the woods behind the house and beckoning John to follow. "Your future awaits you in the otherworld, Jack. We must go."

John followed, aware at once when the shift between the worlds began. Bennett was controlling the passage. John didn't understand how, but he could feel the elf's effortless display of power flickering in the air around him.

Someday John would be so adept. He promised himself that.

For the moment, however, he let himself be led. He tried to open himself to the magic as Dr. Spae had taught him, tried to let the ambiance adjust his perceptions, tried to let the understanding come. And understanding did come. He understood that something was different. Somehow this passage differed from the others that he had experienced.

"Is something wrong?" he asked.

"You sense a difference?" Bennett replied.

John wanted an answer, not a question. Well, he could play that game too. "What are you doing?"

"Taking you to the otherworld."

"More than that."

"Or less. There are places, deeper realms, where time flows differently."

Like in the ballads and stories, where a man spends a night in a Faery hill and finds that twenty years have passed in the real world? Was that to be the result of coming with Bennett?

"You have a promise to fulfill," Bennett reminded him.

He had more than one promise to fulfill, and he would fulfill them all.

They walked on.

As they shifted to the otherworld, Faye's existence became more real. She went from the merest impression of presence, to flickering phantom, to insubstantial but definite wraith, to concrete physicality. Tall, though not so tall as he, her slender form moved lightly by his side, her mane of spun-silver hair floating in the breeze. Faye. She was as beautiful as he remembered her.

How could he ever forget that she was around?

"Do you feel better now?" Bennett asked.

"What?" John replied distractedly.

"This is Faery," he said.

"You're home, John," said Faye.

"Or nearly so," Bennett said. "We must walk a bit farther."

They left the woods and embarked on a trek through a countryside devoid of buildings or other structures. The scenery seemed stranger, more lively, now than it had on the first trip. The multitude of stars overhead were wondrous in number and clarity, not a sight to be seen in the glow of the sprawl. John supposed that he had grown less used to greenery than he once was; the strip of trees along the river near his slump was nothing like a real forest. While growing up, the closest he'd come to really experiencing open countryside had been a few romps in the park, and those tended places offered little of the wild wonder around them. There was no place near his slump that one could go and not see something built by man—he'd always thought that a shame—but here there were no constructs. Curiously, he found himself a little unsettled by the lack, a little unnerved by all the wildness around him.

"Nervous?" Faye slipped her hand into his as she spoke.

"Yeah. I guess. A little." Faye's nearness sent his head buzzing and his blood racing. "And confused."

A lot.

"I'll help if I can," she said.

John found himself thinking entirely too much about one sort of help she might offer. He didn't trust himself to speak, so they walked on in silence. Faye, as she always did, accepted his choice. So accommodating. Too bad they weren't alone. But they weren't and John forced himself to look everywhere but at Faye.

The beauty around him offered distraction. Most of the landscape possessed a haunting familiarity, the way places seem familiar in a dream. A sensation well known to John. He had dreamed of the otherworld both before and after learning that he was an elf—but before, in that seemingly long-ago time, he hadn't known that the places of his dreams were real. Now he knew that those dreamscapes *had* been real. *Were* real. He walked across those dreamscapes now.

He belonged here.

Bennett stopped and suggested a rest. John didn't feel tired, but he didn't feel like disagreeing either. While Bennett and Faye sat, he paced, looking about, searching for he knew not what. Something made him restless. There was a different sort of feeling about this place, an impression of sympathy that struck a chord in him.

"I've been here before," he said aloud, realizing where they were. "The magic pool is just over there, in the woods." That pool was where John had first seen his reflection as an elf. And where he had first seen Faye and realized that she was . . . attractive? Desirable? Remembering and seeing her, palpable and solid, sitting and looking placidly off into the distance spooked him a little.

"You have a good sense of place," Bennett said, apparently oblivious to John's turmoil. "There is time. Would you like to visit the pool again?"

"Yes," John said. Bennett started to get up, so John quickly added, "Alone."

Faye blinked.

"As you wish," Bennett said.

John immediately regretted his abruptness. With Bennett complying, there was no way that she could not. John had said "alone" and now, though he wished otherwise, was committed to it.

He left them to await his return. As before, he found the pond easily enough by sensing and following its emanations, although he hadn't understood what he was doing the last time, ignorant as he had been of magic. In a lot of ways, he was different now. Would the magic pool show him something different?

As he neared the sheltered pond, he seemed to startle something, but John saw nothing except a disturbance among the bushes bordering the water. If whatever it had been was too shy to show itself, he need not feel threatened by it.

He drew nearer the pool and found the surface of the water was as still as ever, mirror-shiny in the moonlight. He went to the spot where the bank projected over the water and sat, a bit back from the edge. By leaning forward he would be able to see his reflection in the still waters, but he was not quite ready to do that.

First he wanted to compose himself, attune himself to the magic he felt in this place. Taking off his leather jacket to expose more of his skin to the air, he let his senses take in his surroundings. The soft rustle of the leaves in the slight breeze. The damp of the moisture in the air above the pool. The soft, springy ground beneath him. The sweet smell of growing things and the moist fragrance of the pond. The play of the starlight upon the water. He had a vague sense of being watched, but that could have been just an echo of his consciousness as he tried to become one with this place. No one and nothing disturbed his communion with the timeless moment. When he felt at peace, he leaned forward to look.

As before, the face of an elf looked back at him. This time he knew it for a true reflection. He stared at the face, at once strange and familiar. It was a handsome face, though long and gaunt and dominated by wide, pale, slightly slanting eyes. Elven handsomeness, he supposed. His reflected ears had finely pointed tips, visible where they poked through silver hair as delicate as moonbeams. This was the face he would wear when the disguising spells were removed.

His face.

But not the one he had worn all his life. Regret, or something much like it, disturbed his peace. The face in the pond rippled as though the water had been disturbed, but it didn't change. It was his face.

Whoever *he* was.

Elf? By birth. Human? By nurture. Where did that leave him? Was he one or the other, or something of each? The latter, he supposed. And where did *that* leave him? Could he be both elf and human? As an elf, he was supposed to be heir to the elven prince Bennett, and to the magic of Faery. As a human, he was a fugitive from corporate society, a streeter in the sprawl of old Providence, and an occasional thaumaturgic student to Dr. Spae. How did it all fit together? *Did* it fit together? Or would he have to choose one over the other?

He wished, wanting to know, hoping for some sign to tell him what he was supposed to do.

But nothing changed.

He sat, alone by the side of pool, looking down at an elf's face. His face. Was that the answer? Would the elf's life soon be his as well?

He closed his eyes and rocked back, not wanting to look at that face anymore for the moment. He became aware of a shift in the rhythms of the place. Someone else was nearby, perhaps more than one person. Opening his eyes, he turned around and saw Faye approaching; she had followed in spite of his stated desire for solitude.

"You didn't really want to be alone, did you?" she asked almost timidly.

She knew him so well. There was the alone of a personal privacy and the alone of privacy shared. She'd known which he'd meant before he did.

"Is Bennett following you?" he asked, to be sure.

"He's still waiting on the hill." She giggled. "He doesn't pay much attention to me."

John didn't have that fault.

"Sprites are beneath his notice," she continued. "I slipped away so we could be together for a while."

She sat beside him, her body close. In the perpetual twilight of the otherworld, her skin was cool against his where their shoulders touched. John put his arm around her and she snuggled close.

"Bennett says you're not a suitable companion for an elven lord."

"Because I'm not an elf like you."

"That's what he says."

"Does it bother you that I'm not an elf?"

"No." He'd been bothered when he thought that they might be related.

"Then it doesn't matter." She smiled radiantly, melting his heart and tearing at his last shreds of inhibition. Her fingers teased across his chest.

He knew what she wanted. He wanted it too. "What if Bennett comes looking for us?"

"Then he will find us."

"But we're out in the open."

"That doesn't matter."

Other things did. "Faye, should we be doing this?"

"Why not?"

There were some why-nots, but John was having trouble focusing on them as she nuzzled at his neck. "What about—"

She put a finger to his lips, stilling his objection. He wasn't sure that he'd be able to talk to her about Sue anyway.

"Nothing matters but now," she said, replacing her finger with her lips.

Desire spurred them both on. Her hands worked at the fastenings of his pants. He tugged on her dress, pulling it up around her waist, then her shoulders. The flimsy fabric was in their way, frustrating their mutual desire for total contact. They parted momentarily to rid themselves of their encumbering clothes, then fell together again on the fragrant grass and moss.

Faye was a lot more skilled than Sue had been. Rather than wondering where she had acquired such skill, he accepted it. No, he enjoyed it. A lot. Faye was right; nothing mattered but the moment. He lost himself in her. After they had shuddered to conclusion and lay resting in each other's arms, she whispered to him.

"You will always be my prince, John."

"Sweet Faye, I've never known anyone like you."

"Will you always remember me?"

"Forever."

She sighed, satisfied. He was too. As they rested in each

other's embrace, John again began to feel that someone was nearby. He listened, unwilling to do more lest he disturb Faye, but she seemed to pick up his shift in mood.

"What is it?" she asked.

"I don't think it's anything." He had heard nothing to confirm his feeling. His statement didn't satisfy Faye.

She squirmed free of his embrace and pushed herself up on her arms. Her eyes took on a wary look as she sniffed at the air.

"John, I think we'd better go."

It was his turn to ask, "What is it?"

"It's time we got back," she said, not really answering his question. Her eyes continued to dart about as she pulled her dress back on. John scanned the trees and brush around the pool as he dressed. If there was something or someone lurking nearby, he saw no sign.

Faye remained nervous until they left the copse that hid the pool. Bennett remained where he had been, sitting and waiting. He smiled wryly at their return together, but said nothing. Instead he pointed to a distant hill.

Over the crest came a rider, mounted on a dark-coated elven steed and leading a train of three other mounts, each as brightly caparisoned as his own. The cavalcade drew closer—surprisingly quickly—and John thought that the dark-haired elven rider looked familiar. When the steeds came to a halt and the rider dismounted, John put the face together with this place, the animals, and another time. This was the elf who had met Bennett during John's first trip to the otherworld, and who had taken Bennett away, leaving John and the others to find their own way through the deceptive countryside of the otherworld. This time, though, the elf had brought enough mounts for everyone.

"I know you," John said to the elf.

"I doubt that," the elf replied. "But we have met."

Bennett rose and made the introduction. "Shahotain, this is my son Jack."

"Jack?" Shahotain raised a haughty eyebrow. "Your name

in the sunlit world, I gather. Will you take another name here?"

"I'll stick with Jack, thanks."

"As you will," Shahotain said.

"As I am Bennett," said Bennett.

Shahotain turned to him and, after a moment, nodded. "The will of the prince."

"The will of the prince is that we be on our way," said Bennett, mounting his steed.

The others mounted as well, John somewhat awkwardly. And then they were away, riding at speed across the hills to an unknown destination.

CHAPTER
8

Carlos Quintero wasn't particularly good at his job, but then he didn't have to be; he was necessary. Even in this age of information, there were still physical commodities that had to be moved, and many of them moved most cost-effectively by ship. And ships required sailors, at least according to union rules.

Used to be that a sailor had a hard life, but that was before Carlos's time and so really didn't bother Carlos at all. Used to be ships were a lot smaller than S.S. *Wisteria*, too. Being on a small ship, now that *would* bother Carlos. He didn't have to worry about that. Container ships like *Wisteria* were bigger than just about anything that had ever sailed.

The big ships were more sophisticated, too. Most of the time it seemed that Carlos was a supernumerary, that ships like the *Wisteria* could sail themselves. And most of the time they could. That was fine with Carlos. It gave him time for other things, like surfing the vid nets.

Weather was a feature of the sailor's life that Carlos didn't care much for, especially cold weather. *Wisteria* was chugging along in the grip of the West Wind Drift just now, well inside the iceberg limit—not that it mattered much this early in the season—and letting the currents do most of the work in taking them across the shortest distance between New Zealand and South America. The weather was as cold as it would get for this trip. Carlos would be glad when they headed up the Chilean coast, gladder still when they made port in California. Meantime, when he didn't have monitor duty, he'd stay in his cabin or in the lounge and stay warm. Why the bridge couldn't have better heating he didn't understand. The lounge was heated just fine, and it was crew space like the bridge. Had a bigger vid screen too. Only natural that he prefer the lounge to the bridge. Too bad he couldn't convince the captain to patch the monitor feeds down here. Sometimes the captain was a little too by-the-book.

As if in response to Carlos's thoughts, the loudspeaker spoke with the captain's voice.

"All hands, this is the captain."

Carlos sneered at the formality. Too by-the-book.

"Our weather radar is picking up a small storm that isn't showing on satellite weather feeds. It's probably just a glitch in the system, but I want everyone ready for weather just in case."

A small storm wouldn't faze *Wisteria*. Carlos hoped it wouldn't fritz vid reception. The non-corp channels often had weak up-down links, and it was a non-corp channel he was watching now. They had all the good stuff.

The show was right on target with Carlos: an exposé on McKutchen Wood. He liked the way the reporter—Lauder, the name was; he'd remember that—was getting to the meat. Lauder had the Wood pegged as a doorway to other dimensions. Carlos had figured that out as soon as he'd heard about the Wood. How could anybody with a brain not know that something was lurking at the edge of reality, trying to get in? It was so obvious! Some things had already slipped into the real world. Places like McKutchen Wood were doorways for otherworldly things. People like Lauder knew. Carlos knew too.

Carlos focused down and forgot about the captain's order. The images on the screen were too compelling. He knew all about this kind of stuff, but had an insatiable need to know more. This Lauder had a good line, a good angle, real perceptive. Carlos knew there were plenty of things that ordinary science couldn't explain. Plenty of real things. Things that people like Lauder had the scoop on. The paranormal was all around.

Not that Carlos had had any personal encounters. But lately Carlos had been seeing a lot more reports about the upsurge in magical things. It used to be hard to find that sort of stuff. Not hard anymore, and the quality of the information was much better. The eyewitnesses were less obviously over the edge, the pictures less fuzzy, and the physical evidence— DNA, for God's sake! Sure, the establishment still said that all the data on this kind of stuff was faked, simply the efforts of crackpots, lunatics, and hoaxers; but the government had a lot to hide. Didn't he know it?

A ship as big and serene as *Wisteria* still had its share of noises. Carlos was used to most of them, so he dismissed the first few scrapes and bumps. Then he began to wonder if the captain's storm had arrived. He ordered the computer to repolarize the viewports, bringing them to transparency. There was no storm outside. He darkened the windows again and went back to Lauder's report.

A sound, like someone rubbing a handful of gravel on the cabin's outer wall, intruded on his concentration. He realized that he was shivering. The room was colder. Definitely colder, but not so cold as to make him shiver. So why was he shivering?

Something scratched briefly against the door to the corridor. A light sound, barely audible. Probably just his imagination. The cold was not his imagination.

"Computer, is there something wrong with the heater?"

"System normal," the machine reported.

"What about the temperature?"

"Temperature within normal parameters."

How could that be? Carlos was shivering; it was cold. There was no point in trying to order a temperature increase; only the captain could do that. There had to be something wrong with the heating system or with the computer monitor. Much more likely the monitor. Computers always sounded so sure of themselves, especially when they were fritzed.

That was it. The computer must be fritzed. He'd call Salmon and get him to take a look at it.

Something moved at the corner of his vision. He turned his head, looking for it. Nothing seemed out of the ordinary. He had seen something, hadn't he?

A thump behind him made him turn. One of the captain's books, which had been on the table, now lay on the floor. Carlos was the only one in the room.

Wasn't he?

A dark, viscous thing, like a snake made out of the very stuff of the night, slithered out from beneath Carlos's chair and wrapped itself around his ankle. His skin burned with a cold so intense that his skin blistered. He screamed.

Belief in the unnatural had its downsides. He knew this was no nightmare—knew it with a certainty that nearly froze his heart—and he knew he could not explain away this monster from the other side that had come to steal his soul.

He couldn't move. As much as he wanted to tear the thing away from himself, he could not. His muscles were solid ice. All he could do was scream. No words, just terror. Carlos screamed and screamed again as the night serpent crawled up his leg. His screams stopped only when the awful thing forced his mouth open and slithered down his throat, and his awareness perished.

CHAPTER
9

The passage of time in the otherworld was hard to gauge. John had yet to see a daytime sky. The stars seemed eternal. Yet he knew that time passed because occasionally he felt hungry, and more occasionally he felt tired enough to sleep. Other than the cues his body gave him and the fact that he was progressing with his lessons, however, there was no hint that the moment was anything other than constant. Trying to figure out the passage of time became less and less important; he had other things on his mind, like magic.

Bennett had kept his promise that John would learn magic, placing him under the tutelage of Shahotain and others. John was learning how to touch and control the energies he had sensed for so long. And learning quickly—because he was in the otherworld, where the magic was stronger? Or because his elven tutors were better magicians, or maybe better teachers, than Dr. Spae? He wasn't sure. It really didn't matter; the important thing was that he was getting better at understanding and controlling real magic. Even more important, he was beginning to understand how much magic had to do with being an elf. Magic, he knew now, was a part of his heritage, a hole in his life that he hadn't known existed was being filled. With each lesson John grew more amazed that he had survived without being able to touch the magic.

It was a whole new life, and a good one. John saw little of Bennett, which was fine. He saw more of Faye—which was finer—and even more of his tutors which—with the new doors they constantly opened for him—was perhaps finer still.

He understood now that he had been born to magic; Bennett hadn't lied about that. And Bennett, the liar, hadn't lied about arranging for John to learn. John wasn't sure what to make of that, but he was sure that he was going to take advantage of it. He intended to learn all that was offered.

At last he was coming into his own!

There was, however, still a matter that disturbed him, a matter that Shahotain had finally agreed to address. They met in the place that John thought of as Shahotain's study, though there was nothing about the place that suggested any study John had known in the sunlit world. There were no books, no desk, no comfortable chairs, just four paneled walls, a planter filled with a riot of vegetation, a pair of intricately carved chests that served as seats when necessary, and a tiled floor of even more intricate and delicate decoration. The place seemed more suited to meditation than to study.

"This is untimely," Shahotain said, not for the first time, when John entered his study.

"You already said you would do it," John pointed out. "Besides, Bennett said the spell would be removed if I came to this place with him. I'm here, and it's been long enough. You're not wimping, are you?"

"I merely suggest that you reconsider."

John didn't want to reconsider. He wanted to be done with wearing a lie. Having his own face would be his first step in making his *life* his own. He was more than ready for *that*. "Let's do it."

Impassively, Shahotain nodded. With that, John felt the power begin to rise. He felt the energies that Shahotain manipulated and knew that an unraveling was being done, but he had little comprehension of the forces involved. Still, he knew the magic touched on him. How could he not comprehend the manipulation of energies so closely tied to himself? But he didn't—at least not fully—somehow the details escaped him. He felt a little like the time he'd watched a mechanic work on one of the elevators in the rezcom where he'd grown up. He saw everything that the mechanic had done, but he hadn't understood the why of any of it. The ritual ended abruptly and Shahotain said, "You may look now."

John took the offered reflecting glass with trepidation. Shahotain had certainly done something. What, exactly, John wasn't sure, but he had felt no harm in his tutor's working. So why was he reluctant to look?

Foolishness.

He looked and saw the elegant arching of his cheeks, the subtle slant of his eyes, and the delicate pointed ears. There was no magic in the glass. What he was seeing was a simple reflection of his face. His true elven face.

"You did it," he said, touching his features to convince himself of their reality.

Shahotain shrugged. "A trivial exercise. You will soon be capable of similar work if your progress continues as it has begun."

"Is that the next lesson?"

"There is no lesson for you now. Go. I have other matters to attend to."

John went, having already learned that Shahotain's forbearance was far from limitless. A bogie met him outside the door with a summons to a training session with Loreneth the Lightspinner. The Lightspinner was educating him in glamours.

John shared such sessions with nearly a dozen young elves. He might have thought of them as his classmates, if they had been more friendly. For all that he was one of them, until now he had not looked like one of them, and appearances seemed to matter greatly in Faery. The other students remained aloof, apparently reluctant to spend any more time in his company than necessary, so John seldom thought of them. He was used to being a loner. Of course he wasn't really on his own. He had Faye to keep him company when he wasn't busy having the secrets of elven magic drilled into

him. Let the others have whatever revels they went off to, he
had Faye.

What would Faye think of his new face?

He would have to wait to find out, since at the moment he
needed to respond to the Lightspinner's summons; she was
no more forgiving than Shahotain. John let the bogie lead
him. Having such servants around was extremely useful; the
elven keep was extensive and, apparently, mutable, but the
bogies always seemed to know their way around. John supposed that otherworld navigation was another Faery magic
he'd be taught at some point.

John's arrival caused a minor sensation among the students. He might have been showing up for the first time.
There was no time to deal with the interest on the part of the
others, since the Lightspinner allowed none. She set them to
work shaping phantoms of sight and of sound. Sometimes
she let them choose the glamour they shaped and other times
she set them to shaping a specific illusion. To John's surprise
he earned a word of praise for his skill in emulating the
nearly silent sound of an elven steed galloping.

After the Lightspinner concluded her lesson and departed,
Duwynt approached John. Duwynt was the elf who had
come at Faye's call to help against Quetzal, arriving in time
to see John and Dr. Spae emerge from what had turned out to
be a dragon's lair. Duwynt had used the incident to nickname
John; it was the friendliest gesture John had encountered
among his fellow students.

Duwynt bowed before he spoke. "Well, Dragon Baiter, it
seems that you really are coming into your own. There had
been some doubt."

"Doubt?" John echoed, unsure of how to respond.

Duwynt only smiled enigmatically and asked his own
question. "Coming with us? Fraoch has composed a new
chanson that she says is her best yet."

The other elves were watching John expectantly. Fraoch,
fairest of the females and of a beauty to make Faye look
plain, smiled dazzlingly at him. Previously she had not both-

ered to look in his direction. Clearly he had crossed a threshold.

John found the sudden camaraderie uncomfortable. Their precipitate acceptance of him seemed based solely on his appearance. What was different other than that? *He* hadn't changed, just his looks. Why had their attitude changed?

He wasn't sure that he really wanted to know the answer. He was sure that he wasn't ready to join them. "Shahotain set me a lesson to practice," he lied.

"Another time," Duwynt said without hint of regret or promise. He rejoined the others. Laughing and joking they left the classroom. John followed them out into the hall. The others turned a corner, and, as soon as the last was out of sight, their voices vanished as though a door had been closed behind them. As it might have done. John didn't bother to go look.

He longed for the comfort of Faye's arms. She would make him feel better. But wait—Faye was born of Faery, as much as Duwynt and Fraoch and the others. Would her attitude change too? He didn't want to think it would, but he found himself in no hurry to find out. The keep seemed awfully confining of a sudden, and he wanted to see the sky above him with no walls around to cut off the view.

One of his privileges was the use of an elven steed, although he had been warned not to stray far from the keep. So far he had been too busy to go anywhere. Now he decided to take advantage of that entitlement and ride out into the countryside. He had no destination in mind, he just wanted to get away.

His steed was ready for him, saddled as if his whim had been anticipated. He shoved away thoughts of the implications. Such uncanny anticipation of his desires was another reason that he needed to get away. He mounted and rode through the courtyard and among the assorted Faery folk going about their business there. No one stopped him. No one even noticed him. Once through the gate, he was free of the keep. He urged his mount to a gallop.

Now that he was moving, he was tempted to keep going and to ride back to the sunlit world, but he knew that such a course wasn't open to him just now. What would he do there? He no longer looked human, and his appearance would raise questions wherever he went. Would Sue recognize him? What about Marianne Reddy—would she know the son she had raised? He could not go back until he learned the secrets of disguising magic so that he could appear in the sunlit world as he had before.

Appearance.

So much depended on it.

He had always hated the corporate prop and the way that the corporate spin doctors were always twisting the truth around, seeking to put a good face on whatever the suits did. They were always worried about appearance. Always lying. He'd grown up believing that lies were wrong. Now he'd been shown that his life was a lie, and the only people who could show him the truth were liars and the servants of the greatest liar he had yet met, Bennett. Life wasn't fair.

Fair? Bear might have said. *Life has never been* fair. *Fair is for a man to be.*

Bear hadn't exactly been fair, but that didn't make the sentiment any less valid. A man had to strive, and a man didn't always succeed. But then, John wasn't exactly a man, and he had the face to prove it.

His mount's course took him near the grove of trees that sheltered the magic pool. By intent? Was the steed responding to some unconscious urging from John? What did it matter? They were here. John reined in his mount. By the edge of the trees, he dismounted and entered the copse afoot.

The place was as quiet and tranquil as ever. Peaceful. He liked that, wanting to soak up the feeling until it filled him and forced out all his worries. He walked to the bank and looked into the pool. The reflection showed him an elf, by look and by dress. By appearance.

Was it really him?

He spent a good deal of time pondering that question without reaching a satisfactory answer. Slowly he realized that he was again experiencing the sensation of being watched. Trying to disguise his search by stretching, he looked around him. This time he saw something. A man, standing almost concealed in the shadow under the trees, was watching him.

John hadn't come here to be gawked at.

"I know you're there," he said, staring right at the man. "Come out where I can see you better."

The figure started at John's challenge and shifted as if to flee. For a minute or so they stood in silence; the watcher's decision to flee suspended and John's challenge unanswered. John began to wonder if he'd been right to acknowledge the man's presence. Maybe he had broken some rule of Faery etiquette. Just when he was sure that the next move was up to him, the watcher took a step toward him.

The stranger emerged from the shadows. John got a good look at him for the first time and was shocked at the watcher's appearance. What he had thought a man was no man at all, but something of a mix between a man and a goat. From the waist up, the creature looked mostly human, with a man's hairy torso and arms and a drawn-out but manlike face sporting a long, scraggly beard; but from the waist down, the creature was a beast. Its legs were back-cocked and cloven-hoofed, making its walk a mincing prance. John was reminded of something he had seen in a vid on Greek mythology.

"Are you a satyr?" he asked.

The long face got longer as the creature's eyes narrowed and its mouth pursed. Its voice warbled. "There's no need to insult me. Though I suppose I shouldn't have expected else from one of your kind, should I?"

The strange creature started to back away, returning to the shadows. John didn't want it to leave, at least not before he satisfied his curiosity.

"I'm sorry," he said. "Please don't go."

The creature stopped its retreat and looked at him with large, mournful eyes. It seemed unsure, ready to flee.

"I didn't mean to insult you." John tried an apologetic smile. "It's just that, well, you look like what I always thought a satyr might look like. If you're not one, what are you?"

"I've always liked to think of myself as a *who*, not a *what*," the creature said with a sniff.

"I'm not very familiar with the varieties of Faery folk. We've established that you're not a satyr, but what sort of being *are* you?"

"You've never seen an urisk before?"

"No."

"There is no surprise in the hearing of that. We are a solitary folk, not much given to involving ourselves in the affairs of the great ones. A mistake I make, most probably, even talking to you. But I've started, haven't I?"

"So it seems." John was intrigued by the urisk's mixture of boldness and diffidence.

The urisk nodded solemnly as if reaching a decision. "Call me Yuri, if it suits you."

"You're the one who should decide if it's suitable. I'm Jack."

"Jack? A great one named Jack? A laugh that is." Yuri brayed to prove it.

"What's so funny?"

Yuri's expression said that John was an idiot. "Jacks are human."

"I've always thought of myself as human."

Yuri blinked owlishly. "I suppose you have. Changelings do. For a while. In time you will get over it. They all do."

John wasn't sure he wanted to "get over" being human, especially knowing so little about the alternative. "What would you know about it?"

"Seen them before, haven't I? They come here, they do. To look into the pool. Like you did."

"And what do you tell them? That they're just like all the other changelings?"

Yuri looked appalled. "Never do I talk to them."

"You're talking to me."

"I am, aren't I?" Yuri sounded surprised. "A chance, I took. I guess I was a bit too lonely. The real surprise is that you are talking to me."

"Why is that a surprise?"

"You're a great one," Yuri said, as if it explained everything.

It didn't, even though John had experienced the deference shown to elves by the so-called lesser folk. "Great ones"— what an arrogant term. Faye had used it once, saying that she wasn't one. "I'm afraid that I don't really understand what makes a great one different from anyone else around here."

"You *are* new come to Faery, aren't you? Well, I guess I'd better enjoy the privilege of your company while I can. Once you come into your inheritance, you'll grow too important for the likes of me. Then, you'll only have time for other great ones. Seen it before, haven't I? I have truly. Should have stayed in the bramble, shouldn't I? Seems old Yuri is not as bright as he thought. Disappointment, nothing but disappointment in dealing with great ones."

John didn't care for the urisk's judgment. Yuri didn't know John at all. "Then why did you bother to speak to me?"

"Thought you were different?" Yuri looked at John sidewise. "I saw you with that sprite. Amazed me, didn't it? Not that a great one can't do as he pleases—I know that—but the way you were with her." Yuri sighed. "Like you really cared about her."

"I did. I mean, I do."

Yuri looked down his long nose. "Really?"

"Sure." Embarrassingly, an image of Sue ran naked through his thoughts. They were talking about Faye. "I really do. Care about her, I mean."

Yuri's eyes narrowed, then he shook his head. "Confusing."

The feelings surging through John were confusing to *him*. Why should they be any less so to the urisk? John wanted to change the subject and think about other things.

"You said you've seen changelings here before. Did Bennett bring them too?"

"Bennett?" Yuri looked thoughtful for a moment. "Ah, the prince, mean you?"

"Don't you know him as Bennett?"

"A new name."

John knew that Bennett wasn't always Bennett, but no one had ever offered another name for the prince. "What's his old name?"

Yuri raised a tufted eyebrow. "Asking me for his name, are you?"

"Yeah."

"His *true* name?"

"Sure."

"You want to know his true name?"

"Yes."

"So do I." Yuri brayed laughter, making John frown in annoyance. When the urisk's amusement subsided, Yuri shifted into a more serious mood. "In this world, closely guarded secrets are true names," he said. "The name by which one knows one's inner self is a powerful magical tool when put to use. It can aid and hinder, bind and loose, and be very dangerous in the wrong hands. Dangerous enough are use names."

"So Bennett is just a use name."

Yuri nodded. "By some lights, a new name is Bennett for your prince, although he has used it for some time now. Before that he liked Beneyt. Gorloys is another he has used."

It seemed suitable that Bennett had used many names. John wondered about the names for Bennett that Yuri had given him. Beneyt was just a variation, and while Gorloys sounded familiar, John wasn't sure where he had heard it before. Maybe in a fairy tale or a legend? Yes, that was it, a legend. In fact, he'd read it in a legend of King Arthur.

Well Arthur, more properly Artos, was Bear—as real as John—which suggested that the other characters were real too. He'd heard Bear mention some of them, though John couldn't remember any mention of someone called Gorloys. He knew that Bennett and Bear had a history; they both admitted it, although neither had ever given John any details. Unfortunately, John couldn't remember anything from the legends about Gorloys. He wished that he had access to a computer. He could run a search, ransacking every Arthurian database he could get access to until he shook something out.

Of course the legends wouldn't have the story straight. Having met Bear, he knew that the popular myths hadn't gotten things quite right, but that there was a core of truth and real people at the center of the legends.

Gorloys, eh? Maybe John could find some clues as to what had happened between his mysterious father and Bear that had raised such bad blood between them. There might be things that John could use in his own struggle with Bennett.

"Too young you are," Yuri said. "You cannot challenge him."

Challenge? Had John really been thinking of something so . . . direct and combative? "I wasn't—"

"Yuri knows your kind. Your face shows your mind, and there shines the thought of challenge."

Was it so? The concept of having Bennett at a disadvantage *was* appealing. John was vaguely aware that Yuri had begun backing away from him, but he was too intrigued by the possibilities the urisk's information had opened up to care. In his mind's eye he saw himself setting Bennett up so that *Bennett* was the one not knowing what was going on, so that *Bennett* was the one asking questions that *John* could disdain to answer. That would be a good twist, wouldn't it? Can't challenge him, eh? There were all sorts of challenges.

"Who says I can't challenge him?"

"Wiser heads." The urisk's voice came from far away.

John looked to see where Yuri had gone and found that he was nowhere to be seen. John was alone by the pool.

Wiser heads, eh? Maybe he couldn't challenge Bennett just now, but the idea of making Bennett dance to his tune was too good to let go of. John knew that he had a lot to learn before he could make it happen. He snatched a twig from the ground and called fire to light its end. The stick crackled as it burned. Calling flame was the first magic John had learned. It was a simple spell, but learning it had been his first step into the world of magic. At some things, John was a good learner, a very good learner. And once he learned what he needed to know—well, then, they'd see who could do what to whom.

CHAPTER
10

Magnus rose when Holger entered the room. Holger felt honored. Holger had worked with Magnus before, though not directly, of course. He felt a thrill of anticipation at the opportunity being offered to him. Magnus was the head of the most successful team in the Department.

Magnus was also a sleeper. Holger's clearance wasn't high enough to have the details, but he knew that much. He'd heard that Magnus had been a ruler, but that occupation was currently unavailable. Even had it been, the world had changed and Magnus's grasp of politics was about fifteen hundred years out-of-date. Yet Magnus had succeeded in reinventing himself and finding a place in the modern world—no mean feat. He had come far and fast in the service—in some ways a greater accomplishment. Magnus was a comer. There were those who said that Magnus might get his old job back someday. If that was so, staying in his good graces was not a bad idea.

But such possibilities were for another day. This day had its own matters.

Abandoning his conference with Security Officer L'Hereaux, Magnus told Holger, "We have an assignment available."

"I'll take it."

Magnus laid down the folder he'd been holding. The screen was readable from Holger's position; it would have details on the assignment, but that didn't matter. Magnus would tell him. Magnus said, "I haven't told you what it is yet, Agent Kun."

"I'm ready, sir."

"Eager, certainly."

Holger didn't say anything. He *was* ready.

"This is a recovery operation," L'Hereaux said.

Holger had experience. "Very good, sir."

Magnus and L'Hereaux exchanged glances. Holger hoped he wasn't playing his hand wrong. He wanted—needed—this assignment.

"It will probably mean operating in the United States," Magnus said.

"I'm ready for hardships," Holger stated. They all laughed at the old joke. "Who is to be recovered?"

"This is the woman," L'Hereaux said as the wallscreen lit, displaying a portrait pic. Full body and casual shots followed to make up a montage. A window with vital statistics opened, but Holger ignored it for the moment to concentrate on the images. She was average height and on the slender side. She seemed to favor drab clothes and unflattering hairstyles. Her most unusual feature was her mismatched eyes, one blue, one green; they were magnetic, even in the pictures. Those eyes disturbed Holger, so he shifted his attention back to the woman's overall impression. She looked to be in her forties, maybe fifties if she had good genes and the wherewithal to pamper them. Not consistent with her apparent lack of interest in fashion. Forties, then, probably midway through the decade. Holger studied the casual shots. He found nothing definite to indicate her profession, but most commonly her expressions were abstracted, as though she were thinking thoughts not connected to what she was doing in the pictures. She looked as if she ought to be wearing a lab coat. He found himself drawn back to the portrait pic. Something about the woman's face was vaguely familiar. A resemblance to an aunt perhaps? Unimportant. Do the job. He memorized the face.

"She's a thaumaturgic specialist," Magnus said.

He had known that. It explained the lab-coat look. A specialist. He didn't like specialists.

"Is that a problem?" L'Hereaux asked.

"Nothing insurmountable," Holger replied. He tried to sound as though he were just stating a fact. He didn't want them dumping him from this assignment just because he didn't like dealing with specialists. "What's her name?"

"Elizabeth Spae."

The name sounded familiar, but when he tried to put his finger on a memory, he found himself thinking of another Elizabeth. Now, *she* had been worth remembering. Elizabeth Spae meant nothing to him. But she mattered to the Department; soon he would be told why.

"She is a renegade," Magnus informed him.

"A very dangerous woman," L'Hereaux added.

"She has taken up with the enemy," Magnus said.

"To be more precise, we have learned that she has done work for a subsidiary of Metadynamics, a corporation whose name you will remember from earlier affairs."

Holger remembered. Metadynamics was a many tentacled, multinational corporation, one of the largest. Several of their subsidiaries were suspected of encountering and sequestering materials within the responsibility of the Department. Under the terms of the United Nations Intelligence Purview Act, Metadynamics's base in North America made the North American Commercial Community's Federal Security Agency the proper investigative authority. The last Holger had heard, the FSA continued to give Metadynamics "uninvolved" status. If this renegade specialist was working for Metadynamics, lack of involvement was unlikely.

"FSA refusing cooperation?" he asked.

"Quite," L'Hereaux answered. "They deny any connection between Metadynamics and Elizabeth Spae. They deny any influence from corporate sources. With Metadynamics a major influence on the NACC government, influence must be presumed. After all, 'Metadynamics makes America dynamic.' "

Holger had heard the slogan.

"There is evidence contradicting FSA's claim. In here." Magnus held up the folder. "You will see that we cannot expect any in-country cooperation."

Holger nodded, understanding the situation. Wedded as they were with Metadynamics, FSA would be hostile to the recovery. That collusion between the agency and the corp was a complication, but not an insurmountable one. He'd overcome similar difficulties. "Who will be leading the recovery team, sir?"

"You are my choice, Agent Kun."

Magnus's faith was reassuring. "Thank you, sir."

L'Hereaux, characteristically, had an additional point. "Agents Linkwater and Pankhurst will be part of the team. Is that a problem?"

"Not for me." If they thought otherwise, he would see that they changed their minds. Or their team.

Magnus looked at him earnestly. "There are those who think you are not ready for this assignment, Agent Kun. The doctors do not all agree that you are completely recovered from your accident and ready for duty. This is a difficult situation and one which must be handled expeditiously. Your record recommends you for this assignment. I see no better alternative and am wagering that you are ready. More than that, I am wagering that you will complete this assignment smoothly and cleanly. This woman cannot be allowed to provide her services to Metadynamics. I am relying on your loyalty and service, Agent Kun. I am relying on you."

"I'm ready to do my job."

"It may be that she cannot be recovered. Such a loss would be regrettable, but our loss cannot be Metadynamics's gain."

"I understand, sir."

One specialist fewer was one step closer to sanity for the world.

CHAPTER
11

"A memento," Bennett said, folding the soft silk over the oblong crystal clasped within argent, helical bands. Supposedly the talismanic crystal that he wrapped so carefully had belonged to John's elven mother. Bennett handed the object to John.

Didn't you need a memory for a memento to mean anything? "What am I supposed to do with this?"

"Keep it safe."

From what? "Is this the help you wanted me to give you?"

"Safeguarding the stone is in your own interests. As to what you agreed, the time of that promised service remains in the future. For now, you must remain here, learning and readying yourself for your new life."

"I thought you were in a hurry."

"Time passes, but not so swiftly that you cannot ready yourself properly. Shahotain says your skills develop steadily."

"Not what he says to me."

Bennett chuckled. "No. He would not. Still, I am pleased with your progress." He said more, praising John. When a sprite came to fetch Bennett, his parting words to John were, "When you are well grounded we will go up to the high court, and you will claim what is yours."

John just said farewell. Bennett's continued promises of an inheritance to come when John completed his studies did little to convince John of Bennett's sincerity. *When you are*

well grounded. We will. You will. In the future. But not now.
The constant deferment rankled like a days-old cut; like such
a cut, the pain of "not yet" had lost its sharpness. John had
grown less anxious about time, immersed as he was in his
studies. Such relaxed acceptance of the rhythm of the otherworld was a change in him, and in its own way a marker of
the passage of time. Surely a fair bit of time must have
passed since he had come to this place, but what measure of
time mattered in a world of eternal twilight? And how important was time after all? Any true student of magic knew
that the Way was a journey with no end, and that a magician's studies were a lifetime adventure. Hours and days
were but petty cycles within the All of the World.

Time might not be important, but timing was, and Bennett
a master of the art. All John had to do was heft the weight of
the gift Bennett had brought him to know Bennett was playing games again. He felt the hardness of the gift beneath its
wrapping of soft silk, his fingers tracing where the roughness
of the ornate silver mount gave way to the smoothness of the
crystal. Just what string did Bennett think this thing would
pull?

For the moment, John didn't care. He wasn't going to let
Bennett intrude on him. There were other, more important
things to care about. If he'd been wearing his leathers, he
would have had a pocket into which he could slip the package. The doublet and hose, which Fraoch said looked so
good on him, didn't offer any place to stash the gift, so he'd
have to carry it in his hand. He wouldn't just throw it away;
even if it had come from Bennett. The crystal had intrinsic
interest, not least its faint residue of old, faded magic. But
that was something for later thought. Now he was expected
elsewhere.

Despite his early misgivings about his fellow students,
John had grown fond of their company, and more than fond
of one in particular. The trials of learning the Way had
forged a bond between them. The other elves were a lot like
his friends from the college fencing team, but better. There,

he had shared mutual interest in the sport but little else. Here, too, his companions shared a fascination with him: magic, a far more absorbing study than anything John had ever encountered. But there was more than shared art. Here his comrades were all elves, like him. They shared the heritage of Faery. True, John still knew little of that heritage, but their kinship was something he felt in his bones. It was sort of like being in a frat—or so he imagined—or a gang; like what he'd known during his time with Bear and the Downtown Dons. But this was better. Far better.

And when John thought about things being better, he naturally thought about Fraoch. He wasn't sure what he had done to earn her favors, but whatever it was, he was glad. The first time they had made love had been—well, John wasn't sure he had the words to describe it, but just remembering it got him excited. He was going to have to make sure that she and he did some private "studying" again soon.

It was amazing to have such thoughts come so casually. After John's first tryst with Fraoch, Duwynt had told him that Gentiano, originally the least friendly of the bunch, had been Fraoch's lover. John had feared the start of some jealous rivalry, but his apprehension had been unfounded. "Time for things to change," Gentiano had said when he next saw John, and had actually offered John tips on how to make love to Fraoch. When John had tried the advice in his next session with Fraoch, he'd been surprised to find that Gentiano hadn't been setting him up. John had been amazed. Gentiano certainly had not acted the way any of the Dons would have if John had ended up with one of their honeys. For all his haughty manner, Gentiano was okay when life got real.

In fact, Gentiano was the first to greet him when John arrived at the hall. The music was already rolling, a lively twilit take on *700 Elves* played by a crew of Faery folk in motley. For all the wild dissonance of their looks, the musicians played well together. John especially liked the bongo beat under the pipes: very danceable. But Gentiano preempted John from joining the sprites and goblins frolicking on the floor, steering him around the crowd and through the bogies rushing about to attend on the revelers toward a quieter corner in the back where the elves hung out. Fraoch and Duwynt were already there, deep in an argument about esoteric applications of the Law of Similarity. They dumped the discussion and met him with smiles and questions about what had kept him, so he told them he'd seen Bennett.

"He give you a present?" Duwynt asked, indicating the package John carried.

"Something like that."

"So what is it?" Fraoch asked.

"Later. The music's too nice to spoil."

Being friends, they let it ride and talked about other things.

A bogie came up with refills, and Duwynt insisted that John try a new liquor that Duwynt had added to the refreshment stocks. The stuff had no smell that he could discern, but it had a kicky, smoky taste that lingered. He liked it. Fraoch said she liked the taste, too, but she hadn't drunk any, only taken the flavor secondhand from John's mouth. He liked that too.

Still, curiosity was powerful. As John knew it would, the talk kept coming back around to Bennett's visit. John was on his third shot of Duwynt's liquor before he let his friends convince him to talk about his visit with Bennett. To have a hand free to unwrap the package, he tossed his glass away, confident that a bogie would snatch it before it smashed against the floor. The bogies were good at catching glasses; they didn't like what happened to them when they missed.

"He gave me this," he said, unveiling the silver and crystal trinket. Seeing it again reminded him of how angry he was with Bennett. "He said it belonged to my mother. My real mother."

The others exchanged glances. There was some kind of undercurrent in those glances, something to which John was not privy.

"You're sure that's what he said?" Duwynt said.

John felt a little peeved by the question. He tucked the crystal back into its wrappings. "My ears work."

"What about your brain?" Fraoch asked. "Are you sure he is not just trying to see how you react?"

"How am I supposed to react? I never knew my mother." *My* Faery *mother. Whoever the hell she* was! "Bennett still won't even tell me her name! Just gives me a gimcrack that might or might not have belonged to the woman and tells me to guard it carefully."

"Looks like he's getting some reaction," Gentiano said.

"Be kind, Gen. Jack's having a hard time." Fraoch ran a sympathetic, soothing hand up John's arm and onto his shoulder. "All the same, Jack, I think that Gen is right. Bennett likes to make people dance to his tune, especially when he thinks that they can't hear the music."

"So you think Bennett's scamming me?"

"There must be some value to the object, why else tell you to guard it?" Gentiano asked.

"More scam," Duwynt said with a shrug.

Fraoch didn't look convinced. "Perhaps. From what Jack has told me, it wouldn't be the first time his father has done that to him."

"Definitely a scam. That's what I'd bet," Duwynt said.

Fraoch hummed thoughtfully. "On the other hand, perhaps it's an honest gift and there is some other reason to guard the object. Perhaps it really did belong to John's mother."

Duwynt looked sharply at her. "You don't think . . . "

"Why not?" she said.

Gentiano laughed. "Yes, indeed, why not?"

"Why not what?" John didn't like being left out of their secrets.

Fraoch gave him a solicitous look. "Names, Jack. Names are worth guarding."

"Names? You've seen it. There's no name on it. There's nothing written on it at all."

"Not all records are written," Gentiano said. "Don't tell me you didn't feel the residue?"

"Don't say it if you didn't," Duwynt said mock-seriously. "We'd have to tell Shahotain that he's a failure. He wouldn't like that."

"I felt it," John said defensively. John still wasn't good at handling it when he was the butt of his friends' humor. "Suppose it does hold my mother's name." Suppose it did. The thought was a little unsettling. So long without knowing and now to have the answer in his hand. "Why would Bennett give it to me?"

Fraoch looked a little surprised, as though he was missing the obvious. "You're Bennett's heir. Who, besides himself, would have a better interest in seeing your mother's name safely guarded?"

"A cheap, naive guardian," Gentiano said.

"But only if he believes the story," Duwynt said. "Do you believe Bennett's gift worth guarding, Jack?"

"I don't know."

"See, Bennett's plan is not working," Duwynt said.

"Jack said he wasn't sure, not that he was unconvinced," Fraoch said.

"He ought to be unconvinced," Duwynt insisted. "Bennett never gives away anything of worth."

"He could have reasons," Fraoch suggested.

"He usually does," said Duwynt.

"Maybe he just means for Jack to have a memento of his mother. Or maybe he intends Jack to puzzle it out, you know, like a *shemiten* puzzle."

Gentiano frowned. "If he'd intended it as a puzzle, wouldn't he have told Jack that the thing had a secret without revealing what the secret was? It can't be *shemiten*. Jack knows what the prize is."

"What's a *shemiten* puzzle?" John asked.

Fraoch answered, "A riddle for an elf child. It's a way to learn about the use of magic and wits to uncover secrets. A *shemiten* is supposed to be a paradigm for life; you know, a search where you don't know what you are looking for, and where you only realize that you were looking when you find the answer to the puzzle. For a child, there is always a prize for solving the puzzle."

"A prize, eh?" John didn't feel like jumping through hoops for anyone, especially Bennett.

"Fraoch, my dear, I hate to say it, but I begin to think that you may be right," Duwynt said. "Bennett loves *shemiten*. If the puzzle is exceptionally difficult, he would find revealing the nature of the prize to be gained a wonderful tantalizer."

"So the prize is supposed to be my mother's name? That doesn't seem like much." Not on the face of it, but John knew that it meant a lot to him. Bennett would know that. So John had recognized the carrot, so what? There'd probably be a stick involved somewhere. *That* was like Bennett, too. And in between? Just what was he supposed to do with Bennett's gift? What was the puzzle? How was he supposed to achieve this prize?

And when he did, then what?

Gentiano nodded knowingly. "Learning your mother's name would give you knowledge you didn't have before."

"Knowledge fuels power," said Duwynt.

"And power fuels magic," said Fraoch.

"And magic rules the world," said Gentiano.

Fraoch chuckled. "*Fuels* the world, Gen."

"Shahotain has his version, I have mine," he returned.

Duwynt sighed and said, "My, but wouldn't it be nice to be a step ahead of Bennett for once?"

"Sweet," Gentiano agreed.

"So very." Fraoch got a dreamy look in her eyes. "We could—what's the phrase from the sunlit world?—give him some of his own medical."

"Medicine," John corrected absently.

Was there a chance here to give Bennett some of his own back? John wasn't sure he could see any way that knowing his mother's name would hurt Bennett. Or her, for that matter. Hadn't Bennett said that she was dead? Whatever his reasons, Bennett was withholding John's mother's name. What a petty, spiteful thing to do. Who was helped by keeping the name a secret? No one, that's who. Who was hurt? John. It seemed a simple situation. Learning his mother's name shouldn't affect Bennett one way or the other, yet the learning was something that Bennett clearly didn't want. Well, hell, *that* was enough reason to find out all by itself.

Or did Bennett *want* John to know? If the gift was a *shemiten* puzzle, as his friends thought . . .

The music that had surrounded them cut off with almost electronic precision. Shahotain had come.

"Go. All of you," he said in a voice without patience.

The party was over. Sprites scattered and goblins ran for cover. There wasn't a bogie to be seen. Gentiano and Duwynt were already halfway to the door. Fraoch took John's hand and turned with him to follow their departing companions.

"Not you, Jack." Shahotain's face was stern.

Fraoch sighed, but dropped John's hand at once. Silently she mouthed, *Later*. John hoped so. First he'd have to survive whatever had put Shahotain in such a mood. He stood, waiting for the storm.

Shahotain's gaze swept John up and down. John felt hot, tried to find some place to put his hands. The package made it difficult. Hard to clasp your hands when you're holding something, hard not to look like you're fidgeting. John noticed the barest flicker in Shahotain's eyes as he took note of John's silk-wrapped memento, but Shahotain's expression never changed. John was reminded of how scary he had thought his tutor the first time he had seen him on that hill near the magic pool. At least then John hadn't had to endure Shahotain's attention for long. The silence grew, and John's trepidation with it, until Shahotain said, "I have something for you."

In Shahotain's hand appeared a transparent box containing a data disk. It might have been sleight-of-hand, or it might have been real magic; Shahotain was capable of either. He held out the disk to John. Taking the offering with his free hand, John saw that there were no labels on either the box or the disk.

"What's this?"

"That's a question I'd look for from the others, not you," Shahotain said in his Disapproving Tutor voice.

John's tension eased. He was familiar with that voice; it was much better than Shahotain's Superior Elf voice. John had a good idea where he stood with his tutor. He tried again. "I meant, what's on it?"

"Information."

The bald, uninformative, elementary answer caught John off guard. Actually, it annoyed him. He expected better from his tutor. "That's the kind of answer I'd look for from Bennett, not you."

"Or one you might give yourself. Under the right circumstances."

Could be. "I haven't seen any computers around here. How am I supposed to read it?"

"You are not expected to read it here."

"Then what am I *expected* to do with it?"

"What you will."

John considered strangling Shahotain. "Why the games?"

Shahotain gave him the cold smile that said there would be no answer forthcoming to *that* question. Then Shahotain surprised him. "The disk contains information concerning a woman from the sunlit world."

John's first thought was that Shahotain meant his foster mother. No, it couldn't be! John just had mothers on his brain because of Bennett's gift. Still, if not her, whom? He had to ask. "What woman?"

"Marianne Reddy."

Hell! He wanted that data, now he was being handed it. "Why give this to me now?"

"It is timely."

Shahotain left him with that remark.

Timely.

There were times when the ways of the people of his

blood infuriated him. Times when John felt more than a little out of place in Faery and weirded out by the strangeness of the otherworld. Faery just wasn't Rezcom 3.

Where Marianne Reddy had raised him as her son.

He had a lot of questions, but he should have been used to that. Some questions seemed determined to remain unanswered. He'd had some answered here, but the answers often seemed to spawn more questions. Some of the questions he wanted to ask didn't seem appropriate to put to his new friends; he really didn't want to look stupid to them. His tutors might have the answers, but he wanted even less to appear stupid to them. Bennett held the answers to a lot of John's questions, but he was about as forthcoming as a stone.

Whom could he turn to?

These days, when the questions got too much, he usually sought privacy. Once he'd turned to Faye as a matter of course. She'd always been there whenever he had wanted another viewpoint. He wanted another viewpoint now, but Faye was not around. That was his fault. Fraoch. There were times when he wished his physical intimacy with her was matched by a spiritual one.

John felt very alone. He needed to do some thinking, get some kind of handle on what was going on. He was going to have to do it himself. Who else was going to help him?

CHAPTER
12

The guard at the apartment door didn't belong to the C-Kure™ rentacops who held the contract on the rezcom. She wore an Armianco uniform. Armianco was the corp that owned the place. Not a real cop in sight, but the monitor beacon proclaiming the apartment a crime scene was a New England Cooperative issue, which meant the locals had at least been here. *Ah, the joys of cooperation.* Charley hoped to God that the corp mooks had managed to preserve some of the evidence.

Charley breezed past the guard, a flick of his wrist displaying his badge. Manny stopped to do the check-in talk, which was fine by Charley. *Better him than me.* Manny would let him know later if he had done any more than waste time. Charley had more important things on his mind than corp etiquette.

Fifteen minutes before they'd gotten this assignment, Caspar had posted an addendum to his Modus 273 file. Caspar was one of Charley's cyberspace ears, a damned good one, and it had been months since Caspar had posted on anything but bad ones, the ones that didn't have the logical explanations that the department said they had. Caspar had posted this location, adding it to the Modus 273 file that hadn't previously shown anything in NEC police jurisdiction. Charley just knew he'd hate the reason, but he needed to find out what Caspar knew that he didn't about how this new incident was connected to the Modus 273 killings.

Armianco's Stamford rezcom, like the rest of the town, was more a part of New York City than the New England Cooperative, but technically all of Connecticut still belonged to the NEC, at least until the amendment went through. Until then, this kind of shit was the NEC's problem, and NEC cops would be doing a job that was too big for them. Too bad New York didn't send any money for enforcement to go with the crime they let slop over the border.

It was a bit surprising that Armianco was being a good corporate citizen and cooperating. They had actually called in the NEC police, even though the deaths had happened on their ever-so-precious corporate turf. Which they only did when it was a mess that they didn't want to clean up themselves. The situation stank, even without the omen of Caspar's modus link.

The apartment stank too, of cold, old death. Charley had scanned the prelim file on the way over, curious as to how bodies could go undiscovered in such a state-of-the-art place as the Armianco rezcom. According to maintenance, the tenant, one Anthony Marino, had called in to say he was going on vacation, and the apartment's systems had been set low, even the Tidibot™ drones were shut down. Nobody from maintenance would have checked the place for another week if the rezcom's electronics hadn't been fritzed in the blackout when Eden Again bombed the Agassi power station. When things came back on-line, a nasty-minded busybody of a supervisor, one Yvonne Browne, had discovered a chance to score points when she noticed the vacation request. Execs like Mr. Marino didn't take off on whimsical vacations; they had to log downtime requests weeks in advance, and Browne knew it. When Browne couldn't find such a request in the log, she had squawked upstairs and found out she wasn't quick enough; there already was an investigation in progress. Execs like Mr. Marino didn't miss work without people noticing. Her yelp put them on the apartment, something that the corp cops hadn't yet gotten around to. Mr. Marino might be a godlike being to Supervisor Browne, but he was still fry to the people who ran Armianco, and by extension their pet cops. At least Marino had been until he'd gone and gotten himself dead. Now he was somebody important and Armianco wanted to know just what the police department was going to do about this tragedy.

The department sent Charley and Manny, though why was unclear. The prelim report had contained lots of details, sordid ones. Mr. Marino had died in the arms of prostitutes, who were also dead. There were drugs involved. Nothing in the report pointed to a case for Special Investigations. Of course, the cause of death remained undetermined, but that was not in itself suspicious; examinations took time these days, especially for corporate citizens. No CoD just meant that the crime wasn't an obvious murder. Charley just hoped that when the coroner's report was filed, it would end their assignment to this case, but his sour stomach kept telling him he was being foolish. Caspar wasn't interested in ordinary deaths, even homicides.

The apartment was huge, wandering off into nooks, crannies, and other rooms. Charley knew from the report where to go. The bodies were in the main bedroom, off to the left. The door was open and the light on. When he laid eyes on the bodies, he popped an antacid tab even though he'd already had the bottle-prescribed limit for the day. He needed it.

What he saw was a trio of stiffs. Mr. Marino's bio listed him as thirty-two. The prostitutes' registrations showed them in their twenties and the DNA scans supported it, give or take a few years. But the bodies looked like old people. White hair. Shrunken muscles. Papery skin. The corpses looked ancient, almost like mummies. The withered husks looked dry enough to blow away if a wind ever penetrated the sacred air-conditioned confines of the rezcom.

He understood now why the report didn't have anything that looked like an SIU crime. This was one of the bad ones. The less data about it loose in the system, the better.

The brief sound of a rush of water from the bathroom caught his attention. There shouldn't be anyone here but cops. Cops didn't wash their hands at a crime scene. So who?

The bathroom looked bigger than his own apartment. From the doorway, the mirror showed him a woman seated on the chair by the vanity. An Armianco ID tag lay atop the shoulder-strapped briefcase near her elbow. She was brushing with a cloth at dark flecks staining the front of her business suit. Charley caught a faint whiff of something that was not perfume, the same odor coming from the john. Bad enough that she was here, but if she had compromised evidence—

He entered the bathroom, warming up to slag her down for interfering in a police investigation, then he realized that he had seen her before. Association chains fired in his brain and his anger cooled. A little. Well, maybe not much, but curiosity overrode it.

"Dr. Spac, isn't it?"

She started at his voice, first looking into the mirror, then turning to look directly at him. When her mismatched eyes focused on him, there was no hint of recognition. Her voice was shaky when she spoke. "Do I know you?"

Charley hadn't needed to hear her voice to cinch his ID; her eyes had done that. "We met a bit over a year ago, Doctor. Norwood Hilton, during their poltergeist problem. Since then our only contact has been on the net." He could see that she was still having trouble placing him. "I'm Charley Gordon. NEC Special Investigations Unit."

"Gordon? Detective Gordon?" Charley nodded politely. She nodded back, forced a smile. "I suppose it makes sense that they assigned you."

Makes sense to whom? "Just doing my job, Doctor. I have to say that I'm surprised to see *you* here. I don't remember seeing your name on the list of witnesses." Not that there were any witnesses, and even if there had been, they wouldn't have been detained here at the crime scene. Still, he thought he ought to at least start the conversation politely.

"I'm not a witness. At least not to the *event* of this abomination."

That was an odd phrasing. "You know something about this?"

"Know?" Her gaze strayed to the door into the bedroom. Her eyes were bleak. "God, I hope I don't *know*."

"You're not making sense, Doctor." *And you're not making me happy.* Spae's postings had always been rational, at least once he allowed for her assumptions, and she'd always been as fast to debunk the garbage as the department PR flacks, sometimes faster. That, plus the fact that she'd put him on the right trail on one of the bad ones when nobody else had been holding a clue, had led Charley to put more faith in her responses than those from the usual run of "investigators." "Why don't we start over. Suppose you tell me what you're doing here."

"Armianco hired my firm to investigate."

"That firm being?"

"Lowenstein Ryder Priestly & Associates."

Charley recognized the name, but wondered why Spae was associated with them; he hadn't heard of LRP taking an interest in his sort of business. They specialized in keeping things quiet and, failing that, putting the best face on whatever dirt their corporate clients had gotten into. That must be why they were involved. He didn't like it. Sure, Armianco had the right to have a private investigation, this was corporate turf; but they shouldn't have had their people on site until SIU cleared access. He wasn't going to push the point. Not yet anyway.

"Do you have a specialty I don't know about, Dr. Spae?" She looked confused, so he added, "I mean, just why did LRP put you on this particular job?"

"Armianco's request. They want to know if there was a connection between this and what happened aboard the *Wisteria.*"

Charley considered popping another antacid tab. "Aboard the *Wisteria*?"

"The ship with no crew. Surely you heard about it? It got a lot of media coverage. Armianco is a major investor in the shipping firm that ran the *Wisteria*."

Yeah, Charley had heard about the *Wisteria*; he'd heard more about the crewless ship than he'd wanted to. For one thing, Caspar had opened the Modus 273 file with the incident, the same file Caspar had logged this crime to. Clearly Caspar wasn't the only one thinking along those lines.

The *Wisteria* incident had been bad enough as an isolated occurrence. The public story had been that the ship came in crewless. Another mystery of the sea. Only the *Wisteria* hadn't come in crewless. When the ship's autopilot started asking the San Francisco Port Authority for docking instructions, there had been a crew aboard. A dead crew. Fearing some unknown plague, Port Authority had gotten the lid on fast and, for a miracle, the lid had stayed on, and the real story hadn't gotten to the media. If this incident was connected to the *Wisteria*, the odds of the lid staying on had just dropped dramatically.

"I can appreciate Armianco's interest," he said. "*Have* you found a connection between what happened here and what happened on the *Wisteria*?"

"God, I hope not." She sounded like she meant it.

"Which suggests that you *have* seen some sort of connection."

"Pray I'm wrong. I could be, you know. The feel isn't quite the same."

"You're not making me happy, Dr. Spae. I'd like more substantive answers."

"I'd really rather do some more work before I say anything."

"What sort of work?"

She started to say something, then caught herself. After a moment of consideration, she said, "Tests."

"Since Armianco has called us in, we get priority on all forensics."

"That won't be a problem, Detective."

What the hell kind of tests was she talking about? Had to be some kind of mumbo-jumbo. If there was one thing he hated more than dealing with the bad ones, it was dealing with people who thought they had an inside line on wherever the hell the weirdness came from. She was losing points with him. He remembered her hints that she knew something. Thinking about the evidence she might have destroyed or compromised, he asked, "Have you started any of these tests yet?"

She shook her head and waved a hand vaguely in the direction of the john. "I had a little problem."

Have a problem, make a problem. "You should have checked in with the department before you came in here."

"Armianco cleared us."

"But not with the department."

"You lose, Gordon," said another voice. Beryle's voice. "News from the Edge" Beryle, the damned tabloid chronicler who just loved to make Charley's stomach do its tricks. Face half obscured by a recording rig, Beryle was entering the bedroom from an adjoining room. *Shit! What's he doing here? This was a crime scene!*

"Notice is on file," Beryle said cheerily. He didn't even look at the bodies as he passed them; he must have already recorded his fill of them. "All nice and legal."

Brazen as ever, Beryle walked right up to Charley. The red "recording" light gleamed evilly from his rig. Charley counted it a grace that the "broadcast" light was dark. Beryle smiled a false friendly smile. "I have exclusive media rights to Dr. Spae's discoveries, and since she's authorized by Armianco to be here, so am I. Finding that the Special Investigations top cop is involved in this is a plus. A real validator. Want to make a statement for the audience?"

"Shut that damned thing off."

"So, you're saying that the police want to cover up the supernatural aspects of this crime."

Beryle's grin invited smashing, but not while he was

recording. "This matter is under investigation. There are no conclusions as yet."

"But lots of suspicions, eh? Tell me, Detective Gordon, is it true that the federal government has ordered you to shut down any exposure of this crime?"

"The feds have got nothing to do with this."

"So you're denying that the government was involved in the summoning of whatever did this?"

"Why do I bother? You'll twist whatever I say. Try this! You're nothing more than sensation-seeking pond scum. Is that quotable enough? Shut the damned rig off!"

"If I don't?"

"I'll have you jammed."

"That's suppression of the press," Beryle said jauntily.

"The man said shut it off," Manny said by way of announcing his arrival. He ripped the rig off Beryle's head, none too gently. Beryle's style of sensational journalism hadn't made him any friends in SIU.

"That's very expensive private property you're holding, ape," Beryle said, rubbing his ear.

"You'll get it back when we're through." Manny stuffed the rig into his coat pocket.

"Now we're really talking suppression. You're going to see a suit on this."

"I got insurance."

"It ain't gonna be enough. Detective Salazar, isn't it? I want to make sure the name is correct on the writ."

Manny was spelling his name for Beryle as Charley went back into the bedroom. Nothing had changed. Mr. Marino and his party girls were still as dead as they had been ten minutes ago. Charley punched in a call to the crime scene unit and told them to bring their SI kit. It was official now. SIU business. He had started to make his next call when Dr. Spae joined him. She avoided looking at the bodies.

"Detective Gordon?" Her expression was earnest. "I'd like to cooperate on this."

"That Armianco's position?"

"I don't know about them. It's my position."

Interesting. "I'd be very happy to have you cooperate, Dr. Spae. I like cooperation a lot. You willing to sink Beryle's tapes?"

She sighed. "David can be difficult to deal with."

Charley had experience with that.

"I'll do what I can," she said.

"And Beryle's suppression suit?"

"There won't be any suit if I have anything to say about it. I think you would like to see whatever did this put down as quickly and quietly as I would."

That so? Very interesting. "You're talking like you've got a lead."

"It's more that I see a possibility. We need to talk."

"I'll be glad to." *It had better not be smoke.* "Soon as I make a call."

Her brow furrowed. "To whom?"

"New federal ruling," he told her. "Everything we log in about cases like this goes upstairs."

She didn't look happy about that. Well enough, he wasn't happy about it either.

CHAPTER
13

John knelt on the verge by the magic pool, the disk Shahotain had given him lying before him. Try as he might, he could conjure no image from the pool. All he saw there was his own reflection, an elven face that had no connection to Marianne Reddy.

Was that his answer? After all, what connection could an elven prince have with a mainline straightline corporate pensioner? Only the bond of love, for a woman who had raised him as her son. Just the guilt of abandonment, for giving up so easily when he tried to discover what had happened to her. She believed John dead. He'd told himself that he had stayed away for her safety. At first that had made sense, what with Mitsutomo so interested in finding John so they could get at Bear; but Mitsutomo was out of the picture now, and what had John done? Sure, he'd visited their old apartment and nosed around a few databases, but he hadn't gotten anywhere and he'd let his efforts peter out. Before he'd left for the otherworld he'd spent more time chasing after Spillway Sue and studying magic with Dr. Space.

John felt like a shit.

Had Shahotain given him this disk just to torment him? No, Shahotain was hard, but he wasn't needlessly cruel. He must have had a purpose. He had often said that John wasn't committed to the Way, and that he was still too attached to the sunlit world. Maybe this was a test, a test to see if John could let go of his past that he might embrace his future.

Maybe Bennett's gift had something of the same purpose. It was another tie to Faery, and another way to connect John to him. Had he known what Shahotain was going to give John? John wouldn't put it past him. Here are your mothers, John, pick one. Pick a life. Your choice, no pressure. But you can't have both, because they come from different worlds.

Did it have to be that way? Two mothers, one mortal and gone from his life, and the other of whom he knew nothing. Well, he had two fathers, too, one an elven prince and the other gone from his life before he had a chance to know him. He hadn't realized before the odd symmetry of that: two mothers and two fathers and one of each unknown. His sets of parents made a strange reflection, almost as strange as the still barely familiar face he saw mirrored in the pool. That face was his, but it wasn't the one he'd grown up with.

Was that reflection an answer, a sign that the John Reddy he thought he'd been was gone, dissolved away in magic? He picked up the encased disk. Even the case reflected his elven visage.

"Your spells won't work on that, don't you know?"

Yuri? John turned his head. It was Yuri, no more than three yards away and leaning on a staff. John had been too wrapped in his thoughts to notice the urisk's arrival.

Pointing with his stick at the disk, Yuri said, "Dead, isn't it? Dead to magic."

"Nothing's dead to magic." That's what Shahotain said.

"Not dead?" Yuri tilted his head to look sidelong at the disk. "Maybe to a great one's magic—a truly great one—but to lesser folk dead enough. A thing of the sunlit world, isn't it? It doesn't belong here."

The disk that offered him a chance to reconnect with Marianne Reddy didn't belong here in the otherworld. With his longing to see her again, maybe John didn't belong here either. His gaze drifted again to the pool and to his image. An elf, no doubt about it, not a mall rat, or a collegiate fencer, or even a runaway and ganger. In the pool the reflections of stars glittered about his head like a crown of fire. He'd been told that he was a royal prince of elfland. As a child he'd dreamed of such a life. Here, it could be his. Would be his. Some of it already was. Here, his dreams were coming true. Maybe he *did* belong here after all.

So why couldn't he bring himself to toss the disk into the pool and be done with it?

"A surprise to see you here, isn't it, Great Jack?"

"Oh? And why is that?"

"It is the changeling way of things. Your life among the other great ones grows familiar, does it not? The lights are brighter, the music sharper and more poignant, the company more suitable to your needs and station. Is that not the way of it?"

Life at the keep *had* been more comfortable than he'd expected.

"A surprise, too, that you are not happy."

"That a personal insight, or just another part of the way of things?"

Yuri didn't respond.

John shifted his gaze from his reflection to Yuri. The urisk was half man, half goat, like some kind of DNA-fluxed chimera, neither one nor the other, but frozen in between, a bunch of bits and pieces that didn't quite blend. Sort of like John. No, that was wrong, John saw as he studied him. Yuri *did* manage to blend it all together. There was a solemn, if forlorn, peace about him, the sort of comfort and acceptance of his lot that John wished *he* knew how to find.

"How do you do it, Yuri?"

"Do what?"

"Find peace."

"Know my place, don't I?"

They were silent for a while, John thinking about just what his own place might be. It was the sort of companionable silence John had once shared with Faye. He hadn't seen her for some time, had been woefully neglectful. He wondered where she was, and in wondering, felt her presence. Nearby.

Yuri reacted to his start. Nodding knowingly as John scanned the nearby trees. "Here she came, to look in the pool. Strange, isn't it, to see a sprite sad?"

"Hush, Yuri," Faye said as she emerged from the shadows under the trees from which Yuri had once watched. "John doesn't need to hear that."

No, he didn't, but he had. He'd never intended to hurt her. It was just—well—

"You are coming into your estate," she said. "Your aura is much stronger. I'm very glad for you."

Her smile was radiant, forgiving and loving, and a balm to John's spirit, but then her presence had always had a soothing, reassuring effect on him. For reasons that he didn't understand, she was treating him better than he deserved. "Why?"

She broke eye contact with him, looking down at her feet. She stole a glance at Yuri, and John thought she blushed. Shyly, she looked at John again. "You're my prince."

John couldn't think of anything to say.

She didn't let the silence drag out. "You're not thinking of abandoning the court to go back to the sunlit world and search for Marianne Reddy, are you?"

He had been thinking of that, but he was a little scared to go alone. "Would you come with me if I did?"

"Of course. But it would be wrong."

Who had been telling her that? "Says who?"

"You would lose so much."

"What about what I could regain?"

"Anything you might regain would pass from you again in time. Think about your new estate. You belong in the court."

Why was she giving him the elven party line? "Bennett tell you to say that?"

Faye shook her head, eyes solemn.

"The speaker of the truth is of no consequence compared to what he speaks," Yuri said. "What you are, you are, Great Jack. Belong to the court, don't you?"

Maybe so. "Everybody is giving me the same line. Pardon me if I get a little suspicious considering that it's Bennett's."

"Why so suspicious, John? Bennett's given you your opportunity to be what you were born to be."

"He's been giving me other things, too." He told them about Bennett's gift and about his friends' speculations concerning the memento. Neither of them seemed to like it when John mentioned the plan to examine the crystal magically that he and his friends had come up with.

"John, you can't be serious about tampering with Bennett's gift," Faye said.

"Why not?"

She blinked, hesitant. "Well, it's not proper. Bennett entrusted the crystal to you. You shouldn't go prying into it."

Prying? Didn't he have a right to know? "If Bennett trusted me, he would just *tell* me my mother's name."

"Consider his reasons, John."

"Damn his reasons!" Faye's sympathetic tone made light of all Bennett's lies and deceptions. "I want to know who my real mother is! How the hell am I supposed to make decisions without knowing all the facts?"

Yuri murmured agreement. John recognized the urisk's ploy to calm him down. There really wasn't any need to be angry at these two, and John told them that he wasn't angry. Not at them. Yuri spoke.

"So, think you that the others are right? Could the crystal hold a clue to your true mother's identity?"

"I guess so. They've been studying magic longer than I have, and they seem to think the possibility is there. Sure, why not?"

"Possibility, yes, possibility there might be."

"Glad you think so too."

"I? That I did not say, but you are right, they should know better than me." Yuri looked at him mournfully. "And they have offered to help you uncover it, haven't they?"

"Yes, they have."

"Thought so, didn't I?" Yuri said, nodding as if John's answer confirmed something. "Considered, have you, what they gain from this?"

What did they need to gain? "They're my friends. They want to help me."

"No other reasons?" Faye asked.

"They don't like Bennett."

"See this as a way to harm him, do they?"

John didn't buy Yuri's suggestion. "Harm him? Not really. It's more in the nature of a prank."

"Names, Great Jack. Forgotten about names so soon?"

Of course he hadn't forgotten. "What can knowing her name harm? She's gone. Bennett said so."

Yuri raised a bushy eyebrow. "Names are still names. Connections can still embarrass. Think you about the politics of the court?"

"I don't give a damn about Faery politics."

"John, there's a lot you don't know about politics here," Faye said.

It was not as if she had ever taught him about Faery politics. It wasn't that long ago that he hadn't known the difference between a sprite and an elf. Sprites might spend time at the court, but they were not part *of* the court. Most of them weren't bright enough to understand politics. What did Faye know about all this anyway. She was probably just afraid that John might anger Bennett. "I don't think there's anything to worry about. No one's going to get hurt."

"No one? If trust you break with the prince, you will embarrass your sire, won't you?"

"Embarrassed? Bennett?" John laughed. "If that's the result, I'm all for it. Serve him right."

They argued some more but John stopped listening. He knew now what he was going to do. He would go along with his friends' plan to wrest whatever secrets they could from the crystal. Bennett might want to keep the identity of John's mother a secret, but John had a right to the information. And have it he would! If uncovering the secret caused Bennett problems, fine. Let Bennett take his lumps.

CHAPTER
14

Benton crawled the bug a little higher, then a little more, until he had a view of the bodies.

"Zoom. Three steps. Do it now."

His comp relayed the order to the bug and the lens eyes obeyed. The wasted face of a victim filled his monitor. He studied the image. It would take proper tests to confirm it— tests he wouldn't get to make, since the cops had this site locked up—but he felt sure. This was one of his quarry's kills all right, and he'd missed it again. He was beginning to doubt he'd ever get as close to it as he had last August.

He crawled the bug back to the edge of the window frame, where it would be less conspicuous, and set it to record. Unlikely he'd learn anything he didn't already know, but it paid to cover all bets. He was glad to see only SIU cops and a couple of corp investigators. If the authorities had any idea what was going on, the feds would be infesting Armianco's Stamford rezcom.

Just as well. Feds got in the way and complicated what should be simple. The longer they stayed out of this, the happier he would be.

He entered what little he had on this latest strike, including his personal evaluation of the circumstances, into the truck's comp. It wasn't good, hard data, but it would give his expert systems something to start working on until he gave them better. He wanted them working out predictive probabilities *now*. This kill was days old; there'd be another soon.

His expert systems, operating with his data and encrypted stuff from his employer, had gotten him close a couple of times now. Close enough that the "resonator" that his patron had supplied had registered the presence of his quarry. Unfortunately, the resonator wasn't very precise. Sooner or later he'd get lucky and the systems would give him a location near enough that he could get to the scene in time to catch his quarry while it was still involved in the kill. Sooner would be his preference; he was running out of continent on which to chase the thing.

For the moment there was little he could do. Time to contact his patron.

The false front of the truck's entertainment center was already down. He popped open the storage compartment and took out the induction headset. Settling the pads on his temples, he checked the contact integrity before initiating the call. The feed to his headwear was clear. Calling up his directory, he eyeballed his patron's number and initiated it. The garage vanished and the virtual meeting room appeared before his eyes.

He didn't like being cut off from the world this way even though he should be safe enough with the truck's minder watching. But you had to play to contract if you wanted to get paid, and the contract specified telepresence meetings. They were paying enough for him to take the chance.

The meeting room appeared empty, but he knew better.

"Benton here," he announced. It was an old telephone habit; there was no need to identify himself by speech. The coded connective handshake that had gotten him into the virtual meeting room was enough, even without the very recognizable image that the telepresence system was showing his patron.

His patron appeared: a well-muscled human shape of smooth, liquid gold with features too perfect to be real; no clothes, not even genitalia. Benton supposed the nearly featureless image was supposed to evoke thoughts of gods, but in these days of high-resolution imagery, it looked more like a digital antique. It had to be a style thing; he knew his patron had access to better, because he knew who his patron was. Anton Van Dieman, up-and-coming suit, a veep actually, at Network Securities, an arm of Metadynamics. Benton wasn't supposed to know, but he'd cheated. Purely in the interest of his own safety, of course. It was always best to know who you were working for. Just in case.

"It has been some days," Van Dieman said.

"It's struck again."

"You're sure?"

"Nothing on the resonator, since it's been a few days, but yeah, I'm sure."

"You say the resonator did not react, but you are sure it was what we seek. How can that be? Was the resonator functioning properly?"

It had worked before and the diagnostic routines checked out. "I'm more worried about the capture device working." *That* hadn't been field-tested—for obvious reasons.

"I begin to think that you need not concern yourself with that."

"Hey, don't fade on me now. We're getting closer all the time. Next time maybe, or the time after that. I'll get it." There was a big bonus for "getting" it.

The golden image waved a dismissive hand. "I do not doubt your prowess, but priorities have changed. I have observed, and appreciate, your diligence in this matter."

Benton's minder flashed notice of a financial transaction. Van Dieman's appreciation was substantial. Benton smiled at the compliment as he listened to his patron continue.

"However, I think it best if you pursue other matters for the moment. This situation has moved beyond the solution you represent."

The situation reported on the wallscreen looked no closer to solution than the last time Pamela Martinez had checked on it. Disturbing. A string of incidents related only by apparent cause of death.

Was this some new monster, or had the old one risen again to plague the world?

As far as she knew, she and her people were the only ones to see the whole picture. Local media and police departments had linked some of the incidents into small chains; no more than half a dozen of the component elements showed up in any of them. Only the National Illuminator™ had gathered several of the chains together, in their terror story of a lethal new retrovirus; but they had included several clearly inappropriate deaths in their count. They did not know the real story.

She looked again at the geographical plot. The dates attached to the plot points told the tale. From the earliest in California to this most recent in Stamford, the unfolding pattern showed an eastward trend. The progression was neither straight nor steady, save for that brief period at the beginning of August when five closely spaced incidents mapped out a straight line pointed at New England. At the time she had thought nothing of it, but now that the killer had struck in New England that line looked more significant. Had it been an anomaly in the data collection, or was it a significant, if obscure, clue? There was no way for her to know, certainly it had baffled her best analysts, but she had suspicions now—fears actually—that this killer might indeed be an old problem returned to haunt her.

The killer had come ashore nearly a year ago when the *Wisteria* had made port in San Francisco. Where it had come from before that was a mystery that only the *Wisteria*'s dead crew knew. That ship's last port before San Francisco had been in New Zealand, but so far there were no reports of similar deaths from there or anywhere in the South Pacific region. *Wisteria* had been boarded somewhere along its route. There were no clues as to where.

The chain of deaths was a waking nightmare. Medical reports on the deaths, where available, looked too much like other reports sealed in Project Charybdis's files. Too much like Quetzal's victims.

"Tell me, Hagen, is it Quetzal?"

"Quetzal is dead."

"A revenant, then? Some summoning left as a fail-safe? An avenger connected to his cult? You understand the manifestations of magic better than I. What is it?"

Hagen frowned at her, clearly unhappy to be sidetracked from the discussion he'd started. "The *Wisteria* killer is an unknown, but a direct connection to Quetzal is unlikely."

"How can you know that?"

"It is the best evaluation my people have come up with."

His *people* were not people at all, but dwarves, another species that had secretly shared the earth with humans for as long as there had been humans. Now, with the world on the edge of dissolving into magical chaos, they had emerged from hiding. Like her they wished to mitigate the effects of magic's rising tide. The dwarves had faced and dealt with the menace of magic before, and that experience was why Pamela valued them as allies. Such experience would give her an edge in positioning Mitsutomo to survive in the chaotic new world that was dawning. Unfortunately Hagen and his dwarven cabal were a secretive bunch, and despite their shared fear of and antipathy for magic, they were far too cautious to trust her completely. She understood that. She didn't trust them completely either.

Could she trust them in this matter?

"I don't believe that we can ignore this problem," she said. "Whatever this thing is, it is killing people *and* it is headed this way."

Hagen glanced at the map, repeating what he had been telling her all along. "Its path is unpredictable."

"But suggestive. I think, Mr. Hagen, that this is one of those situations in which you know more than you are willing to tell me. Am I right?"

"No," he said. She wondered if he had forgotten about the stress monitors in his chair, or if his people had found some way to beat the technology. The chair registered agitation, but didn't confirm a lie.

"I don't care what your people tell you. What do *you* think? Do you believe that it is coming here?"

"Unknown. For your peace of mind, we will institute precautions. However, I believe you are worrying unduly. If this phenomenon is related to Quetzal—an unlikely circumstance—then I believe that its attention will be centered on the artifact recovered from the site of Quetzal's death."

"But we don't have that."

"So you need not worry. The best information indicates that the artifact is still in the possession of the Federal Security Agency, classified under their Project Dark Glass. If anyone need worry, they are the ones." Hagen cleared his throat. "This may be an important manifestation, but it appears a minor one for now. There are other matters more deserving of our attention lest more problems like the *Wisteria* killer be spawned." He tendered a disk. "As I was starting to tell you, I have updated the files on the Pend Foundation, and I believe that you will find their programs more interesting than ever. Especially illuminating will be Dr. Gower's evaluation of certain correlations between Quetzal's projects and certain of the Pend Foundation's environmental programs that seem to be alleviating some aspects of the damage caused by the monster's magic. This is a situation that, I need not remind you, Mitsutomo abetted and must atone for."

Pamela took the disk, but laid it on her desk rather than slotting it. "I've already made my decision. I will allocate no Charybdis funds to the foundation."

Hagen looked crestfallen, but he wasn't ready to give up. "Please, Ms. Martinez. Read the reports. Let me bring Gower in if you have doubts. This is a vital matter."

"I agree," she said, savoring the confusion that appeared on his face. "The Pend Foundation will be receiving major funding from Mitsutomo NAG. Mitsutomo is, as ever, public-spirited. Mitsutomo-sama believes that such a worthy foundation deserves our support. Protecting the environment and reclaiming blighted parts of it are worthy goals. There is no need to be secretive about it. Mitsutomo-sama himself has approved the Keiretsu's support for the foundation." She smiled at Hagen. "He was most impressed by my presentation."

The creeping chaos that threatened the world threatened Mitsutomo as well. And what threatened Mitsutomo threatened her. Evolve or die, the old saw demanded, and she was not yet ready to roll over dead.

Mitsutomo, large as it was, couldn't survive the changes wracking the world alone. Allies were necessary, agents and intermediaries, dedicated entities that could concentrate on specific aspects of the problem. The Pend Foundation would be one of those entities, ready to do some of the work that needed to be done. Helping them might drain some of Mitsutomo's coffers, but it was only money going to the foundation—the Keiretsu's other resources would remain available to be directed at other problems. Even the money wasn't totally lost, the tax relief for charitable contributions compensated quite nicely.

But long-term plans didn't solve today's problems. Her eyes drifted back to the wallscreen. Her mind worried at the nature and goal of the *Wisteria* killer.

Hagen's reassurances weren't enough.

She set her secretarial agent onto the files to purge them of Mitsutomo proprietary material, package the remainder, and post it to the attention of Detective Charles Gordon, NEC Special Investigations Unit. If she was to have allies, she needed to support them, otherwise they would not form the bulwarks that she needed against the chaos of magic.

If one wished to have allies, one had to choose them carefully, perhaps even more carefully than one's enemies. The wrong allies were a greater liability than most enemies. On the whole, Anton Van Dieman thought, he was doing well.

The windstorm raging outside the skyscraper made little impression on the building. At least to ordinary perceptions. He was no ordinary person and was attuned enough to feel the structure sway. As it was meant to do—nothing unnatural there. A capricious shift in the air currents directed a hard gust against the outer wall of his office, rattling the Perspex™ panes. Nothing unnatural there, either. A storm, just a storm. He consulted a weather feed on his comp to confirm his impression that the storm would soon pass. The comp agreed with him. He smiled. His grasp of the natural world had improved immensely over the last year.

A bit over a year ago he had departed Clemsen Bioresearch, leaving behind the empire he had built there. Letting go had been a hard but necessary step in improving his corporate standing. Of course, he hadn't let go completely. The personal, immediate control was gone, but his influence remained through the carefully built network of managers and executives who, through cultured loyalty, intimidation, or coercion, believed their best interests were aligned with his. Most of those he'd left behind considered themselves his allies. He didn't see how any of them could believe that they offered him a tenth of what he could do for them, but he was willing to take advantage of such belief. It made them more useful to him.

He, of course, knew better. There was a vast difference between allies and vassals. An alliance could only be based on mutual and commensurate advantage. Not that there was anything dishonorable about vassalage. Indeed, being able to acknowledge a superior in power or influence was a survival trait that had served him well within the ranks of the followers. But vassalage was not *his* destiny, as his fellow followers were learning. Had not the *telesmon* come to him?

He gazed across the room at the case in which his treasure lay. The *telesmon* gleamed in the soft light, its sinuous curves drawing his eye seductively along its coiling beauty. *Such a delight!*

The Key to the Glittering Path!

It was his! The artifact had already opened for him new glittering paths to power, and had become his window to secrets of magic undreamed of. The more he worked with the *telesmon,* the more he learned and the greater became his rapport with the energies growing in the world. The secrets he pried from the *telesmon* set him apart from the herd, even from his fellow followers. As the followers had done for so long, he continued to work in secret, or nearly so. He had given his fellow followers a taste of his new power and they, at least, had begun to recognize the new order. Hadn't they elevated him to the second circle in recognition of his mastery? His status in the mundane world was rising as well, though he was more circumspect there in displaying his power.

And all this was just the beginning.

He checked the hour. Ten minutes before midnight. Almost the so-called witching hour. Even the uneducated knew that time had power. He needed time, time to consolidate his power, time that his nightmares told him he might not have.

He had not understood the visions at first. How could he? Brief flashes of sensation. A sight, a sound, a smell, all disjointed and meaningless, like the fading fragments of a chaotic dream. It had taken him almost two months to understand that he was receiving clairisensory impressions of killings. Magical killings. He hadn't understood why he was cognizant of those deaths, but he'd been disturbed. Not by the deaths themselves, of course; they were unimportant. His concern arose when he discovered himself drawn to the *telesmon* after each episode. The connection had puzzled him until he realized that the magical killer was connected to the *telesmon* as well. He began to suspect that the entity was what the sacred writings named a harbinger, one of the scourges of the unbelievers, one whose kind would abound on the earth in the final days of the man-blight.

While he conducted his own research, he had set hunters on the trail of the suspected harbinger. When Benton, the best of them, started to get close, Van Dieman had given him a special tool. Drawing upon his rapport with the *telesmon,* Van Dieman had created a resonator to aid the man in detecting the presence of the entity. The hunter had successfully used the device, locating a kill to match each of Van Dieman's clairisensory dreams, but because Benton had never been timely enough to capture it—or even see it—Van Dieman remained in the dark as to its true nature while the entity continued its wandering path across the continent.

Until the most recent kill in Stamford. In the surge of energy when the thing had taken its prey, Van Dieman had felt a jolt that had woken him from his dreams and had left him sure not only that the entity was connected arcanely to the *telesmon,* but also that there was a goal to its wanderings.

It was seeking the *telesmon.*

Was that a knock on the door? No, it wouldn't be. Ms. Emery was under strict orders not to allow any disturbances. Less than competent Ms. Emery might be, but she understood that part of her job. Besides, who would come calling at this hour?

He knew who, or rather what. The harbinger—if that's what it was—was coming to him.

His office was superbly soundproofed, fitted with the most modern materials and technology to absorb unwanted sounds, and it was quiet now. So very quiet. When he tapped on his desk, the sound seemed to come from far away.

His eyes roved the room, searching. He had done what he could to be ready for its arrival, but had he done enough? Was he prepared? He disliked the trepidation he felt; so demeaning an emotion should have been a thing of his past. Still, he could not help but shudder at the growing feeling that he was no longer alone. His darting glances swept the room, searching for—for what? He wasn't sure, but he felt that something had changed.

There! Through the archway into the bathroom. Had that shadow been there before? Nothing in the room would cast such a long, narrow shadow. A gust of wind rattled the window, distracting him. When he looked back the shadow was gone.

Had he imagined it?

A soft, scratchy sound from the bathroom. Was that the sound of claws scraping against porcelain?

Breathless, he waited, watching. Something moved near the credenza. A dark shape, more shadow than substance, slithered across the floor, moving directly toward the pedestal on which the *telesmon* sat within its protective transparent sheathing.

He let go the breath he had been holding. The fear that it would seek him out first ebbed away. A new dread arose. Had he understood correctly? Soon he would know. He touched the prepared function key on his desk. As the panels opened on the *telesmon*'s case, he dropped the wards guarding the prize.

The entity, a serpentine shadow, flowed up the pedestal and began to entwine around the *telesmon*, coil matching coil. The being had an insubstantial quality to it, echoing the translucency under light that was the barest manifestation of the *telesmon*'s power. For a moment, entity and artifact seemed to merge. It was time.

He triggered his trap, finger stabbing the button that dropped the cage of silver wire around the *telesmon*. The metal rang as it struck the base of the pedestal. The magnetic clamps embedded in the cage's wire and in twists inset in the pedestal held the two parts tight, preventing any rebound. As fast as he could, he pronounced the last bit of the formula to quicken the spells woven into the intricate mesh.

The entity surged against the barrier of silver and spell. Through the medium of his spells, he felt the thing's chill touch, knew the potency that it radiated.

What he could do with such power!

"Greetings, Harbinger."

He felt the entity's attention turn to him. That cold eyeless regard threatened to freeze his blood. He wanted to run screaming from the room, but he suspected that would be the worst thing he could try. He faced the entity. After all, what had he to fear? Was he not the Chosen of Quetzal? Was the Key not his? He stood his ground.

Barely.

Keeper, the entity said in a voice with no sound. The word seemed as much statement as interrogative, but its next statement was unambiguous. A command: *Unbind me.*

"Not just yet, I think." There was an order to these things.

The entity tested his spells. Though he would never admit it to another soul, he was surprised that they held.

I remember, it said. *Other times. Not so weak then. Other times.*

Weak? He could barely hold the bindings. He must not let it know that.

Unbind me. I will reward you.

"What is it you offer me, Harbinger?"

I can eat your enemies.

"My enemies—my surviving enemies—are few."

There are many enemies. They hide. They lie in ambush. Can you know them all? I have great knowledge. I see in ways that you cannot.

"My vision is also wide. I know things you do not. Long have your kind been away from the world, and all is not as it was."

I have seen this.

Was that a tremor of disquiet in the thing's voice? He had been waiting for it to reveal a lever. He believed that he saw it now.

"This world is *my* world, and I know its ways. There are dangers to you that you cannot comprehend. I can guide you, show you the dangers. I do not deny your power, but power is not everything. This is an age of information, and knowledge is the greatest tool."

As it has ever been.

"You know the ways of the shadow."

Yes. I can give teaching.

"And you can learn from me things you need to know."

It stirred, radiating a turmoil that he could not comprehend. *Yes,* it said.

He hadn't expected the negotiation to go so easily. "I'm glad that you understand that there is mutual advantage here."

I understand loyalty, it said.

Loyalty, he knew, needed to be earned. Or bought. He touched the intercom. "Ms. Emery, would you come in for a moment?"

He had been putting up with her marginal competence for nearly a week now. Time for his patience to be repaid. He watched her enter, appreciating the youth and energy in her walk. She had gone through an elaborate screening procedure. She believed the extra screening was due to the sensitive nature of the job. As it had, as it had, but not in any way she might have guessed. Her job—her real job—was to serve tonight.

He pointed at the cage. The harbinger would not be visible to her; not yet, anyway. "Would you please bring that over to me?"

A brief flicker of annoyance passed over her face. Menial tasks were not supposed to be part of her job. He saw her evaluate the request. He imagined what was passing through her mind. She was too new, and this was the first imposition he had made. She would let it pass this time. She moved toward the pedestal.

He released the binding and the magnetic clamps. The cage shifted and the harbinger sprang. Emery's startlement when the cage shifted bloomed into terror as she perceived the serpentine shape of the entity. There was no time for her to run. The harbinger coiled around her, wreathing her in shadow. She screamed, a full-throated wail of terror and despair.

He smiled. His office was superbly soundproofed, fitted with the most modern materials and technology to absorb unwanted sounds.

Emery twisted within the smoke that was the harbinger. He watched her begin to shrivel as the entity drained her.

I reward loyalty.

A spectral tendril drifted out toward him. He told himself that he could not show fear, could not let the entity know that he wasn't sure that he could trust it. The pseudopod slipped across his desk, rising up like a snake preparing to strike.

He told himself that he must not move, knowing that he lied to himself. He could not move. He was too frightened.

It touched his forehead, and his mind exploded in a rush of power. Echoes of Quetzal's gift flashed across his memories. The heart. The hot, heady taste of the bitch's essence. This woman's taste was different. Better. What the harbinger shared with him was no secondhand leaving, but the full, wondrous taste of flayed soul. It filled him, expanded him. He discovered that he had only imagined that he knew what power felt like.

When I am strong, you are strong.

Oh, yes. Yes!

The harbinger coiled more tightly around its meal, taking the rest for itself. Van Dieman sat in his chair, feeling the wet stickiness in his pants, watching Emery shrink and wither into a husk. There was definitely mutual and commensurate advantage here. He knew a good thing when he felt it.

Of course, once he learned what the harbinger could teach, once he had grasped for himself the power it offered, he would have no further need for it.

He had not cared for the fear it had raised in him. For the moment he had use for it, but that would pass. Until then, he would look forward to the next feeding.

CHAPTER
15

John's fascination with the mother he'd never known puzzled him. He really knew nothing about her. All he had were the tiny clues that Bennett let drop, and they were even vaguer than Bennett's usual comments. It seemed that she was no longer alive, but obviously she had to have been once, and there had been no hint that she had died giving him birth, so it would seem that she was as guilty as Bennett of abandoning him. So why didn't he feel the same way about her? Why didn't he hate her?

Maybe it was because, in some way, he equated her with William Reddy, the earthly father who had died before John had really formed any memories of him. It hadn't been William Reddy's fault that he was gone. Maybe it wasn't her fault either. He wanted to believe that. He didn't want to think that every elven parent was as cold-hearted as Bennett. But he just didn't *know* anything about her, and there were no public databanks here to search. At least John knew the formal official facts about William Reddy.

He had tried asking about his elven mother and gotten little result. His tutors refused to discuss the subject, telling him that there were more important matters to occupy his time. His friends knew nothing about her, and urged him to try unearthing her name from the crystal. The other folk about the keep—those who did not find sudden, important business elsewhere—pleaded utter ignorance of the doings of great ones. Stymied, he had come to see the crystal as his only link to her.

And that had brought him to the highest tower in the keep.

"It's the only way you'll learn anything, Jack," Fraoch said, slipping up behind him and putting her arms around his waist.

"I still don't understand why we have to do it here. There's nothing in the ritual that demands it."

"Nor anything that forbids it. Here we are isolated, away from the prying eyes of Bennett's spies. He will get no warning in time to stop you."

"You think he would?"

"You're the one who thinks that if he had wanted you to know your mother's name, he would have told you. If he wants the name kept secret, don't you think he'll do what he can to prevent you from learning it?"

"I suppose so."

"You know so." She turned him around and kissed him. "Just as you know that this is the best place and the best time to do what you need to do. Why don't you think about it some more while I help Gentiano and Duwynt prepare the circle?"

He turned to look out over the pure fairy-tale roofs and spires of the keep. The platform on which he stood was so far above the next highest that he might have been flying above it rather than gazing down from crenellated battlements. The sky above was full of stars, glowing in all their glory and whispering promises of magic, love, and hope from their eternal vantage point. They were a million eyes, watching, burning down through a clear sky that somehow defied the mists that shrouded the countryside around the keep. In the otherworld there was never a clear view for any distance, except in the sky. The land around the keep was shrouded in the mists of Faery, leaving the keep's spires an island of reality in a sea of dreams. There were hills and trees and rivers hidden out there, he knew; he'd walked and ridden over that land, smelled the fragrance of the trees, and felt the cold, bracing rush of the waters. Yet it seemed that the towers were the only substance in the midst of mirage. A matter of perception? Maybe. Maybe all of Faery was a matter of perception, a place of desire and dream fulfilled.

His foremost desire now was to know his mother, and the fulfillment of that desire began with learning her name. He turned toward the ritual circle.

Duwynt was taking his place in the north. Fraoch stood to the east, Gentiano opposite her. Once John took his place, each of them would occupy a cardinal point, places assigned according to personality, physical characteristics, and correspondences. The better to focus the energies.

"Time may pass slowly here," Gentiano said, "but we haven't got forever."

Gentiano was right. His friends were here to help him. There was no point and no courtesy in delaying. All that he hoped to gain would only be gained by completing the ritual.

John entered the outer boundary of the circle and closed it behind him before moving to the center. The crystal was already there, resting in the bowl of a small brazier wrought of silver rods carved in the shapes of vines. Small piles of dirt lay under each of the brazier's tripod legs. He picked up the crystal and lifted it above his head, offering it to the view of the stars. Laying it down again, he drew the cleansed knife from his belt sheath and pricked his finger with the tip. Blood beaded. He let a drop fall on the crystal. Just one was needed to link him to it. He spoke the words to energize the link and retreated to his station in the south.

John stood for a moment, gathering his wit and his will. This was to be a complicated sorcery, and he didn't want to make any mistakes. Mistakes were dangerous, and as ritual master, he would bear the brunt of any backlash.

He started slowly, as his tutors had taught him, gathering the energy and channeling it, using it to shift his perspective from the ordinary realm of Faery into the preternatural fields where the magic coursed. Around him the tower seemed to rise, carrying them up into the embrace of the stars, until the bulk of the keep was lost in the mist below, until it seemed that the rest of the universe might not exist at all.

He looked at the object of their efforts. The crystal looked different, pallid and plain. Gone were the facets that had caught and held the subtleties of the light. Gone too were the intricate traceries of the silver mount, replaced by a dull, unattractive banding. He felt a desire to look elsewhere, to find something else of more interest, but the energy of the ritual was strong and he understood that he was experiencing a glamour. He put aside the urgings, but the crystal's uninteresting image remained. Try as he might, he could find no flaw in that perfect image.

"It's well protected," he told his friends.

"If there were no secret here, there would be no need for protection." Fraoch sounded excited. "Try harder, Jack."

He did, but to no avail. Everywhere he pushed or probed, he was rebuffed. "I need more strength."

"We're here to help, Jack," Faroch reminded him, reaching out.

He took her hand, Gentiano's too. They took Duwynt's hands. The four of them linked, channeling their energy together, under John's direction, against the spell surrounding the crystal.

It was still not enough to perturb the crystal's protections.

Hell! There had to be some way to penetrate the wall of blankness. The featurelessness of the crystal's arcane image was not true. There was no way the thing could be as simple as that. He had seen it, touched it, felt it to be more textured. He knew what Bennett had given him and that gift was not what he saw lying in the brazier. He knew—

He saw an answer. There *was* a way to get around the blankness. He'd found a flaw in the spell, and it lay in the nature of the crystal as it related to John. Bennett had given the crystal to him. *Given* it to *him.* That fact was the key to circumventing the spells that protected the crystal's secrets. Not all actions have a magical significance, Bennett had once told him. However many actions, perhaps most, could be *made* to have such significance. Having been given the object—freely—John had been given whatever secrets the object held. The one was the other. The crystal was his now. *His!*

The crystal's pallid arcane image morphed into the brilliant, sharp-edged image he remembered. The web of its silver mounting shone with the fire of the stars.

But no writing appeared. No answers sprang to his mind. No name—no name anywhere.

It couldn't be a cheat! It couldn't!

But wait. There *was* something there—faint, but there. A sense of presence, of person. No one he knew, but someone who was somehow connected to him.

His mother?

"Do you have it, Jack?"

Fraoch's voice shocked John from his feeble grasp on the perception. His gaze slipped from the preternatural to the ordinary. What he saw beyond her was not part of the ritual they intended.

Shahotain perched on one of the battlements. Cold starlight sparkled from the silver studs and buckles on his garments, and from his opalescent eyes. His pale hair writhed in the wind, looking like pallid flames haloing his head. He might have been the leather-clad biker ghost of vengeance from *Interstate 666*^{EM}. But he wasn't—he was Shahotain, looking as grim and frightening as the first time John had seen him.

He leaped down to the wooden floor of the tower and strode into the ritual circle. His presence, unplanned for and unanticipated, ruptured the spell. Energy crackled around the boundaries of the circle and arced, naked and uncontrolled, overhead. John, as master of the ritual, had the responsibility to contain those energies. He tried to hold them to the shape he had built in his mind. Gentiano's hand left his, then he felt Fraoch's slipping away.

No!

The backlash roared around him, blinding him to everything

but the dazzling incandescence of energies struggling to be free. He wrestled them, fighting to channel them down into the grounding of the circle. Their heat burned on his skin. Fire coursed through his veins, threatening to consume him. At least losing touch with his friends freed his hands to make the gestures that would focus his mental struggle, help him rein in the energies. As he made the passes to shape the power, his hands twitched. Convulsed. He was losing it! His back spasmed. His head snapped back. He couldn't hold it! He—

Was flying.

Was—

Hit the battlement. He screamed as stone rammed into his back, its edge slicing through his clothes and flesh, digging for bone and threatening to bisect him. For a moment he tottered over the brink, buffeted by the backlash's raging force, until his groping hand gripped a crenellation. He hauled himself back onto the tower floor, only to be smashed to his knees. Desperate, his head spinning, he gave up trying to hold the energies and lashed at them, trying to beat them into submission. Somehow he managed to hammer the rampant energies into a shape he could comprehend. Slowly, painfully, he forced them back under control and dumped them into the arcane sumps anchoring the circle.

Exhausted, he fell forward. His face smashed into the wooden floor, but he barely felt the splinters clawing at his cheek. He wanted to sleep, but he needed to know if his friends were all right. He found that he needed to open his eyes. It was hard. He wanted to run away from the jackhammers rattling on his skull. So much easier to sleep. But not yet—he needed to know what had happened. He forced himself up onto his elbows, but it still took all his will to compel his eyelids to rise.

He saw Shahotain standing in the center of the circle, holding the crystal in his hand.

"Morgana." Shahotain's tone was at once wistful, surprised, and spiteful. He looked at John. Smiled. "You lose. Little wonder he took pains to hide the truth. Though this little bit of information has cost you, it will cost him as well. Take comfort in that."

John didn't feel comforted at all. Yet all was not lost. Fraoch stood near Shahotain, close enough to snatch away the crystal. "Fraoch," John pleaded. "The crystal."

"Has told us more than we'd hoped," she said. She laughed at him. Laughed, and draped herself over Gentiano.

"Time for things to change," Gentiano said.

John's head was pounding, his vision blurred. It couldn't be. It just couldn't. His friends . . . He was concussed, that was it! Imagining things, having hallucinations. He blinked to drive away the false images and nearly blacked out from the pain. When he opened his eyes again, he still saw what he had seen before. Fraoch hung on Gentiano's arm, laughing at him. Gentiano laughed too.

He felt like an idiot.

"Come," Shahotain said to the elves at his side. "We have things to do."

John wasn't sure if it was magic or his own flickering consciousness, but Shahotain, Fraoch, and Gentiano seemed to vanish. Duwynt remained, staring down at him.

"Another twist for the poor, put-upon changeling." He shook his head. "Morgana. I wouldn't have guessed. I really thought you were his heir. You won't inherit now. With her as your mother, there is no place for you at the court, and all of Bennett's smooth talk cannot make it otherwise. Whatever his plans for you were, they are now in a shambles, but then, so is your future. Was it worth it?"

Then he was gone too.

John rolled over and lay looking up at the traitorous, lying stars of Faery. He closed his eyes. He didn't want to see them anymore.

He felt so *stupid!*

He also felt sick. He rolled over just in time to throw up. He lay there for a long time afterward, afraid that he was going to do it again. When he felt reasonably sure that he wasn't, he got shakily to his feet. He looked at the blackened lines of the ritual circle and the twisted, half-slagged remains of the brazier. *There's sure as hell no more reason to be up here.* He staggered down the stairs.

Everything was quiet. He met no one on the first landing, saw no one in the hallway. The same on the next landing and the one after that. Where was everyone?

Not that he wanted to see anyone.

His back called him a liar, telling him that he *did* need to see someone: a doctor. One of the bogies could fetch him a physician. If he could find one of the bogies. Even in the great hall there were none to be found. The keep was empty, hollow. As hollow as John felt. It suited him. But the keep wasn't a place for him anymore. He needed to get out, to get away.

He went to the stables, ready to ride wherever his steed would take him, but his steed was gone too. None of the stalls were occupied. No surprise there.

He'd been abandoned, deserted by them all.

You won't inherit now. Bennett's promises were no more than trash. *No place for you.* John's life had been taken away from him again.

He needed to be somewhere else, anywhere else.

He headed across the courtyard, went out through the open gate. He lurched as he walked. With each step, he felt like he was tearing up his back, but he didn't care. All that was important to him was to be out of there.

The hill sloped away from the keep. He liked the way it made his progress faster. He wanted to go faster still. The best he could manage was a stumbling quick-step. He didn't care, he was going places. The fog of Faery closed around him, but he could barely tell. His vision was grayed, his thoughts themselves fogged. Faster. Farther. *That* was what was important. He had to get away.

Away.

Far away.

His foot caught on something. He didn't see what, because he wasn't seeing much of anything. Damn, he was in bad shape. He toppled forward, falling.

He fell for a long time.

CHAPTER
16

Holger set an emulator loose in the system and abandoned the computer. He had what he was looking for, and his online probing had tripped enough alarms to activate the device's homing signal. The emulator would make it look as if he were still probing for another ten minutes. If the Federal Security Agency lived up to its reputation—and he had no reason to suspect it wouldn't—their response team would soon be here. He had no intention of being present.

He checked the pulse, breathing, and temperature of the FSA agent they had ambushed. Well within recovery parameters for a man of his size and weight. Holger estimated fifteen to twenty minutes before he started to come out from under the drug. Excellent timing. Linkwater knew his specialty.

The agent would be facing a lot of questions, but if Holger's team had done their job right—and he had no reason to suspect they hadn't—the agent would have few substantive answers. The agency would know there had been a run against them, but the source and the reason would remain mysteries. Sufficient confusion would be generated to allow Holger's team enough time to complete their mission. After that, the agency would know the team's target, but by then the matter would be decided.

Linkwater was with the car, but Pankhurst was waiting outside, keeping watch. He seemed surprised to see Holger.

"Get locked out?" he asked

"No." Pankhurst continued to underestimate Holger. If the man's evaluation of enemies was as flawed, Pankhurst was a weak link in the team.

"You can't be done."

"As suspected, they had an active file on her." Holger tapped the side of his head where the memory chips were. "Downloaded a copy. It will take some time to crack the encryption, but we have their data." He signaled Linkwater to bring the car up to meet them. "Got something else that Magnus will want to know. Dark Glass is more advanced than intel believes. The Americans have specialists, quite a few. I saw indications that they have sleepers as well. It seems that our monopoly may well be ended."

"Doesn't change this mission."

"No, it doesn't."

They retired to the safe house that they were based in to continue on with that mission. While they worked together to break the FSA encryption and uncover the connections to their target, Holger discovered to his surprise that he was a lot faster than Pankhurst. He knew the man's rating; it was as high as his. He hadn't expected that the encephalo-chip interface would make as big a difference as the doctors claimed, but it had. Holger liked having advantages. They kept you alive.

It took them days, but they cracked the encryption, and they were able to study the FSA files on their target. The data were minimal—consistent with the FSA's official responses concerning the Department's inquiries—but they did confirm the target's location and associations. Her current domicile was in Providence, and she was working as a contracted researcher for Lowenstein Ryder Priestly & Associates, a relations firm associated with Metadynamics.

Metadynamics. There were those, Linkwater among them, who said that the megacorporation was, for all practical purposes, the government of this country. Holger didn't believe that, but he was aware that ties between Metadynamics and the government were very strong indeed. And during his recent browse through the FSA database he had not missed the

damning links between Metadynamics and Project Dark
Glass. What puzzled him was that they found no substantive
links between the target and Dark Glass. It was curious that
the FSA, so eagerly building their own teams of specialists,
did not seem to know what their allies harbored. Pankhurst
decided that the recovered files must be plants, intended to
be found by anyone penetrating FSA security, and that the
real files had been buried too deep for Holger to uncover.
Holger had been there, and knew better. Strange though it
seemed, they were working with the real files. FSA just did
not know the value of the target.

But Holger and his team knew. Now, with the Metadynamics connection exposed, they had confirmed that she posed a
security threat. They argued over the extent of that threat, but
they were in agreement on one point: she must be removed
from Metadynamics's sphere of influence. If the target showed
any signs of resistance, they would abandon the recovery effort and shift to sanction. Specialists were too unpredictable,
too dangerous. Elimination was the safest, surest course, but
they were bound to at least attempt the recovery.

Two weeks of surveillance and selected database checks
offered them an opportunity. The target had become a regular customer of V. Price, Antiquarian Bookseller. Holger was
surprised that any merchant could make a living selling actual physical books and nothing else, but Pankhurst's check
revealed no other sources of income. Those checks also
showed that the target regularly ordered books and invari-
ably made the pickups in person. She currently had several
volumes on order. After checking out the location of V. Price
and determining its suitability to their needs, they tapped into
V. Price's dataline and set a flag to report the arrival of the
target's next order. Holger filed his plan and got approval
from Magnus.

They waited.

The day came. Their target walked down Westminster
Street through the chill late afternoon shadows. She wore a
business suit not out of place on the streets at that hour,

though it would be soon. She might have been any suit conducting one more errand at the close of play, except for the walking stick she carried. That was an odd touch, reminding Holger of another time.

Hikes in the hills of England. Cloudy skies, cool breezes.

Not the sort of thing to be cluttering his mind with just now. They had business to attend to. The target had been spotted, and it was time to start the operation. He and Pankhurst cut across on Orange Street and headed for the second entrance to the building where V. Price, Antiquarian Bookseller, was located. Linkwater was already inside, and at Holger's signal, he entered V. Price, ostensibly to browse.

As he walked up the stairs from street level, Holger noted again the bronze plaque proclaiming the building to be the oldest covered mall in the country. That might be so, but it had only the faintest resemblance to what he would call a mall, being a narrow building only stretching the width of a single city block. Times had changed for the commercial world, they would soon change for their target.

Like good citizens, he and Pankhurst nodded when the rentacop informed them that the gate would be closing in fifteen minutes. The guard had already unlocked the storage cylinder that held the folding Secure-M™ mesh screen designed to seal the entrance. The management didn't allow streetlife inside and made a sweep to clear any out before locking up for the day.

The team would be done with its business before that happened.

Pankhurst split off just inside the arch, headed for the interior stairwell. The building had elevators, masterpieces of vintage tech, but they only ran on holidays and special occasions. Holger walked down the main gallery, feigning occasional interest in shop displays. He didn't look up toward V. Price; he didn't need to, having memorized all the pertinent details.

There were three tiers of public space, the main floor and two upper-level galleries, each set back slightly from the one

below it. Only the main floor and the first gallery had commercial establishments, the rest being offices and already
closed for the day. The upper levels were not full floors like
the main one but simply something akin to glorified bal-
conies, barely more than the width of the sidewalks outside
and bounded by metal railings scabby with peeling paint.
Each end had a crossover and access to a stairwell. He
started up the stairwell on the far side from where he had entered, the one the target would have used.

He stopped a step short of the landing, in the sheltering
gloom of the stairwell. Not that the open areas were well lit.
Originally, the structure had relied on skylights roofing the
atrium to let in light, but the ancient frosted panes had been
replaced by Glowsheet™. Now those retrofits were old and
lacked the brilliance preferred by viable shopping establishments. Atmospheric, claimed the mall's PR flacks, but their
cheery hype was doing little to keep the mall viable. V. Price
was one of the few shops still attempting to operate beyond
midafternoon and the departure of the lunchtime shopping
clientele.

All very suitable for what they had in mind.

He waited. Pankhurst waited too, in the opposite stairwell.
There were no shoppers to disturb them. Very suitable.

A buzz behind Holger's ear told him that their target was
about to leave the shop. Linkwater was activating the next
step in the operation. Phones started ringing in the establishments that were still open. The computer agents placing the
calls weren't bright, but they had enough sophistication to
occupy the call recipients for a few minutes, and would keep
any shopkeeper's attention focused inside their establishments. Linkwater himself would distract the staff of the
bookstore. The timing was good; the only person in sight
was a late departure headed for the stairwell on the upper
level of the opposite side of the building. She would be out
of sight in seconds.

The door of the bookstore opened and the target emerged,
a brown paper package under one arm. They'd had no way to

predict which way she would elect to exit, so both he and Pankhurst were prepared to make contact. He tugged on his glove, triggering the mechanism and exposing the prick needles. The needles carried a soporific, not enough to put the target out, but enough to make her tractable.

The target turned and headed toward Pankhurst, who had already started out to meet her. Holger, now cast in the support role, moved out to do his job. Pankhurst stopped ten feet from the target and addressed her.

"Good evening, Dr. Spae."

Having a stranger identify her by name had the predictable effect. She halted, hesitant.

Hearing her name spoken had an effect on Holger, too. Something wasn't right. He stopped. Spae. Her name. A person's name. She stood before him, a real person. The image jostled his thoughts. She was real. The safe appellation of "target" no longer applied.

"I'm from the Department, Doctor," Pankhurst said. "We want you back."

Spae took a step backward. Her head swung around. She would be looking to see how trapped she was. She noted him and looked past him. At the stairs. He was between her and the nearest stairs. She looked back at Pankhurst. "Suppose I don't want to go."

"Your wishes are irrelevant in this matter. Your return is not optional."

"Meaning?"

Pankhurst smiled, not a very reassuring smile. "Meaning it would be better for you to cooperate."

"Or what? You club me over the head and drag me back by my hair? That kind of Neanderthal thinking is why I left."

She swung her walking stick up, toward Pankhurst's crotch. He skipped back, out of range. Spae spun on her heels and started toward Holger. The target was attempting escape. He moved to block her path. His action had been anticipated. Blue fire started to burn along her stick.

Holger came up short. His memory flickered. He had seen

something like that flame-wreathed walking staff before. Flickering flames danced before his eyes. Blasting. Flames reaching out—

Enemy!

Yes, blasting an enemy, that was what he remembered.

She is enemy!

He saw arcane fire, reaching out. Blasting. Blasting . . .

Him! She would kill him!

No! Blasting a thing that was tormenting him, wanting to kill him.

His head was full to bursting with conflicting images.

Fire! Hate the enemy, the enemy hates you. No, helping him. *Target. Enemy. Spae.* Helping him.

He staggered under the onslaught.

The railing caught him hard in the stomach. He folded over it. The floor seemed very close, the tiles spinning before him. He felt as if he were falling, but he could still feel the railing hard against his belly. He closed his eyes, trying to force the vertigo away. His head spun. He gripped the rail, feeling helpless. Visions of blue, blasting flame filled his head.

Why hadn't she struck?

"Kun?"

Her voice. Concerned. That made no sense.

She is enemy! Spae is target!

He forced his head around and looked at her. She was shaking her head, disbelief, concern, and other less identifiable emotions crossing her face.

"It really is you." She stared at him, her eyes deep and probing. He felt naked before that gaze. "My God, Kun. What have they done to you?"

Confused.

She is enemy!

She had helped him, saved him.

Pankhurst was behind her. He had drawn his weapon. No, it wasn't *his* weapon; Pankhurst carried a standard-issue

Glock. The weapon he was aiming was an Arisaka En-
forcer™. Holger hadn't known Pankhurst was carrying one.

Something was wrong. Damn, he wished he was thinking
more clearly. Somehow, somewhere, this woman had saved
Holger. The memories weren't clear, but they were real. He
couldn't let her be shot in the back.

He threw his arm up, sweeping Spae down out of the way.
Move! Fire lit the Arisaka's barrel. Holger's shoulder exploded in pain.

Pankhurst cursed. "I told them you should have been
trashed as a bad job."

The slide of Pankhurst's weapon locked down, another
round chambered. Holger surged across the walkway. The
Enforcer's muzzle followed, Pankhurst's trigger finger tightened. The second shot missed.

Holger knew an enemy when one was shooting at him.

He dived for the wall. He pulled his Glock, setting the
weapon's selector as he did. Pankhurst fired again, missed
again. Holger was shifting too fast for him. Holger squeezed
his trigger, aiming low, below the skirts of Pankhurst's ballistic cloth coat. He let the magazine empty in a spread.
Pankhurst screamed as at least one bullet took him in the leg.
He went down.

But he wasn't out.

Holger was up and on Pankhurst before the man could
bring his weapon back to bear. Holger's left hand closed on
the barrel. It was hot. With a single twist of his torso, he
ripped the pistol from Pankhurst's grip and slammed a knife-
hand into the man's chest. Pankhurst's finger bone and ster-
num cracked almost in unison.

Threat neutralized.

Holger was breathing hard, almost panting. It wasn't from
exertion. If Pankhurst had turned on him, then—

Linkwater appeared in the doorway of V. Price, weapon in
hand.

Holger didn't give him time to take in the situation. Using
Pankhurst's pistol, he shot Linkwater. Three shots, no fi-

nesse. Linkwater slid down against the door frame, smearing it with blood and brains.

Threat neutralized.

Holger was still breathing hard. Spae looked up at him from where she had fallen when he pushed her out of the way of Pankhurst's shot. He could see fear in her eyes. Uncertainty too. She wasn't sure what he would do next. He wasn't sure either.

He knew he had just killed one man, possibly a second, to save her—or was it to save himself?—and still, every time he looked at her, he thought *enemy.* And just as surely knew that such thoughts were wrong. Men with laser scalpels were slicing his brains into tiny fragments.

"Get out of here," he told her. Whether for her sake or his, he didn't know. "Now!"

"What about you?"

"I'll be fine." Like hell. The voice in his head was still screaming that she was enemy. "Go. The authorities will be here soon. You don't want to be here when they arrive."

Or when I start listening *to the voice.*

"Come with me," she said.

"That wouldn't be advisable."

Enemy!

Not! Not enemy! Not!

"You can't go back to them now," she told him.

Back to the Department? No, he was finished there, no matter what he did next.

Dr. Spae made no move to leave.

Alternate solution.

Eliminate threat.

No!

He vaulted the railing. It wasn't that far to drop. He landed, rolled, and came up running. Straight out into the gathering night.

Part 2

TRANSITION

CHAPTER
17

John didn't have to open his eyes to know that he was back in the sunlit world. He could smell and hear it. The peculiar mix of stale urine, garbage, vehicle exhaust, chemical stink, and other noxious stuff was like nothing he'd ever smelled in the otherworld. The sounds were characteristic too: sirens, the whine of distant traffic, drifting notes of a dozen clashing entertainment modes, the buzz and sputter of a failing streetlight. All very familiar.

He remembered running away from the keep, burning with the need to be elsewhere, anywhere. He could guess what had happened. That desire had wrapped itself around his motion, unconsciously—or maybe not—taking him across the barrier between the worlds. Such transitions weren't free, and the crossover had taken all the energy he had left. He must have collapsed on reaching the sunlit world. He still wasn't quite back to himself.

He was lying on his back, which hurt like hell, and not just from the jagged roughness of whatever he was lying on. From the pressure he felt, he was half buried in noxious debris. Just another piece of discarded trash.

But he wasn't alone. Someone was pulling his leg. Fingers fumbled at the lacings of his boot.

"Come on, ya stinkin' stiff, ya ain't got no more use for these. Leggo!"

He was being rolled. John didn't like that. He didn't like it at all. He coiled his other leg and lashed out, aiming for

where he guessed the face of his molester to be. He connected. Solidly. There was a cry of pain and the hands left
him.

Batting away the debris covering him, John struggled to
his feet. He could hear the scavenger doing the same. John
was faster. Looming above the still crouching figure of the
sprawl scut, he looked down at a man who looked every bit
as scuzzy as he smelled. The mook's expression was somewhere between fear and surprise, but his eyes glittered like a
trapped rat's.

"You're one a them Proper Order freaks." He was panting,
clearly letting fear take the upper hand.

"I don't know what you're talking about," John told him
truthfully.

"Well, you ain't gonna get me." The man snarled, showing yellowed, rotted teeth. He backed his statement by pro-
ducing a knife from beneath his coat. He waved it around,
letting it flash in the light. It looked very long, pointed, and
sharp.

The sight of the knife didn't intimidate John as it was apparently meant to do. It infuriated him. Who the hell did this
mook think he was? John gave him the boot he'd been after,
toe right under his chin. The sprawl scut went over backward, his knife glittering off into the dark. This time, he
stayed down.

John nearly went down too. His back was on fire. The kick
had stressed his back injury. His back had been badly
abraded against the keep's crenellations. Shreds of his doublet were stuck in the scabbing, slimy mess. He managed to
get the doublet off without aggravating the wound too badly.
Most of the garment's back was shredded. The doublet had
been a present from Fraoch and now it was ruined.

Like so much else.

He'd get something out of his relationship with the bitch
elf. Tearing the doublet's remains into strips, he wished it
were Fraoch he was tearing into. She'd used him, playing

him like the proverbial fiddle for the pleasure of her master Shahotain. And Shahotain—

God, what a blind idiot John had been.

At least he was quit of the otherworld.

Though where exactly he *was,* he wasn't sure. He stood in the middle of a city block's worth of rubble. He could see a fence of panels and posts bounding the area, walling the vacant lot away from the neighborhood around it. Scattered mounds of trash and garbage and junk and drug debris—lots of drug debris—were evidence that this area had been used as a disposal area. Still was, to judge by the ripeness of some of the garbage and the talus slopes of anonymous dark plastic bags against the fence. A prefab hut of the type common to construction sites crouched in one corner of the lot.

Beyond the fence he could see buildings, most dark, but some were showing light that proclaimed that they were still inhabited despite their derelict appearance. Some of the others had the squatters-owned look with boarded over windows from which escaped the fitful glow of boosted power. The high-pitched cackle of someone wasted on bubble floated across the night. He could guess that this was not one of the friendlier parts of the northeast sprawl.

He didn't recognize exactly where he was, which wasn't surprising given how big the sprawl was, but he did recognize something about the place. All around him he could feel the play of magic. His stay in the otherworld had sensitized him to such things, and made him more open to what his tutors had called the *shai,* the sense of awareness. Wherever he was, he was *aware* that it was one of those places where the walls between the worlds were weaker.

Luckily.

What he had done was stupid. The blind, stumbling transition he'd made could have gotten him into big trouble. Loreneth had told him once about an elf who hadn't made it across. John could have been caught that way, trapped in the dismal gloom between the worlds, until his mind frayed and he became a gray wraith haunting the edges of the worlds, never able to touch anything real.

The bubble dreamer laughed again. *Like that,* John thought. He could have ended up like that, without anything to anchor him to the real world—either real world. It scared him, and made him want to find another place to be.

He gave up his attempt at bandaging his back as hopeless. The shreds of his doublet would have made a poor bandage anyway. Maybe it was better that the wounds not be covered.

The wind was rising, rooting among the trash for scraps and fluttery things to carry off. Its touch on his skin wasn't unpleasant—another benefit of *shai*: he didn't feel the cold the way he used to—but it did remind him that he was not dressed for the streets. Being so obviously wounded made him a target for predators, and he'd been abused enough for one night.

The sprawl scut who had tried to roll him was wearing a coat, some kind of outback duster a couple of sizes too big, its hem frayed and stained from dragging on the ground. Once it had been a nice coat. It had seen hard wear, but it would do for him. As he stripped it from the scut, John told him, "You tried to steal from me. When I objected, you tried to kill me. I think I deserve some compensation, don't you?"

The mook didn't answer. Probably couldn't, even if he'd been conscious, the way his jaw was swelling. Well, he'd gotten what he deserved.

John checked out the coat but found nothing of interest beyond the sheath, roughly sewn into the lining, where the scavenger had kept his knife. Careful of his back, John shrugged into the coat. The fit wasn't bad. A little short in the sleeve, but not all that much. Most of the buttons were gone, but even hanging open it would serve his purpose. He dug the disk case from beneath his waistband and dropped it into one of the pockets. It was good to have pockets again. He hunted up the scut's knife and slipped it into the sheath.

There didn't seem any reason to hang around.

He headed toward the prefab hut. By the way that the

streetlights outside the fence threw splinters of light on the ground over there, he guessed that there was a gate in that corner. The damned thing was probably locked, but the fence was lower there if he had to go over it.

Walking across the rubble-strewn ground wasn't fun. Each step reminded him that he was no gray wraith. No ghost ever had a back that hurt like his. He really did need someone to look at it. Going over the fence started looking more and more like a bad idea.

Naturally the gate was locked.

John scowled at the loops of composite chain and the padlock securing them. It didn't take him long to find a hunk of rebar. In the course of his search he noticed a sign leaning against the hut. Big block letters proclaimed RECLAMATION SITE. The picture showed a park, all trees and shrubs and grass. There even was a little pond with ducks on it. Half the space of the sign was devoted to a list of corporate sponsors. John didn't get it. How long did the suits think such a thing would last in a neighborhood like this one? Shaking his head, he slipped the rebar into the padlock's hasp and popped it. He left the gate swinging wide behind him.

Walking along the fence, he saw that the outside was already so defaced with graffiti that he could barely tell the inspirational RECLAMATION SITE posters from those offering corp-sponsored public services. One, less trashed than the others, caught his eye. It touted an open clinic sponsored by the Pend Foundation. John had seen that corp name on the sign by the hut, but other than that it was new to him. The poster claimed "No questions, no turnaways."

That was what he needed.

The poster had a map, complete with a you-are-here, and enough of it remained unobliterated that John figured he could find the place. A few minutes of walking proved him right. He was just congratulating himself on his luck in getting to the clinic without running into trouble, when he caught his reflection in the mirrorlike surface of the smoked TransShield™ doors.

He stared. It was John the elf, pointed ears and all, walking up to the clinic. John might have left Faery, but Faery hadn't left him.

He couldn't go into the clinic looking like he did. The poster's no-questions policy was for wonkheads, bubble dreamers, and shady sprawl scuts—people who had reasons to avoid treatment for fear of coming up in somebody's computer—and not for elves. How could it be? Elves didn't belong in this world. A living, breathing elf walking into a clinic for treatment would be big-time news, scientific as well as pure tabloid. There would be no escaping the media.

Maybe his back wasn't so bad. He'd be okay. He'd always been a quick healer. He turned and kept walking, hoping he wasn't lying to himself.

He'd been so glad to have the disguise spells broken and his true face revealed—and now, here he was, wishing he could hide it again. The darkness did its bit, and he pulled up the collar of the coat to help, but it wouldn't stay dark forever. He'd have to find a place to go to ground. He really didn't want to end up as the star attraction in a media freak show.

There was one place where no one would be surprised to see that he was an elf—his slump in Providence. If he could get there, he'd be safe. Then he could get in touch with Dr. Spae; she'd had some medical training and she'd helped Bear. She'd help him. All he had to do was get back to the slump without any more trouble and everything would be fine.

He *wasn't* lying to himself, was he?

CHAPTER
18

They had lied to him.

That was one thing of which Holger was sure. Hell of a thing to be sure of. It didn't tell you anything. Not what was really going on. Not why it was happening. Nothing. The only thing it assured was uncertainty.

He was loyal to the Department!

Yes. Yes, he was. Or at least—he had been.

Loyalty is the greatest virtue.

Loyalty *was* important. A very great virtue. But the greatest? What about honor?

Loyalty. Loyalty to the Department. The Department was his life.

Pankhurst staring at him over the sights of a police-model Arisaka Enforcer. Non-reg pistol. Undeclared. The image in his mind wavered. Not a street, but a firing range. Familiarity training. Everyone had an Arisaka and Pankhurst was firing. Holger was confused. It happened on the range.

No, on the mall.

Shooting at him.

The Department was his life.

If Pankhurst was an indicator, the Department *wanted* his life.

Loyalty to the Department sometimes demands sacrifice. On occasion, the ultimate sacrifice. He was loyal to the Department! Loyal! He would sacrifice himself if needed.

But what was needed?

He didn't have an answer. He wasn't even sure what questions to ask. Was he doing the right thing? Had he *done* the right thing? What *had* he done? The images were jumbled in his mind, and the voices had no answer for him. People who heard voices were not considered quite sane. What was the verdict on people who argued with those voices?

The people around him on the street were casting their verdicts. They stared—unobtrusively, of course—and gave him a wide berth, avoided him, made him an outcast. They marked him, as well they should. Prudent of them. He was a marked man. He was a killer, after all.

He stalked through their midst, the way opening for him.

He had come to this city for Elizabeth Spae.

Elizabeth Spae is a renegade. Elizabeth Spae is your target.

She was a specialist. He knew that. Specialists were spooky, untrustworthy. He hadn't had a lot of experience with them, but he'd had more than enough. He'd had experience with Spae.

A clarity of image: Magnus, briefing him. L'Hereaux was there. They were giving him his chance to get back into the active ranks of the Department, giving him his assignment: a renegade specialist by the name of Spae. The name meant nothing to him.

Nothing? But he had known Spae before.

Elizabeth Spae is your target.

That's what they'd told him. But Spae wasn't what they had said she was. He had memories. Then again, maybe she *was* what they said. He remembered her with Mannheim, his mentor. No, that wasn't right. Mannheim was dead. Had been dead for years. He had been killed by magic. Why did Holger think Spae was involved in that? He'd met her after Mannheim was dead. Or did he only think that now? Could she have altered his memories? That must be it. She was a renegade; Magnus had told him so. She had betrayed him, betrayed the Department.

Rogue agents are disloyal.

But he wasn't.

What about Linkwater? An accident, like the other one. Like Leftenant Barkins. That's all, just an accident. Holger wasn't a renegade. Spae was the renegade.

Renegades must be recovered or eliminated.

Department policy. It was a hard policy, but fair. Couldn't jeopardize all for one weakling. You had to do something about renegades. You had to act as soon as you knew who they were.

Elizabeth Spae is a renegade.

Yes, that was right. *She* was the renegade, not him. The Glock nestling in his armpit was the answer for *her*.

Authorized sanction is correct.

There was no magic he'd heard of that a specialist could use to stop a bullet. Specialists were scary, but they weren't untouchable. Not like those things, those nightmare things from the other place. Bullets couldn't hurt them. He couldn't do anything about them. But he could do something about her. Needed to. Spae was responsible for what was happening to him.

Elizabeth Spae is your target.

Target! He was fast, very fast. She'd never see the Glock leave the holster, never notice it until it was pointed in her face. Then it would be too late for her. She'd scream. He could hear her screaming, knowing there was nothing more she could do to mess him up.

But the face wasn't hers. A stranger's face. Not the target. He looked for the target. She was out there. He knew she was! One of the crowd, hiding. He was ready, ready for her. She wouldn't trick him anymore. One shot, one clean shot, and she'd be out of his head forever.

Out of his head.

What the hell was he doing?

He stood in the middle of a crowded street. People were running away. Some just stood and stared like stupid animals. Most cowered or sought cover as he wildly swung the pistol around. What in hell was he doing, pointing his weapon at innocent people?

He slipped the weapon back into its holster and ran down the first side street he found, away from the crowd, away from what he might have done. He had been ready to shoot, he knew he had. He'd seen the face of the enemy on the faces of those innocents.

God, what was wrong with him?

No one followed him. There were no heroes in the crowd, for which he was grateful. After the first block he slowed to a fast walk. This street was less crowded, and no one here knew what he had done. He was a little surprised to find that he was headed toward the lot where they had left the car. On instinct, he guessed. Heading for the escape route.

Not a bad idea.

The car remained where they had left it. He unlocked the door and got in, thankful to be sitting, thankful to be quiet. He needed time to think. Rearming the security systems, he opaqued all the windows, activated the surveillance mask, and made himself an island of isolation in the midst of the city.

But it was only a temporary refuge. He knew that the car could be tracked, and sooner or later they would come looking for it. He doubted that it would be a good idea for him to be found with it.

Just what *had* happened?

Temporary insanity? Natural or induced? And if induced, by whom?

Spae was the obvious candidate. Spae was pivotal in this. But what role was she really playing? He only had the Department's side of the story. Maybe it was time to hear the other side. He checked the chronometer. She would not have had time to reach her apartment building. He could intercept her.

He made the plan into action, spotting her as she approached her building. She was more wary than she had been earlier in the evening, but there was nothing about the car to alert her. Still, she turned and looked at it as he slowed and pulled up to the curb. She didn't run, not even when he opened the door and greeted her.

"I was wondering if I'd see you again," she said.

"I hope we can talk."

"That wasn't talking, back there."

"I . . . know, but I think that it may be important that you and I talk. This street isn't the place to do it."

"I'm not inviting you home."

He didn't expect her to. "This vehicle is neutral ground, Doctor."

She shook her head. "You've locked me in cars before, Kun."

Had he? He didn't remember. "All right, then." He slid across to the passenger seat. "You take the controls."

"So the autopilot can drive us wherever the hell it is you want to get me?"

"The dogbrain is dead," he said, pointing out the shredded electronics under the steering column. He didn't want the car going to a prearranged location any more than she did.

She remained suspicious. "Why should I trust you?"

"I don't know."

She blinked, surprised by his answer. "No prepared bull-shit story?"

"I could ask you the same thing."

"Touché." She got in, leading with her walking stick, and closed the door. She kept the stick between them. "This a Department vehicle?"

"Yes." Holger's eyes were riveted to her stick. He remembered strange lightning coursing across its surface, arcing away into—into something he refused to remember. By force of will, he kept his mind inside the car. "Its systems offer us privacy."

"Except for its own little recordings, of course."

"Same as the dogbrain."

"Really? I don't suppose you can prove that?"

He shook his head. Either she believed him or she didn't. There was no reasonable way to offer proof.

"I suppose it doesn't really matter," she said. "You wanted to talk. Let's start with what the hell you're doing here."

What was he doing? He wished he knew. If she meant what had brought him to Providence, *that* he could answer. "They sent me to bring you in. They told me you were a renegade, that you deserted the Department."

"I resigned. If they're calling that desertion, they don't have a good grasp on reality. And if you believe everything they tell you, *your* hold is pretty tenuous as well."

Holger had a good idea of just how tenuous his hold on reality was. *Never show weakness to the enemy,* Mannheim had advised him. Spae might or might not be the enemy, but the advice was sound just the same. "I'm no starry-eyed recruit, to believe my superiors are beyond reproach."

"But do you believe what they told you?"

"You admit that you no longer feel yourself bound to the Department. Do you also admit that you work for Lowenstein Ryder Priestly & Associates?"

"That doesn't make me a criminal."

"Are you aware that LRP is subservient to Metadynamics?"

"Half the companies in this country are connected to Metadynamics. What's your point?"

"Are you saying you didn't know?"

"I haven't looked into their corporate connections. That kind of garbage isn't important to me. I'm working for a legitimate firm. I'm doing research, the kind of research that the Department, in its infinite wisdom, kept interrupting. *That's* what's important to me. The Department doesn't own me. They never did. Magnus and his people have a little problem understanding that sort of thing."

"What about your oath?"

"What about it?" she snapped. "That oath was a contract. I was doing my part. I came back from the otherworld with more practical knowledge about how magic works than I had gotten in ten years with the Department. I wanted to get a handle on what I'd learned. That takes time. So do I get lab assistance, support of any kind, or even a goddamn pat on the head? No! I get interrogations, innuendo, and suspicion. They treated me like some kind of traitor. Hell, they even threatened to *drug* me, to verify the truth of what I told them. It looks like I got off lightly. *You* they treated like a laboratory animal and made you like it."

"Laboratory animal? You know about the experiment?"

"Is that what they called it? An experiment? Didn't they even give it one of their fancy code names? Code Cyborg, maybe? Or Machine Man? How about Implant Operative? What the hell did they tell you to get you to go along like a good little soldier?"

"How do you know what they did?" He didn't even know all of it.

"Your aura is corrupted," she said as if that explained everything.

Aura was specialist jargon. Weird shit. If that was the kind of answer she was going to give, he didn't want to talk about it. "Let's forget me for the moment. I need to know, Doctor. Do you consider your resignation from the Department to be irreversible?"

"Hell, yes."

"And are you working with Metadynamics?"

"I'm doing my own research with funding from LRP. If that money ultimately comes from Metadynamics, I don't know about it. If the Department has a problem with what I'm doing, they could have sent someone to talk to me. But rational discourse is not their style. You're the proof of that."

"I'm talking to you, Doctor." Rationally, he hoped.

"Look, I've been doing nothing that is contrary to the Department's interests. I haven't released proprietary information, and I haven't told them anything about the Department's programs, capabilities, or goals. As far as I'm concerned, the Department doesn't exist. I'm on my own. There's nothing illegal about that, and nothing that the

Department has any legitimate control over. The Department is just a piece of my past that I'd rather forget. Got it?"

"I hear you, Doctor."

"If I understood what went down back there correctly, you're on the road away from your past as well. If that's true, I might know a place for you."

"Recruiting me, Doctor?"

"Look, Kun. I've got reason to be grateful to you, and not just for today. I pay my debts, when I can."

Pay the debts you can. That's what an honorable man does. Don't worry about the rest. That's what a practical man does. Know the difference between the two kinds of debts. A wise man does. Mannheim's advice.

"I'm not looking for work just now, Doctor."

"Okay, then. Just remember one thing, and you can repeat it to anyone you think might be interested: I don't take kindly to people sending bullyboys to kill me just because I'm not doing my research in their laboratories. Don't start a war you're not ready to fight."

With that she left the car.

Holger slid over and tugged the door closed. His head buzzed too much with it open. Watching her walk away, he considered that his caution had been appropriate. Spae was only one woman, even if she was a specialist; she couldn't take on the Department all by herself. But her threat of war implied allies, which suggested that she was perhaps not entirely truthful about her connections with Metadynamics. They had the resources for a war with the Department, and the Department knew that, and feared it. Or did she refer to darker, more sinister allies from the otherworld? Though he had not set out to do so, he had broken with the Department. Though he would now need allies himself, he was not about to turn in that direction.

He didn't like being adrift. What Spae had told him suggested that the Department had deceived him on more than one score. She alleged a legitimate departure and recounted their continued interest in her with honest, forthright indignation. It had felt true to him.

Assuming he could trust his judgment.

And what about him? The Department had done something to him, something more than the simple enhancements the doctors had told him about. But how much more? And had they used magic? The thought of that possibility made him shudder. But whatever they had used, whatever they had done, who had given them the right? He had accepted the enhancements because he was loyal. He had thought that they would make him better at his job. And he had needed reconstructive surgery anyway, or so they'd told him.

He couldn't remember any accident. They had said it was traumatic memory loss, but now he found himself doubting that statement. How much truth had he been told? Spae was right: oaths were contracts, to be upheld as much by one side as the other. What *did* the loyal man do, when his loyalty was used as a weapon against him?

He didn't like the dark waters he was navigating.

He didn't like the dark streets, either. Time had passed and full night had fallen while he had wandered, pondering his predicament. There were pieces missing, gaps in his understanding, but one thing that he understood too well: he couldn't use the car indefinitely. Its location could be monitored too easily. He hated giving up the peace that its security systems had offered him, but peace wasn't safety. He took what he thought might be useful and safe—from the vehicle and abandoned it.

He hadn't gone ten meters before the voices started in again. Whispers in his mind, warning him, suggesting that he wasn't doing the right thing, advising him to be careful, to think about seeing Dr. Gilmore. Gilmore could help him.

Could Gilmore make the voices stop?

Report.

If he reported to Gilmore, Chartain would know, and Chartain wouldn't be happy about what had happened to Pankhurst and Linkwater.

The bastards got what they deserved.

Pankhurst is loyal. Linkwater is loyal.

Pankhurst pulled the gun! Pankhurst shot first.

Pankhurst is loyal.

Pankhurst turned on him.

Report!

Maybe he ought to. Wouldn't that be the easiest course? They would sort everything out. He could say that he had become confused, which was true. That he hadn't intended to kill Linkwater, to shoot Pankhurst. A mistake. Maybe even a malfunction with the implants. Such things were possible. Hadn't he demonstrated that he was capable of extreme violence motivated by reflexive response? The report had said that. Reflexive response. He had responded reflexively, hadn't he? He did that when provoked unexpectedly. The incident with Barkins had proven that.

Bar—

The troll. He remembered its hairy, horrible face. He remembered that it hadn't been one of the more terrible things, one of the untouchable ones. He remembered how good it had felt proving that it wasn't one of the untouchable ones. He—

He was crying.

Why in hell was he crying?

God help him, he was on the edge. Over it more likely.

Report!

No, there was no need to report. He was done with the Department. Having killed Department agents, he was more of a renegade than Spae. How long did he have before they came after him? They would, he was sure of that. They couldn't afford to let him run loose, with who-knew-what secrets implanted in him, knowing as much as he did about their operations. They had already shown how much they trusted him; they wouldn't believe that he would not trade on such secrets.

No trust.

Where was the loyalty when there was no trust?

He was loyal to the Department.

But was the Department loyal to him?

Loyalty is the greatest virtue.

He wasn't feeling virtuous.

Loyalty to the Department sometimes demands sacrifice. He would sacrifice himself if needed.

He had believed that. Mannheim had taught him that.

But his sacrifice hadn't been self-sacrifice. Pankhurst had decided to sacrifice him. That wasn't part of the contract. The contract was broken, but the voices wouldn't admit to that. They still urged him on as if nothing had happened. Maybe it was him. Maybe nothing *had* happened. He had bad dreams sometimes, very bad dreams that felt real. Maybe this was one of those dreams.

Pankhurst's eye, behind the Arisaka's sight, was very clear. His face was calm, committed.

Pankhurst. Familiarity training. On a firing range.

No! That was not the view Holger would have seen on a firing range.

Except maybe in a dream.

He was confused.

On the firing range.

No, not a dream, not a faulty memory. Real. He was sure.

Wasn't he?

Report!

He had to go somewhere.

The voices told him otherwise. Could they be trusted? He realized that he'd only heard them so clearly here in Providence. Were they a part of the place, some kind of magical perversion of the city, an arcane pollution that affected his mind? He knew that creatures of the otherworld could play odious games with his mind. They had in another place. Another place . . .

Somewhere else—anywhere else—he'd be able to think more clearly. That's what he needed. He needed to think more clearly. He needed to be somewhere else. Soon.

Afoot he wouldn't get very far, very fast. He had abandoned the car. The cabs waiting for business folk to depart the downtown were long gone. But there was a train, and it had service to the airport. That was the answer! From the airport he could go anywhere, somewhere where the miasma of magic wouldn't be rotting his brain.

He found the train station deserted. That was fine. He didn't need anyone observing his departure. The third ticketing terminal he tried was working, and he checked the schedule of commuter runs. Twenty minutes till the next one with a stop at the airport. He could afford twenty minutes. He went out to the platform and sat on one of the benches. It had a good view, commanding both the entrances to the platform and the track in the direction from which the train would come.

The train did come, late, but he didn't mind. No one had troubled him. His departure plan was undisturbed.

The train clacked to a stop, sighing like a weary beast as it halted. As he prepared to rise, he saw that his plan was undone. The confidence he'd begun to feel was a joke. His plans to leave had clearly been compromised.

An elf in a long dark overcoat emerged from one of the cars. He knew at once what it was. He'd seen others like it. A sardonic elven face flashed in his memory. He felt as paralyzed as he had then. As helpless. The elf walked toward him along the platform. Holger didn't move, sure that he couldn't, but not remembering why. No other passengers got off the train, just the elf.

There were implications in that.

Holger didn't want to attract the elf's attention. He tried to pretend that he was unaware of the elf's presence, hoping it would ignore him. He was rewarded. The elf walked past, leaving the platform by way of the ladder to the rail bed.

It was gone, and Holger could move again.

The train was gone, too, long gone. That was for the best. The train, infested as it was by creatures from the other side, was not the way to leave this city.

He needed another course.

Report!

No, no. Whatever he did next, reporting to the Department was not going to be it.

CHAPTER
19

Benton left the bed without disturbing the whore. She'd deny the label if he ever spoke it aloud, but he knew what she was. He also knew how to honor a contract, and part of the one between the two of them was not mentioning the true nature of their transaction. Looking the other way and pretending things weren't what you knew them to be was a big part of Benton's business. In his experience secrets were best kept when you knew what that secret was and from whom it was important to be kept secret—the latter point being the most important, certainly most valuable part. He was good at it, and that's why he got the big bucks. Enough to pay for women like the one who slept on, unaware that he was no longer with her.

He padded on bare, silent feet out of the bedroom, across the sitting room, and into the second bedroom of his suite. The perscomp on the table by the bed was a stripped-down model with only the most basic capabilities. That was fine by him. He only wanted the most basic of the basic, the line connection. He distrusted broadcast connections. He hooked the perscomp to the portable he'd brought up from the truck, and made a couple of inconsequential calls while running a diagnostic. There was a flutter on the line but well below the threshold that suggested a tap. Satisfactory.

He'd chosen this hotel because it offered recharge for electric vehicles. His truck itself didn't run on charge, but it carried a backup system for the electronics, which should be completely topped by now. Such a system offered another advantage to those, like him, with the knowledge and equipment to use it. He sent a coded signal—broadcast, but there was no other option—to the truck's on-board comp. Under the guidance of a dedicated agent, the comp invaded the monitor link on the recharge connection, following it back to the comp controlling the power outflow. From there it jumped into the hotel's main system, connected to the phone net, and opened a link with his portable. The truck and the portable talked to each other, and when they were satisfied that the handshake protocols were all nominal, the portable's screen lit.

"Good morning, sir," the comp said. "What do you require?"

"Review offers, by start date. Now."

"There are no new offers. However, you have seven outstanding contracts. Do you wish to review the seven contracts?"

Seven? He only remembered six. "Yes. By date. Now."

He scanned the list as it came up and saw the anomaly at once: case 71822. That was the hunt for the *Wisteria* killer.

"Query: why is 71822 still open?"

"Client has refused payment on expense invoice."

Most likely a glitch. Using putative begging letters from bogus charities as screens for payments occasionally ran into categorical refusals from corporate accounting departments. "Resubmit. Now. Contingency: if refused, activate collector program three."

"Affirmative."

Then again, maybe there was more to it. "Recover file on contract 71822. Search public databases for similar deaths. Three point correlation. Confine search to New England Cooperative geographical area. Do it now."

"Affirmative."

He knew he'd have to wait. "Secure."

"Affirmative."

He took a shower. When he was done, the comp was still

working, but it had uncovered at least one more probable hit by the *Wisteria* killer. Yesterday, in New Hampshire.

"Query: is client Anton Van Dieman still alive?"

"Affirmative."

Interesting. "Query: where was he yesterday?"

"The only public information available reports him present at a conference in Nashua, New Hampshire. Do you wish a more extensive probe?"

"No." Same place as the killer. Very interesting. "Referent resubmission of expenses on contract 71822, change contingency. New contingency: notify of response."

"Affirmative."

He'd want more evidence to be sure, but what he had was suggestive. He'd been suspicious when Van Dieman had pulled him off the contract; the move had suggested that the client had another game running. He had long suspected that Van Dieman knew more about the killer than he'd let on to Benton. Hadn't he supplied that whatever-it-was—resonator, that's what he called it—that could sense the beast?

Lots of possibilities, little data. Too little to speculate effectively. He'd have to keep his eye on it. He'd seen what the *Wisteria* killer could do, and didn't like the idea that he might encounter it from the other side of the hunt. His ordinary caution in keeping Van Dieman's resonator until the accounts were settled was looking like a foresightful decision. Dealing with these extraordinary situations was still relatively new to him and any edge, even if not fully understood, was welcome as long as it worked.

Le pragmatisme, toujours le pragmatisme.

And, practically speaking, he needed work. He reviewed the other six open contracts. One called itself to his attention, not just because it was the longest outstanding op but because it too was for Van Dieman. Not directly, of course, but Benton had done his homework. He knew who had placed the order to put the strong-arm on the squatters in the Pickman Building.

Working on another of Van Dieman's ops might give Benton the chance to learn whether he needed to watch his back.

He reviewed the file. The op had been a minor one, with Benton serving as a cut-out for his corp client. A test, really, a way for him to prove his reliability and to demonstrate how he handled things. Well, he had managed to sufficiently establish his employability even though the actual op hadn't been completed. The op stayed open in his files because he had never received a final payment, which had been contingent on the corp acquiring the property it desired.

Either they hadn't made the acquisition, or they weren't telling him they had. He had the comp query the records office for any transfers of title on the Pickman Building and got "Last change of title recorded in 1999." So Van Dieman and his people didn't have it.

The failed acquisition wasn't his fault. The streetlife he'd employed had gone missing after going in for the clean-out, but he had gone in the next day and found the place empty. There had been a few signs of violence, but no bodies. The result had been clean enough that the client had been satisfied. Benton had gotten paid, but the streetlife had never shown up to collect her cut. Not his problem.

Now Benton found himself wondering if there might not be something to that disappearance, something extraordinary. At the time nothing had seemed unusual, and it still might be nothing. Street people were notoriously unreliable, that made them expendable, and that—considering that he hadn't been sure that the corp hadn't been setting him up—was why he had chosen to use a local zip artist as an opening move for the op. Had she disappeared—if so, how and why—or had she just flaked out?

Or maybe Van Dieman and his corp hadn't been after the building at all, but whoever had been squatting there. Benton's prelim survey of the place had only turned up one squatter. He hadn't worried about the guy's identity at the time. Had he made a mistake? No, that was a bit too paranoid. If they'd really wanted the guy, they'd have said so;

they knew that he did that sort of thing. Unless all they had wanted was to flush the guy out of hiding.

Too much speculation, too little data.

He needed a place to start, and he couldn't think of a better one than where he had left off.

"Computer, search the following Providence databases: police, welfare, medical; also check private file: fixer offerings. Recover any records referent Spillway Sue. Also recover any records concerning Unregistereds matching file description of referent Spillway Sue. Do it now."

"Affirmative."

He didn't need much to start a hunt.

CHAPTER
20

The southbound commuter platform was nearly empty, just a handful of nightshifters all being careful not to notice their soon-to-be fellow passengers just in case one of them might be a crim planning on working the train. That attitude would work to John's advantage once he got up there. In the past when he'd had no money and needed the public tranz, he'd nicked his way aboard when there were crowds. Crowds covered a multitude of illegal activities on the tranz. There were no crowds to hide in at this hour, but the late hour had its own benefits. The guard in the kiosk looked tired, not very watchful unless you counted how he studied the vid screen throwing lurid glare up onto his face. A small glamour—an apparent fritz on reception—to hold his attention and John was past the gate and on his way up the stairs to the platform.

The glamour was a trick he couldn't have pulled before his training under Shahotain and Loreneth. He was grateful for the ability, but it annoyed him to remember whom he had to thank for it. Everything would have been a lot easier if the hideaway trick that Faye had shown him could be used while he was moving, but it couldn't. He needed other tricks to stay "invisible."

A few more nightshifters plodded up onto the platform, but no guards. John's ruse had succeeded. He boarded the train along with the legitimate users, snatching a discarded faxpaper from the platform as he did. He chose the least filled car and used the faxpaper to put a screen between him and the other passengers; the cars were better lit than the platform, making him all too easy to see. There wasn't much of interest in the paper, whoever had pulled the selection of articles had the most mundane of tastes, but John read it all anyway. It had been a long time since he'd read anything.

He got out at the State House station. The platform was empty save for a single old wonkhead or drunk sitting on one of the benches and having a conversation with himself. John ignored him; after all, who would listen to such a man telling them about an elf getting off a train. John watched as the train left him in a clattering, rattling shower of sparks. Walking to the end of the platform, he found the maintenance ladder, climbed down to the track level, and set out along the right-of-way. Following the tracks was the shortest, safest way back to his old neighborhood.

While he was making his way up to the street from the railroad right-of-way, he got the oddest sense that something had changed in the area. That puzzled him. The skyline looked the same, none of the buildings had been demolished or burned down, and nothing new was going up nearby. The streets didn't look any more or less trashy and there weren't any new symbols among the graffiti on the walls, but he still felt something was different. Then he noticed the SOLD signs on several of the buildings he passed. Most of the signs had several layers of graffiti, so they weren't new. He didn't remember seeing them the last time he'd passed this way.

Trudging up Acorn Street, he got lots of complaints from his back about the steady exertion. Soon, he'd rest.

He got his first look at the tower. The weathered concrete and brick exterior looked unchanged. As more of the building came into sight, he knew he was ready for a rest. Just a little farther.

So far as he could see, his slump hadn't acquired one of the SOLD signs. He'd been afraid that it might have.

As he walked through the door, he knew he was home, and he *knew* even more. Feelings that he had not understood when he had moved into the building made sense to him now. He understood what had attracted him here. This place was one of those close to the otherworld. The magic was brighter here. He liked that. It made him feel more secure.

He hadn't gotten ten feet into the building before Kesh, Metch, and Lep came bounding out of the shadows. They danced around him, babbling excited and incoherent greetings like loyal dogs upon their master's return.

"It's not like I've come back from the dead," he said. "I haven't even been gone all that long."

"Too long for us," Kesh said.

"And how long is that?" John asked.

The bogies exchanged blank looks. As one, they turned to him and shrugged.

"We're just glad you're back, Great Jack," said Kesh.

"We are indeed," Metch echoed. "Most glad."

"Kept this place safe for you, we did," Lep added. "Safe, safe indeed."

"As if you had a part, sluggard," Kesh admonished him.

They began to wrangle over just how much each had contributed to what they hyperbolically called the Defense of the Domain. John listened patiently—more accurately, tiredly. He didn't have the energy to put down the squabble. Soon enough they'd blow out their own fires. He started to doze, coming to attention when the three bogies silenced themselves of a sudden. Gorshin crouched atop a stack of crates, watching, his wings slowly unfurling and furling.

"Smelll blood on yuuu," the gargoyle said.

"Well, hello to you too." John didn't like the avidity with which Gorshin watched him. "Aren't you going to welcome me back?"

The gargoyle ignored John's question. "Hurrtt?"

"As a matter of fact, yes."

The bogies reacted to John's statement with a hubbub of concern, shock, and apologies for their lack of prompt attention to his needs. They insisted he retire to his bed where they would tend his wounds. It sounded like a good idea to

John, so he went along. Gorshin remained behind. Along the way John spotted several of the shyer Faery folk who had moved into his slump. He'd seen so little of them that he couldn't tell how they were taking his return. He tried to stop and talk to the shellycoat who laired in the utility space under the first flight of stairway, but the bogies started to drag him up the stairs. Struggling against them hurt his back, so he went along. He could talk to the shellycoat later.

Having escorted him to his room, the bogies vanished. John shrugged off his coat. He was ready to collapse, but before he could, the bogies were back, each bearing a first-aid kit. Kesh's burden still flaked wallboard from the mounting he had torn from the wall. Despite the chaotic nature of their debate about who knew best how to deal with John's injury, they seemed to understand the use of the medical supplies. Metch demonstrated surprising gentleness in cleansing John's scabbed-over back. John let the bogies fuss over him, their deferential attention reminding him of some of the better parts of his stay in the otherworld. He'd been getting used to such attentiveness. Somewhere in the middle of the bogies' ministrations, he dozed off.

When he awoke it was still dark, though it wouldn't be for long. He was still bone tired, so he couldn't have slept the clock around. Still, he wasn't ready to sleep more, and he wouldn't be until he had a better handle on where things stood.

He dug the disk case out of his coat pocket. The first item on his agenda was determining if the disk was as false as the one who had given it to him. He got up, padded over to his perscomp, and hit the start. And got nothing. A glance out the window assured him that the area hadn't been hit with an outage. The failure was closer to home. He tried the light switch. Nothing. So it wasn't just the comp, power was gone too. He went out to the feeder conduit to check it out. His hacks into the nets had been chopped, leaving the wires dangling and useless.

Without leeches and limpets to nick into the utility company's lines, his tabletop hardware was just so much scrap.

He'd have to score new taps before he could connect again. Normally, to avoid just that hassle, he would have removed the taps before the proles from NEUCO came through on their maintenance sweeps, but it seemed he had been in the otherworld long enough to miss one. When he'd left, the next one had been three months away.

Climbing back up to his bedroom, he worried at the passage of time. Apparently three months or more. Bennett had said that time would be different in the otherworld. John had spent a long while among those treacherous vipers, long enough for them to have gulled him into believing that they were his friends. But how long had it been? Hell, his time sense was shot. Could three months have passed here?

No, that didn't match with the weather. It was autumn out there. He *knew* that. His mother would have said that he was feeling it in his bones. His elven tutors would have attributed the knowledge to *shai* awareness. Three months would have put Providence into winter.

Maybe NEUCO *had* changed its policy. Maybe they *had* done an unscheduled sweep. Other things had changed around here, why not that? Sitting in his slump, without a tap to the nets, he had no way of knowing. It was too near dawn and he was too tired and sore to go hunting new taps, but he had an idea.

"Kesh, how long has it been since you saw Dr. Spae?"

The bogie shrugged. "She only came a couple of times after you left. Gorshin doesn't like anyone here when you're not here."

"We don't either," Metch said.

"Dr. Spae is nice, though," Lep said.

"You just like her because she's foolish enough to talk to you," Metch said.

Lep started to bluster, signaling an imminent outbreak of disputes. John cut it off. "Kesh, I want you to take a message to Dr. Spae."

Kesh gave John a "why me?" look.

"I'll do it," Lep volunteered.

"Lep is better at sneaking about," Kesh said in a rare display of honesty.

John recognized motivated self-interest when confronted with it, even if he didn't understand the motivation. "All right, Lep. You can go. Give me a minute to write out the message, then you're off. I want it delivered straight, no side trips."

Lep nodded solemnly.

John started to look for something to write with. Metch had a scrap of paper ready for him by the time he found a pen. John wrote his note and handed it to Lep. "If you can't get it to her directly, leave it where she'll find it soon."

Lep scampered off. John didn't see that there was much else he could do just yet. It was nearly morning, and he couldn't go outside in the light looking like an elf. He thought about sending one of the other bogies with a note to Spillway Sue, but he knew the Faery folk made her nervous. Besides, he didn't know if she could read. He'd see her soon, soon as he found out what was on the disk. If he'd been away for a while, a few more hours wouldn't hurt. Feeling tired and sore and more than a little depressed, he went back to bed.

It was late afternoon when Metch whispered in his ear that Dr. Spae was coming. He dragged himself out of bed, brushing away the bogies who wanted to change his bandage. His back felt a lot better. Scrounging up a T-shirt, he pulled it on and went to the window. Dr. Spae had come alone, as he had asked. He went downstairs to meet her but didn't bother going to the door; she knew how to get in.

Because he knew she had dealt with elves, he decided that caution was in order. Although she knew that he was Bennett's son, she had never seen his elf face. He wanted to give her a chance to get it set in her mind that he was not an impostor. He waited in the shadows for her, cloaking himself in the same spell Faye had once used to hide him from assassins. She walked right by him.

"Thanks for coming, Doctor," he said, stopping her in her tracks. "I appreciate your promptness."

"I had begun to think that you weren't coming back," she said, turning toward his voice. She looked puzzled not to see him. "John?"

"Didn't I say I'd be back?"

"Yes, you did," she said guardedly. She was searching the darkness for him. Apparently her mage sight was not a match for his spell. "John, is there something wrong?"

Yes, but nothing to do with you. "I'm fine."

"Why are you hiding?"

"I wanted you to have a chance to assure yourself that it really was me."

He dropped his spell and stepped out of the shadow. She gasped in surprise when she saw him, but recovered quickly.

"I see you got the disguise spells lifted." She nodded, eyes wide. "The resemblance to Bennett is uncanny."

She didn't have to insult him. "Seen one elf, seen them all, eh? Did you bring a machine?"

Her mouth twitched a little. Annoyance? She patted her shoulder bag. "I brought my old Romer™. I don't use it much anymore. It's a bit out-of-date. You're going to have to show me how you learned to hide from mage sight."

"I've learned a lot recently, Doctor. Some of which I'd be happy to share with you, but right now I'm not very interested in magic. If the comp's battery is good, it'll do what I want." The disk casing was a bit out-of-date, too. A Sony-mac Romer would be just about the right vintage. He held out his hand. "I'd like to get started."

"I see manners weren't in the curriculum you were studying," she said gruffly, but she did hand over the comp.

Marianne Reddy hadn't raised him to be rude. "I'm sorry, Doctor. I've had a lot dumped on me lately, and I haven't gotten much sleep. I'm pretty tired."

"You're not the only one. You're lucky I came. I half thought that your note on my desk was some kind of decoy. If I hadn't spotted Lep leaving . . . Never mind the alternatives. I'll be honest with you, John, I'm not in the mood for a new mystery. I've had my fill of them lately. I'll feel a lot better if you tell me what this is about."

Why not? She had trusted him. "I've been given a disk. It's supposed to have information about my mother."

"Your real mother or your foster one?"

Real? Real had been raising and caring for him, not pumping him out and dumping him on somebody else's doorstep. "Marianne Reddy."

"I thought you said Bennett wanted to keep you from finding out what happened to her?"

"I didn't get this from Bennett."

"You're trying to make a mystery out of this."

"Sorry." Talking about it made him uncomfortable. Dr. Spae had been his teacher, not his friend. Some things you just didn't talk to teachers about. "Maybe we should just see what's on the disk."

That seemed to satisfy her. With her help, John didn't have to waste any time figuring out the Romer's protocols. When it was time to slot the disk, John hesitated. Was this going to be another hoax? Only one way to find out. He slipped the disk into the Romer. Icons appeared on the screen. The disk wasn't empty, as he had feared it might be. There were Mitsutomo surveillance reports and clippings files that dated back to his disappearance and alleged death. There was a relocation-of-residence order, also Mitsutomo, more recent surveillance files, and even medical records, showing Marianne Reddy to be in good health. Most interesting to John was the termination-of-surveillance order. It would seem that Mitsutomo had lost interest in Marianne Reddy's doings. There was other stuff, too. A lot of material, too much to just skim through. The worth of the data remained to be seen.

There was another thing he needed to know. He set the comp to display the dates on the files. They had last been updated six months after he'd left. In the spring. He didn't like what he was thinking.

"Doctor, I wonder if you could tell me how long I've been gone."

"Don't you know?"

"There aren't a lot of clocks or calendars in the other-world."

"No, I suppose there aren't." Her eyes searched his face; presumably she was trying to find something in his elven features to clue her in on a tack to take. She bit her lip, then tentatively said, "Just about a year."

He closed his eyes, felt his shoulders sag. Bear had told him never to trust an elf. *Time passes differently.* He should have known better. "A year and a day, maybe?"

Dr. Spae smiled, worried and sympathetic. "I'm afraid I don't remember the exact date of your departure."

"The date doesn't really matter," he assured her. Scammed again, and left overdrawn at the promise bank. What *had* he done to Bennett to be jerked around this way?

"A lot has happened while you were away, John."

He could say the same thing. Fraoch's laugh echoed in his ears. Yeah, a lot had happened, but he wasn't going to talk about it.

Dr. Spae, however, had something she wanted to talk about. She told him about a killer "thing" that seemed to be haunting New England. For reasons that weren't entirely clear to John, she believed that the thing was related to Quetzal, but even the hint of a connection chilled him. She didn't have a clear connection that she could point to between this *Wisteria* killer and Quetzal because, she said, her investigations had been frustrated. "They've got me running after a thousand stupid little outbreaks from the otherworld," she told him. "Every time I try to get focused on this whatever-it-is, something else weird comes up, and they send me off to investigate it, pointing out, all too reasonably, that there may only be one opportunity to look into these other things. I can't seem to make them understand how important this threat may be."

"What am *I* supposed to do, Doctor? I don't even know what you're talking about."

She looked at him as if she wasn't sure what she wanted from him. After a bit, she said, "John, I could use your help."

"I'm not interested in helping you hunt down any monsters. We did that once before, and nearly got ourselves killed. I've got a hunt of my own to take care of, one I've put off for far too long."

"You're still not ready to do that. You haven't verified the data yet." She paused a moment before offering him some bait. "At the firm we have good computer access. You could run cross-checks."

He sensed a hook in that offer. "I have my life to rebuild. I know it's not as nice as yours, but it's what I have."

She wasn't ready to give up. "I could get you put on retainer. Money would help your search."

Sure, money would help, but the firm would want to record it all, and that would mean that John would be back in the datanet where he could be spotted by cruising cybercowboys. Covered by an alias or not, he would be making trails that could lead someone to him. He doubted that Dr. Spae's firm had the resources, or the desire, to mask everything that belonged to him. Certainly they couldn't cover him against a megacorp like Mitsutomo. While everything indicated that Mitsutomo's interest in him had faded, he wanted to be sure before he crawled out of the woodwork.

"I appreciate the offer, but I don't think I can accept." So she wouldn't be too put off, he added, "Just yet."

"Think about the future, John. You could make a difference."

"There are a few more things I'd like to get settled before I look to the future."

She sighed, shook her head in resignation. "You've got the Romer now. The communications package has a direct line to my system. Use it if you wise up."

He was impressed that she didn't try any of the levers she might have used on him, knowing what she did. "I'll be in touch, Doctor."

"Try not to get burned," she said as she left.

He would do his best. He'd already been burned enough.

CHAPTER
21

Holger left the city not by leaving the city, but by leaving himself. The solution, once he thought of it, was so simple, so elegant, that he had seized upon it at once. Holger Kun, agent of Department M, put down all those things that marked him. Everything he had so carefully scavenged from the Department's car, everything he had carried with him to that fateful rendezvous with a certain specialist, he dumped in an abandoned warehouse on the West Side. He shed even the clothes he wore, replacing them with items bought in a secondhand store on Wickenden Street. Everything but what they had put inside him. He couldn't leave those things behind—not that he wouldn't have if he could have, but some things were beyond his power.

Evolve or die, Mannheim had said. It wasn't the sort of thing Mannheim usually said. Holger had always thought it must be a quote. It fit now.

His world had changed. Again. Changed so that he wasn't a part of it anymore, not in any way that he understood. All because of a specialist, a person who could touch the magic. He hated magic. The magic leaking into the world was at the heart of the problems. Again. Magic had killed the old world and left chaotic nonsense in its place. As long as magic remained, the world would be nonsense. Magic trapped him in this city and it would kill him if he let it.

Evolve. Or die.

He'd never much cared for the thought of dying.

He would sacrifice himself if needed.

Once, yes. Now, he didn't think so. Who, after all, defined what was *needed?*

He knew for certain something that he needed. He needed to stop hearing the voices. They didn't belong in his head, but they were there nonetheless, a part of him, apart from him. An accommodation was necessary.

He was learning ways to deal with them. Already he knew better than to go near the place where *she* worked. Just like he knew better than to think of *her* name. The voices were quieter when he didn't think in certain ways. By not thinking of *her* name, he didn't have to listen to their lectures, didn't have to reach their conclusions.

But avoidance had its limits.

"Wake up! We cannot avoid responsibility forever," the poster said as he passed.

He kept walking, getting out of its sensor range. He'd listened to the whole message the first time he'd triggered it, intrigued by the deep, compelling voice. He liked the message too. The green, growing world in the visual was beautiful. He agreed that the world needed to be looked after. Humankind had been given the world in trust and had betrayed that trust. Humankind had to face its responsibility, to step up to the challenge of saving the world, to do something, though the poster voice was vague on actual details. A stirring message. The Pend Foundation had chosen their spokesman well. The speaker's voice made Holger want to listen, but in the end he knew that the message wasn't for him. How could he save the world if he couldn't save himself?

Time was passing and that was good. Each day was a new day, a day in which no one found him. Not the hunters from the Department that he knew were out there, not the things from the otherworld that lurked about hunting whatever they could, not the police, not even *her*. They were looking, he knew, looking for the old Holger. The new Holger was camouflaged, invisible, a part of the city, not apart from it. A day in which he called no attention to his presence was the best of days.

Evolution, one day at a time.

His memories were jumbled and it seemed that the more he searched them, sifting for truth, the more he became confused as to what was truth and what was not. When he couldn't stand it anymore, he got out and walked around the East Side. He'd made the Hill his home turf because he liked its liveliness, and because he couldn't imagine the craziness taking hold anywhere near the great university that dominated the East Side.

He favored a neighborhood just north of the old courthouse, near the design school. It was a neighborhood that didn't know if it was on its way up or down, and it had two lives, one for the day and another for the night. That fit him, since he had two parts to his new life. By day he wandered on the streets, anonymous among those with whom he walked. Sometimes he panhandled—to keep the image up; he wasn't yet reduced to relying on it for his simple needs— but mostly he just watched the people and the locale, relishing his nearness to the ordinary, everyday lives around him. By night things were different. A different sort of life emerged after dark, a rougher, less friendly, but no less ordinary life. Sometimes, though, he caught hints of the extraordinary—and when that happened he retreated. At those times, impelled by some atavistic instinct, he climbed up into the bones of the great structure growing on the edge of his chosen ground.

That building was going to be enormous when it was finished. Its girders already touched the sky and its foundation sprawled over several city blocks. It was not a well-liked place by some. On most days defeated preservationists still protested its construction, skirmishing against it with placards and with stickers slapped against the construction fence. That fence surrounded the construction site like the curtain wall of a castle. He liked that. By night, the unfinished building was his haven, his castle keep, the only good place.

He was not supposed to be there, of course, but he didn't let that bother him. The guards that CaranelliCo hired to watch their project were not the best—easy for Holger to avoid. The adjunct security systems were almost as easy to spoof. He'd found the places where neither live nor electronic eyes watched, and there he took his refuge.

From his unwatched sanctuaries hidden among the great structure's bones, he could keep watch. The building would one day dominate the skyline of the East Side, rising as it did against the side of the Hill and stretching taller than the land form from which it thrust. From its heights he could see most of the city. Everything was all laid out before him like a situation map. And he studied that map, looking for the clue that would reveal his way to escape. And he watched the city because, while he watched, he wasn't sleeping.

Eventually, inevitably, he would sleep, and sleeping, dream. He didn't much care for his dreams. They were rambling torments wherein reality changed as he watched, helpless to affect anything. A normal enough situation in dreams, but these changes were different, deeper, more real and profound. He hated being helpless.

He tried not to sleep much.

There was one of the Pend Foundation's talking posters on the hoarding around the construction site. Sometimes, late at night, while he was watching, someone or something would trigger the poster. He would hear its message drifting in the quiet air and filling him with memories of better times, better lives.

But how much was memory and how much was dream?

That was the essential problem that faced him. He had to sort the one from the other, and both of them from the lies. Yet each day the distinctions seemed less clear. He had no benchmarks, no checks, nothing to hold on to. He envied the conviction he heard in Mr. Pend Foundation's voice. He'd had conviction once, in the old days when memories were not traitors.

The poster was talking again. The air was clear and carried

the sound perfectly—directly to him, it seemed. *Mistrust co-incidence,* Mannheim had said. Hadn't he? If he hadn't, he should have. Was this his clue? Holger listened, taking in the message. The message was no different than before, but tonight it touched him. He found himself hoping that when he finally slept, he would dream of a green and pleasant land, but it was a hope without faith. So he sat and he cried, listening to that sincere voice, until finally he slept.

CHAPTER
22

"You wanted to see us, Captain," Manny said.

"Sit down," Captain Hancock told them.

Charley Gordon closed the door behind him as he entered the captain's office. Sitting down was the cue that something unpleasant was going to happen. With the door cutting off the continual clamor of the squad room, the office was as quiet as a funeral parlor. Hancock barely let him get seated.

"I've got a new case for you. Tabloids are calling it the Holyoke Haunting. Falerio and Vuong did the prelim, but they're overloaded, so it's going to you two."

"Like we ain't overloaded, too," Manny complained.

Hancock ignored him. "I want you to get out there this morning and do a face-to-face with the eyewitnesses, especially this Thomas Rudge. He's got a history of hoaxes. I think we can get this one buried if you two dig deep enough."

This wasn't quiet room stuff. What was going on? "Come on, Captain, we've got real work to do. We don't need to be cleaning up Falerio and Vuong's messes. I just got a lead on the Sandowski homicide that—"

"That you can pass on," Hancock finished for him. "The Sandowski homicide is out of your hands."

What? A slow roller churned Charley's stomach acid. "What about the Marino case?"

"Not yours anymore."

Shit! He had only told Hancock about the connection between the killings last week. "It's all of them, isn't it?"

"List of reassigned cases is already in your boxes," Hancock told them.

"Why?" Manny sounded offended.

"You can't do this," Charley said, wishing it were true.

Hancock sat back and glowered. "I don't need any shit from either of you. You've got other cases assigned to you. You'll work on them. You'll work on this Holyoke thing. You'll work on whatever I goddamn tell you to work on. Insubordinate cops get suspended."

Who was going to suspend the monster? The thing that had come off the *Wisteria* was somewhere in New England. Wherever it had come from, it was *here,* and that made it Special Investigations's problem. SIU had made it Charley's problem; a problem Charley hadn't yet solved, and a problem that was still loose and still killing.

"You can't do this," Charley said again. "Captain, we've got a killer out there."

"And there are competent people to chase him down," Hancock retorted. "You can't save the world by yourself, Gordon."

Hell, he wasn't trying to save the *world.* "They haven't got the history on this case."

"They will when you turn over your files. Which you *will* do."

Charley didn't like it, didn't like it at all. Something wasn't kosher. "This isn't your idea. Why are you doing this?"

"Orders from upstairs," Hancock said, stony-faced.

"That's it?" Manny asked with appropriate scorn.

Hancock nodded. "That's all I've got to say. Close your investigations down and log all the data."

"And what's going to happen to that data?" Charley wanted to know. Some of it came from proprietary sources. He'd be burning bridges to those sources if he let the stuff go blindly.

"That's not your concern."

"It's the feds," Manny said, leaving Charley to add, "It's Fletcher horning in, isn't it?"

"The case isn't yours anymore. So stop worrying about it. In fact, you'd both be smart to forget about it altogether."

"I can't forget we've got a killer sitting in our backyard, looking for somebody to suck dry," Charley said.

"You think I like this?" Hancock didn't look happy, but he didn't look like he was going to back down either. "Listen, Gordon. You put a lot of backs up last year with that verrie stunt over Providence. Buzzing the damn city with a flight of corporate Mambas! We don't need you pulling any more crazy tricks like that, got it? A lot of people are still unhappy with you. You understand? You make waves now, you're history. You'll take Salazar down with you. That what you want? It's one frigging case! And not your only one either! Forget your killer. It's good advice, Gordon. Good for your health. Take it."

"This stinks, Captain."

"Easy, Charley," Manny said, dropping a hand on his arm.

Like he needed restraint. Like he was going to strangle Hancock.

"Listen to your partner, Gordon. This isn't worth your job."

Maybe so. It sure wasn't worth anything to stay and argue.

When they got back to their cube, Manny looked around to see if anybody was paying attention and, satisfied that they had as much privacy as one got in the squad room, quietly asked, "You gonna do it?"

Worried about your job, Manny? "Yeah. This is a no-win. They'll strip it out of our machines, if we don't hand it to them."

Manny nodded, satisfied. "Hancock's right, you know. We oughta forget this one."

"Yeah." Hancock could suck rocks. No way Charley was going to forget.

So he didn't forget. What could he *do?* There wasn't a hell of a lot he *could* do. The investigations weren't really going anywhere. Despite the wealth of data Pamela Martinez had dumped on him, he had been unable to discern a pattern to the killings, unable to get a handle on what drove the killer. The victims were too dissimilar, the locations too different. The only constants were the victims' conditions and the fact that all the killings happened at night, but that bit wasn't news in an SIU investigation. The best he'd been able to do was plot a track from San Francisco, where the thing had gotten off the *Wisteria,* to New England, where it seemed to have decided that it liked the climate.

Spinning wheels didn't help anybody, and spinning wheels was all he had done. Maybe whoever was getting his files would have better luck. He doubted it. He started stripping out the stuff he'd gotten from Martinez and couldn't verify from another source. Then he went after Caspar's contributions.

Thinking about Caspar, Charley figured he ought to let Caspar know before his cybernetic ear dropped something new in the *Wisteria* killer's Modus file. It was late in the week and the address Charley had for the ear might not be any good anymore, but Charley felt like he ought to try. He popped an e-mail explaining that he had just been taken out of the loop on Modus 273 and there wasn't any point in sending any more connections.

Caspar might have been waiting on-line for him, given the speed at which a response landed in his box.

Suspect connection between current termination and other terminated investigations, was the meat of Caspar's message, but the bones were in the appended list of cases. Some of them Charley recognized, some were unknowns. Most of them weren't even from the NEC. Out of Charley's jurisdiction, but clearly not out of Caspar's sphere of interest.

Charley was interested, but who had the time? He had half a dozen investigations to close down, write up, and gift-wrap for—whom? He'd guessed Fletcher and his feds, but Hancock hadn't confirmed or denied. No real reason to hide federal involvement. The *Wisteria* killer had left bodies in a couple of dozen states. Clear interstate crime. So why wasn't Hancock talking? Who was really calling the shots?

There were times when Charley wished he were back on the streets.

CHAPTER
23

John didn't know if Spillway Sue had changed her slump, but the door at the bottom of the alley stairs was locked. Someone was living there. Recalling how much difficulty he'd had tracking her down before, he decided to wait and see who came home.

The alley was wide enough for vehicles, but somebody had once decided to deny passage and had built a cinder-block wall across it. Somebody else hadn't liked the idea and had blown a hole in the obstruction. He could still see the scorch marks on the remains of the barrier and the fragmentation scars on the walls of the nearby buildings. There were enough cinder blocks left against Sue's building to offer a seat, so John took it. The spot got him off the damp ground and out of the way while staying close enough to her door to watch and wait, but not so close she'd take his presence as an immediate threat when she returned.

He let his legs dangle and idly kicked his feet against the concrete, scuffing his fine green elven boots. They were good boots, without a doubt the best-fitting pair he'd ever had, deserving of better care, but they were elven and he had little concern for such things at the moment.

While he waited, he watched the thick clouds plow across the night sky. They promised more of the rain that had slicked the afternoon streets and brought the first fall leaves, tamping them into sodden, brown masses. Not that there were a lot of trees, in this neighborhood. Pure urban around

here. Through a gap in the buildings he could see the south-
ern end of the Hill. There were trees there, many of them already well on their way to winter barrenness thanks to the
rain. Unlike the urban barrenness, nature's would give way
to renewed life in the spring. Mankind's stripping of the
green just went on and on.

Gloomy thoughts for a gloomy night.

He didn't have to be here. He could be back at the slump
baby-sitting his automated effort to verify the information on
the disk. But what would be the point of that? He'd taken the
best course, having rigged a cuckoo and set loose half a dozen
agents to do data searches. The searches would take time—
had already taken hours; there wasn't much he could do to
speed it up, and the little bit of boost that he might give could
be dangerous. The cuckoo was his cutout to keep him safe
from tagalongs that could all too easily run him down if he
was doing his hunting live. The minimal contact he'd have
with the agents when he dropped in to pick up whatever they
had sieved carried a risk of picking up a tagalong, but only a
minimal risk. Minimal risk was the key to safe hacking.

So he was here, hoping to find Sue. Not for the first time,
he wondered if he was doing the right thing, and—not for the
first time—he figured out the answer. The processing loop
got shorter every time he went through it. Sue had been the
best thing to come into his life since he'd fled Worcester.
How could he *not* do this? He had to see her and let her
know he was back. She'd understand. Their relationship had
barely gotten off the ground, but it had a heart to it, a soul.
She *would* understand.

The sound of voices out on the street told him that his wait
was over. One of the voices belonged to Sue. Four people
appeared at the mouth of the alley. She was with a trio of
guys. Male guys. John listened as they exchanged banter.
The talk was friendly, easygoing street stuff—end of the day,
see-you-tomorrow stuff—and John worried that one of those
three wasn't going to keep walking.

Sue was wearing a floppy hat, the sort of thing she'd worn

before she met him. He'd liked the look then, he liked it now. The hat made her look like an old-time adventurer, in a funked, retro way. Her clothes were as eclectic a mix as ever, maybe more so given the extra layers she wore against the chill. But her look was only an outward expression of her self. It was the person inside the clothes John wanted. She didn't have Fraoch's ethereal beauty and she never would, but she had a liveliness, a warmth, that radiated from her. He was getting hot just seeing her stand there.

His fear that she might have found someone to replace him looked unwarranted. The guys shoved off and she entered the alley alone. He had thought about using the same routine he'd used with Dr. Spae, to give Sue a chance to know it was him before showing his elven face, but he got too involved watching her to think about spells. Staying inconspicuous wasn't a problem; she didn't notice him until she was halfway to her door.

Upon seeing him sitting on the wall, she didn't back up, or call her friends, or even reach for a weapon. She stayed cool, collected, squinting a little because the light didn't give her a good view of him. Sue set herself, hands sweeping back her long outer vest to rest on her hips, and looked up at him, deceptively casual. John wasn't deceived. She'd be ready for fight or flight, whatever made the most sense. Streetwise, Spillway Sue was.

He noticed a bit of dead-black ballistic plastic peeping out from just behind her wrist. The black shape was grooved like a pistol butt's. When had she started carrying so openly?

What else was different?

She took the initiative, proving that not everything had changed.

"You're sitting on my turf, friend," she said, neither hostile nor friendly. "Ya got business or is this a social call?"

"It's nice to see you again, Sue."

She didn't respond at once and when she said, "Tall Jack," she didn't sound like she believed that she had recognized his voice correctly.

"Haven't answered to that name in a while, but yeah, it's me."

He dropped off the wall and—thankfully—landed grace-fully. As he approached her, he dragged off the watch cap that the bogies had found for him; he'd been using it to cover his ears. Time to stop hiding.

Her eyes narrowed and her face went hard when she got a good look at him. The sudden shift to hostility hit him hard. What she said hit harder.

"Not a nice trick, Bennett. Watcha want with me?"

Her words had the element of surprise, like getting a solid rabbit punch to the gut from a kindergartner. "I'm not Ben-nett," was all John could think to say.

"Ya can drop the voice, okay? I'm wise ta ya."

Her misidentification angered him. Holding his hand be-fore him at chest height, he summoned flame to it. She flinched as the flickering flames appeared. He knew she didn't like magical things, but he wanted her to see.

"Take a good look. I'm not him. Never have been. Never will be."

She obliged him, searching his face. She was quiet for a long time, her brow dipping slowly into a furrow of confu-sion. Her mouth opened slightly. Her head gave the tiniest of shakes. "If ya can change your voice, ya can change your face."

"If I were him, why would I bother not doing it right? Come on, you know I'm me. This is my real face. You asked me once why I didn't look like Bennett; well, now you can see that I do. At least when there's no magic disguising me."

"Magic's for school brats ta believe in."

"You know better than that. You've seen it. You've even been to the otherworld."

"Been a lot of places, ain't all of them real."

"I'm real, Sue. This face is. Touch it and see for yourself."

For a second, she looked like she might take him up on the offer. Then her suspicion took hold again. "Suppose it is you. What am I supposed ta do?"

"Say hello? Invite me inside?"

"Hello."

That was one. "And?"

"I'll pass."

"Why?"

She threw up her hands and stomped toward the wall. She spun before she reached it. "Whaddaya mean, why? Ya shimmied out on me, Tall Jack!"

"I didn't mean to."

Her face was pinched in a scowl. "Looked like ya walked out under your own power ta me."

"I came back as soon as I could."

She laughed. A bitter, mocking laugh. "As soon as ya could? Tell me another one."

Her attitude cut him, but there was a familiarity to her obstinate disbelief. A real, close-to-home familiarity. Hadn't Bennett claimed to be unable to visit John during his youth? John hadn't believed him. And now here was John telling the truth and not being believed.

Maybe Bennett hadn't been lying either.

John didn't like being on the other side of such distrust. It hadn't been his intention to be away so long. He didn't really deserve her scorn. He certainly didn't want it. He wanted things to go back to the way they were.

"It's true," he told her. "Where I was, time was, well, different."

"Drop the puppy-dog look. And don't give me any magic shit. I ain't buying."

"If you won't let me tell you the truth, how can I explain things to you?"

"Truth? I ain't no corp prole who don't know how ta wipe her ass unless the suits give her vid instructions. I got a lot more ta me than a cunt and a pair of boobs. Ya want truth? I'll give ya some! Save your stories for some starry-eyed virgin outta the rezcoms. I know why ya came back. Ya came back 'cause ya got a little bored. Decided it was time for another romp with Stupid Sue. She won't mind, ya said ta yourself. I'll just pop in, throw a little razzle, grab a couple of quickies, and be off again. No fuss, no muss. Back ta the glam with a 'See ya, Sue. I'll be back.' Ya like empty promises all glossed up with a bunch of slick words and soulful looks? Well you're the only one, dode. I think it'd be a good idea for ya ta take your fancy face and poof before I cram your lying bullshit down your throat. Ya *can* just go poof, can't ya, being an elf and all? Come on, let me see ya do it."

"Sue—"

"Come on, magic man, go poof."

What could John say? Sue thought he was running a scam on her. What proof could he offer her that he wasn't doing what she thought? Anything he said was just words. From her point of view, she was justified. How could she know of the strangeness of time in Faery? How could she understand it when John, who had been there, didn't understand it?

"It's not that way, Sue."

"Poof!"

With a gust of wind that snatched away Sue's hat, the promised rain arrived in sheets. Sue didn't go after the hat. Neither did John. They stared at each other, getting wet.

Finally she said, "No magic?"

"I can't do that kind of magic."

"I ain't as stupid as you think I am." She turned her back on him and went down the stairs to her door. Stiff-shouldered, she worked her key in the lock. She tugged the door open and shot him a look. "Ya follow me and I'll shoot ya dead and sell your body parts. Probably get a good price for your eyes, too."

She went through and closed the door. He heard the bolt slide home. More bolts too, security locks.

John stood in the rain, the world all sodden and gray around him. He stood there for a long time, but Sue didn't come back out. She wasn't going to, and no amount of hoping was going to change that. On his way out of the alley, he picked up her hat. It was already soaked and would be worthless trash by morning if it sat out in the rain. Turning it over and over in his hands, he walked down the street, his elven boots kicking up spatters of murky water. His feet were dry inside the boots, protected by some elven magic. His face wasn't dry, though. There were no elven magics for that.

CHAPTER
24

Holger recognized the voice coming from the bank of monitors in the shop window. The sound drew him like a magnet, recalling to him the thoughts that had led to his first tolerable night since the incident at the old mall. The words weren't important, starting as they did in midsentence and vanishing the same way. It was the voice.

He crossed the street and stood before the shop. Its window was filled with video monitors, stacked side by side and atop one another so that dozens of screens poured their light out onto the sidewalk and into Holger's eyes. The screens in the center stayed with a single channel while those along the edges shifted channels, finding new images to exhibit, a ripple of change running among them, switching each to a new presentation as it passed. A selector—preprogrammed or random, he couldn't tell which—jumped from screen to screen until it chose one to replace the central images. Sound from the chosen slice of the media bombardment was shunted to speakers, offering it to the sidewalk and to Holger's ears. The fickle, mutating outer screens were not allowed the dignity of sound. While Holger sought the source of the voice that had arrested his attention, each of those vid images competed for his regard, sought to steal his eyes. Eyes were so much more capable of taking in the chaos of the world, and so much less confused by it than ears.

Holger's eyes were not confused. Among the wall of images he found a face that evoked the strangest combination of memories: memories of dark places dared, blurred memories of standing side by side against danger—memories that Holger could not possibly conceive of being attached to that face, for they were things of his childhood, things of dreams and wonder and imagination. Though he had not yet heard the voice again, he felt certain that it belonged to that face.

He knew that face. The hair was cut shorter, the beard more fashionably trimmed, the clothes right out of *Gent*[EM], but the face was familiar. He knew those eyes. They were the sort of eyes one never forgot.

He wanted to hear the voice again, to know the message that this man carried for him. He waited, patient, as the world flowed past around him. Some cursed him, some jostled him, some ignored him. Their reactions were unimportant. He wanted to hear the man speak. He remembered this man as one who could be trusted.

A true memory or a false one? Or merely an embodied hope?

Holger studied the face. He *did* know this man. This was a man with many names, as Holger had been. In memory, this was a confused man, a man out of his proper place, as Holger was. On the vid, the man looked different. He had changed, had clearly become a man who had a place, a man with answers. All Holger had were questions.

Sound snatch by sound snatch, Holger learned that the man was appearing on an infoshow for the Pend Foundation, publicizing the organization's commitment to revitalizing the world in all its natural and proper order. Very Green. Very idealistic. Holger sensed an intense and honest commitment to the avowed goals, an integrity that he found himself craving with the intensity of a soldier's after-battle thirst. Holger needed to see this man, in person, to talk to him, to learn from him the secret of the peace he had achieved; but how to contact him?

Infoshows normally fed a steady stream of advertising and contact information through a strip at the bottom of the screen; but the shop had co-opted the feed channel, dumping its own ads atop the originator's messages. Holger didn't want to buy what the shop was selling, he wanted the information it had taken away. He had to wait through fifteen cycles before the sound snatches coincided with a segment of the infoshow in which contact information was given. Holger didn't mind the wait. In a lot of ways, his waiting was over.

If.

If the man was what Holger believed him to be, and not just a faulty memory.

CHAPTER
25

The physical kill and the gushing rush of power from the feeding that followed echoed and enhanced the thrill of the corporate kill, making the Nashua acquisition all the more satisfying. Tonight's prey was tasty, surprising in its richness. For the moment, Anton Van Dieman was sated. His alliance with the harbinger had opened very satisfying, very rewarding avenues.

Besides the raw taste of power, his ally brought the great gifts of knowledge and understanding. The harbinger had become his tutor in comprehending and manipulating all things arcane. Van Dieman was an eager and attentive student, far more than he was for any human teacher. He had already outstripped the most advanced among the followers, to become their leader in all but name. Some were calling him the new Quetzal, though they did not think he knew. That pleased him.

So much was open to him that he had a little trouble choosing from among his opportunities. So much to gain, so many scores to settle, so much to achieve. The world lay before him, opened to him by the secrets that the harbinger whispered to him in the night. Such insights had already brought him advantages in the business world, and he had increased his power and improved his position through applying his new understandings almost as much as he had through direct application of his improved arcane skills. Network Securities Corporation, a major player—soon to be *the* major player—within the Metadynamics corporate family, was his now. And once he led the corporate family, it would not be long before Metadynamics was the undisputed leader of the commercial community and, by the most obvious of extensions, of the world.

Unfortunately his ally and teacher had an active, insatiable hunger that was a potential source of danger. He understood the hunger well. Who could deny the delectability of the feast? But the appetite was dangerous nonetheless. Remembering how Quetzal selected his sustenance, Van Dieman had guided the harbinger's hunts, steering it toward the detritus of society and away from those who would be missed. The time of revelation was not yet upon them.

Discovery of their hunts would be inconvenient at best, and the effort necessary to deal with meddlers would most certainly interfere with their work. The work to open the Way would not bear interruption. He would not permit himself to be balked. His mundane power, great though it was growing, would be increased immeasurably once the Way was opened. He had no intention of losing his opportunity to control such authority.

Unfortunately, tonight's prey had been more than the derelict he appeared to be. He had fought the implacable coils of the harbinger. The futile struggle should have added piquancy to what the harbinger had shared with Van Dieman; it should not have left a lingering aftertaste of taint. There had been something untoward about this one. Siphoning off a living being's energy was a curiously impersonal thing. Nothing of the person came through. There had been nothing to tell Van Dieman what had made this man different from their other victims, but he felt sure that there was a difference. When the harbinger finished with it, Van Dieman examined the husk.

There was a tiny lump behind the man's right ear: something inorganic lay beneath the skin. Van Dieman focused a tiny fraction of the fresh energy still coursing through him and slit the skin with surgical precision. The object he removed, a subcutaneous processor and communications unit, lay glistening with blood on his palm. Tiny fibers, now broken, trailed from it. His own Network Securities Corporation trafficked in the chips that empowered such devices.

So many possibilities.

He concentrated on the unit, seeking its source through psychometry. As with so many modern devices, the images of origin were diverse, diffuse, and mostly worthless. Yet he sensed dedication, both to the man who now lay a lifeless, withered corpse at his feet and to something greater, something to which the man himself had been dedicated: the Federal Security Agency.

Van Dieman had not been informed of any FSA operations in this area. Was the agency watching him, or had he and his companion coincidentally stumbled onto some unrelated operation? He had learned to suspect coincidences. With so much power focused through the harbinger, it was too much to expect that this agent they found in their path was there by accident—which meant that the agency had deliberately put this man near him.

Not unwise from their point of view, he supposed—he would have done the same in their place—but foolish to get caught at it. What was behind this? Were they aware of his program to suppress all the records of the harbinger's activities? Had his cover-up aroused suspicion in some quarter? He knew that there was no official awareness of his intimate connection with the harbinger—he'd made sure of that. It had been so easy, as their principal arcane adviser, to tell them what was important and what was not—so easy to feed them lies and be believed. Now he saw that the ease might have been illusory and that his efforts might not have been as successful as he had believed. Clearly they did not trust him completely. This agent's presence suggested that uncontrolled, and therefore dangerous, elements might lurk within the forces he had gathered. How much did they know? How much did they guess? For the moment he could only wonder.

Steeling his fingers with arcane strength, he crushed the device to powder. Would that he could dispose of the agent's body as easily. This husk could not simply be abandoned. It must be disposed of in such a way as to leave the agent's masters wondering about his fate.

The harbinger remained quiet, unconcerned by Van Dieman's worries. Doubtless his companion did not understand the danger. Oddly, that reassured him, for it proved yet again that the harbinger, for all its power, still needed him. The modern world was not the one that the harbinger had known of old, and that was still Van Dieman's greatest power over his companion. By that knowledge he constrained it, and with those constraints he ruled it, but the situation was changing. With each new prey that they took, Van Dieman's power grew stronger, and the secret chains of mastery that he was forging grew stronger as well.

As if aware that his thoughts touched upon it, his companion stirred. He reached out to the shadowed coils to offer reassurance of his presence and devotion, and sensed that it was not as calm as he thought. A strange restlessness resonated through the harbinger.

"What is it?"

Ah, hear them. They sing.

He heard nothing. Through their link, he felt that the harbinger's attention was on the sky. He looked up, seeing nothing but a few stars burning through the sprawl glow. He knew there were more stars, many more, and with his arcane sight he could see them in all their glory.

They are calling.

"The stars?"

The others. I must go.

Go? Van Dieman was not ready to surrender his access to the ways of power. "Our work is not yet done."

Not yet done, the harbinger agreed. *The others want to join us.*

Others? How much more powerful would he be if he controlled others of its kind! "There are more harbingers waiting to come here?"

More. They cry in the darkness, seeking the way.

"And we can help them find it?"

Open the way. Not here.

An image of the *telesmon* appeared in his mind. The Key. "Where?"

South, it told him. *To the place where time shivers, to the window where the shell of life is weakest.*

"Of course." He would take it wherever it wanted to go. But first, "We must dispose of this husk."

Unimportant.

"This one is not like the others. This one may bring the forces of the opposition if his death is known."

Yes. Very well. Leave it to the fire.

There was fire, springing to life all around them, filling the alley with heat and lurid light. Enwrapped in power, he felt no discomfort. Fire would serve. Fire was a cleansing agent, capable of obliterating things beyond the abilities of modern science to reconstruct. There were still some agents one could rely upon.

Pamela Martinez could rely upon numerous agents, but she was coming to doubt that Hagen was one of them. Hendrik Hagen had been her right-hand man in the restructuring of the Charybdis Project, and eager to help. But he fought—and continued to fight—her establishment of Thaumatechnics, the successor to the project that would utilize what they had learned. He complained that the new corporation would do more to encourage the arcane than to suppress it. Pamela preferred to think that Thaumatechnics and its programs were a viable effort to control the magic and prepare for its inevitable spread. Early market positioning was absolutely vital to eventual dominance.

Hagen's foot-dragging was only one of the obstacles Pamela saw hindering her efforts to define Mitsutomo's future role. Entrepreneurs and small companies were already developing preternatural resources. For the moment, the new companies dealt in fringe stuff and special interest pandering, but she knew better than most that those companies were just the beginning. Most of the Keiretsu's major partners had once been hungry young start-ups, each riding the crest of a single specialized product, technology, or service. She understood what catching the wave meant. She did not intend to get left behind.

At least as great a threat was the possibility that a rival with resources comparable to Mitsutomo's might have the same insights that she had so laboriously gathered through the Charybdis Project. Mounting evidence suggested that such a fear might be justified. Metadynamics, for example, had recently made some real estate acquisitions of questionable value—questionable, if one were not aware that their newly acquired parcels appeared to be loci of preternatural activity. And if one were aware, one found additional questions to ask. How much did Metadynamics know about the use of magic? What were their sources? What plans did they have to take advantage of the changing world?

Some of MetaD's recent actions had disturbed Hagen enough that he had come to her, even though, by his own admission, he had no idea of their rival's goal.

"What makes you sure that Metadynamics is involved?" she asked him.

"At the moment, the evidence is admittedly circumstantial, but I expect confirmation within forty-eight hours. However, considering how formidable Metadynamics has proven in less, ah, esoteric arenas, we cannot afford to take any chances."

She didn't like to take chances, and he knew it. "We cannot afford to create unnecessary enmity, either."

"Agreed, but a prompt response may be necessary. A recent report suggests that Metadynamics may be about to step up their programs. Several of our street contacts confirm that one of their regular freelance agents—Benton by name—is once again in the Providence area. You may recall that he was involved with last year's attempt by Metadynamics to acquire a certain property in that district."

"The Pickman holding."

"Exactly."

She remembered the case because it had been her first hint that someone at Metadynamics was aware of the changes. The property was an old factory, completely outdated, belonging to a nearly defunct, family-held publishing firm. She had seen no obvious value to a conglomerate of MetaD's size and interests—unless she assumed that they had observed what Mitsutomo's own agents had observed, and that the property was indeed a locus of otherworldly activity. MetaD's attempt to buy the property outright had failed. Pickman Publishing had rejected MetaD's generous offer out of hand, and that had seemed to end the megacorp's interest in the property.

But now it seemed that Metadynamics had not been discouraged. Hagen had uncovered a systematic buyout of nearby real estate. Piece by piece, the properties surrounding the Pickman Building were being purchased by holding companies. Hagen had electronic records showing several of those holding companies to be controlled by members of the Metadynamics family, and he said that he would soon be able to prove that all of them were tied to MetaD.

"So now they're trying to acquire all the property surrounding it?" None of Hagen's documents suggested a reason. "To what end?"

"Observation? Containment, perhaps?" Hagen shrugged uncomfortably. "We have insufficient data."

"Then we must obtain some data."

"Efforts are being made, but I do not think we will see timely results."

How could she know what was timely if she didn't know what was going on? "Perhaps there is another way to forestall whatever it is our friends at MetaD are planning. I'll have Duncan arrange an offer on the Pickman property."

"Any offer will be refused," Hagen said confidently.

Why was he so sure? "Is there something you're not telling me, Mr. Hagen?"

"I am not prepared to discuss the matter further at this time, but be assured that the property will not be sold."

More of his dwarven secrets? She disliked being prodded to action while information—possibly vital—was withheld. So far Hagen had always steered her in a direction that offered some significant gain or avoided some pitfall, yet something about the dwarf's attitude hinted that this time the interests of Mitsutomo and Hagen's secret masters might not be coincident. It would be best to have Duncan arrange some independent verification of the situation. In the meantime . . .

"We'll make the offer nonetheless." Hagen might be wrong, and if that was the case, she would enjoy telling him so. "However, just in case you are right, we will buy whatever adjacent properties MetaD has not already acquired."

"A reasonable course of action."

She hoped so. She was involving Mitsutomo primarily to satisfy Hagen's interests, though any chance to hinder a rival like MetaD was not to be snubbed. Such holding action was unlikely to harm the Keiretsu, but she didn't see the profit in it. Yet. Once she learned what MetaD was after, she would make sure there was profit for the Keiretsu, and for herself.

Hagen rose from his seat. "If that is all?"

"Have we begun to work at cross-purposes, Mr. Hagen?"

Her question clearly caught him off guard. He schooled his expression, studying her stonily for several moments before replying. "I remain as committed as ever, Ms. Martinez."

Committed to what goals? To hers and Mitsutomo's, or to those of his fellow dwarven conspirators? She had never thought to doubt his dedication, just his allegiance.

"I recently received a message from Detective Gordon," she said, calling a copy and the attendant files to the wallscreen. "It seems that he has been ordered to close his investigation of the *Wisteria* killer. I would like an explanation of your role in this."

Hagen read Gordon's note. He didn't bother to open the accompanying files. "I had no role in this."

"You wanted the investigation stopped."

"I discouraged *your* interest in the matter, yes, but I have not interfered with the police investigation. The matter more properly belongs in their sphere. Let *them* deal with this aberration inflicted upon us by the otherworld."

"This particular aberration is being ignored." Which had not turned out to be the problem she had feared it might be. The killer's destination had not proven to be Brookfield or the facility where Quetzal had been held, and none of the recent incidents had touched upon Mitsutomo or any of the Keiretsu's dependents. The killer was one problem that had not come knocking on her door. Since she had apparently been wrong about the creature's connection with Quetzal, perhaps her suspicion of Hagen's motives was wrong as well. "So you had nothing to do with burying the investigation?"

"Nothing. Gordon cites federal interference, which implies FSA and Dark Glass. That *is* an issue of concern. I will look into the matter."

Her source, a congressman on the FSA oversight committee, had told her that the investigation was being dead-ended, labeled a hoax, by Dark Glass. She declined to tell Hagen that bit of information, preferring to see if his "look into the matter" would uncover it. She'd give him a chance. What he reported would tell her something about where he stood.

CHAPTER
26

The outside of the office building gave no sign that Holger's destination lay inside. The lack of an identifying logo gave him a moment of doubt, but only a moment. The street number on the wall confirmed that he had found the right building. What had he been expecting?

What *was* he expecting?

He was no more sure of that than of why he had come.

But come he had. He was here. He gave a tug on the outer door and it swung open on well-oiled hinges. The supposedly silent screech of the security system drilled at his head as he entered. He wasted no time in the entry, ripping hard on the inner door to open a way into the lobby. There were people there, staring at his precipitous entrance, but he didn't care. The closing of the inner door cut off the annoying whine. Unknotting his facial muscles, he blinked a few times and looked around. The people were gone, leaving him alone in the lobby.

The lobby area was T-shaped. He stood near the entry, at one end of the cap. An anonymous door lay ahead at the opposite end of the cap. To his left, down the upright of the T, two pairs of elevators. To his right, a glassed wall revealed a reception area with an untenanted desk. The letters on the door proclaimed it the law firm of Cohen Masters and Norton.

Not who he was looking for.

The wall of reconstituted marble framing the elevator entrances held the usual controls and a set of bronze plaques that had the names of the building's occupants, organized alphabetically by floor. All the names were presented in subdued serif letters, one plaque to each of the organizations. There were eleven names, thirteen if he separately counted Cohen Masters and Norton. The plaques were of varying sizes: small where several organizations shared a floor, larger where one had a whole level to itself. The largest, proclaiming possession of the top three floors, was also the newest. The screws holding that plaque were still shiny brass, not chemically aged as was the nameplate itself. No artificial dignity for them. The letters on the plaque were no larger than those on any of the others; they seemed almost lost in the expanse of the bronze. Holger nodded as he read the name. Pend Foundation.

He punched the call button and the doors immediately opened on a waiting car. He was not asked which floor he wanted, so he looked to the controls. The two uppermost touchpoints were covered by a panel, inaccessible. The Pend Foundation offered only one point of entry. He touched the button and stood staring blankly at the elevator opposite until the doors closed, then at the doors of his car. The ride was smooth, almost unnoticeable. No stops interrupted his transit; he was pleased.

The doors opened on a reception area furnished in greens and golds and browns. The space was crowded with verdant growing things and caressed by soft, indirect lighting. He might have stepped into forest glade, or an advertisement for the foundation's Re-Green℠ program, or—*No!* He didn't want to think about that possibility, even if he did associate it with the man. The man hadn't liked being *there*. He wouldn't have duplicated *that place* here. To put thoughts of that place out of his mind, Holger focused on the ordinary, twenty-first-century things around him: the Cavendell™ wood-trimmed dish chairs, the stone-and-stump table with its vid readers and flimsy zines, the Glazz™ receptionist desk with its Sonymac Escritoire™ system.

A secretary sat behind the desk, a university-issue vid reader propped before her. She was dressed in the old-fashioned style of frilly, high-necked blouse and long skirt in vogue among female radical Greens of her age group. She even wore glasses. He flashed on ID shots of similarly dressed women. Hardened, harsh women committed to a dangerous program of reform by terrorist threat. He hadn't seen her face before but her lack of makeup, long hair, and clothing was their look. Idealistic fashionable imitation or ideological livery? The answer to that question would tell him much about the foundation's practices, hiring and otherwise.

The furtive glances she threw his way while he stood and stared at the reception area were those of a nervous young girl ill-prepared to deal with someone of his appearance. Her discomfort at his approach was apparent. He didn't care. He wasn't here to see her. He stood at the desk until he tired of her pretense that she was so engrossed in her reader that she hadn't noticed that he was there.

"I want to see him."

She looked up then, but still didn't meet his eyes. Afraid to, he supposed. Dangerous trash from the streets. He wanted to smile. He might be just that sort of thing now. She seemed to think so, but her voice was polite when she spoke. He gave her points for that.

"Whom do you mean, sir?" she asked.

Which name? He wasn't sure. Without making a decision, he answered, "Bear."

"We have no Mr. Bear on staff, sir."

Something flashed on her console; Holger saw its reflection on the lenses of her glasses. The secretary excused herself and picked up a handset. What she was being told wasn't for him to hear, but he heard it anyway. The secretary was to be calm, reassuring, and to take him to office C. Did she understand?

"Yes, sir," she said into the handset.

Holger hadn't recognized the voice of the man who had

spoken, but he went along. She led him to a door bearing the letter C. The room's lights came on as the door opened. She gestured for him to enter, and stepped clear so that he wouldn't have to pass too near her. The office was dominated by another Glazz desk, this one an executive model smoked to near opacity. Beyond the desk was another door, closed and unmarked. Wooden paneling made the room dark, the opaqued windows darker still.

"Please be seated," she said. There were only two chairs in the room, one on either side of the desk. No mistaking where he was supposed to sit. "Someone will be along to see you in a moment."

She closed the door. He heard a lock click, sealing him in the room. Curiously, though, he felt better almost as soon as the door closed. His mind felt clearer, less fuzzed than it had for—how long?—too long. He sat in the chair, listening to the buzz of ultrasonics in the walls, and waited.

His seat was positioned in the exact center of the room. A calculated position, most likely. The placement focused him on the desk and the door behind it. A psychological power thing, or something more sinister?

He didn't get time to puzzle it out. The door beyond the desk opened, revealing a stocky, bearded man. The man walked into the room and took the seat at the desk. To all appearances, this was the man Holger had seen on the video screen. But this was no man. There was no heat to this man. He might have been made of dreams, all air and thoughts and memories and desires.

"You're not real," Holger said to him.

The false man's eyes slid a fraction to one side like a news anchor looking off screen when he didn't believe what his TelePrompTer told him. When his gaze returned to Holger, he said, "You are speaking to a telepresence projection."

"I don't want to speak to a telepresence projection. I want to see the real man. Why are you doing this?"

"A precaution. I'm sure you can understand. Just whom are you looking for?"

"You."

"You don't sound very sure."

He wasn't. Had he made a mistake coming here? "The man I knew wouldn't hide behind a dummy."

"Are you sure of that, Mr. Kun?"

They knew who he was. *Had* he made a mistake? The projection looked like the man he sought, but projections could be synthesized. What could be digitized could be manipulated. Who really controlled the image? "The man I knew wasn't afraid to look another man in the eye."

"The man you knew didn't understand the century in which he found himself."

The image vanished. The door opened again and the man entered the office again. To all outward appearances he was identical to the first—but this one burned with the fire of life. This was the real man.

Another man followed, shorter, stockier, and more heavily bearded. Holger started to reach for the weapon he wasn't carrying. He aborted the futile motion. Old reflexes, and, on a closer look, triggered inappropriately. He had never seen this man before.

"Very jumpy," the short man said. "Still working for Department M, Mr. Kun?"

Maybe his reaction *hadn't* been inappropriate.

"I believe he thought you were someone else, Wilson. Someone I myself would have considered shooting on sight." Bear turned his attention to Holger. "What brings you here, Mr. Kun?"

Holger was looking at the answer. "You."

Bear folded his arms, wrinkling the fine fabric of his business suit. "You were more polite the last time you sought me out."

"Things are different now." Very different. He had come here hoping that they could be more different still.

"You certainly look different," Bear observed. "And the circumstances are different. We don't have any commandos creeping about with mayhem on their minds."

Holger didn't like remembering the place, the strange elf place that was as much museum as palace, but he remembered the commandos who had assaulted the place and tried to kill them. He remembered fighting the men in black. Bear had fought them too. They had won, then the elf had come back and nearly stolen their victory. Holger didn't like remembering that. Bear had saved them. With the sword. The elf wouldn't face Bear when he had the sword in his hands. Holger smiled at the memory.

"Who says he doesn't have mayhem in mind?" Wilson asked. He waved a hand at Holger. "Looks to me like good camouflage for an urban hunt."

"Camouflage for the hunted," Holger said. He wanted Bear to understand.

"Hunted?" Wilson didn't sound as if he believed. "By whom?"

It was hard to say. "The Department."

"You want us to believe that you've left them? Hard to believe that they'd let you go, considering how much they obviously have invested in you." Wilson scratched at his beard. "Artos, he's more likely a stalking horse—if not the hunter himself. They're still looking for you."

Holger looked to Bear. "They don't believe in you. Only Spae believed, and she isn't with them anymore either. They want her, too, more than they do you. They don't believe that you are who you are, but I believe. I saw you with the sword. I remember."

"He's babbling," Wilson said.

"They did things to me. I don't know what. I didn't ask for it. I didn't. They broke the contract. They sent me after Spae. They told me she was a traitor, but they are the real traitors. They broke the contract." He knew that he said more, told them about the attempt against Spae, about his flight, about the voices. He knew he was prejudicing them, because to them, he must sound like a madman.

"I think that sedation might be in order," Wilson whispered to Bear.

"No needles!"

Holger kicked the chair away as he regained his feet.

Wilson crouched, protective of Bear. Bear himself didn't flinch. He just watched Holger, eyes calm, assured. Holger saw the strength there, strength that he needed, assurance that he needed.

"No one here is going to hurt you, Mr. Kun," Bear said.

Holger took the promise as truth.

"Put down your weapon," Bear said.

Weapon? Holger *was* holding something. He looked down. He didn't remember ripping the arm from the chair. He dropped it.

"You know, Mr. Kun, I think I have some idea of what you are going through." Holger saw understanding in Bear's eyes, sympathy without pity. "We warriors have to look out for each other."

"I showed you how to fire an H&K Viper," Holger said.

"Short bursts," Bear said with a smile. "I kept forgetting. Still, what you taught me saved my life. I have not yet had the honor of returning that gift."

"The sword," Holger said to remind him. "I saw you use it. I remember."

"I wasn't fighting for you."

Holger remembered. "You fight for us all."

"Don't confuse the legend with the man. There was no King Arthur of Camelot, no Round Table of noble knights in shining armor. It's all legends and stories and lies."

Not lies, not when there was truth at the heart. "Not all. You're real."

"Real, yes, but no fairy-tale hero."

"Heroes are for kids." And desperate men.

"If I believed that you believed that . . ." Bear shook his head. "I am a man, Mr. Kun, not a hero. A man, just like you. Don't shake your head at me. You may not believe it now, but you will."

"You're better than me."

"We're both men. Men are fallible, and they make mistakes, but real men own up to and fix their mistakes. Some die trying. What mistakes are you trying to fix, Mr. Kun?"

"I—" He didn't have a clear answer. "You—"

"I can't fix your mistakes for you, but I can give you a chance to find them and fix them yourself. A chance, Mr. Kun. That's all you really want, isn't it?"

Holger's knees felt weak. He let them go. The carpet was soft and thick where he knelt. He looked up at the man who knew his heart so well. "I will be your man, of life and of limb—"

"Fealty is a bit after my time."

Holger blinked, confused. "You'll not take my oath?"

"I didn't say that." Bear's smile was radiant with the warmth of absolution. "But not just yet. There are a few details yet to settle. Wilson, help Mr. Kun get cleaned up. I believe that he will be joining us in our fight."

CHAPTER
27

John wasn't surprised to find that the rezcom where Marianne Reddy was supposed to be living belonged to a member of the Mitsutomo Keiretsu. Once upon a time, he would have been pleased to see how well the corporation was taking care of its dependents. But "once upon a time" was a part of his past, along with other childish fairy-tale stuff like living happily ever after.

The Dupree rezcom sat in a pocket of rural Massachusetts, in the middle of a deadsville triangle of three sleepy little towns off the main highways. The public tranz from the nearest rail was the rezcom mall's courtesy bus, and that was only a twelve-seater.

John took a walk through the property to scout it out. The Dupree rezcom was a lot smaller than any of the Benjamin Harrison Town Project rezcoms, and had a lot lower security. The mall entrances were wide open; property safeguards were left to the individual shops, as shown by the decals for a dozen different rentacop operations. John saw secured access points only at the entrances to the residential area, and those were minimal—nothing more than keypad doors, and half of them were propped open. As far as he could see, there were no cameras and no guards. Even the main entrance foyer was unattended. If Mitsutomo was doing surveillance on this place, they were being deeply subtle about it. Such subtlety would have flattered John, if he'd believed in it; watching this place on the chance that he might show up couldn't be high enough among their priorities to rate such expensive attention.

So he was free to do what he had come here to do.

He walked around the mall again, telling himself that he was just making sure that he wouldn't encounter any unexpected problems, but knowing he was really putting off doing what he had come here to do. He'd been less scared when he and Dr. Spae had been chasing Quetzal. Back then, he hadn't had time to think about what he'd been doing.

It was nearly Halloween, the time of year when the spirit world was close and the dead rose to walk again, and the mall stores were ready for it, where they weren't laying out Christmas decorations. Skeletons and ghosts and gravestones and vampires abounded in festive, commercial gaiety. It seemed that everywhere he looked, giant pumpkins grinned at him with lopsided smiles. Hollow smiles, they were, ignorant smiles; all flashy advertising style and forgotten substance. There was grim, hard truth behind those symbols, a truth that had been lost somewhere along the line while the otherworld was farther off than it was these days. *The lights are on in there, Mr. Jack O'Lantern, but is anybody home? Do you know what your duty is, O Great Orange Guardian of the Home?*

Home.

He'd been wanting to go home for—how long? Now here he was, on the threshold and hesitating. She wasn't going to come out looking for him. He had to go to her. No one else would tell her that one of her dead was coming home.

The residential area was quiet and empty. He walked through the corridors constantly expecting to meet someone, but he never did. At last he stood before the door and the nameplate confirmed what Shahotain's disk had told him. Marianne Reddy lived here. He pressed the bell.

The woman who answered the door was his mother. She looked older and more worn, but he had no trouble recognizing her. She opened the door wide, with all the assurance of the protected. Knowing how easily he'd entered, John felt a little queasy about her lack of caution, but he smiled. Squinting at him curiously, she spoke first.

"Do I know you?"

"Yes." Her blank look told him that she didn't recognize him. *It's okay. It really is. No surprise.* He'd known that instant recognition wasn't likely. He dragged off the wool cap that hid his hair and ears. "It's been a while. I've changed quite a bit."

"I know your voice." Now she looked puzzled, and a little disturbed. "But your face isn't at all familiar. Are you made up for some reason? Of course, it's almost Halloween, isn't it? If you're doing some kind of promotion, I ought to tell you that I do all my buying on-line."

"Still watching *Happy Lifestyles*ᴱᴹ?"

She blinked in confusion. "Why, yes. How did you know that? Are you from the network? Are you doing a survey?"

"No, no survey either. I'm John."

"That was my son's name."

"It still is."

Her friendliness vanished. Looking at him suspiciously, she solemnly said, "My son is dead."

"No, he's not." *I'm not.*

"I don't think I want to talk to you."

She started to close the door. He slapped his hand up onto it and held it fast. She struggled for a moment to shove the door closed. It wasn't a contest. Her strength apparently exhausted, she staggered back away from the door. The panel flew wide. John entered.

"Wait. I'm not going to hurt you," he said in what he hoped was a reassuring tone. To validate his words, he stayed near the doorway, afraid that going any deeper into the apartment would alarm her further. It was time for the alternate approach that he had hoped he wouldn't need. He should have known better. He'd had it easy with Dr. Spae and Sue; they had both already known that John was really a changeling elf. "I've got some papers here you need to see."

She backed away, putting a table between them.

"Really, Mrs. Reddy." He was surprised at how much it hurt to address her formally, but it seemed necessary. He had to go one step at a time. John produced a printout. "This is a copy of the public records report filed on the Armory incident. It includes a bio on John Reddy. Look it over. Especially the physical data. The man who died in the museum was five inches shorter than your son."

She wouldn't take the report. He put it down on the table, shoving it toward her. She stared at it as if it were something dangerous.

"Whatever is in there is wrong," she said. "It must be a clerical error. Yes, that's it. Johnny died in the fire."

"Look at these, then." He offered her another report and an ID card. The report he'd gotten out of public records. The card was one of the things he'd picked up from his old room the last time he'd gone looking for his mother. "The public database has the same data as the incident report, but they're both wrong. Look at the height on the ID card. You know that card's John's. You know how tall he was."

She stared at the card, not at the data but at the picture. Her expression softened. He started talking, reminding her about incidents, recalling things they had done together, and describing their old apartment. She'd know they were true. She'd know that only he could know about them. She stared at the picture while he talked. Finally he ran down and slowly, very slowly, she looked up at his face. Her lip trembled.

"Who are you? How do you know these things?"

"I'm John, Mom."

"No." She shook her head. "No. Johnny's dead."

"I'm alive, Mom. Alive as ever, just different. It's kind of hard to explain."

Her head shook steadily now. "I don't want to talk to you anymore. You're . . . not right."

Exasperated, John snapped, "What's not right is you not giving me a chance to explain."

She started at the crack in his voice. "This is very cruel, what you are doing. Get out of here. If you don't go right now, I'll call down to security."

"This isn't Rezcom 3, Mom. There's no security to call down to."

She edged toward the end of the table away from him. "I'll scream. I will!"

What a cruel joke. He'd finally gotten his reunion with his mother and she was going to scream and call the cops to get the crazed creepoid out of her life. Hell, this wasn't what he'd wanted. He looked at the terrified woman before him. She looked as though she might have a heart attack at any moment. Or go into screaming hysteria. This wasn't what he'd come here for.

There didn't seem any point in staying, and there were a lot of good reasons for going. He headed for the door.

There was a man in the hall, a big hard-looking guy who stared right at John. The hall lights were bright and John hadn't pulled his cap back on. He stood revealed as what he was, but the man didn't act surprised. He spoke in a matter-of-fact voice.

"It's not a mask, is it?"

"No, it isn't." Elf, human, what did it matter? John didn't have a home or family anywhere now. "What the hell is it to you?"

"Profit."

As John saw the gun start to come up, he dodged backward, into his mother's apartment. Something whizzed down the corridor, through where he had been standing. Whatever it was whirled and twirled and grew as it traveled, until it struck the wall at the corridor junction with a sticky splat. He had a good idea what it was; he'd seen vids of the Paris rioting in '03; the police had used guns that shot an immobilizing mass of gooey foam.

The man in the hall swore. Marianne Reddy started to scream.

"Get down!" John yelled at her. "Hide!"

She didn't move, just stood screaming and trembling. John started toward her, intent on getting her out of the way. Reaching the table, he realized he'd forgotten to close the door. The gunman was in the doorway. He had a different weapon in his hand now, not a capture gun.

"Don't move. Don't even breathe," he said. "Except when I tell you." John froze; he didn't dare do otherwise.

"Very good," the gunman said. "Now, step away from the woman."

"You won't shoot. You want me alive," John said, hoping he was right.

"It's the first choice, but it's not my only option."

John wasn't about to bet his mother's life on the chance that this stranger *wouldn't* shoot. He stepped away.

"You can stop yelling now, ma'am," the gunman told her. "I'm with the police. It's all right now."

Marianne Reddy paid as much attention to him as she had to John. The gunman didn't look happy. He kept his gun pointed at John and indicated the door with his head.

"Come on, you. We're leaving."

John hesitated.

"I could shoot her to shut her up," the man said.

The gunman sounded like he just might. John edged past him into the corridor. The man followed him, closing the door; Marianne Reddy's screams were cut off. The gun disappeared into the man's coat pocket.

"Don't get any ideas," he said. "I don't mind putting a hole in the coat. Now, put your hat on."

"You're not a cop," John said, doing as he was told.

The man chuckled. "It's a private firm."

"Mitsutomo."

"Nice guess."

John felt like an idiot. "I should have known they hadn't given up."

"I said it was a nice guess. I didn't say it was right. Come on, get moving. You and I have places to be."

The gunman directed John toward the stairwell. The residential corridors that John had found pleasantly empty now seemed appallingly deserted. They encountered no one in the stairwell, either. Bypassing the main entry level, they went down another floor, through a utility corridor to a back entrance, and outside.

"We walking?"

"Panel truck. End of row."

John saw the truck. The walk to it was long and open, the only cover being past the truck where a strip of buildings backed onto the parking lot. A lot of open space between them and the truck, plenty of chance to be seen—only this end of the parking lot was as deserted as the rezcom's corridors.

John had to think of something, or this mook was going to drag him off to God knew where. He needed the cavalry to arrive, or a magic trick to—Magic? John didn't know of any magic that would stop a bullet, or make him fast enough to outrun one. But there were other kinds of magic, and he had an idea of what he might try.

As they reached the truck John stumbled, going to his knee near the back of the truck. The gunman stiffened, the muzzle of his weapon straining against the fabric of his coat. John had come very close to getting himself shot. He tugged at his boot lacing. "Boot lace is loose."

"Fix it then. You almost got yourself shot. You might not be so lucky next time."

"My thought exactly."

Head bent, John worked on the lacing. Watching his captor, he tried to guess how gullible the man might be. If John got in the truck, he would lose his last opportunity to run. Time to take a chance.

Touching on his own fear, John cast an audible glamour behind the man. A scream sounded. The gunman's head twisted to check it out. As soon as the man's eyes left him, John threw himself into a backward roll. He tucked around the corner of the truck, to put its bulk between him and the gunman. He conjured another glamour, the sound of running feet pounding toward the buildings, something to cover the sound of his own crabwise motion toward the truck's far side. The gunman appeared at the truck's fender, his pistol out. To John's relief, the man didn't look at him. The mook's attention was directed toward the apparent source of John's false sound. The weapon's muzzle shifted with the man's stony glare, searching the shadows in unison for his escaped prisoner. At the man's feet John stayed quiet, finding the shadows where he wouldn't be seen.

After a very long time, the gunman shook his head, puzzled. "How the hell is he masking his thermal sig?" He stared into the darkness for another long time before putting his pistol away. "Next time," he muttered as he turned away.

John felt him enter the truck. Was this the time to really run? He thought about the vehicle's rearview mirrors. No, the magic had worked so far; he'd trust it a bit longer.

The truck started quietly, hinting that—like its driver—it had more to it than its battered surface showed. John waited until the truck left the parking lot before standing up. He watched until it ran up the ramp and disappeared onto the highway. He was safe.

But what about next time?

Whoever the gunman was, he had tracked John to Marianne Reddy's place. Once John had feared that he would bring danger home with him, but he thought that those wild times were over. Clearly there was to be no end to them. If he tried again to convince Marianne Reddy that he was her son, he might bring the gunman or others like him. Such men might not be content to leave an old woman out of their affairs, especially if they figured out the connection between Jack the elf and Marianne Reddy. He couldn't do that to her. She might have forgotten him, but he couldn't forget her.

He jumped when a voice spoke from behind him.

"Nice use of glamours, Jack. Loreneth taught you well."

Bennett.

John turned and glared at him. "Hell of a time to show up."

"I knew you'd come here sooner or later."

"Hope you've had a long, cold wait."

"Not long, certainly not by any reasonable time scale. As to being cold, you know better than that. This weather's far too mild to affect elves like us."

"I'm not an elf like you."

Bennett smiled and raised an eyebrow. "You haven't slipped back into denial because of Shahotain's little game, have you?"

"*Game?* What do you mean game?"

"Plot. Scheme. Ploy. Machination. Call it what you will. His profit from it is fleeting. He will regret what he did to you."

Was that anger on Bennett's face? John couldn't believe it. "Going to try the avenging father trick?"

"Would that make you feel better about me?"

"No. I'd know you were only doing it for whatever problems he caused *you.*" Though John wouldn't mind seeing Shahotain get what was coming to him. "Why should I want anything to happen to Shahotain? He's done more for me than *you* ever have."

"Meaning he gave you the disk that led you here? Where do you think he got that disk?"

"Not from you."

"Not directly. I could have arranged for you to have that information at any time. He used stolen knowledge to further his own ends."

And you never do that. "If you knew where my mother was, why didn't you tell me when I asked?"

Bennett gazed into the sky. He sighed. "And just how did it go, in there? No, you don't have to tell me, I can see the answer in your face. Still, it might have been worse. You're here, alive and free, and you now know that changelings can't go back to their old lives."

"I knew that," John lied. "I know I can't go back. I just wanted her to know I'm not dead. That I still— What the hell's the point of telling you this?"

"You need to say it. Isn't that reason enough? Get it out of your system. It's time to face the fact that Marianne Reddy is not part of the life of Jack, an elf. It's hard, I know—"

John slapped away the hand Bennett reached toward him. "What the hell do you know about it!"

"I understand better than you think," Bennett said, staring again at the sky. When he looked at John again his eyes glittered, despite his human guise. "I wanted to spare you this pain; the transition to knowledge is always hard."

John didn't need the bastard's false sympathy. "Just leave me the hell alone!"

"Very well." Bennett took a step backward, into the shadows beyond the streetlight, and was gone.

Part 3

♕

DARKNESS COILED AROUND HIM

CHAPTER
28

For all the sustenance from the harbinger's feedings, Van Dieman still had a taste for good food such as Loch-Olber prepared. Chef Gambino was quite inventive with the sauces he created to complement the lobster. Considering the trip he and his companion were going to take, he had decided to indulge himself, and Loch-Olber's was tailored to refined indulgences.

The harbinger, nestling close and comfortable, enwrapped him in coils invisible to the ignorant mundane throng. It shifted against him slightly, stirring like a dog catching a familiar spoor in its sleep. He scented something too: a certain tang in the air, a scent of magic, or, more properly, a scent of magician. With senses attuned by his association with the harbinger, spotting the source was simplicity itself. An unfamiliar man was being seated at a booth on the far side of the dining room. Though he was a stranger, his companion was not. Dozens of parties, political gatherings, and business conventions had acquainted Van Dieman with Pamela Martinez.

He knew from his predecessor Nakaguchi's reports to the followers that Martinez had for some time been clandestinely investigating the rising energies and realities of the new age. The Dark Glass files on her suggested that she was continuing her futile work to contain the blossoming magic. That information, along with his own investigations, had revealed her part in the awakening and subsequent destruction of Quetzal. Van Dieman supposed that as a good Follower of the Glittering Path, he should be contemplating revenge against her, but he was not. Had the Feathered One still been among them, Van Dieman's position would not have become half as commanding. Looked at in a certain light, his current prominence was due to Martinez and her undercover network of magic haters.

Everything he knew about Martinez suggested that she would be working against magic, but here she was consorting with a mage. Did she know the nature of the man with whom she shared her table? A fine irony if she did not. But she could be very aware of what the man was, and her presence here might not be coincidence. Could she have learned of Van Dieman's activities? Was she out to destroy him as she had Quetzal? Was the mage accompanying her a recruit in a strategy of fighting fire with fire? If so, she was making a mistake. Her companion's aura was weak, weaker than Van Dieman's had been even before he had the augmenting strength of the harbinger. If she intended to put her man against him, she would lose.

He decided to finish his meal, and to observe them as he did. He noted what seemed to be a celebratory air. An affair was the obvious conclusion, but with a mage? Martinez was known for the force of her convictions, one of which was the distrust of all things magical. Could she put that aside to consort with a mage? It seemed unlikely, unless she had deeper reasons. But the longer he watched the more he became convinced that there was nothing more than a business relationship between the two. Whatever the case, something had gone well for them.

If Martinez and a mage were celebrating, there must be something of interest in the cause. What might it be? He could set the usual assets in motion to search out the reason, or he could attempt to scry it out himself, but neither approach would give him a quick answer. He was here and they were here. He would try the simple, direct approach. If that failed to yield significant results, any data he gained would provide a springboard for one of the alternative methods.

The mage noticed Van Dieman as he crossed the room. He could see it in the way that the man stiffened in his seat. Martinez noticed her companion's reaction and looked up just as he arrived.

"Good evening, Ms. Martinez. No, no, don't get up. I have only a moment. I was on my way out when I saw you, and I thought I would stop and assure myself that there were no hard feelings over the last Defense appropriation?"

"Senator Hidoshi still seems to prefer pork over practicality," she said, indicating that there were indeed hard feelings, which didn't surprise him. In fact it pleased him, because it meant they'd hurt Mitsutomo.

"Yes, well, a man in Hidoshi's position does have to consider his constituency. Perhaps Mitsutomo will have better luck next time." Time to include the mage. "I don't believe that I know your new associate, Ms. Martinez?"

"Abraham Gower." The man's eyes flashed at Martinez as if she had betrayed him. She ignored his reaction. "Abraham, this is Anton Van Dieman, president of Network Securities Corporation. Congratulations on your promotion, by the way." He brushed aside her complimentary remark, knowing it for mere formality, as she added, "Too bad about Slaton."

"Yes, quite unfortunate." For Slaton.

"Heart problem, I heard."

Frightened to death, actually, courtesy of the harbinger. "He did not take sufficient care of his body. Not uncommon among higher-level executives. But you and I know better, don't we?"

"Are you implying something, Mr. Van Dieman?"

"Nothing more than the obvious. Slaton was a sluggish old man. His fate shouldn't surprise anyone. The old must make way for the new. It is the order of things. Don't you agree, Mr. Gower?"

Gower paled under Van Dieman's attention and had trouble finding words. This Gower was not a follower, Van Dieman would have known the name. Gower had learned whatever magic he knew from a different tradition, though the tiny pentacle he wore as a tie tack hinted that it was a related one. The man's sensitivity was sufficient for him to know Van Dieman for a mage, and to judge by his nervousness, he recognized Van Dieman as his superior in the Great Art. Van Dieman enjoyed the man's discomfort. Martinez stepped in.

"Most things happen in their proper time, but certain things seem to happen at, shall we say, *convenient* times."

He smiled at the spite in her tone. "Convenient is an interesting word. In some ways, I would think that Slaton's death came at no more convenient a time than the demise of *Kansayaku* Nakaguchi."

Gower looked nervously at Martinez, but she kept an admirable stone face. Still, his hint that she had done for Nakaguchi as he had done for Slaton had quieted her. Was she vulnerable on that front? Van Dieman knew that she had nothing to do with Nakaguchi's death—Quetzal had handled that—but Martinez had covered it up and taken advantage of it. Would she have acted if Quetzal had not gotten him first? Her eyes said she was capable. At the very least, she was guilty by desire.

"But enough of that," he said. "Good fortune, however come by, is a matter for celebration, is it not? If I may be so bold, what brings you and Mr. Gower out on the town?"

"Mr. Gower is part of a new venture," she replied guardedly.

"A new venture? Always cause to celebrate. I, too, am opening new avenues."

"Shall we trade secrets, then?"

"I don't think my associates would care for that."

She had expected no less. "Nor would mine."

There was nothing more to be gained with this ploy. What did her petty secrets matter? If Gower was the best she could muster, she and her associates were no threat. Her insolent obstruction of his whims was an annoyance of the sort he still had to endure in order to maintain appearances. "Things will be different when I return."

"Oh? You're taking a trip?" she asked with false innocence and real interest.

To the cold mountains in the heart of ice, the harbinger said sleepily in Van Dieman's mind. The longing and desire churning through its dreams excited him. For the moment, he needed to hide that excitement.

"Yes," was all the answer he gave Martinez. He made his good-byes politely. Martinez returned them just as politely, just as full of empty cordiality. He left them. They were the past, dreaming of the future—a future that they, in their ignorance of the Glittering Path, could not know as a false dream. The coils of the harbinger caressed him. Anton Van Dieman was not ignorant of the order of things to come. He was no false dreamer. He had the will and the way—and the future was going to be his!

Pamela liked to think that she had a grasp on the future and the path she needed to get there. She didn't like it when rivals intruded upon her unexpectedly and threatened that future. Van Dieman's recent succession to power within rival Metadynamics meant a shift in the balance of commercial power. She was still assessing the ramifications of that change and adjusting her assessment of what it meant to her company and her plans. She knew too little about Van Dieman and *his* plans, having paid insufficient attention to normal business matters, while being bound up in launching Thaumatechnics. Had her inattention cost the Keiretsu? Clearly the man had plans and had meant to disturb her by hinting at them. Unfortunately, he had succeeded. *Things will be different when I return.* What did that mean?

Gower had another question.

"Who was that?"

"I told you," she said, annoyed. "Anton Van Dieman."

He was still staring at the door through which Van Dieman had departed. "I know you told me his name, but do you know what he is?"

She had told him *that* too. If he kept up this idiot act, she would reconsider his appointment as president of Thaumatechnics. "What are you talking about?"

"He has darkness coiled around him."

"Abraham," she said, exasperated. "I would appreciate your speaking plainly. I am in no mood for mystic mumbling."

Gower seemed to come to himself. "I'm sorry, Ms. Martinez. I, uh, I was taken somewhat off guard by him. He has a very strong aura, the strongest I've seen since—"

"Since what? Don't stop there."

"Since Quetzal."

Now it was Pamela's turn to be caught off guard. "Are you saying that he's a sleeper?"

"I hadn't considered that." He thought about it for a while. She let him; his unique perspective was one of the things that made him valuable. Finally, he said. "No, I don't think that he is a sleeper. He is a mage, though, that much is clear. One of significant power. Yet there is something else about him, a strangeness that I haven't seen before, something dark and nasty."

"Hagen says that there are more than one kind of sleeper."

"I considered that. Yet the sleepers are human, are they not?"

Who the hell knew? Too many things mixed up in the chaos were *not* human. "Hagen hasn't said otherwise."

"Exactly. How much do you know about Mr. Van Dieman?"

"He's the new head of Network Securities, largest and most powerful of the Metadynamics corporate family— which makes him a most powerful man indeed, considering that MetaD is one of the Keiretsu's greatest rivals. He's been a fast riser; he only recently became a significant player. He's reportedly ruthless to opponents and openhanded to supporters. An ambitious fellow, by all accounts." She thought about what she was saying. A rival's evaluation report on *her* would describe her in much the same terms. She knew few details concerning Van Dieman, and the real story would lie in the details. Until now she'd had only peripheral dealings with Van Dieman, and she hadn't needed to know details. But there would be many details in the Mitsutomo databank, and what was in that bank was hers. She *would* know more by tomorrow.

"Nothing unusual in the psych evaluations?" Gower asked.

"That's a strange question."

"I have no doubt that he is a dangerous man. Your remarks about the convenience of Mr. Slaton's death stirred something in him."

"Are you suggesting that he actually *had* something to do with the man's death?" For all her ambition, she had never killed to open a job slot. If Van Dieman had, he might have provided a lever with which to remove him from the playing field, mage or not. "You say my remarks stirred him? Was he feeling guilt? Satisfaction, maybe?"

Gower looked uncomfortable. "I wouldn't dare to be so precise. I know that your comments touched him. Warmed him, I am sorry to say. Beyond that I can't be sure. There was so much that was strange about his aura."

"Abnormalities?"

Gower became suddenly reluctant to talk. She had to prod him.

"I cannot give you clinical certainty," he said at last.

"Tell me what you *think*. You wouldn't be where you are if I didn't value your opinion, Abraham."

"When you asked him about his trip, there was—I don't know how to explain this—another voice, that was not a voice, his but not his. It was very disturbing."

"Another voice?" Lunatics heard voices, and sometimes those voices told them to kill. "Is he insane?"

Gower gave a nervous laugh, fiddled with his tie tack. "I am afraid that the Art and its manifestations have not been refined even as precisely as psychology. The data necessary for a mage to turn out an evaluation report full of probabilities are still being gathered. We work in a young field. Consider how long it took psychology to emerge from personal opinion."

She didn't need a psych eval to know that he was avoiding something unpleasant. "And what is your personal opinion of Mr. Anton Van Dieman?"

"Insanity is built on disharmony," he said. "That man has conflict within him, but there is a fundamental harmonic that I don't think would be there if he were insane. To be honest, Ms. Martinez, I am afraid that he is *not* insane."

There was another explanation for voices in a person's head, an older explanation. She hated thinking that it might be a real explanation, but so much that she had once thought unreal had become commonplace. "You are not suggesting demonic possession?"

"I don't think I've ever met a demon." Gower's eyes strayed to the door. His fingers caressed the amulet on his tie.

"Abraham, look at me. Would you know one if you saw one?"

"I would hope so, Ms. Martinez." His eyes were bleak, frightened. "By God, I would hope so."

She wouldn't let his fear infect her. There had to be a better explanation than demons. A more reasonable one. Didn't there? Demons were just things made up to frighten children and unrepentant sinners. There weren't any *real* demons. Were there? Hagen would know. And if he didn't, there were answers elsewhere. She would find them. She would.

"I think there's more research to be done," she said, and signaled the waiter to bring the check. She drank down the last of her espresso. She'd call from the car to have more ready when they reached the office. She was not going to be sleeping much tonight.

CHAPTER
29

Holger heard voices, but they weren't the voices he'd grown accustomed to. These were deep, gravelly voices. They were discussing him, conjecturing on his condition, considering abstruse technical details that somehow applied to him. These voices weren't telling him what he believed in, or suggesting courses of action, or even just babbling at the edge of coherency. The voices that had done those things were quiet, as quiet as they had been in the car and in Bear's office. They were gone.

He was sure that they would be back.

But he was content with his reprieve, save for the smell. *That* smell again. Chromed steel and ozone and tile and disinfectant and latex. It was the hospital smell, the sickness smell. Even knowing that he was sick, he hated it.

Tentatively, he tested to see if the restraints were there. They weren't. The restraints belonged to a different time, didn't they? He'd grown unsure of his place in time lately.

He smelled the stink and listened to the murmuring voices. He tasted something metallic and harsh on his tongue, and against his skin he felt the play of air chuffing from a blower set somewhere above and behind him. Four of his five senses told him that he had left the dreams behind. He opened his eyes to confirm that he was awake and immediately feared that his senses had betrayed him.

Wires trailed from pads stuck against his skin, pads he couldn't feel. The wires led to machines, machines monitored by short, stocky men in white coats. Bear's friends, that's what he'd been told.

He closed his eyes, but the men in the white coats didn't go away. Behind his eyelids they wore black coveralls studded with pockets and equipment. Round black helmets covered their heads, hiding their wide faces and bushy beards. They were coming for him! Gunfire! The dwarves were rushing forward, attacking.

"Modulate the alpha rhythm," a distant voice said.

Doctors didn't carry guns. Something was wrong.

"Calm down, Mr. Kun. Calm down. You are among friends. No one is going to hurt you."

Friends? With guns? No, with lab coats. Doctors, trying to help him. He knew that. He'd been told that by a friend. Friends were what he needed. A whispered voice, not directed to him, spoke.

"I think it would help if you spoke to him."

"All right." Bear spoke as quietly as the stranger, then again, louder, to Holger. "Everything will be all right, Mr. Kun. Relax. You're in good hands."

He wanted to believe that everything was all right. Bear sounded so sure, so believable. He opened his eyes, but he couldn't see Bear until—against a stranger's whispered advice—he came into view from somewhere beyond the foot of the bed.

"You've been asleep for a while," Bear said, patting Holger's shoulder reassuringly. "You're safe. Well guarded."

He wanted to believe that he was safe, wanted to believe that he could trust this man. Holger remembered that he had already trusted Bear. Bear had taken him to his friends, and had convinced Holger to let them examine him. Holger had agreed to that examination and the sedation that Bear's friends had said was necessary. Holger had trusted Bear, trusted him with his life.

"Now what?" he asked.

Bear looked across Holger to one of the doctors, who had just come into Holger's range of vision. Holger had met this one before—he was the one who had come in with Bear at the Pend Foundation. Wilson was his name.

"Now we consider some of our options," Wilson said. "From what you told us before we started poking around, I'd say that you are unaware of how extensively your bodily systems have been modified."

He had told Bear's friends about the modifications of which he was aware, although he hadn't told them everything that the Department's doctors had told him about the capabilities of the implants. But this man spoke of *extensive* modifications. How extensive? Perhaps the Department's doctors had not been honest about how much they had done to him. Just what *had* they done to him? "What sort of modifications?"

"To begin with, as you suspected, there was a tracer signal emitter. A simple subcutaneous implant, nothing special about it. We've already removed it and sent it on a journey far away from here."

That was fine by Holger.

Wilson looked at the screen of the pad that he held. He nodded in satisfaction. "Your reaction to the tracer's fate is encouraging, Mr. Kun. This record will go a long way to convincing some about your sincerity."

Holger didn't care. "What else?"

"The mastoid commo receiver you mentioned is not standard issue. It is, we believe, the source of some of your 'voices.' When you are out of contact with the ECSS net, as you are now, the occurrence of voices goes down—but only some of the voices go away, yes? I thought so. If you are willing, we believe that we can disable the receiver without danger to you."

Again, fine with him, especially if it quieted the voices. He'd risk "danger" for that. But Wilson's answer was incomplete. "You said *some* of the voices."

"That is correct. We believe that we have identified another source in a systematic monitor which seems to react to specific stimuli by triggering counterstimuli. When the triggering stimuli is specific, the response is specific as well, apparently in the form of memories. We believe that some of the stimulated reveries are based on real memories while others may be altered or completely fabricated experiences. With less specific stimuli, the system responds less specifically, triggering neurochemical emitters to overwhelm your honest reaction with simulated needs or emotional states. We believe that translation of the system's signals into intelligible images is probably responsible for some of the voices as well."

The Department's doctors had given him false memories. They had tried to take away his past. He'd had an "accident" once before. If *that* memory was real. How much had they stolen from him and replaced with their lies? "How can I tell which memories are real?"

"That won't be easy. With time and careful monitoring, we may be able to help you sort them out. No promises."

Always *maybes* and *somedays*. Never any promises. All right, then, he could play the hand he'd been dealt. He'd have to live in the present and let the past be the past, whatever it was. When he encountered a suspicious memory, he'd just have to be suspicious. He didn't like being suspicious all the time, but he had survived such paranoid times before. *That* was a memory of which he *was* sure.

"Tell him the rest," Bear said.

The rest of what?

"Very well," Wilson said reluctantly. "Mr. Kun, there is an extensive network of microfibers paralleling much of your neural network. High-density clusters of these fibers occur in several areas, suggesting subprocessing units at those locations. Near several of them we have detected implanted objects displaying chemical compositions consistent with nanocomputers. We believe these units to be similar to standard medical signal control and interpretation units, such as those used for treatment of sensory and motor control disabilities. Such an interpretation is supported by the presence of several linked nanocomps in the regions of your cerebral hemispheres and cerebellum. We have also detected several dispensers whose locations suggest that they contain neurochemicals such as stimulants, depressants, and curiously enough, memory enhancers.

"The biotechnical and cybernetic implants are very sophisticated. We are impressed. However, no matter how sophisticated the hardware, the software is what drives your enhancements, and its capabilities will take significantly longer to assess."

Holger didn't understand the biological details, but he understood that he had been taken advantage of. "What's it all for?"

"As I said, the software is the key, and its nature still remains unknown. However, from the placement and nature of the hardware, I speculate that the implanted systems were intended to do more than improve your physical performance. I suspect that the designers intended to affect some of your higher cognitive functions as well."

He didn't like the sound of that. "Which higher cognitive functions?"

"I cannot be exact. That software issue again. However, I believe that they intended to control you, Mr. Kun, to own your heart and mind."

"They brainwashed me?"

"A crude term, but perhaps applicable," Wilson said.

"The stuff they put in to control me, can you take it out?"

Wilson frowned. "Very risky to you, considering how deeply some of the fibers have infiltrated your nervous system."

"How risky?"

"At the moment, I would place your probability of emerging with your mind intact at less than ten percent. There's a fifty-fifty chance you wouldn't survive the surgery at all."

"Lousy odds."

"I wouldn't care to try them," Wilson admitted. "But given more time to study our data and make some more tests, we may be able to improve the odds. Should we try, Mr. Kun?"

He didn't like the idea of the Department controlling his life. They had taken what he had given and demanded more. He hadn't even had a chance to offer. They'd just taken it.

"What have I got to lose?" His mind. His life. Nothing important.

The bastards! The deceitful bastards had stolen his life! They had gutted him and rebuilt him in the image they had wanted. What he had been wasn't good enough for them. What he had given insufficient. Who had given them the right to do what they had done to him?

"The news is not *all* bad, Mr. Kun," Wilson said with exasperating cheeriness. "You have improved eyesight and hearing. Some of the other modifications allow you to perform well beyond the capabilities of a normal man of your strength, by stimulating your brain to produce stress chemicals such as adrenaline and epinephrine. And the dispensers could well be supplying more potent concoctions. We are certain that you are capable of what is colloquially called hysterical strength, and that you will be able to ignore quite severe injuries that do not actually preclude physical function. Additionally, your reaction speed should be quite high. In short, you are stronger, tougher, and faster than an unenhanced man. We cannot yet determine by how much. Perhaps with a series of tests that I have in mind—"

"You've done enough tests for now," Bear said. "And you've filled this man's ears with too much. He needs quiet and peace."

"But we're not fin—"

"Yes, you are finished. For today, anyway." To Holger, Bear said, "They will talk forever if you let them. They don't care whether you understand, either."

"I want to sit up," Holger said. He wanted to see more of where he was. Bear helped him up, helped him strip away the sensor pads too. The doctors, not one of them taller than Wilson, gathered up their computer pads and coffee cups and left. When only the machines were watching them, Holger asked. "Who are they?"

Bear looked at him quizzically.

"Them. Wilson and the ones like him. They're not . . ."

"They're dwarves."

They couldn't be—could they? Bear hadn't sounded as though he was making a joke. "Like in stories?"

"They are real as you or I. They are my allies now, as they once were long ago."

"Can you trust them?"

Bear nodded. "They have helped me out quite a bit. You could do worse than trust them. Play them fair and they will play you fair, deceive them and earn their enmity. They are a long-lived people, Mr. Kun, and their memories for grudges outlive them."

"But—" Dwarves in black suits charging forward, weapons firing. "They tried to kill you. Kill us."

"They opposed the return of magic to the world, in a way that they thought might be effective. We—got in their way. It wasn't personal."

Holger had always taken personally any weapons fire directed at him.

"You look troubled, Mr. Kun."

He *was* troubled. Each time he thought about the dwarves, he was reminded that he ought to report such things to the Department. The thought disturbed him, because he suspected he knew it was prompted by the Judas wiring inside him. But he was disturbed on a level deeper than that. Some older memory fired his distrust and apprehension. The details were unclear, but the implications unpleasant. *The present,* he reminded himself. *Stay in the present.*

"Have you ever held a command in battle, Mr. Kun?"

"No."

"I have. Sometimes you have to send men, good men and friends, to their deaths. You know it when you give the orders, but you give the orders anyway and pray that the outcome will be worth their deaths. You pray that their lives will buy what you need bought. Later, if you're right, you'll have the chance to pray for their souls and your own, but when the need presents itself in war, you do what you have to do. The dwarves were fighting a war. They did what they believed they had to do."

Holger understood the principle. He might not have commanded in a hot war, but he had commanded operations, and he understood expediency. But he also understood that friends were friends and the enemy was the enemy. Confusing the two was dangerous, ultimately deadly. "They had no right. It wasn't our war," he protested. "We weren't their soldiers to expend."

"You're wrong. It *was* our war. It *is* our war, and I am a soldier in it."

Holger was missing something. "But you fought them. You killed some of them."

"Yes, I did. I didn't know who they were at the time; but even if I had known, I would have fought to stay alive. For while we are fighting the same war, we do not always agree on the strategy. They and I have been allies before, as we are now, but allies do not always agree on strategy. They set a course without consulting me, a course that from their point of view made sense. I might have even agreed, had I known their plan and agreed with their goal. However, I was not consulted when they drafted a plan that allowed for my death so that the end could be achieved. I do not care for strategies that call for me to sacrifice myself. I like to flatter myself that I can find better solutions. They are a bit more sanguine about such things."

"How can you work with people who tried to kill you? How can you trust them not to try again?"

"Their motive is gone. Caliburn is drawn, and the magic that bound it is loose. There's nothing that they or anyone can do about that now. They understand that."

"But we spoiled their plan. Didn't you say they hold grudges?"

Bear nodded. "They pride themselves on their practicality.

The general who devised that strategy is gone, as are a number of good men, all in the service of a failed plan. There is no point pursuing a grudge against me—or you, if that's what worries you. I am valuable to them now. As I said, we fight the same war."

"If the dwarves are not the enemy, who is?"

"The serpent lovers who have fallen under the sway of darkness and want to drag us all down with them. They are behind much of the woe of the world and they are the most dangerous foes we face."

"Who are they?"

"They are fools and idiots, power-hungry self aggrandizers. They have abandoned all that is good and wed themselves to the creatures of the outer darkness, the haters of life and eaters of souls. The things that they worship are enemies of all living beings, including themselves, but they are blinded to that truth. We must fight the serpent lovers now as good men have always fought them and their lies. It will not be an easy battle for they are a subtle, crafty, and persistent foe."

"And the dwarves fight this war too?"

"Yes. They knew that the convergence of worlds would make it possible for the serpent lovers to call their unnatural masters. They sought to prevent the possibility by preventing the release of magic."

"And killing you would prevent the release of the magic that was holding you in the otherworld."

"They were too late for that. But there were greater magics encasing Caliburn. Those they sought to keep in check."

So the dwarves had thought that they had a good reason to kill Bear. Holger still felt unsettled, distrustful. "Are they listening to us?"

"This is one of their places. Don't they have the right?" Bear shrugged. "What about your Department M, are they listening?"

"I don't work for them anymore." He felt his head, the hard spot behind his ear. "I don't know if they're listening. They might be."

Bear smiled. "I like honest answers."

"I didn't come looking for you to betray you."

"All right, why *did* you come looking for me?"

"I'm not sure."

That answer, too, seemed to satisfy Bear. "If it makes you feel better, Wilson tells me that they are blocking the transmissions to and from your commo thing. I don't understand the technical details, but they say they can keep your former masters from hearing. I believe them."

"Then I will too. But I don't understand why they want to help me."

"They are not helping you because they are altruistic," Bear said. "They are suspicious of you and even more suspicious of your former masters. Some of my friends believe that you may be a spy."

"I can understand that, but I'm not. At least not intentionally." Lord, he did not want their fears to be real. If they were, he was less in control of himself than he could tolerate. "If they are so suspicious, why are they bothering?"

"They're bothering because I asked them to."

"Why are *you* bothering?"

"Because you came to me, Mr. Kun."

"Aren't you suspicious of me?"

"In former times, my life depended on being able to judge a man quickly. I needed to be able to see into a man's heart and gauge his strength. I got rather good at it."

"What about—"

Bear didn't let him finish. "Not perfect, Mr. Kun. Perfection is not for this earth. Do you think that I'm wrong about you?"

"I hope you're not."

"I don't think I am. We worked together before, remember? Your present uncertainty and confusion will pass when you realize what you are looking for. Deep down, I think you know."

Did he? He knew that he felt yearnings. His own? He thought so. "I want to help."

"I would be pleased to have your help. If you're feeling up to it, I need a refresher on modern firearms. With all the work of getting the foundation going, I'm afraid I've neglected my arms practice. If you want to help, you can start by helping me there."

"Arms practice? Are you expecting trouble?"

"The worst kind."

CHAPTER
30

Walking the route had been easier when Bennett had led the way, but John managed it well enough. Unlike the last time, he felt the unevenness of transition where an otherworld hill faded and he stepped onto the surface of the elevated garden of the Nikko Hartford. The builders had removed the hill in the sunlit world, the better to site their multitowered construct. Was it only luck that the congruency remained between the Faery hill and a pocket park set two stories above the sunlit ground, or had the architect dreamed of the land as it should have been and included the park in his design as an apology for the rest of what he was doing? Whatever the reason, the match had served Bennett last year and served John now.

John's trip through the otherworld had been short—as short as he could make it—and if he had been able to think of a better way to avoid going through the hotel's street-level lobby, he would have taken it. At least he hadn't been seen.

Standing at the entrance to the elevator shaft, he looked up at the tower that held the luxury suite where Dr. Spae had stayed when she was working out of her office in Hartford. She was staying at the suite now, according to what her synth secretary had told John. He took the elevator up, using the security code he'd used before. The door rotated open on a darkened entry, and only then did John realize the lateness of the hour. He went in anyway. He could wait for the doctor to rise in the morning, but he wasn't about to spend the time till then standing in the elevator.

The place was as fancy as he remembered it, but it looked more lived-in now. The corp must have gotten a long-term lease for the doctor. Here and there he saw clothing that couldn't be hers and had to be Beryle's. So she was still seeing him. Beryle was some kind of journalist who specialized in the fantastic and John had been seeing his byline a lot more frequently these days, but John had never much cared for the guy even if Dr. Spae liked him. What she saw in him, John could only guess. At least John didn't see Beryle's portable, which probably meant he wasn't here right now. Off on assignment, probably.

A lot of books had been added to the wall shelves by the fireplace. John was starting to look them over when he began to get the feeling that someone was watching him, someone not entirely friendly. He tried to muster his magical defenses as he turned.

Dr. Spae, clad in one of Beryle's T-shirts, stood in the doorway to her bedroom, blue fire flickering around the ends of the staff in her hand. The flames died and she lowered the staff.

"Jesus, for a minute I thought you were Bennett," she said.

"Seems to be a common mistake."

"You do look a lot like him."

"Like father like son, eh? Not much of my mother in me is there? Either one of them." John knew that he sounded bitter.

"You've tried to see Marianne Reddy, haven't you?"

She must have been paying more attention to his problems than he'd thought if she could put her finger on the cause of his distress so quickly. He told her about his disastrous reunion attempt and the nearly greater disaster that had ended it. She shook her head at his foolishness in the first case and nodded approvingly at his handling of the second, agreeing with him that it would be best if he not go back there. He didn't mention Bennett's belated and unhelpful appearance.

Still, it felt good to have someone listen sympathetically. He had been right to come to her.

"I could use a little help, Doctor." He pointed to his face. "Not exactly man-on-the-street looks. Not the sort of face I should be wearing while someone is hunting me."

"You haven't learned to disguise your appearance?" She sounded surprised. "I would have thought that they would have taught you that. Bennett is accomplished at it."

"I never really had a chance to learn the trick. Besides, there's not much need *there* to pretend that you're human."

"No, I suppose not." She sat quiet for a while, thinking. "I suppose we can work a variation on one of the glamours you already know. We should at least be able to get that humanizing shift Bennett uses."

"It doesn't much matter what I look like, so long as I don't look like an elf."

"But you are an elf, John."

"I don't have to like it."

"You have to accept what you are."

"Why? Nobody else does."

She looked at him sternly. "Nobody? Very melodramatic, but hardly accurate. That kind of fuzzy emotional thinking won't help your magic."

"Magic runs on emotion a lot more than you like to think, Doctor."

"Otherworld wisdom?"

"If you want to call it that, go ahead. I'd call it empirical knowledge. I'm not entirely dim, you know. I can figure out things for myself." Elves hadn't gifted him with *everything* he'd learned since he'd last seen her.

"Maybe we should just try to do some work here," she said slowly, tightly.

Clearly she hadn't liked the tone of his last remarks. He was being a dode. Pissing the doctor off wasn't the way to get her to help him. He mumbled an apology, which she accepted gruffly, and they got down to testing John's knowledge of glamours and their construction. Working with the magic, they slipped with surprising ease into their old working patterns. John found that he had missed the interplay of student and teacher, and the thrill of manipulating the magic just to see what he could do. She showed him what he should have seen all along, and he felt a little stupid that he hadn't seen it for himself. Just as you had to understand, at least partially, the nature of what you were trying to duplicate in a glamour, you also had to understand something of what you were disguising, if you wanted to hide it well. Thus, to hide himself—an elf—he had to understand that he *was* an elf. Without such a basis, any glamour would be transparent at best. Okay then, he'd be an elf. What did he have left?

"That's it!" Dr. Spae exclaimed. "You've got it! You look like the old John Reddy."

The irony of that made him laugh.

Well, he'd gotten what he had come here for. "Thank you, Doctor. I'll be going."

She stared up at him as he stood. "And just where is that? If you're thinking about going back to your slump, think again. If the hunter was tracking you, he almost certainly knows about that place. He's probably watching it, waiting for you to come back."

"Let him watch. He won't see anything. I've got a way in that he can't watch." A hunter from the sunlit world couldn't lay an ambush along a trail in the otherworld.

"Maybe you do, but you can't spend your life holed up in there."

"I don't intend to." He didn't know what he *did* intend, but he'd figure it out.

"I still have a place for you," she said. "The firm can use you."

Exploit the elf, eh? He remembered her desire to get Bennett to work with her. All her talk about learning about how an elf lord did magic, about learning the secrets of the otherworld. "As a research subject?"

"John, you're being deliberately offensive."

"Isn't that better than doing it accidentally?"

"It would be better if you didn't do it at all. You've picked up Bennett's habit of turning things around on people."

Had he? "Maybe I can't help it. Maybe it's part of being an elf. You said I should accept being an elf."

Dr. Spae didn't look happy at getting what she had asked for. "You want to be an elf? Okay, try this. I've been studying my elf lore. We've dealt in magic, you and I, and that's put a bond between us. I've helped you, now you must help me, and since we struck no specific deal, *I* get to say how, and *you*, Mr. Elf, will go along."

"I know those stories too, Doctor. Doesn't the human always get burned in the end when she forces the elf to do something that he doesn't want to do?"

"I'll take my chances."

"Very traditional of you."

"Respect for tradition is very strong in mages. Elves, too."

He did feel as though he ought to go along with her. "Suppose I buy into this. What is it you want of me?"

"I want your help in an investigation."

"Is this the thing you were working on that had to do with Quetzal?"

"It is."

Should he be surprised that he no longer felt the fear that he'd felt not so long ago? It was not as if there was anything to be afraid of; Quetzal was dead and gone. What the hell? He didn't have anything better to do. "Okay. Sure. Why not?"

"Great. It's taken me weeks to clear enough time to look into this. Maybe I ought to take your arrival as an omen."

Maybe he ought to take his leave after all.

Dr. Spae disappeared back into her bedroom. He could hear her opening and closing doors and drawers. She kept talking as she dressed.

"The first thing we do is check out the scene of the crime."

"The railroad tunnel?" Quetzal might be gone, but a dragon lived in the otherworld version of that place. Dealing with a dragon was above and beyond the call.

"No," Dr. Spae replied. "The university. Specifically the building where Quetzal found the *telesmon.*"

"Doctor, it's been over a year. Surely anything of interest was taken away long ago by the police or some curious student."

"Maybe not. I checked with a friend on the police force. They just conducted a cursory search of the building back then, and they did that only because the door was left open. They didn't find anything out of place, but then, even SIU wouldn't know what to look for."

"And you do?"

"I've got some ideas."

She told him about some of those ideas on the drive to Providence. From her arcane reconnaissance on the night they had confronted Quetzal, she knew which room Quetzal had visited when he was there. That room was an office, one of the benefits accruing to a certain endowed seat. The current holder of that seat didn't use the office, preferring a more modern, more spacious one in the main geology building on the north side of the campus. The place was essentially vacant, not even used by the graduate students who occupied every other office in the building.

"How do you know all this?" he asked.

"Research, John. As I've always told you, research pays off."

What she called research, John called obsession. He knew better than to argue with her.

They couldn't find a parking space near their destination, so they had to hike up the hill. As they approached, John remembered the last time they had come here. Even daylight couldn't dispel the dark and frightening memories.

"Dead and gone," he said—apparently aloud, because Dr. Spae asked him what he was talking about. "Quetzal."

"Dead, yes. I'm not so sure about the gone part."

The gates to the main campus were open. They walked in just like the throngs of students hustling along between classes.

"Try and look as if you belong here," Dr. Spae advised. "It's the best disguise."

Once upon a time, John *had* belonged on a campus. He remembered how to act. They walked along, student and teacher pretending to be student and teacher. The humor of it buoyed John up, until they entered the building. It was cold inside after the heat of the bright fall sun, dark and cheerless. Dr. Spae led him down a narrow staircase. It was even darker down there. The narrow corridor was made narrower still by piles of crates and large, oddly shaped geological specimens all covered in dusty sediments of neglect. Dr. Spae pointed to a door.

"That's the one."

"You sure we can get in?"

"The car isn't the only thing I borrowed from David." She held up a key card. "This should open the lock for us."

There was no maglock on the door, just an old-fashioned mechanical one.

"I guess this is worthless," Dr. Spae said, starting to put the card away.

John snatched it from her. "Maybe not."

He slipped the card between the door and the jamb, levering it up until it contacted the bolt. If the lock was the right kind . . .

Feeling the bolt start to slide, he smiled. He held the bolt back as he turned the knob. He'd done it—old Trashcan Harry would be proud. John swung the door open and returned the card to the doctor with a flourish.

"A man of hidden resources," Dr. Spae commented. "You sure you don't want a job?"

"I am your bondservant," he reminded her—adding, with a wicked grin, "for the moment."

"Okay, then. Moment by moment."

She preceded him into the office. The room was small, with barely enough space for a chunky old steel desk and its chair, a narrow table against one wall, and a set of bookshelves. Everything was as dust-covered as the neglected debris in the corridor outside.

"You sure somebody has been in here during the last century?" John asked.

"Look at the dust on the floor," Dr. Spae said.

There were furrows in the dust, and faint footprints, and some other scuffs. More than one somebody; there were footprints of several sizes. "Chair's been popular." The dust on the seat and back was nearly rubbed away.

Dr. Spae started to browse around. John leaned against the bookshelves and watched. Since she wanted to play the "binding deal with an elf" game, he'd go along, doing only what she asked him specifically to do, and because she hadn't told him what she was looking for, he couldn't know what to look for and so couldn't look and stir up the dust the way she was doing. Maybe there were some advantages to being an elf after all.

He got bored fast, and started staring at the wall opposite him. There was something about the wall, though. He couldn't quite figure out what, but something about it wasn't right. He tried looking at it in the sideways manner Loreneth had shown him for piercing glamours, but that only made him sure that the wall was not what it appeared to be—which, he had to admit, was a find in its own right.

"Doctor, take a look at the wall."

She looked, then looked down at the floor. "Look at the scrapes the desk's legs have made in the dust. It looks as if the desk was moved away from the wall, then back again."

Dr. Spae faced the wall, mumbling under her breath. Reaching out with both hands, she laid her palms against the wall and said, *"Occultus sese ostendunt."*

A faint ochre glow outlined a door-shaped section of the wall. It didn't take them long to find the latch that opened the secret compartment. The false panel concealed a closet full of shelves. There was a lot of dusty stuff on the shelves.

"What have we here?" Dr. Spae said, poking at the objects on the shelves. Most of them seemed to be objects of painted wood, stone, or bone. A couple had feathers stuck to them and looked like preindustrial party favors. Most of the stuff seemed to be abstract carvings and dusty, dried-up leather bags. There were one or two other things and she handed him one of those. "See what's in that."

The object was wrapped in brittle, crumbly paper. The yellow stuff flaked away at his touch. The lower layers were less fragile, and they had printing on them. John got the object unwrapped, saw that it was another of the party favors, and put it down on the desk. The wrappings were far more interesting. He'd never held a real newspaper in his hands before.

"What is it, John?"

"The *Providence Journal Bulletin* for April 10, 1937. I don't think anyone has touched this thing since then."

"Forget the wrappings. Do you know what these things are, John?" She held up a knife and a wand that she'd taken from the biggest of the leather bags.

"Ritual tools."

"That's right. And these?" she asked, indicating the collection of odd objects.

"Objets d'art?"

"These are fetishes and power charms from a dozen different primitive cultures. Whoever held this office was interested in more than geology."

Fetishes and charms? Not one of the damned things held any power. "So he liked souvenirs."

"You don't hide souvenirs behind a false wall. These are magical artifacts."

"Maybe *you* don't hide such things, but this guy—who knows? He obviously wasn't running full-bore. There's not a one of those things that's got even a whiff of magic to it. They're all dead."

She looked at him as if he'd spoken a foreign language. She looked at the collection again, and after a bit, she nodded thoughtfully. "They *are* dead. Of course, they come from a time when the power wasn't there, but their forms and symbology are good. Or maybe it's just that they couldn't hold their power through the years." She studied them some more. "What's this?" She snatched something from the far back corner of one of the shelves. "Now *this,* this is not dead."

John looked at the thing. It was a shard of clay with some marks on it. The fragment had held power once, but the destruction of its physical integrity had sundered the bonds of magic as well. He could sense the drained and shattered dying spells upon it. "What is it?"

"Part of a binding, I think. The symbols look a little like something I saw once on what was purported to be a djinn's bottle."

"Solomon's seal?"

She shook her head, not the least bit impressed by John's display of scholarship. "Not Solomon's. Another sort. I've never seen an attribution given to it, though I've seen some of the symbols—this one for instance—on other occult objects."

The symbol she pointed out was a tiny six-pointed star with something inscribed in its center. John had to squint to make out what appeared to be a stylized eye.

"The guardian eye," Dr. Spae said. "At least that's what Rabbi Guildermann called it. I think that this may be part of the magic that hid the *telesmon* Quetzal took from here."

"But that fragment was back in a corner. Where's the rest of the seal? It's not like anybody was in here to clean up after Quetzal."

Dr. Spae got a strange look on her face, as though she were finding out the medicine she was taking had been flavored with something that actually tasted good. "Oh, no? Remember I told you that this office is part of an endowment? Well, it once belonged to the man who made the endowment. And you know what, that man is still carried on the university rolls as a professor emeritus."

"That would be the guy who wrapped up the fetish?" Dr. Spae's nod confirmed it. "But if this was his office and he wrapped up the fetish when he was using it, he'd have to be well over a hundred years old now."

"Yes, I should have seen it sooner. My friend said that the police hadn't found anything out of the ordinary here. Nothing about the false wall."

John saw where she was going. "And Quetzal wouldn't have had any reason to close it up again."

"He'd gotten what he wanted. What did he care about the rest of this stuff?"

"But someone else must have cared to hide this stuff away again."

"Someone who built the false wall," Dr. Spae said. "Someone with secrets to hide."

CHAPTER
31

The light rain coming in off the bay made Benton more dependent on thermal images than he liked. He needed the amplification to navigate through the fields of the airport's corporate reservations, but the burning wreck spread across the runways polluted his vision every time he tried scanning in that direction. There was a lot of noise and activity out that way. Fire engines were still making their wailing arrivals as the conflagration threatened to spread to the air cargo terminal.

Not his business.

His business was the man in the topcoat standing by the jitney. Benton moved toward him. At the gate to the Metadynamics sector Benton nearly stepped on someone sprawled on the concrete. He stopped to check out the body and found a withered husk of a man, dead. The corpse wore a Metadynamics security uniform, officer rank. There was no blood or other sign of violence that Benton could detect. He'd need a medical report to confirm it, but Benton suspected that he knew what had killed the man. He looked up at the topcoated man standing by the jitney, oblivious to the rain and watching the fire.

Why chase what's coming to visit you anyway, eh, Mr. Van Dieman? Is that why you called off the hunt for the Wisteria *killer? Did you know it wouldn't kill you too, or did you just take a chance?*

The man in the topcoat spoke without turning. His voice was soft and carried farther than it should have. The clarity

of the man's words was better than Benton's ears should
have provided.

"Ah, Mr. Benton, so good of you to come on such short
notice. I trust you passed the police line with little trouble."

"Bypassed it."

"Yes, exactly. They can be so tiresome." Van Dieman
waited until Benton got closer, within normal conversation
range, before speaking again. "You know what happened
here?"

Benton had been listening to the police and emergency
bands on the way to the airport. He'd caught the media's
take on the situation as well. "I know about the missile. First
news reports are talking terrorist bombing."

"This incident has disrupted my plans," Van Dieman said
peevishly.

A burning aircraft was spread over three of Logan's runways and the airport was shut down. The aircraft's crew of
four and two other men were dead. Six people dead—seven,
if you counted the MetaD security man—and Van Dieman
was upset about having to postpone his travel. Typical.

"This was not some random act of violence," Van Dieman
said. "I was the target."

"Evidence?" Or paranoia?

"My departure was unscheduled, yet there was a pair of
assassins waiting aboard. No one outside of my company
should have known about this trip." Van Dieman's voice
turned hard. "I suspect a leak in my security forces."

That explained the condition of the security officer.
"There were assassins aboard?"

"Two squat, toadlike men. They failed, but their backup
almost didn't. The missile struck just as we were lifting off.
Stabilizing the aircraft's flight until it could be landed was
most difficult. Had I not—well, let's just say I was very
lucky. However, I am left in an uncomfortable situation. I
cannot trust my corporate security, and I have no time to
weed out the traitors. Therefore, if I am to be spared any fur-

ther troublesome interruptions, I must look elsewhere. I have chosen to turn to you, Mr. Benton. The opposition made manifest tonight demonstrates the physical danger of my traveling without escort. I recall that your résumé includes bodyguard work. In fact, your record is excellent in that regard, is it not?"

"I like to think so."

"I will require, I think, two teams. One as escort and a second to eliminate any hostile shadows."

"Expensive."

"Name your price."

Benton quoted him triple the usual fee. "Plus expenses, of course."

Van Dieman didn't even blink as he rattled off an authorization code. "Arrange the transfer of funds, and I will confirm it. How soon can you assemble the teams?"

"I'll put the call out as soon as we confirm the contract."

"Good."

Benton quoted him the boilerplate details. Van Dieman didn't even bother to contest most of the clauses that favored Benton and his agents. Clearly, the man was worried. And that made Benton worry.

"I'll be able to do my work better if I know who I'm supposed to protect you from," he said.

"If I knew the source of the threat I would be commissioning you for quite a different sort of work." Van Dieman turned his gaze back to the burning plane. "You will arrange my travel personally. I prefer to resume my journey tonight, but stealth has apparently become paramount, and completion of the journey is more important than timeliness. Within limits, of course."

"The police won't want you to leave."

"Their desires do not concern me. Make the arrangements."

"Skipping on an investigation will add to the expenses."

"Do it. Do whatever you need to do, and remember that I will not countenance a repeat of tonight's incident."

Benton had seen how Van Dieman dealt with imperfect security. "There is something I still need to know. Where are we going?"

"Antarctica, Mr. Benton. Just get me there, and I will take care of the rest."

CHAPTER
32

Benton proved efficient. His immediate solution involved bribing their way aboard one of the few aircraft leaving the airport, a verrie flight to Kennedy Airport. The police would not object to Van Dieman's departure, because they would never learn of it. Once at Kennedy, the transportation options multiplied a hundredfold, a strategic advantage that Benton said was important. Van Dieman approved of the plan.

They boarded the verrie moments before its scheduled liftoff and were seated in the first row of the cabin. Another of Benton's arrangements: the better to be off the craft quickly when they reached Kennedy. Van Dieman settled in. The craft didn't offer the comfort or amenities that he was used to, but the flight would be short enough. He could tolerate traveling among the less advantaged.

Not a hundred feet off the ground, the harbinger surged against him, tightening its coils painfully. He yelped in surprise and pain. The harbinger began to howl like a child ripped from its mother, drowning out Van Dieman's questions. Its thoughts were chaos, full of loss and confusion and dread. His own thoughts dissolved into the harbinger's, were tossed free. He floated, detached from his mortality. He saw his body convulse.

Benton reacted quickly, attempting to restrain Van Dieman's thrashing limbs with sheer physical force. He shouted for the flight attendant, who rushed to their side. Her strength was nothing compared to Benton's; she did little to control

Van Dieman's convulsions. For his part, Van Dieman fought to calm the harbinger. The creature fought against him, refusing to listen to him. His body mimicked the flailing of the harbinger's shadowy form.

The pain of spasmed muscles edged into Van Dieman's disembodied consciousness. He hated pain. He watched helplessly as his head slammed again and again into the seat back. This was not right. The harbinger's panic was pointless; the indignities it was imposing on him were unacceptable. More than he hated pain, he hated the offense to his dignity. He used his hate to beat against the harbinger, to force it back under his control.

With the help of the copilot, Benton and the flight attendant began to control the thrashing of Van Dieman's body. With the increasing physical restraint, Van Dieman found it easier to force his will on the harbinger. Regaining access to its inchoate mind, he forced calm upon it, beating the rebellious beast down into submission. With it cowed, he was able to return to conscious control of his body.

"You may take your hands from me now," he said. "I am all right."

"Are you sure, sir," the attendant said. "I think we ought to—"

"I said I'm all right! Leave me alone!"

Rocked back by the power he put into the command, she obeyed him. Van Dieman slumped in his seat, glaring at the copilot, who returned to the cockpit without another word.

Van Dieman felt the eyes of the passengers upon him. He had made a spectacle of himself—or rather the harbinger had done it for him.

Foolish creature, he admonished it silently.

Unnatural, it responded. It still jittered at the edge of panic. *The earth is too far. Return. Must return at once.*

We will return to the ground soon enough.

Too far.

The harbinger moaned and complained for the entire flight, but under his strong control, there was no repeat of the strange hysteria that had gripped the creature. It shifted and twitched, settling down only when he reassured it. But its periods of calm grew shorter and shorter. Van Dieman's patience had worn thin enough to break by the time the pilot announced their descent into Kennedy.

Not much longer now, he told it as he might speak to a child.

Too long. Too long.

There will be longer times.

No!

Yes. This method of travel is necessary to reach the place in a timely way.

He could feel it assessing the truth of his statement. He sensed its distress.

What must be, it said. Coiling tightly around him, the harbinger shifted. Its consciousness dimmed below the point at which he could communicate with it. The harbinger had withdrawn that way before, and its retreat offered Van Dieman no cause for worry. He knew that the harbinger had come back to him when he felt its surge of joy as the verrie's wheels touched the earth.

As Benton had arranged with the verrie's pilot, the craft put down at the edge of its owners' parking area, as far as possible from prying eyes. But Van Dieman's episode with the harbinger had complicated their arrival: an ambulance and a team of paramedics stood by with the ground crew. Per prior agreement, Benton departed through the copilot's hatch on the side of the verrie away from the terminal while the pilot fussed with the landing, centering local attention on the craft. Through a window, Van Dieman watched him sprint unmolested toward the baggage gate. Once inside, he would begin making further arrangements.

Van Dieman had been supposed to exit with the other passengers, anonymous among them. There was no record of his leaving Boston; there would have been no record of his arriving in New York. To the authorities back in Boston, Van Dieman might as well have simply disappeared. In truth, the media were already reporting him missing in what they were calling the "NSC Aircraft Bombing." Metadynamics and Network Securities Corporation flacks were, of course, denying that he had been on the doomed flight. Van Dieman had been wise in priming them to cover his trip. An incident such as the one at Logan might well have sparked stock runs or even a takeover attempt—there would certainly have been an internal power struggle—and he was not ready to surrender any of his hard-won gains. Money and mundane power would still matter in the new world that was coming.

Unfortunately the plan had developed a hitch: the people aboard the verrie. Thanks to the harbinger's fit, they would remember him. All that had been gained by his secretive departure from Boston would be lost unless he acted. He needed to silence these witnesses—quickly, effectively, and in such a way as to hide his hand in it. One of the passengers coughed, suggesting an idea.

Pneumococcus bacteria lie dormant in the lungs of almost every person on earth. They do not threaten a healthy person. However, if activated and energized with arcane force, the disease could blossom; and if accelerated by that same force, the disease could strike swiftly and fatally, congesting the lungs and suffocating the victim.

A waste of fodder, the harbinger complained.

There will be more. For now I think it best that what is done here not look like your usual feeding, he told it. Losing his temper with the captain of NSC security in Boston and allowing the harbinger to ingest the man's essence had been a mistake.

The harbinger growled incoherent complaint, but lent its strength to his plan. In less than a minute surprised passengers and aircraft crew died choking on their own fluids. But to gain the full advantage of what he had done, he needed to be well away before it was discovered; and to do that, he still had to deal with those waiting on the tarmac. It was a small matter to make himself appear to be the verrie's pilot. Not an exact likeness, of course, just a uniform and insignia—

enough for the ground crew to respond to. He opened the
passenger hatch and extended the stairs. The paramedics
were waiting at the bottom when he reached it. They needed
no urging to board.

"You!" Van Dieman shouted to the milling ground crew.
"Come on! They'll need your help too."

The signs of authority affected them strongly. It didn't
hurt that Van Dieman added a compulsive push to their reactions. The ground crew followed the paramedics onto the
verrie. Van Dieman did not need to climb back up; his hand
on the railing was sufficient to connect him to the shell containing the magic he shaped.

He dealt with the new arrivals as he had with the crew and
passengers.

Let the authorities here wonder at the plague ship that had
arrived on their doorstep. The quarantine would delay inquiries long enough for Van Dieman's needs.

Benton was making the arrangements for the next leg of
the journey, summoning the requisite aid and taking the precautions he deemed necessary. Caution was indeed advisable
now that this new, unknown opposition force had entered the
picture. Van Dieman decided to arrange some precautions of
his own. The public comps in the main terminal allowed him
to make the necessary calls with sufficient discretion.

Finishing his arrangements, he realized that he was hungry, as he often was after working magic. The harbinger hun-
gered as well; he could feel the gnawing intensity of its want.
He'd done what most immediately needed to be done, and
there was time before he was to meet Benton.

"We'll find you something soon," he told the harbinger.

Even an airport as large and busy as Kennedy had dark
and quiet corners.

A system as large and busy as Mitsutomo's main database
offered many places to hide bits of information. The decker
Pamela employed knew most of the dark corners, those

places where the furtive could stash things they didn't want others to see. Normally Pamela left the ferret work to her decker, but occasionally she did her own snooping. She liked to keep up on what was being hidden away, especially when it affected her place in the organization.

One of her special interests of late was seeing just what, among the steady flow of information into the Thaumatechnics data store from former Charybdis Project sources, was being diverted or dumped by the esteemed Mr. Hagen. Take, for instance, the latest file deleted by Hagen: an SIU sign-off report on an incident.

Normally the system picked up any reports where the Special Investigations Unit retained interest in a case. This time a flag calling for any unusual data on a related item in old Charybdis files had brought in one that SIU had passed on. The old file was on one Marianne Reddy, a Mitsutomo dependent. Sörli had put a watch on her as a part of his program of surveillance on probable agents of the otherworld. After a museum fire of suspicious origin in which Reddy's son had been killed, she had been sequestered under surveillance. Nothing had turned up in connection with her, but her old apartment had been the site of several "visitation" events, all verified by Gower. Nothing new had shown up for over a year; the case had been closed down, surveillance terminated, although apparently someone had missed shutting down Sörli's flag. This new report, involving a prankster and a police impersonator, sounded like a strange harassment crime, but it had nothing otherworldly except the Halloween costume worn by the prankster. SIU had—quite reasonably, it seemed—signed off on it. So why had Hagen bothered to delete it?

A matter for another day.

Today, she wanted answers from Hagen on his sudden reawakening of interest in the *Wisteria* killer. She kept her face neutral as he entered her office and took his place in the chair. He knew about the sensors in the chair and showed no hesitation in sitting.

"Shall we get right to business, Mr. Hagen?"

"I am at your disposal, Ms. Martinez."

"Good. Let's start with you telling me what has motivated your renewed interest in the *Wisteria* killer."

The sensors registered only mild surprise. He shrugged. "The creature itself is of little consequence. It has, however, apparently been harnessed by interests at odds with our own. That is what must concern us."

"Us? Why not return the matter to the police? Didn't you originally declare it a matter for them?"

"I did. Unfortunately, the situation is now beyond their competence, the scope of this matter having broadened considerably. The creature, or possibly merely the study of the thing, has opened new avenues for its controllers."

New avenues? Van Dieman had used the same phrase last night. "Just what do you mean?"

"You have not read the new analyses that I posted to you this morning?"

She hadn't, but it would not do to admit that. "Maybe I just want to hear you say it out loud."

"Out of character for you," he said with a brief, sly smile. "What is important is that the particular otherworldly intrusion dubbed the *Wisteria* killer has become inextricably connected to one individual in particular. That individual belongs to a rival organization, an organization with programs addressing the redevelopment of magic in the world."

"Names, Mr. Hagen."

"Anton Van Dieman. Metadynamics."

What connection? Pamela wished she had read Hagen's report. "Give me the highlights."

"We can now correlate the *Wisteria* killer's most recent activity tightly with the presence of Van Dieman. It stalks whatever city he is in. We believe that this is the final proof necessary to confirm that Van Dieman is magically active. His potential as a threat has greatly increased.

"During the period of Van Dieman's association with the creature, several affiliates of Metadynamics, including Van

Dieman's own Network Securities Corporation, have shown interest in occult matters: recruiting psychics, acquiring property where or near where we have documented other-world intrusions, building databases of unexplained phenomena, and even collecting specimens of unnatural beings. They have made no overt moves to match your own formation of Thaumatechnics, but such a move can only be a matter of time. Commercial rivalry, however, may turn out to be inconsequential. We have disturbing reports of Metadynamics activity around several of the sites associated with Quetzal."

God, would that specter never be laid to rest? "Including Nakaguchi's resonator sites?"

"Every one."

That was the answer she hadn't wanted to hear. Gower hadn't yet puzzled out the complete purpose of those arcane devices, but he was certain that they would have a deleterious effect on their immediate areas, possibly on the world as a whole. The resonators were, in Gower's words, "aligned with the malign." If Van Dieman and MetaD were involved in activating those things, perhaps they too were aligned with the malign. "Van Dieman is advising the FSA on Dark Glass, isn't he?"

Hagen nodded. "You begin to appreciate how dire the situation has become."

Appreciate? No. You needed hard facts to appreciate a situation. But did she feel dread? Yes. You didn't need facts to be afraid. "If you and your cabal have been following these developments, why didn't you act sooner?"

"We believed that the situation was under control. We miscalculated. The matter has now gotten out of hand."

Now gotten out of hand? "You *have* been conducting an operation."

"Not utilizing Mitsutomo assets, I assure you."

The chair said that his statement was truth, ninety percent certainty. Still, he was officially a member of the Keiretsu family. Actions that brought blame to him brought blame on the Keiretsu. The scandal involving Nakaguchi was still fresh. She did not want to have to deal with another rogue.

"I will not support illegal actions," she told him.

"Have times changed, Ms. Martinez? No, don't take offense. I understand. The problem is that Van Dieman is leaving the country. It would be easier to stop him here."

"Then he wasn't on the plane at Logan."

"He was there." Truth again. "Else there would have been no need to shoot it down."

Hagen knew too much to avoid the obvious conclusion. "The NSC aircraft bombing was your operation?"

"It would have been better had the gunner let the craft get over the bay."

Not only did he not deny the attempt, he gave her additional details. "So you tried to kill him and failed. Now you want the Keiretsu to get involved. Are you sure Sörli hasn't come back to run operations for your cabal? How many innocent people did you kill? How many more did you endanger?"

"How many more will *he* kill? That is the question that must be asked, Ms. Martinez. Make no mistake; he must be stopped."

The creature certainly needed to be stopped. But Van Dieman? "We don't even understand the threat he poses."

"All the more reason to stop him."

A paranoid's logic. Still, she was not surprised by the statement. She recognized the determination in Hagen without needing it confirmed by the monitor. "You will proceed with your plans whether I offer aid or not."

"Yes."

"The Keiretsu cannot be involved in the murder of business rivals."

Hagen looked disappointed.

Van Dieman might or might not be a dire threat. The killer creature certainly was dangerous. She had long ago learned that what one could not control, one might still direct. That seemed the only course left her, unless she wished to adopt dwarvish tactics.

"An attempt to eliminate the *Wisteria* killer would be a worthwhile endeavor. Very public-spirited. Especially if documented. It is conceivable that the creature might claim another victim before it could be stopped."

"Ah, Ms. Martinez, I must confess that for a moment I doubted you. I am ashamed. You are a most perspicacious employer."

"Mr. Hagen, as a perspicacious employer I choose employees who are both wise and careful, those who understand the needs of the Keiretsu. You are still employed by the Keiretsu, yes? Do we understand each other?"

"I believe we do."

"I hope so, Mr. Hagen." She killed the monitor on the chair and tapped the control to open the office door. "Now, I think that it's back to work for both of us."

CHAPTER
33

Holger felt much better when he awoke with the morning sun shining in the window of his room at the Pend Foundation headquarters building. He had gone to sleep apprehensive about sleeping in an unshielded room, but the dwarves had been as good as their word, and he had passed the night undisturbed by voices in his head. He was surprised at how light he felt with that burden lifted.

Unless, of course, they had lied about doing anything and the room *was* shielded against transmissions. But that was paranoia, wasn't it? It was hard to put away the paranoia after living for so long in a world that it ruled.

Someone had entered the room unnoticed while he slept. That someone had recovered his stashed clothing and gear, and brought it here. He didn't remember telling them about the stash, but he wouldn't be surprised if he had. He'd been strung out pretty far. He checked the pile. Everything was there, even his weapon. The fact that the Glock was loaded suggested a certain amount of trust on his hosts' part.

In among the gear was a Shilson Detector™, a device that would let him determine whether or not the room had any of the standard shielding schemes. Using it would say that he didn't trust the dwarves' word. Were they watching to see whether he did use it? Was that why his gear had been brought to him? If he used the device he would know whether the voices were gone or just taking a vacation. He would know that the dwarves had done him a good turn. But what did it say about him that he would prove their trustworthiness by such a distrustful method?

He needed to know, whatever they might think about him. He needed a point of reference. He needed to know whether his new acquaintances told truth or lies. If checking on them offended them, he could apologize, blaming his apparent distrust on caution. Contemplating his deceitful intent, he thought of Bear's trust in the dwarves. Bear believed them. Shouldn't that be good enough for Holger?

He wished it were. But not yet. Taking up the device, he ran the start-up diagnostic, then ran through the scan programs until he was sure that the room was clean of protections. The only localized electromagnetic disturbance was consistent with a security system monitoring the windows. Not the door, he noted. Not even a signature for a video camera.

They hadn't lied.

And he hadn't believed them.

He started when a loud knock sounded on the door. Ashamed to be caught with the device in his hand, he tossed it onto the pile before responding. Bear stood there, dressed in a Bard Taliesin T-shirt with the sleeves ripped off, sweatpants, and athletic shoes. He looked like an ex-pro athlete ready for a workout, but Holger knew better.

"How are you feeling?" Bear asked.

"Better than I have in weeks," Holger replied honestly.

"Good. Up for some exercise? I could use a partner. Ever work with a sword?"

"I've had a little bit of kendo, but I've done a lot of escrima work. The art uses sticks, but the principles are supposed to be applicable to swords."

"Escrima? Never heard of it." Bear shrugged. "But if you think it will work for you, we can give it a try. Sticks, you say? Long or short?"

"Short? Sometimes two."

"Two?" Bear nodded as if he understood. "Mostly edge work then."

"No edges. I said sticks, remember?"

"No edges, right. No points either. Sounds undisciplined. Even Vegetius understood the use of the point."

"Don't assume I don't."

Bear raised an eyebrow, then smiled. "This could be interesting. When you're dressed, the gym's at the end of the hall."

Holger didn't take long to dress, less time than it took to locate suitable clothing in the closet and bureau. They weren't his clothes, but they were sized to fit, a full wardrobe of business and casual clothing. His final selection was a sweatshirt emblazoned with the words "If found, return to CIA (drop in any mailbox)" surrounding what he recognized as the logo of the old spy organization.

Bear had left the gym door open and Holger followed the sounds of clanking weights. The gym wasn't big, but respectable for a private one. Half of it was crammed with assorted exercise machines, while the rest was open space lined with equipment cabinets. In one corner a new computer console gleamed amid a tangle of wires. An inner doorway led to a small locker room and beyond that was another space from which Holger could hear the sounds of a shower. Bear put down the weights and gave Holger the cheap tour. They ended at a set of cabinets full of wooden weapon replicas, padded garments, and plastic helmets, as well as more conventional fencing gear. Bear selected a suite of protective equipment for each of them and got Holger into his. Holger was helping Bear lace up his body armor when Wilson came out of the locker room.

"What do you two think you're doing?" the dwarf asked.

Bear hefted a wooden broadsword. "We're going to do a little sparring. A warrior has to stay in shape and keep his skills up. You never know when you're going to be in a fight."

"You want to fight, you use a gun. Swords! Swords have been out of style since before I was born." Wilson shook his head. "You spend too much time thinking retro, Art."

"And you spend too much time with machines," Bear retorted. "I intend to test Mr. Kun's mettle, and I intend to do it my way."

"All right, all right! Who am I to get in the way of archaic fixations? But before you get Mr. Kun all excited, let's take a precaution or two, eh?" Wilson went over to the computer console and came back with a handful of sensor pads. He held them out to Holger. "Here, put these on."

Suspicious but trying to remain polite, Holger asked, "What are they?"

"They're just ordinary medical sensors to monitor heart rate, perspiration level, stuff like that. You won't even know you're wearing them, but they'll let us know if you start shifting into overdrive. We don't want any training casualties."

"We'll be fine. It's just a friendly practice," Bear said. "Mr. Kun doesn't need your monitors."

"I think he does," Wilson said, staring resolutely at Bear. Bear glared back.

"I'll wear the monitors," Holger said.

"I will too," Bear said, taking them away from Wilson. "Where the hell do they go?"

Wilson helped them attach the monitors, then fussed at the console until he was satisfied that the sensors were functioning correctly. "All right then, we're set. Go ahead and beat each other silly. I'll be watching."

They finished donning their protective gear and went on to selecting their weapons. To Bear's surprise, Holger found several pairs of escrima sticks among the wooden weapons. When Holger pronounced them overly heavy, Bear said, "What did you expect from practice weapons?"

Bear selected a wooden sword longer than Holger's two sticks put end to end and they went at it. They circled each other, shifting *en garde* stances and gauging each other's reaction. The first passes were tentative, stick slapping against stick. The tempo picked up. Bear caught Holger by surprise several times. The stinging slaps and bruising pokes only spurred Holger on. He tried harder, using some of the tricks Mannheim had taught him, and Bear scored less often. After a few unsuccessful exchanges, Bear started circling warily, attacking in flurries that usually ended with Holger putting a solid blow through Bear's defenses. Bear just gritted his teeth when that happened and set up for another go. Each time Bear pushed it up a notch, striking a bit faster, a bit harder. Holger met him with a measured response, matching speed and power. Bear came back fighting harder and more fiercely. Sticks clacked against sticks, occasionally thwacking against protective gear. Holger struck Bear far more often than Bear scored against him. Bear threw himself against Holger's defenses, threatening to overwhelm them. Holger fought back, losing himself in the whirl of combat. He fought. His opponent wouldn't give up. Each time Holger beat him down the man got up again. Holger pummeled him, stick on stick, stick on flesh. Again and again, until the man stumbled back. Again, until he fell. Again. Again. A—

Someone was holding Holger's arms, pinning them to his side. The grip was strong. He started to wrest himself free, but then he heard the shouting.

"That's enough, Holger Kun! Fight's over! It's over."

Wilson's voice. Wilson's grip. Holger stopped struggling, and looked down at the groaning Bear at his feet. Holger realized that he had slipped into the berserker madness, apparently his last and lasting gift from Department M. The escrima sticks dropped from his nerveless fingers. He had no words, unable to think of any way to apologize to the man he'd beaten. His ears filled with thunder and he began to shake.

"Are you all right, Art?" Wilson asked.

"Been worse." Bear rolled over onto his back and looked up at Holger. "How about you?"

Holger didn't know what to say.

"He's come back to earth," Wilson said. "He'll be fine."

Holger realized that not all the roaring in his ears was internal. The building was vibrating slightly as the noise of an aircraft engine beat against it.

"Verrie coming in," Holger said.

"Scheduled?" Bear asked Wilson.

The dwarf shook his head. "I'll go check it out. You'd better get cleaned up, Art. We might need you presentable."

"I was about to call it quits anyway," Bear replied, somewhat out of breath.

While they were dressing after their showers, Bear said, "I think that I'm glad those sticks weren't swords. I haven't had such a drubbing since—well, never mind. You handle those swords well for a man bred to firearms."

"You're pretty good with firearms for a man bred to swords."

"I hadn't thought you a flatterer."

"I'm not. You really are pretty good, allowing for—"

"Don't make allowances." Bear's voice was a whip crack. "There's no room for unrealistic evaluations on the battlefield. A man has to know what he can and can't expect of himself. His commander has to know even better."

Holger was taken aback by the outburst. "I'm sorry. I didn't mean—"

"I know. I'm just—well, never mind. Let's forget it, okay?"

"It's forgotten." It seemed strange to be pardoning Bear; Holger was the one who needed forgiveness.

"You're a good man, my friend. Would that Wilson and his lot were so accommodating."

"I thought the dwarves were your allies."

"Oh, they are, they are. They have done a lot to set up the foundation and to get me oriented in this modern age—and I won't deny that I am grateful for it—but for all their goodwill, they're still dwarves and not humans. I'll be happier when there are more people like you around. I need men I can trust."

"I will try to be one."

" 'Try to be one,' not 'am one.' " Bear slapped Holger's

shoulder. "By the Lord, I find your honesty refreshing. Have you any brothers, Mr. Kun? I could use them, especially if they fight like you."

"No brothers."

"Too bad. Let's hope we don't get to the sharp end before we get a few more recruits, eh?"

Bear had hinted before that trouble was coming. Holger was ready to help him. "What kind of an op are you planning? What's the target?"

"I don't think you understand. Didn't your Department M bosses ever explain to you about the sleepers? The once-and-future stuff? The promised return in a time of great peril?"

He knew the legends, but as a recovery ops agent he hadn't been involved in sorting the legends from the truth. He'd just been responsible for bringing in the target, and he'd left the sorting out to the doctors and the specialists. "They never told me much."

"Did they say that the time had come for the sleepers to awaken?"

"Yes, they did." That much they had told him.

"And did they tell you why?"

"No. I don't think they knew."

"I'm not surprised. The world has grown remarkably complex, and sometimes the enemy is hard to see without a mirror. The peril is out there. Several perils, in fact. You can see them if you open your eyes and look around."

"You mean the return of magic?"

"I know some people are afraid of that, but there's been magic before and it didn't destroy things—except when serpent-loving idiots misused it. Don't get me wrong; I don't like it, but I don't think it's the real danger. The *real* problem is that the earth is dying—unthinking people are killing it. People who don't understand their place in nature, people who lack ideals, and people who just plain don't care. The dreams are dying, and the earth with them. I ask you, my friend, what's the point of living if you have no dreams?"

"Better no dreams than nightmares."

"You're wrong there. Nightmares have meaning. They give you something to fight against."

"How can you fight what you don't understand?"

"People have been doing it for centuries. You don't have to understand your enemy to fight him, although it helps. You just have to understand that he *is* your enemy, and do what you believe needs to be done. If you're on the right path, you'll win out. Eventually. Otherwise what's the point? Without dreams there's nothing, just surviving day to day like an animal. I, for one, believe that man is more than an animal, and I know that you, my friend, believe that too."

He had, once. Listening to Bear, he was coming to remember that belief. "I will fight at your side."

"Any battle, Mr. Kun?"

"Any battle."

"I will fight the battles that need to be fought, but that won't always mean combat. A good warrior knows when to fight with swords—or guns—and when to fight with words. This world is a lot bigger than the last one I knew. It needs different answers. I think I've got a few. I know that some of the people I'm working with are *sure* that they have some of the answers. I think they may be right. I *hope* they are. Otherwise, I see little chance to heal this world. The Pend Foundation is my way to work against what I see is wrong. The foundation is opening doors, getting people to listen. We've gathered some influence already. I hope for more. Call it my dream, my hope to heal the world. I'd like to have you be a part of that dream."

"Do I get to be a knight?"

"You know, I'm still not sure I understand all the freight that this knight stuff carries, but I do have a round table down in the strategy room, and you're more than welcome to sit at it." Bear smiled. "Right now, however, we need to see about our unscheduled visitors."

Holger went along with Bear, who made no objection. Holger was glad of that. Walking at Bear's side seemed the right place to be.

CHAPTER
34

The house might once have been nice—maybe about a century or two ago. It huddled under the bare trees of its corner lot, awash in a sea of leaves. The path to the porch was nearly covered, nearly an unblazed trail. The shabby property sure didn't look like the home of somebody who could endow a chair at a major university.

"Are you sure this is the place?" John asked.

"It's the address of record," Dr. Spae replied. She led him up the walk and onto the porch, which thumped hollowly under their feet. Pointing at a row of mailboxes fastened to one side of the door, she said, "See? J. Daniel Carter."

"How can you be sure it's the *right* J. Daniel Carter?"

"Is there a reason for all this negativity?" she shot back. *Other than not wanting to be involved in this?* ". . . No."

The door had no call box or keypad lock, not even a buzzer. Dr. Spae tried the door, opening it to reveal a hallway. They entered.

The old house was sectioned into apartments, shown on a faded map hanging by the door. According to the mailbox, Carter's apartment was "A," formerly the front rooms. They walked down the short hall and around the corner to the door. The "A" that had once been nailed to the wood was gone, its former presence shown by a lighter tone on the dark wood and three small nail holes. Dr. Spae knocked.

There was no response.

"Maybe we should have called first to see if he was home," John suggested.

"No phone," Dr. Spae reminded him as she knocked again.

They waited again to no effect.

"Did you hear something?" Dr. Spae asked. John hadn't and said so. She frowned meditatively. "I'm sure I heard someone in there."

She knocked a third time. Almost immediately John heard a mechanism trip on the other side of the door, and slowly the knob began to turn. Half a revolution later the bolt slid free of the catch plate and the door opened, but only the slightest, the barest of cracks. They looked at each other. Dr. Spae put her hand to the knob and opened the door farther.

"Mr. Carter?" Dr. Spae's voice was tentative, not at all like her usual tone.

The apartment was a single room, barely bigger than the hall and all unlit and shadowy. The walls had wainscoting of dark wood; the lighter walls above were so age darkened that John couldn't tell if they had once been patterned, or if the vague shapes he saw were from his imagination. Most of the space was filled with a bed, a huge, gnarly four-poster draped in an unwrinkled, faded spread. In one corner, next to a small table piled with dishes and glasses and mugs, squatted a humming refrigerator surmounted by a compact microwave crowned by a two-burner hotplate—the kitchen. In the opposite corner was a desk cluttered with papers that piled like autumn leaves against an antique-style computer so old that its plastic casing was yellowed. The far wall was dominated by a bay window, its panes covered with venetian blinds angled closed so that only faint strips of outside light leaked between the overlapping slats. Set in the alcove of the bay, its back toward the door, was a rattan chair of the high, round-backed sort that furnished all the bars in Pacific Intrigue[EM], the kind of seat that the beautiful enemy spies always favored so that they could make a dramatic appearance when they rose from the chair's concealment. Like those chairs, this one was occupied. The weave of the chair was just loose enough to show the silhouette of the occupant, presumably J. Daniel Carter. The only things visible about the man were his hands, liver-spotted with age, and the fingernails were long and ridged, almost claws.

"Come in and close the door," said a dry, raspy voice. "You're letting in a draft."

John couldn't feel any air moving at all.

Dr. Spae stepped into the room and tugged John along. She closed the door behind them, cutting off most of the light. Now that they were inside, John became aware of a strong odor of mold and decay. How wise were they to accept the invitation? At least the bed lay between them and their shadowy host. Of course, there wasn't much room to do anything; John would have to get Dr. Spae to move just to open the door again.

Dr. Spae spoke. "Mr. Carter, my name is— "

"Elizabeth Spae," the fragile voice finished for her. "Doctor of occult philosophy by training and practice if not by degree, and your companion, who is other than he appears, carries the name John Reddy. Consider yourselves introduced. I had expected you somewhat before now."

"How did you know we were coming?" Dr. Spae sounded more curious than surprised. John thought she ought to be a little more worried.

"I see much better in these latter days. I see things that were hidden from me in the past. Unfortunately, I see much that I do not care to see." He coughed lightly. "You were at the university. In my office. You found my closet. I was surprised that you took so long to go there."

John didn't care for the man's attitude. "I suppose you know why we came to see you, as well."

Carter laughed a laugh just this side of a cackle. "Motives are murky things, are they not? Even after all these years of heightened awareness, I cannot see into the hearts or delve the depths of minds. Would that I could—that I could have long ago. But such vision is not given to me. Concerning motives, I am as blind as the most mundane and benighted unbeliever. Were I to guess, I would say that you have come because you want to know about *it*."

" 'It'?" John found the vehement distaste that Carter put into the word unsettling.

"That which we, in our ignorance, uncovered and brought back here to such woe. The talisman of the worm."

"Talisman of the worm," Dr. Spae repeated thoughtfully. "That would be the *telesmon* that Quetzal took from your hidden closet?"

"Name not the feathered serpent!" The passion in the withered voice caught John by surprise. It must have done the same to Dr. Spae; she looked a bit stunned. For several minutes no one spoke, then the old man whispered, "His heart was as cold as the clime from which we disinterred the talisman. I felt the barrenness when the serpent broke the seal around the talisman. But you two knew his nature, for you fought him, risking your souls to stop his evil. I salute you, unrecognized heroes. Know that your deeds are not wholly unrecognized, even though the greater world remains ignorant of the debt it owes to you."

John's unease was growing. "You know that we fought Que— the feathered serpent? How?"

"I felt the serpent's touch," Carter said. "I saw the flares of power. I heard the earth swallow him, heedless of his cries."

The old guy sounded as though he'd had a front row seat for the battle. Not only that, it sounded as though he'd known that it was coming. How could he have—unless . . . yes, there was a scent of power around this strange old man. John no longer had any doubt that this man was more than a simple geologist. He felt apprehensive about Carter's place in what was happening, and remembering how helpless he'd felt going up against Quetzal, he wondered where the old man had been then. "Carter, if you knew the bastard had copped your toy, why didn't you do something? We could have used help."

"I can sense much, but do little. The price to be paid, I surmise, " Carter replied regretfully. "In my youth I was always disappointed that the more manifest aspects of the Art seemed not to be my gift. I did not appreciate the subtler gifts. By the saint's mercy I have gained enough wisdom to know that the strength and will for action is not given to all. Those who have the ability must do, others must aid as they may. We all have our place in the grand plan. Once the Feathered One rose, time became short. Now, though time grows shorter, yet there is a moment in the turning of the stars, and we are met. You have come seeking understanding. It is small repayment for your heroism to tell you what I know. Ask your questions."

Dr. Spae pounced at once. "Tell us about the *telesmon*. Where did it come from?"

"Its origin is unknown, Elizabeth."

"Then tell me when and where you got it," Dr. Spae snapped. Clearly Carter's mystic mystery attitude was rubbing her fur the wrong way.

Carter seemed unfazed. "Ah, so long ago. So cold. A summer colder than any winter New England has ever shivered through. I had never been so cold. So much was strange to me. There were bones in the earth there, the bones of great beasts. Dinosaurs, Galthier said. How could brute reptiles survive in such a climate, I asked. How would they warm themselves in frigid Antarctic days, let alone in the long night of Antarctic winter? Taylor's and Wegener's theories of continental motion were mocked in those days. I was young and knew no better. Now we know that the land at the bottom of the world was not always cold, and I suspect that Galthier was right about the bones belonging to the dinosaurs, though no specimens remain to prove or disprove the origins of those ancient bones we found."

"What's with the bones?" John interrupted. Carter's rambling explanation wasn't exactly suited to the situation if time was as short as he claimed. "I thought you were going to tell us about the *telesmon*."

"I was telling you, John. It was in searching near the place of the bones that we found what we later regretted."

"Before you go on," Dr. Spae said, "just where are you talking about?"

"Antarctica, Elizabeth," Carter replied. "Hadn't I said that?"

"No, you hadn't."

"I thought it quite a coup. Brilliant young stratigrapher to chart the lay of an unknown continent. Had I known what was in store, I think I would have refused the university's offer."

"You were on a university expedition? There was nothing about that in your record." At least none that John had turned up rooting around the university database.

"You will not find *any* records of the university's expedition," Carter said confidently. "I destroyed them all in 1938. All save one, and that one is gone now, too; you buried it along with the thief who stole it. No one would know of our ill-starred exploration at all were it not for H.P.'s story. Had I greater fortitude I should never have drunk so much, but there was so much to forget. I suppose I thought that telling the tale would purge me of the horror. I was wrong, of course. H.P. listened too well to my tale and ignored my later protests that my ramblings were but liquor-inspired fantasies. He said that he understood every word that I had said, and why not? It was the truth. But even *he* knew that it was a truth that could not be fully revealed. He became as haunted by the truth as I. His solution to rid himself of it was to make a fiction of it."

Carter was drifting off the topic again. "Who is H.P.?"

"H. Patrick, my brother."

John realized that he was blinking like a light-stunned owl. Fiction? H. Patrick, as in H. Patrick Carter? Antarctica? University expedition? It couldn't be, could it? "This fictional story—it wouldn't be 'Among the Mountains of Madness,' would it?"

"You know it? Tell me, John, has the tale currency even in your realm?" Carter asked.

John had no idea if the tale had reached the otherworld; he had read it while in high school. Apparently Dr. Spae wasn't on-line.

"What is this 'Among the Mountains of Madness'?" she asked.

"It's an old horror story," John told her. And here Carter was, telling them that the events in that story were real.

"Yes, quite a horror story," Carter said. "H.P. realized that no one would believe the truth if he told it baldly, so he called the truth fiction and told the story to the world. It eased his mind, I suppose. I still cannot decide whether it is fortunate that the world never took it for more than fiction."

"What has this got to do with the *telesmon?*" Dr. Spae asked.

"Ah, as I was saying, when we first found the stones, Galthier thought that we had found more bones. He was very excited and said all sorts of things that embarrassed him later. He should have asked me before he made his pronouncements. To me it was quite clear that the stones weren't on the same horizon as the bones. Different horizons, different times. In any case, as we worked, it became clear that the stones were not petrified bone; but it didn't end our interest in them, because it also became plain the stones were *arranged*. We had found something quite unexpected. We had found the remains of a temple, on the order of the great henge on Salisbury plain. In the center of the temple, under a cairn of rock, we found the talisman of the worm. That night the troubles began, and by morning we were in full retreat for the coast. Half our party was dead or mad by the time we reached the ship that took us away from the cold, white land.

"Though my fellows were ignorant of the source of our travails, I believed I knew: the talisman. I took the talisman to those who were better versed in such things than I. We puzzled over its nature. To be perfectly frank, we did not know what we held in our hands. Oh, we knew that it was an arcane artifact—I had known that the moment the last stone was lifted from the cairn—but we did not recognize the power that hid in it."

John listened to Carter's tale, flashing on details from the story Carter's brother had written. In the story, the thing the scientists found had acted as a focus for some malevolent energies, but they hadn't known the danger. None of the fictional protagonists had been able to sense the power of the talisman beyond formless feelings of dread and unease. Yet, here was Carter admitting to sensing something of the thing's aura. If Carter had been able to sense anything from the talisman, he should have been able to understand that it was a menace. John hadn't actually seen the *telesmon*, but he had known that Quetzal was carrying the thing when they'd cornered him in the tunnel. Even hidden, it had exuded peril. "How could you not have known how dangerous the thing was?"

Carter sighed, a mournful sound. "The energies were thinner then, John. Much thinner, and I was not so adept at seeing them. We had no one among us of your accomplishments, Elizabeth. Though we knew the talisman had power, we had little understanding of its potential. Still, older and wiser heads recognized its malign orientation and we took precautions. Had we known better, we might have done more; but as it was, we did our best. We could not anticipate the return of the feathered serpent and his interest in the artifact. How could we know that he would awaken with it?"

"You keep saying *we*," Dr. Spae observed. "Who else is involved?"

Carter did not reply immediately. When he finally did speak his raspy voice was even softer than it had been. "Have you ever heard of the Order of St. Lazarus, Elizabeth?"

Dr. Spae shook her head. "Are you saying that you are part of some sort of secret society dedicated to the occult?"

"If that is what you heard, Elizabeth, then perhaps I said it. There are those who stand in opposition to the deluded fools who would open the way for the worm. They stand guard in secret because they must. Such covert vigilance has a cost. Though we sometimes lose some who would willingly join our ranks because of our secrecy, yet we cannot recruit openly. We must remain hidden from those who offer harm. We remain a small and necessarily select group, but we who are the enemies of the worm are united—as we must be—for the worm is strong, strong in power and strong in its hatred for life. The worm's ability to sway weak minds with false promises is immense, and the influence of the enemy is great. Even among the members of the expedition there was one of the Followers of the Path, the greatest and most dangerous of the cults in service to the worm."

"The Glittering Path?" Dr. Spae asked.

"So you do know of them, Elizabeth."

"*He* spoke of the Glittering Path," she said. Her voice trembled a little. "He asked me about Luciferius."

Carter murmured assent. "Ah, the great prophet of the followers, publicist and apologist for the worm. Behind lies and false promises of worldly power and wealth he hides the truth—the worm's path is death, and its followers are damned."

"So you hid the *telesmon* from these followers."

"Because we recognized the sign of the worm, we hid the talisman and warded it as best we could. But our knowledge is not that of our ancestors, and we did not recognize the true danger, else we would have tried to destroy it."

"You muffed it major," John said.

"Omniscience is characteristic of God, not man." Carter's voice was weary. "It is clear now that the talisman of the worm is indeed a *telesmon* of great power and perhaps of greater significance. It may even be the key that the followers of the Glittering Path seek."

"Luciferius's key to the stars?" Dr. Spae asked.

Carter chuckled bitterly. "The key to damnation for mankind."

John wasn't sure that he bought all the stuff about cults and worms, but Carter's conviction and Dr. Spae's accepting attitude to Carter's tale were persuasive. In his brief near-encounter with the *telesmon,* he'd felt enough of its evil to be glad that it was where no one could get at it. "Good thing the *telesmon* was buried along with the guy who stole it, eh?"

"It is not," Carter said.

Dr. Spae looked as shocked as John felt. Carter's three short words evaporated his belief that the *telesmon*'s danger had been suppressed. John felt a little sick.

"Elizabeth, you know one who can confirm this," Carter said, his voice calm and matter-of-fact. "Ask of the man who seeks secrets only to hide them, of him who takes the commonwealth's coin to protect the public from a threat unacknowledged."

"What's with the riddle?" John asked. If they were looking at trouble, they didn't have time to mess around with riddles. "If you know who it is, just say so."

"Riddles may protect as well as puzzle," Carter said. "Why do you pretend not to know? Never mind. Let it be. Elizabeth understands. That is enough."

Dr. Spae asked, "If the *telesmon* isn't buried, what has happened to it?"

"It is in unclean hands and it is moving," Carter said. "A mage carries it southward. I think that I know where he is taking it. Given the malign aspect of the stars, where else?"

"So you think that this mage is taking it back to Antarctica," Dr. Spae said.

"To the temple, Elizabeth. He means to use its power to open the gates of hell."

Up until the "hell" part, John had bought Carter's scenario. "You can't mean that literally."

"The difference that makes no difference is no difference," Carter said. "The mage must be stopped."

"He can't be as bad as Que— the feathered serpent. He won't have the knowledge."

"Do not underestimate him, Elizabeth," Carter admonished. "You will need great power to oppose him."

"We stopped Quetzal," John pointed out. How bad could a wannabe be?

Carter gave a sharp intake of breath at John's mention of the name. "An impressive feat, but you were lucky. The mage who holds the talisman of the worm may not be the equal of the feathered serpent, but he has allied himself with a monster of the outer darkness. And he controls the talisman. A very dangerous combination. You will need help."

Need help? "What makes you think we're going after him?"

"Hush, John. Of course we are." John gaped. His reaction went unnoticed by Dr. Spae; her attention was focused on Carter. "Go on, Mr. Carter. You say we'll need help. Do you have any particular help in mind?"

"Yeah, like are *you* going to do something?" If Dr. Spae wanted help, this guy and his friends were prime material. Hadn't they been the ones to open the can of worms in the first place? "What about your St. Lazarus guys? You gonna help us or what?"

"I'm glad you're in, John," Dr. Spae whispered to him.

So she had noticed. And, *hell*, he had said *us*, hadn't he? Somewhere along the line he had gotten involved. He was angry with himself for losing his detachment. Well, he couldn't let the doctor face this creepoid alone, could he? It had taken both of them to bury Quetzal.

John shot his anger at Carter. "If this mage is so bad, we'll need all the help we can get. We need more help than your damned riddles. What are you going to *do* to help?"

Carter didn't stir. "As you, I fear to face this mage, John. Among the servants of St. Lazarus there are neither arcane nor mundane warriors of sufficient stature. You and Elizabeth have fought the agents of the worm before, you must fight them again."

"Not the right answer," John told him.

"Only too truly the right answer," Carter countered. "We servants of St. Lazarus serve as we can, according to our gifts. We have offered you knowledge in the hope that you—

both of you—as proven warriors, will do what we cannot. Yet we fear that the two of you are not strong enough, and so we tell you this: there is, free upon the land, another talisman of power, one more benign in nature. It is strong. It is near. And you, both of you, have brushed against its power and not been seared. It may be possible that one of you may be given the grace to wield the talisman. The cause is just, and each of you has resisted corruption by the darkness. Shoulder your burden. Face the worm. Do what must be done. Be the heroes that the world needs."

John had always dreamed of being a hero. So why was he terrified of getting the chance?

"Where do we find this talisman?" Dr. Spae asked. She might have been asking for directions to the local mall for all that she sounded concerned about the course of action she was committing them to.

"As I said, Elizabeth, it is near. In fact, it is in a building in this very city. I take its presence as a sign. Yet it is not my place to offer its use. Go to the seeker of secrets of whom I spoke before. He knows not the keeper of that most potent of talismans, but he knows the path to where it lies. Ask his aid. I can say no more."

CHAPTER
35

The babble of voices poured into the squad room, over-whelming the ordinary bustle and noise.

"What about the Kennedy Plague aircraft? Any truth about a new strain of bubonic coming out of Boston?"

"The Proper Order rumbled last night. Are you investigating the cult aspects of the gang?"

"Is it true that the mayor of Pawtucket has been abducted by a UFO?"

"Word is that the Holyoke Horror has struck again. Any truth to that?"

"Is it true that you have apprehended the *Wisteria* killer?"

"I've got a source who says that you have Anton Van Dieman's mummified body in the morgue. Is that true?"

"Is it true that the Newport oil spill has been quarantined because it's really an extradimensional toxic waste dump?"

"Is it true that—"

"Is it true—"

"Is it—"

Manny got out a final "No Comment" as he shut the door and cut off the ruckus.

"Jeez, I hate it when a day starts this way," he said to anybody in the squad room who was listening. Most weren't; someone had leaked where the Special Investigations Unit had set up its headquarters; and every detective on the squad had run the gauntlet themselves as they came on shift.

305

Manny joined Charley at the coffee machine. "What stirred up the piranha?"

Charley understood the attitude, having only come through the crowd of reporters a few minutes ago. "Phase of the moon? Who knows?"

"More like a ratings sweep. A good weird happening is worth a point or two." Manny poured himself a cup of coffee. "One of those esteemed fourth-estaters shouted something about the Proper Order being out last night."

"Yeah. District 30. Vuong and Falerio got liaison with Gang Related."

"Better them than us."

Charley had to agree. Crimes related to the Proper Order gang were currently being shuttled back and forth within the department. The gang, while responsible for a lot of typical violence, didn't fit the mold in a lot of ways—not least that it had seemed to come out of nowhere last year. The gang's soldiers perpetrated vicious acts of violence and had so far eluded all pursuit as if they could vanish into thin air. That insubstantiality, along with their gang members' appearance and reported "abilities," were what kept getting SIU dragged in. Some of the other guys speculated that the gang was from . . . somewhere else . . . and Charley was afraid that they might be right. Worse, the gang was getting more active and starting to attract media attention. He was just as glad as Manny that this latest incident hadn't landed in their laps. They had enough to deal with.

When he got to his desk, Charley found a priority message flasher on his terminal. The source line was missing, and when he logged on and pulled up the call, he understood why. Casper, the friendly ghost in the machine, had dropped by.

>>22.10.29 * 07.23.18.79 * xxxxx.xxx
LOG #10 29.1 PRIORITY 1
TO: GORDONC@NECPOLNET*0004.13.00*874334
FROM:<UNKNOWN>
RE: DUTY. MODI UNNUMBERED.

MESSAGE:
INTRODUCE SPAE TO PEND FOUNDATION. PERS. ATTEN.

While Charley was pondering the implied connections and meaning, he got an incoming call from Dr. Spae's synth secretary. Coincidence? Charley would have loved to think so, but he was just too sure that this apparent coincidence was connected on strings that he couldn't see. The secretary wanted an appointment for him to meet with Spae, suggesting Heddie's restaurant downtown. Curious, he agreed.

He was a little late getting there, having gotten tied up trying to square away the paperwork on a case. He still hadn't finished with it. Soon as the meeting was over, he'd be heading back to the office. Charley didn't want to have to explain to Captain Hancock why the report wasn't waiting for him when he arrived in the morning.

Heddie's was gearing up for the happy-hour crowd, enough people to keep the place busy but not so many that he and Spae wouldn't be able to talk. He spotted her while he was waiting for the hostess. She was sitting with a kid who looked like streetlife. Charley abandoned his wait for the hostess and headed over. Just in case, he popped on his Tsurei Seeing Eyes™ so he'd have a recording of the meeting.

"Who's your friend?" he asked as he arrived.

Spae hesitated. "John Bennett. He is something of a student of mine. John, this is Detective Gordon."

The kid might be a student of hers, but Charley was sure that she hadn't given his real name.

"John." Charley gave the kid a friendly nod. This was Spae's show and he was willing to allow some leeway, but he still made sure to get some good frames of the kid on the Tsurei, in case he needed to run him down later. Charley took one of the empty seats. "So what did you want to talk to me about, Doctor?"

Spae looked surprised. "What do *I* want to talk about? You set up the meeting."

It turned out that Spae had found the meeting on her schedule and assumed that Charley had set it up. Fair assumption, but wrong. "Somebody has gone through a lot of trouble to get us together."

"I was planning on contacting you anyway."

"Oh? Why?"

Again the hesitation. "I've got a lead on the *Wisteria* killer. It's a being called a harbinger."

He'd thought this meeting might have something to do with that case, since it was the only thing he'd worked with Spae on. He'd expected her to bring up the killing at Kennedy Airport. Maybe she didn't know about that. It came as no surprise to him that she was still working on the killer. So she'd found a name to pin on it; that piqued Charley's curiosity. Not that he could do anything about it. Whatever her harbinger was, it had moved on. Besides . . . "You're talking to the wrong man. The whole thing was kicked upstairs to the feds, and you know what? It's not a problem anymore. Read the papers, check the nets. The whole thing was just a hoax."

"We both know that the creature is real and must be stopped."

"You're not the first to suggest that." He'd already been offered an opportunity to go along on a cowboy action to settle the *Wisteria* killer, courtesy of Mitsutomo. The offer had even come over the chop of Pamela Martinez, but Charley had said no thanks. One reason was that he'd already done cowboy work for Martinez, and this summons didn't have her flavor. The other big reason he was happy to share with Spae. "What you're talking about is way too far beyond the law. A man's got to know his limitations."

The kid at Spae's side smirked and spoke for the first time. "Gotta keep the commonwealth's coin coming in, eh?"

"What are you talking about, kid?" The kid just grinned at him. Charley turned to Spae. "What's he talking about?"

"Ignore him," she said.

"More than happy to," Charley said. "But there are some

things I can't ignore. So if there's nothing else, I have to be getting back to my job."

Charley wasn't really surprised that Spae wasn't ready to let him go. She'd been holding something back; his attempt to leave had been designed to get her to the point.

"Actually, there is another matter," she said, as if cued. But then she hesitated. Reluctance, or was she just groping for a place to begin? She found her start point. "Last year there was an incident in the old Providence railroad tunnel. A cave-in. I'm told you know something about that."

The Quetzal affair. He'd been acting on the edge of the law then. Was she going to pressure him to go along on this *Wisteria* killer hunt? "Suppose you tell me first how you know about that business?"

"I—" Spae started, then looked at the kid. "The two of us were in the area at the time."

The kid didn't look happy to be included. "Just how much are you going to tell him, Doctor?"

"He needs to know that we have an honest interest in this, John." To Charley she said, "You do know about the incident?"

"I know something about it." Having been there—not officially, mind you. Apparently they didn't know he had been there, but they had some clue that he'd been involved. So what was their angle?

Charley remembered the two streeters who had gone into the tunnel against his warning. A woman and a tall skinny guy. He looked across the table at Spae and Bennett. A woman and a tall skinny guy. They hadn't been found inside and it had been assumed that they were buried in the cave-in along with the monster. If Spae were wearing ragged street clothes instead of her suit she might look like—"Are you telling me that you were there?"

"Yes," Spae said. "We—John mostly—were responsible for the cave-in."

Quite a claim. Charley took another look at the kid. If what Spae was saying was true, ignoring him wouldn't be bright. And if what Spae was saying was true, Charley and a lot of other people had a lot to thank him—and her—for. But the tunnel had been guarded at both ends and searched from front to back. The only people the search had turned up had been dead. "You couldn't have been there."

"Why? Because *you* didn't see us?" the kid asked.

"Yeah," Charley said. He realized that he had just admitted to being there.

"Let's just say we left by another route," Spae said.

"A side tunnel?"

Spae sighed. "I really think you would prefer not to know."

People who caused cave-ins and disappeared into thin air? Maybe she was right. Then again, maybe not. Clearly they knew about Quetzal and what had gone down. Charley had been left with a lot of questions that night. If he answered their questions, they might answer a few of his. "What is it you want to know?"

"Was something brought out of the tunnel?" Spae asked. "A small object, sort of an abstract sculpture."

"Maybe." Charley remembered the thing he and Hagen had found. He wanted to shiver, recalling the way it had seemed to vanish in the light of their flashlights. "What's this sculpture supposed to be?"

"It's—it's connected to what Quetzal—do you know that name?—was trying to do."

"I've heard the name," Charley admitted. "What's this statue got to do with him?"

Spae spun him a tale about magic talismans and secret cults and some kind of super ritual that the statue was a part of, something that was going to send the world to hell in a handbasket. If he hadn't worked with her, he would have called the guys with the jacket that buckled in the back. Instead he listened, and things started clicking into place. Martinez had connected the *Wisteria* killer to Anton Van Dieman, but only with circumstantial evidence. Charley hadn't thought about the tunnel stuff until now. Van Dieman was the name of the suit who'd been with the feds when they'd busted into the tunnel, the guy who'd taken the statue. Two Van Diemans? Unlikely. This mess had too many connections for coincidence.

"This is way the hell out of my league," he said when Spae finished.

"Tell us about the *telesmon*," Spae insisted. "Where do you think it is *now*?"

Odd emphasis on the "now." "Your thing, whatever it is, went home with the feds. A suit named Van Dieman seemed very happy to have it. He's probably got it on his desk or something."

"Who's Van Dieman?" the kid asked.

"Trouble," Charley replied, trying to make it convincing. "He's a big league corp honcho with federal connections. Understand?"

"So you won't help," Spae said.

"Like there was something I could do. I'm just a cop, Doctor. The feds took your statue, just like they took the *Wisteria* case."

"Then we'll have to get help elsewhere," she said.

She was missing a connection. "If you're thinking about trying close to home, think again," he told her. Her confused look confirmed that she didn't have the picture. "Look, there's only so much I can say, you know. Just don't go diving in without looking. There are some big boys who are probably up to their necks in this one. People who just might have a say in what happens in your life. They play to win, Doctor."

Her eyes narrowed, suggesting that she was finally catching on.

"Let's just say that if you like your job, you might not want to be getting in the way of whatever the hell is going on." Charley continued, "You might want to try some reading before you go to bed tonight." He slipped a disk out of his pocket and put it on the table. It held the *Wisteria* files— source erased, of course, but all speculation included—that he'd gotten from Pamela Martinez. Let Spae make what she could of Martinez's ideas.

"That's it?" the kid said, taking the disk from the table. Charley thought about stopping him, but Spae didn't seem concerned. Charley let it go. The kid flipped the disk up and caught it, looking from it to Spae. "So much for him being helpful. This ain't no benign talisman."

Charley didn't care for the way the kid seemed to dismiss him. "Look, kid, I don't know anything about any talismans, good or bad. Maybe I can't give you the kind of help you came looking for, but I might be able to point you in the right direction." At least he hoped it would be the right direction. There were players in this, and relationships between them that Charley hadn't identified. Charley didn't like not knowing; he was trusting Caspar on this, and Caspar hadn't yet double-crossed him. For the sake of Spae and the kid, he hoped this wasn't the first time. "Someone I know thinks you need to contact the Pend Foundation."

Spae looked puzzled. "Why them?"

"My friend didn't say."

"Your friend got a name?" the kid asked suspiciously.

"Yeah," Charley said, but he didn't offer it.

"I understand your reluctance to name your source, Detective," Spae said. "But you must understand our position as well. How can we know that your source is friendly to our endeavors?"

"You've got mutual concerns," he told her. "He opened the files on *Wisteria* for me."

"This is not a time for questioning the motives of allies," Spae said. "Could your friend be the one who arranged this meeting?"

Charley hadn't thought of that. Caspar was a whiz in computers. "Maybe."

"Perhaps John and I had better visit the Pend Foundation. Their headquarters are here in Providence, are they not?"

"South Main Street. Got their own building near Wickenden."

"Thank you. Of course, there are other things that need our attention and we'll be looking into them as well." Spae and the kid got up. Charley started to as well, but Spae motioned him to sit. "Stay for dinner, Detective. It's on my card. Enjoy a good meal while you can. Consider it a 'thank you' for services rendered."

Not often he was offered a free meal, especially for such minimal "services." He suspected another motive, though. "Doctor's orders?"

"A strong recommendation."

He had refused to join her crusade, and now she didn't want him following her and possibly messing up whatever it was she was planning. He understood that. If she was going to bring Metadynamics and the feds down on herself, it was easy to see how staying out of this was in Charley's best interests. "Whatever you say, Doctor."

There was some more polite, pointless, conversation-ending talk before they headed for the door. Charley realized there was something he ought to do. Spae and the kid were at the door.

"Hey, Dr. Spae!" he called. "Good luck. You too, kid."

He suspected they'd be needing all the good luck they could get.

CHAPTER
36

The Pend Foundation might own their own building, but to judge by the sign outside, they weren't the only tenants. Nor were they particularly security conscious. Though it was after business hours when John and Dr. Spae got there, the main doors were still unlocked. The vestibule held a magcard call box and was filled with a high-pitched buzz that suggested that whatever was installed to watch the lobby was glitched. John looked for cameras and didn't see any. Dr. Spae opened the inner door and barged into the small lobby. She went straight for the elevators while John was still looking for which floor they were headed to. "Top three," he told her as he hopped aboard. The doors nearly snapped closed on his coattails. The building only had a dozen floors and the ride didn't take long. The elevator door opened, and they found themselves facing the muzzles of half a dozen automatic weapons held by dwarves in black SWAT suits.

John decided that maybe he was wrong about the laxity of the foundation's security.

One dwarf among the welcoming committee was not pointing a gun at them. He was taller and slimmer than the rest and his beard was shot through with gray. When he spoke, he sounded as though he had a sore throat.

"Curious timing for a visit."

"Sörli?" Dr. Spae said it as if she didn't really believe it.

"Common enough mistake," the dwarf said. "Hagen's the name, Dr. Spae."

"You know *my* name?"

"We know quite a bit about you, Doctor," said another voice. "About both of you, actually. Hello, John."

The new speaker came into view: another dwarf. This one wore a suit. It was John's turn to do a recognition trip. "Wilson."

Wilson flashed John a smile that lasted a microsecond. "Now that we're done with the introductions, suppose you tell us why you're here before someone gets the urge to un-cramp his trigger finger."

"We were told that something we're looking for was here," Dr. Spae said.

"Something or someone?" Wilson asked.

"I don't understand your question," Dr. Spae said.

John thought that he might understand. When last seen, Bear had hinted that he was going back to the dwarves. John, to see if he'd guessed right, said, "Listen, Wilson, we didn't come here to waste time with you. Let us see Bear."

"I told you they knew," Hagen said.

Wilson gave him an annoyed glance. "If they didn't, you just told them."

Dr. Spae had her own take. "If Bear's here, that must mean—"

"That we ought to talk to him before we say anything else," John finished.

Dr. Spae shut her mouth and went along. Together she and John insisted on talking to no one but Bear. The dwarves didn't like the idea.

"Secure them and tranq them down before they can interfere," said Hagen by way of solution. "We're wasting time."

"A commodity we have in only slightly greater quantity than information," Wilson said. "Given the matter to hand, it should be obvious even to you that we may be dealing with synchronism here. If so, we would be remiss to ignore it."

"They are a security risk," Hagen insisted.

Wilson waved a hand to take in the armed dwarves. "Bullets remain faster than spells."

Telling John and Dr. Spae to follow him, Wilson led them away from the reception area. John wondered if the concession might be a ploy, but he went along. So did Dr. Spae. What other option did they have? Hagen and the black-clad dwarves fell in behind.

Wilson took them through an office and up two flights of an internal staircase. They encountered no one. The level they debouched on was of an entirely different character from the lobby's wood and greenery; its wallscreens and banks of long narrow desks with computer stations reminded him of vid versions of military command centers. At one end was a slightly raised platform in front of a blanked view window. Wilson went straight to the door in that wall, palming the lock. The room beyond was a commander's office, to judge by the central dais surmounted by a single chair and the cluster of lesser chairs ringing the edge of the raised area. One of the wallscreens displayed an annotated map of North America. The light from the screen streamed across the room like that from a cathedral's stained-glass window, illuminating the two people in the room's center.

Bear, looking fit and healthy, was seated in the commander's chair, and Dr. Spae's old partner Holger Kun stood at his side. Bear was wearing a business suit, which made the dark-bladed sword lying across his knees look more than a little out of place. Kun wore black fatigues and web gear, the same pattern as that of the dwarves, and had an H&K Viper slung over his shoulder. Both men looked to the newcomers as they entered.

"Kun? What the hell are *you* doing here?" Dr. Spae burst out.

"Good evening, Doctor," he said.

"Mr. Kun has joined my staff, Dr. Spae." Bear nodded in John's direction. "We seem to have changed partners."

"This is not, like, a permanent arrangement," John told him.

"Really? Well, whatever the arrangements, the two of you have delayed the start of an important operation. I would like to say that I am happy to see the both of you, but I'm not sure that I should. Given your associations I have to wonder if you might oppose the success of our operation."

"We don't know anything about your operation," John told him.

Bear looked to Dr. Spae, who was now staring at the wallscreen. "Is that so, Doctor?"

"I think you might be surprised," she replied.

"How so?"

Dr. Spae indicated the wallscreen. "If I understand the map correctly, I'd say that we are after the same man."

"But do we have the same goals?" Wilson asked. His fingers played on the controls set into the arm of one of the subordinate chairs. The room's lighting came up as the wallscreen blanked. "Your associations suggest otherwise."

"What do you mean by that?" Dr. Spae asked testily.

"Consider the elf," Hagen said, gesturing toward John. "After denying his connections with Bennett, he goes with him, not once but twice, and the second time to train in the otherworld. Hardly the choice of someone opposed to Bennett's schemes."

"Bennett's got nothing to do with this," John protested. "I'm here because I agreed to help Dr. Spae."

"Do you deny that you accepted his call to training?" Wilson asked. His tone was only marginally more polite than Hagen's.

John shrugged. "What's the point? You've already judged and condemned me."

"Jack, your decision to deal with Bennett was a choice you made for yourself," Bear said. "Such decisions have consequences. At the very least, they make you less trustworthy in some people's eyes."

"People like you?"

Bear looked solemn. "Among others."

"Yeah? Well, too bad. It seems like I'm spending most of my time these days telling people that I'm me and not him, so I suppose another time isn't going to hurt. I'm *me,* not *him.* Got it? I'm through with Bennett. Relationship flatlined. Game over. Program ended. He's got nothing I want."

Bear looked at him thoughtfully. "Honestly?"

"You think I'm lying? You want me to take a lie detector test?"

"Wouldn't do any good," Wilson said. "We don't have any calibrations for an elf."

"Then I guess you'll just have to take my word for it." John didn't really care whether they did or not.

"We don't have to take your word for anything," Hagen said.

"Hagen," Bear said, clear warning in his voice. He sat with Caliburn across his knees, his fingers caressing the hilt. "This issue does not concern you and yours; it is between Jack and me. If he says that he has turned his back on Bennett, I believe him."

Had John heard right?

Hagen sputtered. "But he's an el—

"I know what he is!" Bear roared. The dwarves, even Hagen, looked abashed. John was a little stunned himself. He knew what Bear thought of elves, and he'd known even before this loud admission that Bear knew John was an elf. He was even more astonished at what Bear said next.

"More importantly, I know *who* he is. His word is good enough for me. I took him as my *comes,* and he has proven loyal. My *comes* he was, my *comes* he is. Do you wish to question the evaluation?"

No one said anything.

"Even good men can be misled for a time," Bear said. "Jack says he's here because of you, Dr. Spae. I know you less well. What *about* you, Dr. Spae? Mr. Kun has told me quite a bit about you. He speaks highly of you, but he also tells me that you work for Lowenstein Ryder Priestly & Associates. Is that correct?"

"What does it matter who signs my paycheck?"

Hagen snorted. "Your paycheck? Is that how you define your loyalties?"

Dr. Spae ignored him and spoke to Bear. "If Kun has told you anything about me, you know better than that."

"Loyalties are important," Kun said impassively.

Dr. Spae stared at Kun. Something passed between the two former Department M agents. John could only guess what. Spae nodded as if something had just made sense.

"This is about the connection between Metadynamics and the monster, isn't it?" The edge in Dr. Spae's voice told John that she was nearing the end of her patience.

"What connection would that be, Doctor," Wilson asked with mock innocence.

"Don't patronize me, you scraggly bearded rock hopper!" Dr. Spae exploded. "I know the danger here better than you! If you think I'd have a part in aiding Van Dieman and his pet monster you should be shot before you infect anyone else with that insanity. Besides, I don't think you can afford to cut us out of this operation."

"And why is that, Doctor?" Bear asked.

"Because you're playing catch-up and there isn't enough time left for that."

"We are quite prepared to chase down Van Dieman, and to deal with him and his 'pet monster,' " Hagen said.

"Chase him all you want, little man. You won't catch him. Not in time, anyway. He's got too good a lead. *We*, on the other hand, know where he's going." Dr. Spae smiled at the dwarves. "Like us or not, you need us."

"I would wager that we could say the same, Doctor," Wilson said. "You came here to do more than talk to Art, didn't you? There was something else you sought. Yes, your eyes answer when your tongue does not." He turned to Bear. "See where she looks. They came for Caliburn."

"We came looking for a talisman," John said. "We didn't know it was Caliburn."

"But I'd guessed," Dr. Spae added.

John snapped a glance at her. She hadn't confided her suspicions to him. Had Caliburn's identity as the talisman been hinted at in the files Detective Gordon had given them? John wished he'd ignored her statement that there wasn't anything important in those files and gone ahead and scanned them after she had finished with them. *Too little time,* she had said. *Can't afford to waste it.* What else was in those files that he ought to know?

Hefting the sword, Bear said, "So you wanted this, to deal with Van Dieman."

Spae nodded. "He has a *telesmon* of great power. It's going to take another to counter it."

"You would be the one to know," Bear said. "Tell me, Doctor, are you willing to kill Van Dieman to stop him?"

"Yes," Dr. Spae answered.

"With your magic, if need be?"

Dr. Spae hesitated, but her answer was still "Yes."

"I believe you," Bear said. "You think him that dangerous, then?"

"I do. He believes himself to be what Luciferius called the Opener of the Way. He may be right."

"So he *is* of the Followers of the Glittering Path," Hagen said.

"What matter which cult? We knew he was a serpent lover," Bear said. "Our war has always been against them, whatever false face they wore. Will you fight any harder now that you know the name of his cult?"

"No," Hagen admitted. "But I do like knowing just who it is that we're going up against."

"It is clear that you understand the danger, Doctor," Wilson said. "And you understand the press of time. Let us waste no more of it. Tell us what you know. Where is he going?"

"Only if we're in on the hunt," Dr. Spae said.

"All men—ah—people of goodwill are welcome in the war against the minions of the Wyrm," Bear said.

"I want a specific assurance that you'll take us along to confront him," she said.

"Don't you trust us?" Wilson asked.

"You have to ask?" she shot back.

"You're in," Bear said.

"I want to hear it from them," Dr. Spae added, looking at Hagen and Wilson.

"Since Art vouches for you, you have a place," Wilson said. "Now will you tell us what you know before it is too late for all of us?"

Dr. Spae told them what she and John had learned from Carter. The Antarctic destination clearly came as a surprise to Bear and the dwarves. Wilson and Hagen moved to seats at the chair consoles. Wallscreens sprang to life, cascading through maps and data fields as they reviewed options. It was, they concluded, just possible to intercept Van Dieman if he continued his slow, stealthy approach to the polar continent. New plans were contrived. John listened carefully to the proposals for ambushes along Van Dieman's route. To him, the only place that seemed to be a likely site was what Hagen called the "choke point" at McMurdo Station. The Antarctic research station was the only place they could be reasonably sure that Van Dieman would show up. As the discussions got more focused, John faded out, bored by the logistical details.

Bear turned to John. "What about you, Jack? Are you ready to take on this battle?"

Hell, no! As he had learned, real battles weren't as much fun as virtuality battles, but there were some things you couldn't let go. "I'll do what I have to do."

"Good man."

John had forgotten how much he enjoyed praise from Bear. He wondered whether this new phase of their relationship would be as good as their time among the Dons. No, not as good—better. All he had to do was look around at the Pend Foundation's material wealth to see that it would be better, at least more comfortable although possibly more dangerous. Thinking about danger, he wondered anew about something he had noticed when he had first arrived. "How come you aren't suited up like the others?"

"Because I'm not going."

How could that be? "Why not?"

"Van Dieman is not the only agent of the Wyrm. We are engaged in a war; stopping him is but one battle."

"I thought this was like Armageddon or something."

"It may be, or may not. I'm no prophet, to tell one way or the other. Everything we know says that it's important, but other things look important too. A man can't be in two places at once, and there are matters that require me to be here. Believe me, I'd rather be fighting, but I don't see that there's a better allocation of forces to be made. I feel better about it with you and Dr. Spae going."

"But what about Caliburn? We need it to counter Van Dieman's *telesmon*."

Bear looked at the sword, turning the blade slightly so that light flashed along the strangely dark steel. "It is something of a remedy against hostile magic, but it is much more than that. Sometimes I think that I can see the health of the land mirrored in its steel, but such visions are fleeting and hardly clear. When I look at it now, I am troubled and wonder if I was wise to seek it out. This age is not much for swords.

"I hope that all the trouble we went through to get it back wasn't in vain. You know, Jack, when I first woke back at your slump, I thought that I had lost it, and I wasn't sure whether or not to be glad; but it turned out that Wilson and his people had held it safe for me. They made quite a ceremony about returning it to me, especially for a people who profess to dislike all things that partake of magic." He looked down at the sword. "Some burdens, it seems, one can never lose."

"It's a good thing you didn't lose it," John said. "We need it against Van Dieman. We need *you.* "

"I think you're right that there is a need for the sword," Bear said. "But I'm not so sure about the other. Or rather, I *am* sure that you're not the best judge. The sword is needed, yes; but you know I am not the only one to have ever carried and used this."

John suddenly saw where Bear was headed. He remembered the palace of the Lady of the Lakes. He had handled Caliburn then. He hadn't known how to unlock its power, but back then he hadn't needed the secret; he had needed a sword more than a talisman. The situation was different now, and Bear wasn't locked in a spell this time. Bear would be able to tell John what he needed to know. The loan of the sword would confirm Bear's trust in John.

Bear started to stand and John backed away to give him room. The others stopped their discussion and turned to look. That was fine by John. He didn't mind their watching. Bear cleared his throat and spoke.

"Mr. Kun, would you do me the honor of carrying Caliburn into this battle?"

What?

"I thought I was supposed to be your *comes!*" John was embarrassed to hear the hurt in his own voice.

Bear handed the sword to Kun before turning to John and saying calmly, "Caliburn is not for your kind to use."

Holger was stunned by Bear's offer. He was holding Caliburn before he realized that he had accepted the offer.

Caliburn, the sword of King Arthur.

Holger had grown up knowing the weapon by the name Excalibur; he could not recall the number of times that in the dreams and daydreams of childhood, he had drawn the sword from the stone to vanquish the enemies of Christendom and bring justice to the oppressed. But this was no dream. Holger held in his hand the most famous sword in the world. A distant voice urged him to report the acquisition of such an item, but he ignored it.

Caliburn was not meant for your kind either, Department M.

Not for your kind, Bear had said to John Reddy, and the kid wasn't taking it well. Holger thought that maybe Bear ought to say something else to the kid, but if any explanations were to be made, they were Bear's to make. Bear let his bald statement stand, and the kid didn't challenge it with more than a blazing glare that shifted from Holger to the sword to Bear, where it stayed.

Bear seemed to find the mission more important than Reddy's hurt feelings. "So do you have a timetable yet?" he asked Wilson.

"Since the destination has some special requirements, we're looking at a little delay, but I think that we can get delivery of the necessary supplies in about an hour. The delay shouldn't affect intercept."

"Good. Keep Mr. Kun informed. He's in charge now."

Hagen's expression soured a little at that announcement. The dwarf had expected otherwise. Well, so had Holger, but being placed in command of the field op was not as great a surprise as being entrusted with Caliburn. Still, having command of it put this op into new perspective for Holger, and a lot of details that he had only superficially noted suddenly became more interesting to him. While the others attended to their own last-minute details, he put himself in one of the console chairs and reviewed the plan and its timetable. He wanted to make sure that he had all the details right. He left it to Hagen to ensure that the others completed their own preparations.

The supplies Wilson spoke of were cold weather suits and special lubricants for their weapons. They arrived on time aboard a verrie that looked too sleek for its public bus markings. Ten minutes later, leaving Bear and Wilson on the roof of the Pend Building, the team was on its way to rendezvous with the long-range Mitsutomo-owned transport aircraft that awaited them at T. F. Green Airport and would carry them most of the way to their destination. The transfer at Green went without a hitch. Holger could only hope that the rest of the op went as smoothly.

Holger used the first part of the trip to review the McMurdo Station site plans. McMurdo had once been dependent, directly and indirectly, on government sponsorship, but as public support for such distant and seemingly frivolous operations had waned over the years, corporations had taken over the burden of the day-to-day aspects of the base as well as nearly all the research projects. Station operations were now controlled by a consortium of corporations. The U.S. government remained involved, using its military forces for resupply of the base and to provide transportation to and from the station, but the bill was footed by the consortium. One member of the consortium was Mitsutomo, and Hagen's connections had gotten them the necessary clearances for the team to visit the base.

Ostensibly they were an evaluation team checking into the progress of facility reconstruction at McMurdo Station. Almost a year ago, the station had been devastated by a fire, of officially unknown origin. Dr. Spae's data suggested an origin—an origin that implicated the harbinger creature, since two of the bodies recovered from the wreckage of the base fit the profile of the creature's kills. Whatever had caused the fire, McMurdo had been closed down since the beginning of the last Antarctic summer. The corporate sponsors had begun rebuilding the station, but planned research was still off-line; only construction, transport, and weather crews were on site, and they were operating at skeletal levels. Holger was glad of that; the chance for collateral casualties in a place as confining as a cold-weather base was high. He reviewed Hagen's corporate clearances; they looked sufficient to generate plausible orders that would keep uninvolved parties clear of any danger.

The involved parties were another issue.

Holger considered the resources available to his strike team. The core was the dozen dwarven commandos, headed by Hagen. Holger had seen them go through some drills and knew that none of the dwarves were novices. If they were as steady as the dwarves he'd faced in the otherworld, they'd be good troops.

Dr. Spae and John Reddy were supposed to be the magical arm of the operation. He'd worked with Spae before and had a good idea of her measure. She was impulsive but dogged, and her skills had improved dramatically since their trip to the otherworld. According to reports the dwarves had shown him, she was capable of things he didn't care to think about. In fact, he tried not to think too hard about her at all, because it tended to rouse the voices, and he was tired of their lies about her.

Reddy was problematical. He was an elf—something Holger still had trouble accepting—and the dwarves distrusted him. Failure of confidence could destroy a mission team from within, and Holger could only hope that the dwarves would have the discipline to avoid that pitfall. He wasn't sure that he could expect the same from Reddy. He remembered the kid as a team player and steady enough in the otherworld, but Reddy had clearly seen some hard mileage since then. Still, when they'd been facedown in the pot, Reddy had broken Bennett's spell and saved them. That went a long way with Holger, and he hadn't yet had the chance to even thank Reddy, let alone repay the debt. Given the kid's reaction to Bear giving Caliburn to Holger, this wasn't the time to try. He hoped Reddy wasn't prone to letting jealousy and disappointment rule him.

Holger wasn't about to second-guess Bear's decision.

Logistics were much better than he could have hoped. They had good tech, which Wilson had informed him was ahead of the cutting edge, being of dwarvish work. He was willing to believe it after the demonstration they had given him. The cold suits were certainly better than anything he'd seen in ECSS service. Their weapons, from personal sidearms to the heavy gear four of the dwarves were carrying, were all of proven battlefield reliability.

He would have been happier if they'd had better control of their transportation to the site. Relying on Mitsutomo pilots bothered him a little, but so far they had shown a reassuring lack of interest in their passengers and their passengers' business; and they would be out of the picture as soon as the team was landed at McMurdo.

Additional resources, personnel or matériel, were limited

at the ambush site, and the team would be working to keep the resident personnel as clear of danger as possible. It would mean no additional help, but it would also mean no witnesses and no collateral casualties. The trade-off was reasonable, especially since their brief was to stop Van Dieman quietly. But if quiet wasn't possible, the mission had to go ahead however necessary. They had to stop Van Dieman and his monster regardless of witnesses and casualties.

But could they do the job? They were facing an enemy of mostly unknown resources. Holger found that very uncomfortable.

They knew that Van Dieman was traveling with conventional security. Hagen's Mitsutomo analysts reported that Van Dieman's bodyguard consisted of an assortment of mercenaries and Metadynamics personnel the latter presumably men who Van Dieman considered personally loyal. The bodyguard was likely under the command of a freelance operative called Benton, not Registered but listed in several unpublished databanks as an expediter with a good record of success. The spotty record that the dwarves had been able to supply suggested a man of strong physical assets and stronger covert skills. He would be a formidable opponent, but he was the sort of opponent with whom Holger had been trained to deal. Aside from Benton, the composition and capabilities of the bodyguard were unknown, but several other freelancers previously associated with Benton had made sudden trips to New York during Van Dieman's stay, and a handful of Metadynamics personnel had taken trips to Kennedy about the same time and then disappeared. Holger reviewed their stats: muscle and security specialists all. Some of the forces that Benton had gathered had been told off to provide a cover team; it had already been encountered by the team of dwarves in direct pursuit. After studying the reports, he estimated a minimum cadre of three with a probable maximum of eight would be accompanying Van Dieman.

But men, however well trained and equipped, weren't Holger's greatest worry. That was reserved for the creature that Dr. Spae called a harbinger. Tactically, the monster was totally unknown, but clearly capable of killing. Just the thought of its presence made Holger want to reconsider his involvement, but he couldn't back out now. He could only hope that Spae would have the means to deal with it.

They had hours of flight to go, plenty of time for talking. He'd need that time to try to work out some of the rough spots in his team. The loan of Caliburn was the mark of Bear's trust, his faith that Holger was in control and that Holger could do what needed to be done.

Holger didn't intend to fail that trust.

CHAPTER
37

In a continuing misunderstanding of his role, Juarez, the leader of Van Dieman's most loyal band of followers, sought to interpose himself between Van Dieman and Benton. Van Dieman was beginning to think that the man really was too obtuse for his position—an opinion that Benton had expressed more than once during the long trek across the world. Before Benton could restate his opinion, Van Dieman ordered Juarez to let Benton approach and relate his news.

"Fischer reports a new contact with the pursuit," Benton reported. "They have accessed the transaction files of Suong Transport and the specification files on the *Briz Bane*. This is a more serious compromise of security than the San Diego encounter."

Fischer was the head of the team they had left behind to foil pursuit, and Suong Transport's *Briz Bane* was the ship that had launched the Mitsubishi-Hawker Petrel™ in which they were now traveling. The security breach Benton alluded to was a clash between Fischer's team and the pursuers, shortly after Van Dieman had departed San Diego. At the time, Benton had feared that the pursuit would be awaiting them when they reached port, but red herrings had been sufficient. Now, no doubt, Benton feared that the pursuit had picked up their trail again, at a time when red herrings and misdirection could have little value because their goal was clear. But that also meant the goal was near.

"They are too late," Van Dieman said.

The harbinger uncoiled from the depths in which it hid, as if it could sense that they were near the end of the penultimate flight. Van Dieman looked out the window of the verrie. The broken ice at the sea's edge was gone now. Solid ice below. Whiteness stretched to eternity, broken only by the dark smudge ahead that was McMurdo Station. No one could catch them now. The station's airstrip control had already given them clearance to land.

"Recommend direct flight to the destination, if possible," Benton said.

He'd known that McMurdo was not the ultimate destination, because of Van Dieman's insistence on acquiring a more suitable craft than the Petrel. The verrie was a good craft, and well suited to its ship-to-shore role, but not as completely adapted to the rigorous Antarctic conditions as the Omni Dynamics Snowhawks™ that served McMurdo Station. The Snowhawk was a frigid-conditions variant of the rugged Skyhawk™, a milspec utility verrie and workhorse platform for most of the Northern Alliance Defense Organization and a good many other militaries as well. A Snowhawk could make the trip into the interior in weather that would ground the Petrel. And a Snowhawk *would* make the trip, just as soon as they commandeered one.

And as soon as the harbinger ascertained just where they were going. It had communicated to Van Dieman the nature and importance of their destination, but lacking an understanding of maps, it could only give him vague impressions of the location. It asserted that it would know once they were on the ground. Sensing its assurance and eagerness, he believed it.

"We proceed as planned," Van Dieman told Benton.

Behind and above him the pitch of the engines changed. Hydraulics sighed and moaned as the craft's stubby wings began to rotate in their mounts, shifting from horizontal flight mode to vertical for the final approach to the pad below.

The harbinger's presence touched his mind. He offered i

the use of his eyes to look down at their destination. It accepted, and he felt a sense of something akin to nostalgia as
their gaze drifted over the fire-wrought devastation that
marred so much of the station.

Something else stirred in the harbinger's mood. Concern.

Something was not right.

Van Dieman extended his senses, searching for the source
of the unease he now shared with his companion. All appeared tranquil, calm, quiet, as it ought to be. *As it ought to
be?* The harbinger thought not, and he agreed. There should
have been some ground crewman awaiting them, but there
was no one in sight. McMurdo Station, a facility big enough
to house two thousand people at the height of summer occu-
pancy, appeared to be deserted. No people? Though the corporate sponsors had ordered an official shutdown, that could
not be so! There were crews here to work on the reconstruction. Where were *they?* He saw no one, sensed nothing—but
it was a curious nothing that hinted at something lying beneath it.

And then he knew. The *nothing* and the *no one* were
wrong. The *as it ought to be* was a lie. They were landing in
the jaws of a trap!

Holger watched the slowing Petrel with trepidation. Electronic communication with the verrie had been perfunctory,
just the minimum. Hagen's patch into the base's net allowed
them to control that communication, feeding the incoming
flight an artificial rendering of the station's air traffic con-
troller. There had been no indication that their substitution
had raised their suspicion. So why was the Petrel hanging
there? Why was the pilot hesitating?

"He knows we're here," John Reddy said.

How?

The Petrel started to tilt, her nose shifting to the east. She
was refusing to land.

"Is he running?"

Spae answered him, "He's bypassing us. All that work for nothing."

With the verrie headed away from the prepared landing spot, the binding they had laid out to hold the harbinger would be wasted.

"You said he'd have to land here and switch craft," Kun said.

She shrugged. "Maybe he isn't intending to go as far inland as we thought. We'll have to chase him."

The Petrel had almost cleared the base perimeter. The craft was gaining altitude, presumably preparing to shift to horizontal flight mode.

"Fighting on his ground is not advisable."

"Well, we're not going to catch him here," Spae pointed out unnecessarily.

She was right; the catch option had closed. The Petrel's engines were tilting. She was gathering speed.

"Corey, Nasham, hard spill," Holger ordered through the radio link.

The two dwarves popped the tops on their concealment shelters at the eastern edge of the base perimeter. They emerged, folding out the sighting mechanisms of their Gendyne Hunter II™ shoulder launchers as they ran to take up firing positions. The Hunters were the same model that the dwarves had used in their attempt to take down Van Dieman's aircraft in Boston. One had nearly gotten Van Dieman and his monster then. Two should be more than sufficient. Almost in unison the rockets screamed away from the launchers, trailing billowing tails of exhaust through the chill Antarctic air.

John knew what had tipped off their enemy, because he'd felt Van Dieman pressing against his spell of illusion cloaking the ambushers. That nonphysical touch had felt slimy, somehow, but assured and competent. John was sure that the mage had seen through the spell and warned his companions about it. Kun's solution was blunt and direct: a pair of sur-face-to-air missiles.

John watched the contrails stretching out toward the flee-ing Petrel. The fluffy white lines looked innocuous, but they were tipped with death. Those tips grew closer together, con-verging on the dark shape of the Petrel.

The contrails rippled, as if the missiles at their heads were flying through rough air. One went corkscrewing away, reaching for the upper atmosphere, no longer a threat to the Petrel. The other missile began to arc to the left, curving back to the spot from which it had come.

John and his companions stared in disbelief.

The missile screamed over their heads and disappeared be-hind the bulk of the station, hitting a second later in an ex-plosion that threw ice and rock and snow in a geyser taller than any of McMurdo's buildings.

"That was no conventional missile defense," Kun said. "If he can do that, how did they manage to down his craft in Boston?"

"Maybe they caught him by surprise. Maybe he's im-proved his spells. Maybe he's just more powerful now," Dr. Spae said. "It doesn't really matter how. We've got a serious problem."

"Can't you use one of the Snowhawks to shoot him down?" John asked.

"No armament," Kun reminded him.

Antarctica was still demilitarized, all heavy weapons pro-hibited. The antiaircraft missiles they'd used were among the proscribed armaments.

"Looks like we chase him after all," Dr. Spae said.

Having felt Van Dieman's touch, John preferred the idea of taking him down from a distance. "But you said that the closer he gets to his destination, the stronger the harbinger will become. It would be better to stop him now. Maybe if we fire all four launchers at once, he won't be able to stop them all."

"Don't be so sure," Dr. Spae said.

"I'm open to suggestions," Kun said. "Is there no spell you can apply?"

"I thought you wanted the magic passive until we cornered him?" John asked

"No point in that anymore," Kun said. "If he recognized the camouflage illusion, he knows we've got at least one specialist."

"Agreed." Dr. Spae looked unhappy. "He'll be ready to counter any magic directed at him."

John had an idea. "What if he's busy doing something else?"

"The missiles?" Kun asked.

"It might work," Dr. Spae said thoughtfully.

The missiles were only part of John's idea. "More than that. What if instead of trying to do something to *him*, we went after the verrie?"

"He'll be watching for arcane attacks. If an attack is directed anywhere in his vicinity, he'll counter. Overt hostile magics are almost as easy to block as they are to detect."

John had anticipated that response. "But what if rather than trying to make something happen, we made something *not* happen?"

"What are you suggesting?" Dr. Spae asked.

John explained.

"It may be the best chance we have," she said.

"Very well," Kun said. "We'll try it."

While John and Dr. Spae riffled through the doctor's tools and supplies, quickly gathering whatever they could find to ritually enhance their spell, Kun arranged the mundane aspects of the plan. There wasn't much time before the fleeing verrie was out of sight.

Fortunately, Hagen had already ordered the two missile-armed dwarves on the western perimeter up to firing positions that commanded the eastern horizon. When John and Dr. Spae signaled that they were ready—they weren't, but they were as close as they were going to get in the time they had—Kun gave the order to fire and four missiles arched into the sky.

Coincident with the rising smoke and flame of the missiles, John and Dr. Spae launched their astral essences. Dr. Spae, more experienced at projection, led the way. Their speed was that of thought, and they closed the distance faster than the rocket-powered missiles. They slipped past the roiling energies with which Van Dieman battered the incoming missiles, and skirted the darkness coiling around the fuselage of the Petrel. John was glad that they weren't going to do their magic any closer. They approached the starboard engine heedless of what would have been dangerous for physical forms, for neither the whirling rotor nor the churning vortex it created had power to affect their immaterial presences. They alighted on the great cylindrical housing that covered the throbbing power plant driving the rotor.

John touched the engine and felt the heat of the fire inside. It was the fire he had come to deal with. He spoke to it, addressing it by the names he had learned in the otherworld. He told the fire of the frigid air all around it, and of the ice below, and of the cold. He especially told the fire of the deep, deep, deadening cold.

Benton thought they were cooked when he heard the pilot's bleating report of two antiaircraft missiles coming for them. The man was a hireling and had no combat experience. Benton was down the aisle and into the cockpit doorway before the pilot started evasive maneuvering. One glance at the radar screen told Benton that the man's effort's were worthless. The missiles were too close.

Then the threat was gone—one missile heading for orbit and the other back the way it had come. Unnatural. Benton looked to the nearest source of unnatural happenings. Van Dieman was sitting in his seat, eyes closed. To the casual eye he might look asleep, but Benton's was not the casual eye. Van Dieman's temperature was elevated, his blood flow more consistent with serious physical activity than with sleep. A dark, smoky haze hung about his body, but there was no scent of anything burning. Weird. The very sort of thing that Van Dieman had once hired Benton to observe and bring back to him.

Unlike some of his teachers, Benton believed in cause and effect. He'd seen the effect, the redirection of the incoming missiles, but he could see no connection to a cause. Just a suspect. Benton couldn't prove it, but he felt certain that Van Dieman had been responsible for their salvation. In the world Benton understood, such a feat should have taken some very fancy electronics. However Van Dieman had done it, he hadn't done it with electronics.

Still, one had to accept what was, and Benton was happy to accept a save from missiles that would have blown their aircraft to component parts—even if it did leave him feeling unsure about the nature of his employer.

He ordered the pilot to shift to level flight. The faster they were away from McMurdo, the better. Taking the Petrel inland wasn't a good solution, but it beat landing in enemy-occupied territory. Benton had no idea of Van Dieman's limits, but he doubted they were infinite, and where there two missiles, there could be more. The airspace around McMurdo Station was not healthy for them.

When nothing immediately rose to challenge their flight, Benton breathed a little easier. He watched with satisfaction as the base crawled closer to the edge of the map screen. A warning buzzer killed his hopes of an easy escape as four incoming targets appeared on the Petrel's radar screen.

Four surface-to-air missiles.

Van Dieman had dealt with two. Could he deal with four? He'd better be able to, the Petrel didn't have the juice to do anything.

"Forget the evasion," he told the pilot. "Go for speed."

It wasn't much of a hope.

He knew it was no hope at all when one of the engines coughed.

Had they been hit? No, there had been no shock of impact. The radar screen showed the incoming missiles wobbling in their flight. One was already diving back toward the ground.

Then what had happened?

The starboard engine coughed again and died. The Petrel tilted. The pilot fought to compensate for the loss of lift and thrust on that side. If they had been in vertical flight mode, they'd be spinning to destruction. What difference did it make? They were going to be easy prey for the missiles now.

Benton checked the radar just in time to see two of the missiles collide. The Petrel shuddered from the shock of their self-immolating explosion. The last missile veered off course. They were safe.

The port engine emitted a stuttering series of coughs and died as completely as its partner.

Safe?

Whatever had gotten them had gotten them good. They were going down. The idiot pilot was fighting the controls, his copilot trying for a restart. Benton shoved the pilot out of the way and reached down to hit the emergency releases on the tilt hydraulics. The Petrel shuddered and bucked as the massive engines made an inertia shift into vertical flight position. Benton waited anxiously for the vibration that would indicate that the housing had completed the arc and the locks had engaged.

The Petrel was still dropping. Unsecured, Benton was tossed against the cockpit door frame. The craft yawed and he was thrown to the floor. The Petrel leveled out. The locks must have engaged, allowing the rotors to catch air. His ploy had worked! The blades were free-rotating, cushioning the verrie's fall. The landing would be hard but it wouldn't be devastating.

CHAPTER
38

Van Dieman was not surprised when his enemies sent more missiles after him. Indeed, after he had disposed of the first two, he had expected them to send more at once in the vain hope that their first failure had been a fluke. Their delay had puzzled him—until he heard the first sputtering of the Petrel's engines and realized that he had been made a dupe. The second missile attack had been only a diversion. While he had been disposing of the missiles, the enemy mage had been engaged in a subtle but devastating attack.

They were too close to the ground for him to draw upon the harbinger's power to arrest the Petrel's fall. The craft hit hard. A spike of jagged rock tore through the verrie's belly, demolishing all in its path, including one of Benton's men. The Petrel's nose tilted down. The fuselage strained against its impalement, twisted, and, with a rending screech shredded. Frigid Antarctic air whipped into the cabin as the shattered verrie heeled over. The port engine housing jammed against the unyielding ground. The overstressed structural members in the stubby wing snapped and sent lethal shrapnel whirring through the wreckage.

Pain chewed its way into Van Dieman's back and left leg. He screamed in agony and outrage at the darkness seeking to suck him down. He fought against it. In a haze of flashing stars, he tore out the sharp fragment of aircraft composite that had embedded itself in his knee. The lacerations he incurred in his hand were nothing next to the fires that lit his insides.

"Heal me," he ordered the harbinger.

You are broken. Energy is needed for more important things, the creature replied distantly. The harbinger's dark, serpentine image floated above him, but its attention was elsewhere, longing for their now seemingly unattainable destination.

More important? How dare the creature imply he was not worth its effort! "You have the power to heal my injuries. Do so."

No reward for the useless.

"Useless!" The creature's temerity went beyond all bounds. The fire of Van Dieman's anger overwhelmed the pain. The harbinger needed a lesson. He could whip it down, teach it its place—but this was not the time to engage in a dominance battle with a servant chafing at its bonds. The harbinger was right on one point: energy was needed for more important things. Once they were free from these ambushers, however . . . "I could compel you by the terms of your binding, but I am magnanimous. I will merely point out that your goal—our goal!—is still unachieved. You need me, for you have no hands to carry the *telesmon* to its appointed place. You still need me."

Still, came the reluctant response.

Van Dieman knew that it understood. "Take away this pain. The path remains closed unless you do so!"

The pain went away so quickly that it might never have been. A hardness probed at his abdomen. The harbinger's head dipped to that point and nuzzled him. A jagged ceramic shard emerged, passing through his clothes without tearing a thread. The harbinger dropped the shrapnel into Van Dieman's hand. He marveled at it, imagining the damage that such a thing must have done to him. The pain and damage were gone, made nothing by the harbinger's power.

Van Dieman smiled, not from relief as a lesser man might, but from pleasure—the pleasure of his exerting his will upon the rebellious harbinger, and knowing that he was still in control. There was also, of course, the anticipation of showing the harbinger its master's strength.

But the ending of the pain brought back the input of his other senses. From outside the wreck of the Petrel he could hear gunfire.

The harbinger's discipline would have to wait.

He extricated himself from his seat. The *telesmon*'s case was wedged in the ruin of the forward locker. The carrying case had done its job of protecting the precious contents, but would no longer do so, mangled as it was. Van Dieman removed the precious treasure and clutched the *telesmon* to him. Making his way across the uneven floor, he looked at the gaping hole in the Petrel's side. Benton and the rest of Van Dieman's surviving bodyguards had spread out from the wreck in a skirmish line and were moving across the ice field back toward the McMurdo airstrip. From positions at the edge of the buildings, the enemy was firing at them, trying to stop them.

A groan from the cockpit caught his attention. He turned and saw the copilot staggering into the cabin. Beyond him the pilot lay sprawled and dead, impaled on the steering yoke.

"Santiago," Van Dieman said. He read the name on the man's bloodied flight suit as he silently ordered the harbinger to strengthen the man. His servant reported the copilot fit. "Are you well enough to fly?"

"No ship," he replied, slowly but coherently.

"That is a temporary condition," Van Dieman told him.

The harbinger radiated fierce, anticipatory joy.

Holger didn't like the way the firefight was shaping up. Carey was dead and Hagen down, wounded and out of the fight, taking cover before exposure did for him what the enemy's bullets had not. They were now outnumbered locally, and they hadn't managed to put down even one of the six hostiles who had emerged from the wreck of the Petrel. Half of Holger's force was still crossing McMurdo Station from their posts on the far side.

The magical assets didn't offer any help. Spae and Reddy were attempting to weave some kind of magical net to throw over the harbinger should it appear, and weren't available for countering the mundane hostiles. The range of the firefight meant that this wasn't the sort of brawl in which a sword, even a magical one, would be useful. This phase of the op was pure muscle—the kind of fight he preferred.

Only he preferred to win.

He caught a flash of movement out by the wreck of the Petrel. Squinting, he could just make out two figures emerging from the wreckage. One wore an Arctic flight suit, the other a tattered business suit. A business suit? That one had to be the specialist, Van Dieman. Any normal man would have been down from exposure by now.

Holger popped up the image enhancer on his Viper. It was a long shot, not the sort of thing the Viper was designed for, but he knew how to compensate for the drop-off in the Viper's 5mm round. With a bit of luck, this op might soon be over.

But if luck was involved, it was bad.

The image enhancer fuzzed. Holger tapped the reset, trying to clear it, but the magnified image did not return. He got nothing but gray. He snapped down the scope and looked with his own eyes.

What he saw made him shiver.

A rolling wall of opaque mist had risen from nowhere and was drifting toward him from the Petrel.

Dr. Spae cursed, dropping the link between her and John, and he felt the change in the magical ambiance at once. Anxiety gnawed away the last vestiges of his focus. There were spells loose. Van Dieman hadn't been killed in the crash. He and the harbinger were active.

And John and Dr. Spae weren't ready for them.

John looked toward the wrecked verrie, expecting to see some kind of unholy monster rising from the debris, but he couldn't find the craft at all. Some kind of ground fog had come up, concealing it. Then he realized that perhaps he was seeing something monstrous and, if not unholy, at least unnatural. The fog reeked of arcane crafting, sizzling with roiling energies of magic that blinded the inner eye nearly as thoroughly as it did the outer.

Van Dieman's doing.

Something dark and hungry moved in the depths of the swirling opacity. John was intimidated by the thing he felt out there, but he knew that the thing was why they had come. *That* was what they were supposed to stop.

If they didn't do it soon, they might not be able to.

The fog rolled across the ice plain toward the McMurdo airfield. It appeared that Van Dieman wanted his Snowhawk ride into the interior after all.

"Come on, Doctor. We've got to beat him to the verries."

Dr. Spae didn't move. She just stared at the cloud come to earth. " It's so powerful."

John tugged on her arm. "If we get to the airfield we may be able to activate the trap."

"I don't know if it's strong enough."

John didn't know either, but—"It'll have to be."

At least they wouldn't have to foot it to their personal Armageddon. They had the little two-seater GoMo™ all-terrain vehicle they had used to haul the doctor's gear. John got Dr. Spae into the passenger seat, hopped aboard, and kicked the engine to cranky life. Icy pellets of firn sprayed as he peeled out.

Now all they had to do was outrace the fog cloud, get past the gauntlet of the firefight, and activate the spells that they were afraid were too weak to do what they needed to do.

* * *

Benton was unaware of the fog until it rolled over him. The drop in ambient temperature accompanying the vapor was additional evidence of its uncanny nature. More weirdness from the hand of Van Dieman? Then the bastard wasn't dead, as Benton had thought when he'd abandoned the Petrel.

That meant he was still under contract.

Benton couldn't see the front edge of the fog bank, but he suspected the dense grayness was engulfing everything between the Petrel and McMurdo. It wasn't hard to guess Van Dieman's intentions.

Benton shivered, despite his thermal suit, when something unseen moved past him in the fog.

This was not the time to stay put. "Everybody up!" he ordered over the tactical frequency. "Now! Head for the airstrip! They can't see us through this soup."

He didn't know if that was true. The enemy might have enhancement scopes, but they probably hadn't anticipated such an eventuality. He hadn't. Fogs like this weren't part of the normal seasonal weather.

Rather than be paralyzed by the lack of visibility, the best course was to try to take advantage of it, hoping the enemy was similarly disadvantaged. If he was, that was his loss. Cover like this favored the attacker, allowing an unobserved approach.

Benton had an advantage his men lacked. He didn't need a scope to pick out the flickering thermal images against the cold glare of the ice that were the actors in this farce. Watching his men start moving, he waited for a response. There was none. He started after them.

Movement was tricky, because the footing was uneven, and his enhancements didn't help him there. Cold rocks and ice against cold rocks and ice were as invisible to him as to fog-blinded normal vision. Still he made better time than the others. Natural superiority, he supposed.

He had passed the straggling Juarez and Van Dieman's other surviving toady when he spotted another person moving on a converging track. He knew from the squat shape it was one of the enemy. He ripped a burst with his KAR-99 and cut the figure down.

Someone fired back and he knew he wasn't the only one with enhancements. The fire was too on-target to be a response to the sound of his own shot. The enemy's shot missed Benton—barely—but caught one of his own men behind him. Benton shifted into high gear, leaving behind the moaning casualty. Benton knew from Juarez's shouting that he wasn't the wounded man. Not that it mattered which of the toadies had gotten hit—at this point they were just excess baggage, something Benton did not intend to be. He raced for the airstrip, heedless of the risk of a fall.

CHAPTER
39

Van Dieman dragged Santiago through the concealing fog, heedless of the man's whimpers. Santiago's whining grated against his nerves, and Van Dieman considered killing the man just to shut him up, but he couldn't afford to do that; he still needed a capable pilot. When they reached the nearest of the Snowhawks, Van Dieman flung the pilot against the hull of the craft.

"Open it up," he ordered.

Santiago took a moment to realize what he had been brought to, then scrambled to comply. His haste was gratifying, perhaps even necessary. Van Dieman could sense another presence in the fog. He turned to see one of Benton's men approaching.

With Van Dieman's gaze upon him, the man abandoned his stealthy approach and approached with a swagger. This one was called Chase. Van Dieman remembered because he liked this one the least of all Benton's thugs. Chase had never been properly deferential.

"Made it I see," Chase said. "We were coming to get one of the Snowhawks. We were going to come back and get you."

Van Dieman didn't believe that. Underlings of Chase's sort only performed when they were being watched.

"The others have not gotten here yet," Van Dieman said. "You must destroy the other aircraft before joining us. There must be no pursuit."

345

"Sure," Chase said with uncharacteristic eagerness. He ran to do Van Dieman's bidding.

The fog was no barrier to its master's eyes. Van Dieman watched Chase head for the next Snowhawk down the line. He waited until he saw Chase start to open the cabin hatch, then turned and boarded his own verrie. He had no intention of waiting for Chase or any of the others to join him. They were unimportant, save that their actions would continue to occupy the enemy for a bit longer. He no longer needed them to assure that he and the harbinger would get the *telesmon* to the place that awaited. The only one he and his companion needed now was Santiago.

"Take us up," he told the man as he joined him in the cockpit.

"But the fog," Santiago complained. "I can't fly in this fog."

"What fog?"

The air was clear again. Van Dieman wanted no impediments between him and the glory to come.

When Holger saw one of the hostiles fire, he fired back. He missed the man and got one of the others. There was something in the fog that was distorting Holger's vision—he should *not* have missed the shot.

When his target took off like a rocket-assisted rabbit, he guessed that his man was Benton, the hostile's commander. Who else would be likely to display unsuspected abilities? Fog-piercing vision for one, and now unnatural speed. Could he have done something to cause Holger to miss his shot? Whether he had or not, Benton was clearly the most dangerous of the bunch.

Perhaps this was why Holger was here; this might be the part of the fight that was to be his.

Benton was headed for the airfield at full speed, but he had to round an outbuilding to get there. Holger had a shorter course, and he took it. Caliburn, in the scabbard at his back, slapped against him as he ran. He was waiting when Benton rounded the corner.

The mercenary was no fool. He knew Holger had him. He skidded to a stop and dropped his weapon to the ice. Holding his hands up, he strolled closer.

"Stop right there," Holger told him.

But he didn't. Holger wasn't a fool, either. His finger tightened on the trigger of his Viper. Benton twisted away. The bullets only ripped through the mercenary's parka.

God he was fast!

Too fast! Benton changed his evasion to an attack. His foot came up and around, catching Holger on the arm. Hand numbed, he lost his grip on the Viper. It went sailing away.

Both without guns. No matter. Holger went at the mercenary with his hands. The quickness and ferocity of Holger's attack must have caught Benton off guard, because he did nothing more than defend himself in the first exchange. It was Benton's speed more than his skill that saved him from Holger's hammering blows.

"Who the hell are you?" Benton panted as they circled each other warily.

But—as Holger had guessed—the question was intended more to provide a distraction than to elicit an answer.

Benton attacked, striking with dangerous skill and speed. Department M had rebuilt Holger for battle; someone had done the same for Benton. This would be no easy combat. They fell to it. Strike and counterstrike. Grapple and counter. Holger slipped into the intense concentration needed to deal with a threatening opponent. Openings were offered, taken, and countered as the combatants tested each other in the realm where failure was lethal. Rhythms emerged, only to shift dangerously before advantage could be taken. Strike and counterstrike. Time was meaningless. Grapple and counter. Only the opponent mattered. The fight. Searching for an opening, probing until—an opening. Holger shifted lines and launched a kick, but Benton's speed saved him again. The mercenary got an arm up to deflect Holger's foot.

Benton tried to turn the block into a grab—unsuccessfully—but he did manage to shift Holger off balance. Holger threw himself back as he went down, away from his dangerous opponent. Holger landed on his back.

For an instant, the fight was suspended.

The hard steel against Holger's back shocked his brain awake. Could this really be what he was here for? He was carrying Caliburn and this mercenary agent, for all his uncanny speed and strength, was certainly not a problem worthy of the great sword. What if Benton was only a delay, a distraction to keep him from getting Caliburn where it needed to be?

He couldn't afford to take that chance. He had to end this fight. Now!

Caliburn might be a great magical talisman, but it was also a sword and could do a sword's work. Getting to his feet, Holger reached back and grabbed the hilt. In response to his tug, the breakaway scabbard opened. Holger drew Caliburn smoothly down over his shoulder and took up *chudan-no-kamae* stance, aiming Caliburn's point at his opponent's throat.

When unarmed man faced armed man, the outcome was inevitable, unless the unarmed man was significantly superior in skill or physical abilities. Holger didn't think Benton was that good. What did Benton think?

The tension went out of the mercenary's body. Straightening from his fighting crouch, he held his hands wide of his body, a strange smile on his face.

At that moment Holger's reserve team arrived—not exactly late, but not on time either. Over Benton's shoulder Holger could see a Snowhawk lifting off. He left Benton with the dwarves and sprinted for the airfield.

The rolling fog bank caught John and Dr. Spae before they'd gotten halfway to the airstrip. John slowed the MoGo—not enough to be truly safe, but some concession to the drastically reduced visibility was necessary. Every time

John swerved to avoid an obstacle, Dr. Spae yelped and clutched the grab bar.

"You're worse than Kun," she shouted.

He wasn't about to tell her that the only driving he'd done before this was at a video arcade.

Without warning the fog was gone and John found that they were rolling along beside the hangers by the airstrip, headed away from where the Snowhawks were parked. Somehow he had gotten disoriented. He spun the MoGo in a tight turn and gunned the engine, hoping they weren't too late.

The rotors on one of the Snowhawks were spinning up to speed.

No time left. Knowing that he couldn't drive and help activate the trap grid at the same time, he hit the brakes. Dr. Spae began reciting the first phrases of the spell before they skidded to a complete stop. John took her hand, throwing himself into the link that would add his strength to hers.

They weren't fast enough. In a swirl of white, the Snowhawk lifted. The contact with the earth was broken and the chance of tying the harbinger down lost.

New gunfire erupted, announcing that the more mundane battle was rejoined.

"He's gotten away," Dr. Spae said despondently.

"Chill down, Doc. A Snowhawk's a verrie like any other. We brought him down before. We'll just do it again."

John took control of the link and launched their projections after the departing Snowhawk. But Van Dieman had learned their trick. This time John couldn't get near the fire in the heart of the engines. Van Dieman had anticipated their attack and set his pet creature to weave an armor of darkness around the Snowhawk's engine.

Hell, they were back where they'd been before the first missiles had been launched. Only this time, they didn't have any missiles to send after the fleeing verrie.

Kun came pounding toward them across the air strip, covering the distance at surprising speed.

"Looks like we chase him after all," he said when he arrived.

John drove the MoGo and Kun paced alongside. They headed for the nearest Snowhawk. As Kun was opening the cabin door, Dr. Spae said, "I didn't know you were a qualified pilot, Kun."

"I'm not."

"But I am," said a voice from inside. Hagen.

"So this is where you went to ground," Kun said.

"And a good thing too," Hagen said. There was a bloodstained pressure bandage around his leg, but he seemed okay, if a bit pale. His gun was pointed toward the back of the Snowhawk's cabin. "Look what I caught sneaking around."

Climbing aboard, they saw that Hagen had captured one of Van Dieman's bodyguards.

"I believe he had some idea about sabotaging this craft," Hagen said.

"That's what Van Dieman wanted," the man said. "Actually, I had a rather different plan in mind."

"I'll just bet," Dr. Spae said.

"As I told your short friend, I've seen enough to know that helping Van Dieman is the last thing I ought to be doing. I think you have the right of it. He's got to be stopped."

"And you want to help?" Dr. Spae didn't sound like she believed him.

"As a matter of fact, I do," the man said.

Hagen snorted. "And just who the hell are you to do that?"

"They call me Chase. Not that names should matter." Chase swept his gaze across all of them. "And I think that you can use all the help that you can get. I also think that we're wasting time sitting here and arguing. Van Dieman's getting away."

That was certainly true.

"We can't trust him," Hagen said, voicing John's thought.

"I'm not so sure," Kun said. "I think he does want to help. And he's right—we can't afford to waste time. Let's get this thing into the air. We'll sort things out on the way. If we decide not to believe him, we can dump him out the door."

"Good enough," Chase said.

Hagen grumbled, but he said, "Help me up into the driver's seat."

Benton found it a little embarrassing to be under detention by a half-dozen guards none of whom came any higher than his chest, but six guns were higher odds than he wanted to bet against. He let them lead him to one of the construction shacks scattered across the station. The shacks were among the few structures with intact roofs. Czerkas and Juarez, one of his guys and one of Van Dieman's, were already incarcerated inside. They were both wounded; Czerkas had a pressure splint around his left arm, and Juarez's head was swathed in a bloody bandage. One of the shrimp guards used the muzzle of his weapon to issue Benton an invitation to join them. Two of the midgets started removing potentially useful items from the workshed-turned-prison cell.

"So the hotshot couldn't cut it either. No reward for you," Juarez said with a sneer.

Benton ignored him. "Czerkas, you okay?"

"I'll live."

"What happened to Chase and Reg?"

Czerkas didn't look at him. "The midgets caught Reg right when the fog lifted. Chase I didn't see. Got to the verries, I think. I heard a shot from over that way after the first one went up."

Benton had heard the shot too. It had been from a Viper, one of the shrimps' weapons. Czerkas would know that too. Since there had been no return fire, and no verrie had gone north—their plan if they'd captured one—Chase had to be considered MIA at best. More likely he was as dead as Reg.

"You failed the Opener of the Way," Juarez said. "Great will be his retribution for your failure to give your all."

"Yeah? I don't see where you gave *yours*," Czerkas said.

Juarez touched his bandage. "I was not at fault."

Benton shrugged. "Well, retribution comes when it

comes. I know my limits. We did our job, and it didn't work out. There'll be another day. There always is."

A second Snowhawk lifted off and roared overhead, headed east.

"Only if they win," their dwarvish guard said.

"Whatever you say, Shorty."

The guard didn't react to the sarcasm. Once his buddies finished clearing out every visible useful item, the guard backed out and closed the door on the prisoners. Benton listened to the lock dropping in place, a rudimentary thing by the sound of it but strong enough to keep an ordinary man penned in.

"They're determined little buggers," Czerkas commented.

"They cannot hold back the momentum of time," Juarez said sanctimoniously.

The guy had the charm of three-day-old fish. "Maybe, maybe not," Benton said as he walked to the door. "Now why don't you just shut up for a while?"

Benton listened until he was sure the area outside the door was empty, then he levered the door handle down until the retaining bolt snapped. Good thing the shrimps' tactical leader had rushed off without filling his team in on Benton's capabilities.

"Czerkas and I are going to be gone before whoever comes out on top gets back. You can come along too, Juarez, if you think you can pull your weight."

"You have no faith," Juarez said as if it were a condemnation.

"Maybe not, but I have money in the bank and I intend to spend it."

He scanned the area looking for any sign of the guards. They seemed to be well occupied elsewhere. Fine. He took off for the nearest cover, running hard, but not so hard Czerkas couldn't keep up. For a miracle, Juarez wasn't enough of a bastard to yell for the shrimps.

CHAPTER
40

Sitting in the Snowhawk's cockpit, Van Dieman had a much better view of the land over which they flew than he'd had from the cabin of the Petrel. The magnificence of the Transantarctic Mountains lay ahead of them and through gaps between the peaks he could occasionally glimpse a sparkle from the great East Antarctic Ice Sheet beyond them. But the glacier was not their destination; *that* lay among the mountains. Despite the pilot's grumbling about the state of the Snowhawk's engine, they were making good time.

"Weather's closing in," Santiago said, pointing to the sky above the mountains.

The skies were graying, true, but Van Dieman knew that it was magic and not weather that was closing in. He could feel the harbinger squirming, overcoming its fear of flying and reaching out in response to the land below them. He could hear its silent song.

Close. The timorousness that the harbinger had shown on previous flights was gone. It was full of confidence and filling with power. *Very close. Soon now.*

"We will be there soon," Van Dieman said.

The harbinger's song increased its tempo.

The first of the Dry Valleys that they reached was something of a shock after the icy plains that lapped against the mountains. The walls of the valley were steep, like the vertical walls of the desert canyons of the American Southwest. In fact, the vista might have been an old black and white photograph of those badlands. The exposed faces of stone were striped bands of light and dark standing in sharp contrast to each other. Spills of eroded dolerite and sandstone skirted cliffs in sooty-looking talus slopes that flowed down to blend with the rough glacial till that floored the valleys. Nowhere was there any vegetation, any hint of color.

They flew down a long valley and popped up over a rise into another. Side canyons branched off from the main valley. Their flight offered them only glimpses of those lesser branches as they flashed by the rough shouldered mountains standing sentinel at the entrances. One of those canyons held more than geological wonders. One of them—

There.

Van Dieman sensed the point on which the harbinger's attention centered. He directed Santiago to take the craft into the side canyon. As the Snowhawk banked between the shoulders of the mighty cliffs that flanked the entrance, Van Dieman saw that the harbinger was already at work. Its song was not silent here—the eerie melody audible and reminiscent of a lost, lonely wind.

Soil whipped along the canyon's floor, flowing around the larger stones and boulders of the glacial till that blanketed the ancient water-etched basement of the formation. As the harbinger's song grew stronger, the arcane winds moved faster and faster. Stones and pebbles joined the whirling cloud of dust. Faster. Small rocks were added to the dance. A hollow began to appear in the center of the canyon floor at the focus of the whirlwind. The harbinger's song shrieked louder, more compelling and more insistent. The boulders that had stood proud of the till were whipped up into the vortex as the bowl in the soil grew wider and deeper. New boulders appeared like mountains rising from the sea.

But they were not ordinary boulders, for each was long and flat, and there were sixteen of them, four widely spaced sets of four, each set arranged in a rectangle. As more and more of the canyon's fill was drawn up into the harbinger's whirlwind, the boulders were revealed as lintel stones capping monolithic uprights. The tips of other upright stones appeared, stretching in curving arcs between the rectangles. As the new stones appeared, it became clear that they described a circle. One end of each rectangle was a part of the circle. The rectangle of capped stones stood at the quadrant points, their structures offering an entry into the inner precincts of the circle.

Van Dieman understood the privilege of being allowed to see the temple revealed. It was an honor to be present when the gateway was uncovered. It was the time foretold. They had come to the time of the Opening.

The vortex expanded with sudden violence, flinging its lithic burden wide and away from the revealed temple. No boulder, no rock, not even the slightest pebble touched the Snowhawk, enveloped as it was in the power of the harbinger. The verrie continued undisturbed on its approach. In the center of the half-kilometer depression, Van Dieman could see the black altar stone at the heart of the henge. The coiled and entwined whorls carved into the altar's surface were aglow with arcane power.

"What is my role?" he asked the harbinger.

No need for hands.

The obliqueness of its response puzzled him.

Then pain radiated from his left knee and he looked down to see his pants soaked with blood. His back exploded with fiery agony and he nearly fainted from the pain. His insides burned. He understood then that the harbinger had not healed his injuries, but only masked them. It had taken the pain away and made it possible for him to walk and act, but it had done no more than that. Now it had removed that veil and abandoned pretense. And in that moment Van Dieman knew that the harbinger had never been bound by his power. The devious creature had only pretended to be subservient to him. He understood that he had been betrayed. He had been systematically misled and used.

"Liar!" he named the harbinger.

It did not answer his accusation.

"Liar! Is this how you reward the faithful?"

Death, you feared. Life, you wanted. Reward, you asked.

"Yes! Yes! I want to live!"

Life you shall have.

He felt the harbinger's attention shift to Santiago. It took the pilot, draining the life out of the man, but none of those energies, sweeping so tantalizing near, touched him. He understood that the harbinger had left behind fragments of the man, shreds of knowledge and splinters of skill. He felt the harbinger slip into the shell of Santiago and manipulate the little that remained to direct the Snowhawk's course. Paralyzed by the pain, Van Dieman could do nothing but watch as the altar stone grew closer, looming ever larger as the verrie rushed toward it. The harbinger had found a way to deliver the *telesmon* to the necessary spot.

The Snowhawk crashed, but Van Dieman was barely aware of the new violence done to his body, awash as he was in agony. New pain forced its way through his wretchedness as ceramic composite fragments from the verrie's fuselage, and razor-edged shards from the windscreen, tore through his body. Crumpling metal mangled his legs and ground his flesh to hamburger. His wounds should have killed him, but he lived.

Life you shall have, the harbinger had said. He knew the words for a curse.

Smoke filled the air and Van Dieman's lungs. There was fire in the cockpit. Something oily and viscous began to drip onto his shoulder. Fuel or lubricant, its precise nature didn't matter. Whatever it was, it was highly flammable. He called to the harbinger, begging it to save him. Beating his fist bloody against the wreckage that imprisoned him, he screamed promises to the creature. He was willing to do anything for it. Anything!

"Just don't let me burn!"

The harbinger ignored his pleas.

It was singing to the stars.

* * *

Holger was impressed by Hagen's piloting skill. Once they reached the mountains, the dwarf shifted the Snowhawk into vertical mode for maneuverability and kept it there, but he never throttled back. The verrie pitched and yawed as Hagen flung it about, climbing to skim over a ridge or banking to avoid a cliff with the barest of margins. It was a wild, nerve-racking ride, but they steadily closed on the Snowhawk that they pursued.

The Dry Valleys through which they flew were strange, the bare ground out of place in this continent of ice. It seemed wrong somehow. He wanted to close his eyes and make it all go away, but he couldn't. Van Dieman's verrie was ahead of them somewhere, and every pair of eyes were needed to spot him. Holger had a duty.

Caliburn lay in his lap—the only way to carry the sword, since he'd had to take off the back-slung scabbard to strap into the verrie's seat. The sword's quick release scabbard exposed most of the blade; Holger ran his hand along it, feeling the cool calmness of the dark steel. The worn leather of the grip felt comfortable under the fingers of his hand. He was flying into battle armed with a sword and an automatic weapon.

Strange, but somehow right.

The strange had become his commonplace. There was no reason for an iceless valley in Antarctica to seem strange, was there? It was what it was, as he was what he was. There was nothing to do but accept it.

"What's that?" Hagen pointed to what looked like a column of smoke rising from somewhere ahead of them.

Holger squinted to see it better. What appeared to be smoke was windborne soil and rocks twisting in the grip of a monstrous dust devil.

"The work of the harbinger," Dr. Spae said. "We must hurry."

"Nice of it to tell us where to look," Hagen commented.

"Keep low," Holger said. "We want to get as close as possible before they see us."

"Don't have to tell me twice."

Hagen dropped the Snowhawk so low that Holger thought they were in danger of making an unintended landing. The verrie arrowed toward a break in the wall of cliffs, a side canyon that seemed to be the one from which the telltale column rose. They banked hard, heading for the mouth of the side canyon.

As he got his first glimpse of the canyon, Holger spotted their quarry. Van Dieman's Snowhawk was headed directly for the sediment-laden whirlwind.

"What have you got that sword for?" Chase asked.

An incongruous time for that sort of question.

"*You* ought to know," John snapped.

Any surprise at the kid's remark was blown away as the vortex exploded outward, hurling its burden away from the center. A sheet of soil and rocks engulfed the verrie in front of them and hurtled toward their own. Reflexively Holger brought his hands up. Caliburn's point struck the roof of the cabin, the weapon's steel ringing like a gong. He'd forgotten he was holding it. Lucky he hadn't taken Hagen's arm off.

Hitting the airborne debris was like hitting a wall. The Snowhawk shuddered under the hail of stone. The cabin was filled with the thunder of the pounding they were receiving. The fuselage dented, bulging inward where the heavy stones struck. The verrie's windscreen pitted under punishment, then cracked. Just as the fury of the unnatural storm seemed to abate, the windscreen shattered. The cold wind swept into the cabin, carrying lacerating shards of Transparex along with the last of its burden of sand. The Snowhawk nosed down, dropping like a stricken bird.

And all through the buffeting Caliburn tolled softly and continually like a distant mourning bell.

Somehow Hagen regained a measure of control over the craft and fought it back to an even keel.

Holger was surprised to find himself barely scratched by

the barrage of unconventional shrapnel. "Everyone all right?" he asked.

"Nothing serious," Spae reported.

"Wrong," Hagen contradicted. "Listen."

The steady throb of the Snowhawk's engines fluttered and shifted to a ratcheting grind.

"Land," Holger ordered. "We'll have a better chance on the ground."

"Like we have a choice?" Hagen's hands fought with the controls of the pitching verrie. "This bucket's had it."

John felt a flash of annoyance at Chase's question about the sword. "*You* ought to know," he snapped without thinking.

But why should Chase know?

There was no time to wonder. Something out in front of them surged and the energy in the vortex precipitously peaked. With hurricane force, the whirling cloud of soil and rocks exploded toward them.

Somehow the Snowhawk managed to survive the ersatz storm, and Hagen managed to get the verrie down for a safe landing. The battered aircraft sat at the edge of a huge bowl-shaped depression in the center of the canyon floor. In the center of the depression stood a truly enormous stone henge, and in the center of the henge lay Van Dieman's crashed Snowhawk.

It appeared Van Dieman had absolutely no luck with aircraft. Smoke—real smoke this time—was rising from the wreck.

Kun was the first out of the Snowhawk, but he didn't go far. He stood at the lip of the depression, the sword Caliburn in one hand and a Viper machine pistol in the other, staring down at what lay below. One by one they joined him. Hagen, hampered by his wounded leg, was the last. The air was the coldest that John had felt since he'd arrived in Antarctica, but that wasn't what made him shiver. The wind made a keening sound—only there was no wind.

A monstrous serpentine shape, made of shadow, lay coiled beside the wreckage of Van Dieman's verrie. It was huge, bigger than any snake John had ever seen in a nature vid. And no snake outside a fantasy epic had ever had eyes that burned with fire as this one's did. No one needed to be told that this creature was the harbinger.

"This doesn't look good," Kun said.

What Kun was seeing might not look good, but what John was seeing looked worse. The great serpent shape coiled around the wrecked verrie looked even more loathsome to arcane sight than to the mortal eye. But what truly unnerved him were the other serpents, smaller and more ghostly, that spiraled down from the darkening skies and wove among the henge stones in a twisting, torturous dance. John watched in horror as one of the whirling spirits left the stones and squirmed across the open space to join with the harbinger and add its essence to the shadow creature. The great serpent quivered, moaning orgiastically. The ululating wail notched up in volume and the sky darkened further. Another of the lesser beings started wriggling toward the harbinger.

"At least Van Dieman's out of the picture," Chase said.

"How do you know?" Hagen asked.

"He's trapped in the wreck," Chase said with a confident smile. Something about his expression was very familiar.

"Then it's just the harbinger we have to deal with," Dr. Spae said, staring at the monster.

Chase nodded. "Isn't that enough?"

Yet another of the small shapes slithered to the harbinger and was absorbed. The creature's hue darkened fractionally, becoming more substantial.

"It's getting stronger," John pointed out.

No one said anything, No one moved. John knew that they had to act. They had to do *something*! He felt strangely reluctant to act.

"Deadly," Dr. Spae said, sounding awed. Her eyes were riveted on the harbinger.

Maybe reluctance was not so strange. It was suicide to try to attack such a creature. Wasn't it?

"We've got to do something," Kun said.

His wavering tone suggested that he didn't know what, but his words galvanized Hagen to action. The dwarf put his Viper to his shoulder and ripped off a burst, then another. His aim was good, but the bullets passed through the harbinger as though it was not there. Beyond the serpent the slugs kicked up clots of dirt and spanged off the wrecked verrie.

The harbinger raised its head, slowly, menacingly. Its blunt, wedge-shaped snout turned toward Hagen. Jaws gaped wide. With a hissing that John felt rather than heard, the harbinger exhaled a stream of noxious green steam that shot toward Hagen like a laser blast. Better for the dwarf if it had been a laser beam; it would have been kinder. The deadly steam splashed across his chest, dissolving his thermal suit and eating away flesh and muscle. Howling and thrashing, he fell to the ground. His spasms lessened to twitches and diminished further until he lay still, a smoking cavity in his torso. The stench was awful.

John couldn't look at the fallen dwarf for fear of vomiting. His eyes unwillingly drifted to the harbinger. It stared back; its blazing eyes of cold fire sweeping across them, and John was sure—absolutely sure—that they didn't have a prayer.

CHAPTER
41

As soon as he saw it, Holger feared that this harbinger was kin to other supernatural things that he had encountered. That fear stopped him from firing his Viper. Hagen had fired, though, and his shooting hadn't had any effect—just as Holger had suspected. The thing coiled beside the wrecked Snowhawk was one of the *real* nightmares, immune to the weapons of ordinary men.

He watched in awe as the harbinger struck Hagen down. The dwarf died a painful, terrible death. A pointless death.

Holger realized that he was backing away from the stone circle, away from the harbinger that he had come to slay, and he felt ashamed. He forced himself to stand his ground. It was hard; he wanted to turn and run. He didn't know where he would run to, but anywhere was better than here. Anything was better than facing that monster. He didn't want to let Bear down, but what could he do? That thing in the circle was powerful, much more powerful than any man could hope to overcome.

He was worthless here, as worthless as the day that he had failed Mannheim. The anguish of self-loathing for his failure warred with the need to run away, and drove him to his knees. His vision blurred as tears froze his eyelids together.

Worthless!

* * *

Van Dieman retained a fragment of the link that he'd once had with the harbinger. Through it, he felt the magic that the creature was working on those who had pursued him. Before the crash, before the harbinger had betrayed him, he would have applauded its action. He would have enjoyed watching his pursuers stand hopelessly by, filled with despair, while the harbinger achieved its aims. He would have relished the irony of their having come so far only to stop themselves by their own fears and uncertainties.

But those emotions were gone from him, burned away in the flames that ate his body.

All he had now was pain.

John watched Kun fall to his knees. Now he was really scared. Kun was supposed to be the big brave warrior, and even he was afraid to face the harbinger. If Kun couldn't face it, what was John supposed to do? What could any of them do against such a monster?

"Take hold of yourself, Jack."

It was Chase speaking to him, shaking his shoulder. Why wasn't the guy quaking like the rest of them? And why had he used the name Jack? No one here did that. There was something odd about Chase, something that made John forget about the harbinger for a moment. He looked into Chase's face and saw that Chase was—Bennett.

"I replaced Chase some time ago," Bennett said.

"What the hell are you doing here?"

"The Wyrm is the enemy of all who love life, and this is my fight as well. Had I known earlier that you had planned to hunt this thing down, I might have joined you sooner. As it happens, I was pursuing my own course to stop the madman and the creature, but your ambush at McMurdo forced a change in plans. Now there's no time for subtlety. We have to act."

"We can't beat it," John told him, though Bennett surely knew. It was so obvious.

Bennett scowled at him. "That's what it wants you to think, and you're being weak-minded enough to oblige. You've let human thought patterns corrupt your will. You're an elf, Jack! Look to your blood! You are a prince of Faery, and no servant to the will of that deceptive corruption down there!"

"You ought to know about deception," John shouted back. All the lies Bennett had told him came flooding into his mind and along with them the one true thing that Bennett had told him, that he was an elf. "And you can drop the lies about being a prince. I know better now."

"No lies," Bennett said solemnly. "Right now you're the one hiding behind lies. Some are the Wyrm's lies of despair, but you can rise above that, if you set aside your own lies. The very face you wear is a lie. Look at yourself!"

Yeah, like there's a mirror handy.

"Accept yourself, Jack, or you are lost. We all are lost. I cannot stop the harbinger alone."

No one could stop the harbinger alone. Maybe no one could stop it at all. If an elven prince like Bennett couldn't do, what good was a changeling elf like John?

An elf.

John.

The desperate dread he'd felt concerning the harbinger receded a little when John thought about his being an elf, and that realization opened for him the truth. The despair that he had thought born of his fear and appreciation of the harbinger's power wasn't real. It was coming not from within, but from the harbinger. It was a spell, an illusion distantly akin to that which masked his true face. It was a lie. John dismissed his disguise spell, letting go of the illusion, and with it the harbinger's debilitating untruth.

Standing revealed under the Antarctic sky as the elf he was, John felt as if a burden had been lifted from his shoulders. The harbinger's spell, or was it something else?

"The harbinger can't really touch an elf with its despair can it?" he asked.

"It cannot," Bennett replied. "Its breed has subtler traps for our kind, although direct violence is their preferred response to us. They are more than capable of terrible violence."

John had seen what the harbinger had done to Hagen. Being an elf would not have saved him from that fate, had the harbinger directed its venomous spell at him.

"We must free your companions from the creature's influence. Only together do we have a chance to defeat it." Bennett offered his hand. "Trust me in this, and I will lead the way."

It was a hell of a lot to ask. John glanced down at the monster, growing more bloated and powerful each time it absorbed one of its smaller brethren. There was a hell of a lot to be lost, too.

He looked to Dr. Spae. She stood transfixed, staring at the horror at the center of the henge. Kun knelt, crying, shoulders slumped. Caliburn lay on the ground before him. Both Kun and Dr. Spae were enmeshed in the harbinger's spell. They were not elves, and thus were not immune. They needed his help.

John took Bennett's hand.

Power joined to power, they first explained to Dr. Spae about the harbinger's lies.

Holger was letting people down. Not just Bear far away, but people right here. Dr. Spae and John Reddy for two. Bennett the elven prince for another, though Holger didn't remember him arriving. They knew he was not the craven coward he was acting, which shamed him all the more to be paralyzed as he was. He was worthless!

They needed him. He could almost hear their voices, pleading for his help. But what good was he to them? He was too terrified of the creature down there, too sure that he had no hope against it.

The others needed him—they said so. They needed him even more than Mannheim had. There had been nothing that

Holger could have reasonably done to save Mannheim. He knew that now, even believed it. Mannheim was beyond help, but these people weren't. And he was failing them.

He held his hands to his eyes. The warming circuits in his gloves radiated only the faintest heat through the insulating layers, but it was enough to melt his tears of shame.

This was no time for tears.

The past was only memories, many good, some not. But he couldn't live there. The present was where he lived, and if he didn't do something about the present, there would be no memories, good or otherwise.

This was no time for memories either.

He looked at the dragon on Caliburn's hilt. Getting to his feet, he looked down the slope at the harbinger and recognized the face of the dragon. *This* was what he was here for. *This* was what Caliburn was here for. He bent and took up the sword. Raising his eyes to heaven, he touched the sword's steel to his brow and said, "*Morituri te salutamus.*"

It was time for a man to take fate into his hands.

He started down the slope.

Agony. Misery. Suffering. Wretchedness. Pain. Torturous, racking, excruciating pain.

Hell.

The harbinger had given him what he asked for: eternal life.

An eternity of anguish.

What a dupe he had been!

Hand in hand with Bennett and Dr. Spae, John watched Kun rise from his knees. The three mages' combined strength was barely enough to deconstruct the spells of despair the harbinger still sent to them and toward Kun. But barely was enough. Kun took up Caliburn and strode determinedly down the slope toward the henge and the monster that waited within the stone circle.

The harbinger had quadrupled in size and looked more like a dragon now than like a snake. Kun was going up against the monster with only a sword. John thought it suicidal. "He'll be killed. The harbinger will just spit up its poison and fry him."

"You forget, Caliburn protects against magical attack," Bennett said.

"Caliburn didn't protect Kun from the despair," John pointed out.

"The despair is more a part of the harbinger's nature than a spell, and Caliburn has always been in tune with nature. I would say that Caliburn did not recognize the spell-enhanced projection as an attack."

"What about the harbinger's other magic?" Dr. Spae asked.

"As I told Jack, the time for subtlety is past. Any magic that the harbinger throws against Holger Kun will be overt. Caliburn will contest such magics."

"Then why don't we attack with Kun?" John demanded. "Dr. Spae could throw the bolts from her staff. You must know some kind of battle spells."

"It's not our place, Jack. We must continue toward Holger Kun, for if he slips back into the creature's influence he will be lost. We must work with all our will to support him, for as he draws closer to the harbinger, the potency of the creature's influence will grow stronger. Holger Kun must not be allowed to succumb to that influence. He is the sword. We must be the shield."

Through the ritual link, John could feel the rightness of Bennett's words. Still he yearned for a more active role, wishing he had a sword of his own and could stand behind Kun in the fight. Having brushed against Kun's essence in the effort to help him throw off the harbinger's sway, John had seen a bit of the man's heart. John understood now a little of why Bear had given Kun the sword, and his unwarranted jealousy was gone. Each of them had his part in this battle, and if John didn't concentrate on his own part, Kun might fail in his. He set to with a will to shred the harbinger's scourge of hopelessness and give Kun the chance he needed.

Holger entered the stone circle through one of the lintel-capped structures that looked like a gateway. As he entered the inner precinct, he was slammed by the stench of corruption and decay like that of a battlefield on a hot summer's afternoon. He gagged and fell choking to the ground, retching until his stomach ached and his throat burned.

The harbinger laughed at him. He could feel the amusement reverberating in his head.

Behold the dragon slayer.

That was what he had come to be, but curled in a tight fetal ball, he wasn't doing a very good job.

Behold the frail and unfit man, the flawed vessel into which petty tyrants pour their hopes.

Holger managed to force some of the bile back down his throat. He struggled to his hands and knees and looked at the harbinger. He almost retched again. The thing had grown, and it bloated larger as he watched. It was more dragonlike now, having grown scaly limbs and clawed feet. Fetid and twisted, it had none of the majesty vid makers put in their dragons. Such a loathsome thing had no place on earth.

"To hell with you," he told it.

He got to his feet and forced himself to advance toward it. As he got closer he caught the scent of burning flesh amid the overall miasma of death.

The harbinger's fiery eyes watched his approach.

Turn away and live. Stay and die.

Beowulf the dragon slayer had gotten a funeral pyre. But first he had beaten the dragon. Of course, the dragon had given him his death wound in the fight.

There were worse ways to go.

The harbinger reared, radiating distaste and affront at his approach; no cobra had ever made such a menacing threat display. To back up its threat, the creature spat its venom at Holger. The deadly green poison sizzled toward him. But it never touched him. Caliburn rang like a bell, tolling out defiance. The harbinger's spittle dissipated in the air.

As Bear had said it would, Caliburn was preserving him from the enemy's sorcerous weapons.

He didn't want to give the harbinger another opportunity to try any spells. Shouting a wordless battle cry, he attacked. He swung the sword hard, aiming for the harbinger's throat. The creature whipped its head aside. Holger swung again and this time the harbinger interposed a claw. Caliburn screeched as its edge skittered along the talon's impenetrable hardness.

Holger attacked in a flurry, striking as hard and as fast as he could. He had to win quickly. Given the creature's size and nature, it would have reserves of endurance far beyond his own. If he could wound it soon and slow it down, he might have a chance. He saw an opening in its flashing defense of fang and talon, and struck.

But the opening was a deception. Fending Caliburn away with its claws, the harbinger struck at Holger. Its head snapped forward like a striking snake's and only speed born of biotechnical implants saved Holger from being bitten in two. As it was, one of the thing's teeth scored a burning furrow along his left arm. The pain energized him, unleashing the strength of berserker fury that was the Department's gift. He rained blows on the harbinger, slipping away from its claws, dodging its jaws, and attacking, always attacking. His fury drove it back.

Yet still he could not kill it. The harbinger's control of its density defied his best efforts. On one stroke Caliburn might clang against scales as hard as adamant, while on the next it might pass through the creature's substance as if it were no more than smoke. Holger fought on. The harbinger had hurt *him* physically; there had to be a way to hurt *it*.

His fighting rage faltered as adrenaline-stoked muscles

burned away their fuel. Claws of fire raked across his side, ripping through his thermal suit and deep into his flesh. He felt and heard some of his ribs splinter. There was an excruciating moment of agony, then he felt nothing of the wound. But he could smell the death stink of it. His time was almost gone.

The harbinger struck him again, this time with the back of its taloned forefoot, and knocked him down. He could barely breathe. He sure as hell wasn't going to be able to get out of the way. It slithered nearer and loomed over him. The raw stink of its fetid breath made the earlier stench as nothing.

As a child he'd dreamed of being a knight and fighting dragons. In his dreams, the knight always won.

The harbinger rose up, fanged maw gaping to swallow him.

Van Dieman's world was suffering. His body was afire and would burn forever. The reward of the faithful—his reward—life eternal. Everlasting agony.

The darkness, the dread darkness he had so feared since he was a child, was denied him. He had been a foolish child. Now that it was denied, he longed for such sweet surcease.

He felt the faint touch of the harbinger. Its distant amusement was oil on the fires of his torture. It had been so very kind to him, and such kindness deserved reward. He owed it.

Oh, how he owed it!

Though his tongue was blackened and split, he said, "I give you a gift, Harbinger, freely and with all my will"—and he used the link to send the harbinger all the agony he knew. He lost nothing by it. He had more than enough pain to fill the world.

The harbinger threw its head back and roared, not in triumph but in surprise and pain. Holger didn't understand why—maybe the magicians had hurt it somehow—but he knew this was his last chance. He had to get up. He had to take advantage of this opportunity.

But he was weak, exhausted.

Where was the superhuman strength that the dwarves had said he was capable of?

Spent. Gone.

The doctors of Department M had built into him mechanisms to increase his strength, but they hadn't told him how to use such advantages. He wished they had. He needed that sort of edge now, needed their gifts just one more time before his life bled away.

He could hear voices again. They weren't the false memories that had been crammed into his head, but true memories—of friends long gone, of his parents, of his mentor Mannheim. They were reminding him that a man was more than flesh and bone, more even than what man's technology could make him. They were the voices of Dr. Spac and John Reddy urging him to find the strength to get up. Bennett called to him more distantly, reminding him of the sword.

Caliburn, Bear's trust, placed into Holger's hand to use.

To honor.

Not to abandon.

Though his muscles tore with the effort, he forced himself to his feet. His vision was blurred, but he could see the harbinger writhing on the ground before him. Its thrashing was lessening. It was recovering itself. He could not allow that. Raising Caliburn above his head with both hands, he turned it point downward. His arms shook as the serpent's head turned to him, and its eyes sought him out.

Health, it offered. *I can give you your life back.*

Legs wobbling, arms trembling, he felt his blood pumping from the wound that the harbinger had given him. It could heal him, he knew. But at what price? The Department's doctors had healed him, given him new life, and that price had been high. What greater price would this servant of the outer darkness exact?

If you use the sword, you kill your hope of life. In this place there is no help for you but me.

It was true. He'd never reach a doctor in time.

I have tasted death. It is dust. Dust and nothingness. You need not die.

He didn't want to die.

Life. Life forever.

He did want to live. But how could he live without honor?

"*Retro me, Satanas,*" he said.

And he drove the blade down, through smoky armor and insubstantial flesh, into the heart of the harbinger. A deep gonging note filled the air as Caliburn drove in and through, ramming itself into the ground below. The sword didn't stop until its point ground into stone.

The harbinger shrieked, shrill enough to shatter glass, but what shattered was the dark glass of its bodily form, exploding into a dozen pieces. A smaller form remained beneath, dark and pustulent, but no larger than it had been when he had first seen it. That shape spasmed, once, then lay still. Slowly it faded into nothingness, and Holger saw that he had impaled a cracked piece of smoky crystal that looked as if it had been shaped by a madman's hands into the image of a snake or a worm twisted upon itself.

Holger turned his back on what remained of the beast, and saw Dr. Spae and the others running down the slope toward him. It was over. He tried to walk toward them, but his legs buckled and he fell to his knees.

God, he was tired.

He pitched forward onto his face.

He'd done what he needed to do.

"Is he dead?" John asked. He mustn't be. Kun had beaten the harbinger. It wasn't fair that he die.

"Not yet," Dr. Spae said from where she knelt beside the dying man. She was crying. "But he will be soon. I don't think he'll survive the trip back to McMurdo."

"You're assuming that there will be such a trip," Bennett said. "The aircraft is damaged."

"I'll get McMurdo on the radio, and if I can't do that, I'll set the beacon," John said and ran to do it. When he returned Dr. Spae was seated on the ground beside Kun. She had kindled an arcane fire to warm him. Bennett had stepped a couple of yards away, and stood looking at Caliburn and the remains of the *telesmon* that the sword's gleaming steel impaled. John joined him. "Nasham and the dwarves are coming out in a pair of Snowhawks. They ought to be here in less than an hour. Do you think Kun has that long?"

"He was a warrior today. A hero," Bennett said staring at the sword. "Heroes seldom survive their great victories."

"Isn't there something you can do? Some kind of healing spell? Something?"

Bennett shook his head. "Nothing I know."

John suddenly wanted to think about other things. "We need to bring the sword back to Bear."

"I wouldn't advise that," Bennett said. "It's pinning the Wyrm to the earth. This closes the gateway that the Followers of the Glittering Path sought to open. The evil of the harbinger's kind is shut off from the earth and the convergence will proceed cleanly. Of course, if you care to test yourself against such monstrosities again, you could tamper with that arrangement."

"I think he's right, John," Dr. Spae said. "Caliburn has fixed the beast and closed the way."

"We can't just leave it sitting out here," John protested.

"I will bury this place again before we leave," Bennett said. "You can go back to Artos, and tell him that his man did what needed to be done, and let him decide if he wants his sword back. Your work for him will be done. You can return with me to the otherworld."

"Return? To what? Shahotain and the others made it clear to me that I don't belong there. Not with Morgana being my mother."

Bennett's eyes narrowed momentarily. "They were never meant to know about Morgana. They would not have learned about her had you not helped them."

"Don't try to put it on me! I don't even know why having Morgana as a mother is a problem. Hell, I don't even know who she is!"

"Do you want to know?" Bennett asked softly. "I will tell you all about her if you return with me to the otherworld."

John wasn't sure he wanted to know. Morgana, whoever she was, was as tangled in elven politics as Bennett was. He just knew that learning about her would get him in a deceitful mess, and he wanted no part of it.

"I don't think so," John said. "My place is here in this world." He had things he wanted to do. Among them, taking another shot at explaining things to Spillway Sue. "I am not going back to the otherworld."

"Don't be ridiculous. You are an elf."

"I know that."

"Then you know that this world is not your place."

"Isn't it?" John distrusted Bennett's insistence. If Bennett wanted him back in the otherworld, there was surely a scheme under way, and John had no interest in furthering Bennett's schemes. He'd had enough adventure, and more than enough of being Bennett's pawn. He had a home to go back to. "I think my place is where I choose to make it."

Bennett looked surprised. John had scored a point, though that didn't seem very important just now.

"You *have* learned some wisdom," Bennett said. "But do not think I have forgotten your promise."

John was about to tell Bennett where to stuff his talk of promises when Kun spoke.

"John?" Kun's voice was weak, barely audible. John went at once to his side and put his hand into the groping hand of the dying man. "Tell Bear—"

"I'll tell him that you're a hero."

"No."

"You are," John protested.

"Just a man, doing what he had to do."

Holger Kun said no more.

They stayed by him, and did what they could for him. It did not seem to be a time for words, and they said little to each other until the verries came to take them away. It was more than an hour before the dwarves arrived, and by then it didn't matter for Holger Kun. Neither John nor Dr. Spae said anything to the dwarves about the cairn that they had built, because it wasn't the dwarves' business. They boarded the Snowhawks, leaving Bennett behind to do as he said he would, and flew back to a world freed of the shadow of the harbinger and its voracious kind.

Epilog

The verrie came in for its landing without raising a lot of dust. A woman climbed out of the cockpit, shapely despite her military cold-weather flight suit, and walked toward him, smiling. She was as beautiful as an angel. There was no name strip on her uniform, and Holger questioned that.

"Call me Nym," she said. "I've come to take you away to the sleep that is the hero's reward."

Good. He wanted to sleep. He was very tired.

He took her offered hand, and she helped him up. His hurt was an old memory, fading further as they walked to the aircraft. He climbed aboard, nodding to the pilot and copilot as he took a seat. They were beautiful, too. He wondered what the crew might be doing when they got off duty.

The verrie lifted off. On the ground below Dr. Spae, John Reddy, and even Bennett waved good-bye.

ABOUT THE AUTHOR

Robert N. Charrette was born, raised, and educated in the State of Rhode Island and Providence Plantations. Upon graduating from Brown University with a cross-departmental degree in biology and geology, he promptly moved to the Washington, D.C. area and entered a career as a graphic artist. He worked as a game designer, art director, and commercial sculptor before taking up the word processor to write novels. He has contributed three novels to the BattleTech™ universe and four to the Shadowrun™ universe, the latter of which he had a hand in creating, and is now developing other settings for fictional exploration.

He currently resides in Springfield, Virginia with his wife, Elizabeth, who must listen to his constant complaints of insufficient time while he continues to write as well as to sculpt gaming miniatures and the occasional piece of collector's pewter or fine art bronze. He also has a strong interest in medieval living history, being a longtime knight of the Society for Creative Anachronism and a principal in La Belle Compagnie, a reenactment group portraying English life in the late fourteenth century. In between, he tries to keep current on a variety of eclectic interests including dinosaurian paleontology and pre-Tokugawa Japanese history.